THE STORE

THE STORE

T. S. Stribling

WITH AN INTRODUCTION BY

Randy K. Cross

THE UNIVERSITY OF ALABAMA PRESS
Tuscaloosa & London

Second Printing 1994

Library of Congress Cataloging in Publication Data
Stribling, (T.S. (Thomas Sigismund), 1881–1965.
The store
Bibliography: p.
I. Title.
PS 3537.T836S7   1985   813'.52   85–1045
ISBN 0-8173-0251-4

INTRODUCTION

Randy K. Cross

IN THE WINTER of 1930, T. S. Stribling rented a house in Fort Myers, Florida, and began work on *The Store*, the second volume of his Southern trilogy. The first volume, *The Forge* (1931), focuses on the Vaiden family and the demise of the Old South, exemplified by the death of Jimmie Vaiden in the final chapter of the novel. In *The Store*, Stribling resumes the narrative after a lapse of twenty years; it is now 1884, the year in which Grover Cleveland becomes the first Democratic president elected since the end of the Civil War. With the domination of the Republican party removed from the South, men like the ambitious Miltiades Vaiden are presented with the opportunity to take the reins of power.

Although *The Forge* lacks an identifiable protagonist, by the end of that novel Colonel Miltiades Vaiden has emerged as the central character and maintains that role throughout *The Store*. Yet *The Store* is more than a book about power. It is the chronicle of an age. After its publication in 1932, *The Store* became a popular success in the United States and in Europe, and in 1933 it would be selected for the Pulitzer Prize over *Mutiny on the Bounty* and Ellen Glasgow's *The Sheltered Life*. The Pulitzer jury at Columbia University announced that "*The Store* was selected chiefly because of its sustained interest, and because of the convincing and comprehensive picture it presents of life in an inland Southern community during the middle eighties of the last century."[1]

The views of the Pulitzer jury were shared by many leading critics of the day. Gerald Bullett, in *The New Statesman and Nation*, wrote that *The Store* "is a first-rate book of its kind, a good story filled with diverse and vital characters; and much of it cannot be read without that primitive excitement, that eagerness to know what comes next, which is, after all, the triumph of the good storyteller."[2] Even more laudatory was Rich White's review in *Time:* "Written in the great tradition of well-peopled novels, the book successfully commingles impartial observation and ubiquitous sympathy, tinged with a faintly sub-acid humor. In pitch, scope, execution it is easily the most important U.S. novel of the year."[3]

In *The Store*, Stribling presents the essence of an age through the everyday lives of his characters. Herschel Brickell of the *North American Review* credited Stribling with the "ability not only to rebuild and vivify a period, but to people it with living human beings."[4] In *The New Yorker*, Robert M. Coates compared Stribling to Mark Twain in his abilities to convey the "very life and movement" of a small Southern town: "Groups move chatting under the trees or stand loitering in the courthouse square, townsfolk gather at political 'speakings' and drift homeward separately afterward; always, in their doings, one has the sense of a whole community surrounding them, binding them together."[5]

Stribling's finest efforts came when he wrote of the people of his native land. As a child, Stribling spent his summers on his grandfather's farm near Florence, Alabama, and he later completed college at the Florence Normal School (now the University of North Alabama). He was admitted to the Alabama bar in 1905 and practiced law in Florence for about a year before beginning his career as a professional writer. Born in 1881 only a few miles from Florence in Clifton, Tennessee, Stribling knew firsthand the realities of the post-Reconstruction South. "I was born into it," he said, "and when I get out of it, I'll die out of it."[6]

This post-Reconstruction period, when poor and middle-class whites were wresting power from the wealthy landowners, provided the social and economic landscape for *The Store*. Aristocratic planters, once the figures of financial and political strength, had been stripped of their power by the devastation of war and the economic sanctions of the carpetbaggers' regime. The imposing antebellum plantations supported by chattel slavery were carved into small tracts of land tilled by sharecroppers and tenant farmers, black and white. As General Beekman had predicted in *The Forge*, the reins of power were passing to the landlords and merchants. Under the new system, sharecroppers were forced to mortgage their future cotton crops with merchant landlords in exchange for the food necessary to see them through the fall harvest. Rarely did the value of the crop match the bill owed at the store. Consequently, thousands of farm families across the South faced the burden of impossible debts that increased year by year. As C. Vann Woodward has pointed out, the lien system "came to be more widespread than slavery had been, for it was no respecter of race or class; and if it be judged objectively, by its economic results alone, the new evil may have worked more permanent injury to the South than the ancient evil."[7] Not until industrialization in the South became more widespread in the 1880s and 1890s could most Southerners begin to escape the oppression of the new economic system.

Governor O'Shawn's campaign speech for Grover Cleveland in *The Store* stresses the inequities of an economy dependent on Northern industrialism:

> "Look you, my fellow citizens," he inveighed, "Yankees buy up your cotton at five cents a pound; they manufacture it into shirts, sheets, socks, and what not, and send it back to you.
>
> "But do you get it at five cents a pound? Not by a long chalk! No, they begin with a manufacturer's charge of six cents a yard on calico. The Yankee wholesaler adds two cents more; the Yankee jobber another cent. Yankee railroads tax the South one tenth of a cent per yard. All this is understandable. I agree to it.

A manufacturer, even a Yankee manufacturer, must live, although God alone knows what for!" [p. 5]

With the virtual disappearance of yeoman farmers (like the
Vaidens in *The Forge*), Southerners of both races, for the most
part, were left with two choices: they could continue to work as
sharecroppers or tenant farmers, or they could seek jobs in the
growing cities. Whatever the case, it was the local merchant
who benefited most from their labors. As Miltiades had recognized twenty years earlier, "the man who bought from them
and sold to them would be the man in all probability who,
finally, would receive their earnings."[8] Thus, Stribling could
hardly have chosen a more fitting title for the second novel in
his trilogy, for the store, and all it represented, was the central
symbol of the postwar South.

At the beginning of *The Store*, Miltiades is forty-eight years
old, impoverished, and distressed that his life in Florence has
become one of shabby gentility and boredom in the company of
his fat wife Ponny. Miltiades' prewar role as overseer of the
Lacefield plantation and his subsequent prominence as soldier
and organizer of the Klan in north Alabama spoke well for his
ability and promise. Yet by 1884 he has lost all momentum; he
is adrift, living off the dwindling resources of his wife's inheritance, trapped in a system that would seem to hold no place for
him. Whatever potential he may have had lies buried under the
ruins of the Old South that spawned him.

Yet, if Miltiades has been defeated by circumstance, that
same blind and unpredictable force works to save him in *The
Store*. Fate and circumstance, rather than Miltiades' own initiative, are the catalysts of his rise to power. The first step in his
journey—the clerkship in Handback's store—results from his
chance discovery of his employer's black mistress, Gracie.
Through a series of coincidences, Miltiades is able to steal five
hundred bales of Handback's cotton. The shallow depth of the
river, which brings the daring Captain Dargan to Florence in

search of trade that other, more timid captains would avoid, and the early return of the black deck hands who have been fired for shooting dice prove decisive in Miltiades' future. Even when he faces imprisonment for his crime, Milt is saved from prosecution when Handback's search of the Vaiden home precipitates Ponny's death. Indeed, events throughout the novel are motivated by a determinism over which, Miltiades realizes at last, he has had no control. Shortly after his son Toussaint is lynched, Miltiades muses that "if his boy had not started an injunction against him . . . if Bradley had not lost the deeds . . . if Sandusky had not been admitted to the bar . . . a long string of 'ifs' upon which every life hangs suspended" (p. 569).

Years later in his autobiography, *Laughing Stock*, Stribling would again speculate on the inevitability of fate: "It surely is a strange thing how incidents, trifles in themselves, penetrate one's life and grow and grow and change its whole pattern, while other matters of apparent great import fade into nothing."[9] Thus it is with Colonel Vaiden. His position as overseer on the Lacefield plantation, his valor in the war, and his leadership later in the Klan have failed, in the end, to deliver to him the prominence and wealth that have been his life's ambition. Instead, his fortune is linked to a late-night walk along a deserted street, to the depth of a river, and to a game of chance played by deck hands hundreds of miles away.

Even if an avowed thief could rise above his inherited social and economic position in Florence, Alabama, in 1884, former slaves and their descendants could not. As he had done in *The Forge*, and ten years earlier in *Birthright*, Stribling examines in *The Store* the problems of race relations in the South. The decades following the war produced few advantages for blacks; in fact, their plight was often worse than in antebellum days. Granted a freedom that they could not exercise in a closed society, they were bound by the strictures of the white man's law without the benefit of its protection.

Gracie and Lump, both former slaves, realize that they can never be first-class citizens in the South and that their well-being depends, finally, upon amiable, if subservient, relations with whites. As Handback's mistress, Gracie is spared the abject poverty of her black neighbors, but she is haunted by the thought that some day her sins will be atoned for by the death of her white son Toussaint. Lump, who to Gracie is "a kind of carping, fault-finding voice of God," warns of the consequences of her adultery:

> "Do you know whut de Bible say? Hit say, Cuss be de seed ob de scarlet woman! Hit say she sins an' wipe huh lips an say, 'I have done nothing'.' Dat's you, Gracie Vaiden, sinnin' an' wipin' yo' lips an' saying you ain't done nothing'! But cuss shell be yo' seed, Gracie Vaiden! He shall be struck down an cas' in de fiah. . . . De Bible say hit!" [p. 34]

Gracie is Stribling's wisest and most loyal character, and she knows that her relationship with Handback is the only possible key to Toussaint's future happiness. Without the money that Gracie receives from Handback, Toussaint can never hope to escape the burden of his black inheritance.

Throughout the novel, the underlying motivation behind all of Gracie's actions is the welfare and salvation of her son. Even when Handback offers her a new life with him in New Orleans, she refuses on Toussaint's account: "If I go off and leave him he's sure to marry some dark girl. Then he'll be lost again. He'll be a nigger . . . his children'll be niggers . . ." (p. 371). Gracie's attitude is reminiscent of Captain Renfrew's in *Birthright* when he learns that the black protagonist, Peter Siner, plans to marry a black woman:

> "No, Peter; no," quavered the old man. "For yourself it may make no difference, but your children—think of your children, your son growing up under a brown veil! You can't tear it off. God himself can't tear it off! You can never reach him through it. Your children, your children's children, a terrible procession

that stretches out and out, marching under a black shroud, unknowing, unknown! All you can see are their sad forms beneath the shroud, marching away—marching away. God knows where! And yet—it's your own flesh and blood!"[10]

Gracie knows that Toussaint's hope—and that of his descendants—lies in the North where he can get an education and, perhaps, marry a white woman, thereby severing all ties with his black ancestors. Like Captain Renfrew, Gracie understands that the South is an unequivocal white man's land and that it will remain so for generations to come. Her son's refusal to accept this unalterable truth, however, marks him for destruction.

From the beginning, Toussaint is doomed by pride and defiance. His reluctance to shine white men's shoes, his public questioning of Miltiades' honesty, and his fight with Alex Cady are indicative of Toussaint's refusal to live the life that the white community expects of him. The pleas from his mother and the biblical warnings from Lump that "Them as hol's they haid high shall be brought low" have little effect on his attitude. Like Peter Siner, Toussaint is motivated by a mistaken belief that his actions will produce far-reaching advantages for all blacks living in the South. Although Peter is armed with a Harvard education and Toussaint with light-colored skin, neither is able to overcome the barriers of racial prejudice. Even Toussaint's decision to marry Lucy Lacefield and remain in the South is an act of defiance, a symbol of his determination to fight against the injustices to which he and his race are subjected.

Once married to Lucy, Toussaint's fate is sealed. His notions of equal rights and a life independent of the white race are encouraged by the fatal optimism of his wife. Lucy's statement that she wants Toussaint and herself to lead their own lives, not "too close to white folks," prompts a predictable response from Gracie: "Too close to white folks . . . why, everything we get is from white folks" (p. 467). As representatives of a new genera-

tion of blacks, Toussaint and Lucy are not content with their
social and economic inheritance. They are, as Miltiades ob-
serves, "these new uncomfortable colored people who are
springing up in the place of the good old-fashioned nigger"
(p. 467). When Toussaint takes Miltiades to court at Lucy's
insistence, he encounters an even greater obstacle than white
man's law: tradition. In his closing argument at the trial, Governor O'Shawn declares that "politically, religiously, socially, and
agriculturally, the South is and of a right must be now and
forever, a white man's country!" (p. 548). Only after Toussaint's
death is Lucy able to see the futility of her efforts at reform.

Ironically, for Gracie, Lucy, and her unborn child, Toussaint
has become, through his death, the savior he has imagined
himself to be. While his efforts are futile on a grand scale, they
ultimately provide his family the opportunity for freedom. In
the aftermath of Toussaint's violent death, his people look to the
North, and in the novel's closing pages they leave Florence
aboard the steamer *Rapidan*. In so doing, they acknowledge
what Stribling saw as the Negro's only alternative in that time
and in that place: to remain in servitude or to leave and seek a
better life outside the South.

Toussaint's death is coincidental with the final realization of
Miltiades' dream, and it is here that Stribling brings to an end
the second volume of his trilogy. The thrust of the narrative has
brought Miltiades out of poverty and seemingly hopeless in-
ertia and prepared him for the events of *Unfinished Cathedral*.
By so doing, Stribling examines the various forces behind the
political, social, and economic changes that ushered in the New
South. *The Store*, however, derives its main strength from
Stribling's ability to weave together a series of disparate characters and events. The aristocratic Drusilla Crowningshield;
Gracie, a former slave; Alex Cady, a poor white; Jerry Catlin,
the intellectual; the merchant Handback; and the mystic Landers: these characters personify the various classes brought together in the post-Reconstruction South. Thus, it is not

Miltiades' story alone, but the collective experience of all the varied characters that makes *The Store* an enduring portrait of an age.

NOTES TO INTRODUCTION

1. John Hohenberg, *The Pulitzer Prizes* (New York: Columbia University Press, 1974), p. 92.
2. Gerald Bullett, "New Novels," *The New Statesman and Nation*, May 14, 1932, p. 621.
3. Rich White, *"The Store," Time*, July 4, 1932, p. 39.
4. Herschel Brickell, "The Literary Landscape," *North American Review* 234 (September 1932), 283.
5. Robert M. Coates, "Problems of the Old South and of the Artist Today," *The New Yorker*, July 2, 1932, p. 39.
6. White, p. 39.
7. C. Vann Woodward, *Origins of the New South 1877–1913*, Vol. IX of *A History of the South*, ed. Wendell Holmes Stephenson and E. Merton Coulter (10 vols.; Baton Rouge: Louisiana State University Press, 1971), p. 180.
8. T. S. Stribling, *The Forge* (New York: Doubleday, Doran & Company, 1931), p. 510.
9. T. S. Stribling, *Laughing Stock*, ed. Randy K. Cross and John T. McMillan (Memphis: St. Luke's Press, 1982), p. 230.
10. T. S. Stribling, *Birthright* (New York: The Century Co., 1922), p. 214.

THE STORE

IN RESPONSE to his wife's uncertain inquiry about the political speaking, Colonel Miltiades Vaiden called back from his gate that he did not think there would be any ladies at the courthouse that evening.

By laying stress on the word "think" the Colonel not only forecasted a purely masculine attendance in Courthouse Square that summer evening in Florence, Alabama, but at the same time he subtly expressed his own personal disapproval of women appearing at political gatherings at any place or time whatsoever.

The heavy wife in the doorway hesitated at the Colonel's implication. She had wanted to go. She felt the gregarious impulse of fleshy persons to foregather with crowds, to laugh and fraternize with the audience, to propel her large body among her lighter fellows with the voluptuous and genial ruthlessness of a fat person. However, on the other hand, her feminine fear of being the only woman in the audience stood in her path.

But behind these two antagonistic impulses lay another cause of depression which the ponderous wife knew too well but which she never frankly had admitted even to herself. This was that her husband did not want her to go with him to this or to any other public gathering; it was . . . that he was ashamed of her.

This fact wavered in the woman's mind until she expelled it by calling out:

"Oh, Mr. Milt, there'll be a lot of leading men down there, I expect. Maybe some of 'em will offer you a—a better position. . . ."

At this mention of position a disagreeable tickle went

through the husband's chest, but he answered in an impassive, corrective tone:

"Not likely such a topic will come up at a political meeting, Ponny."

"Well . . . if it does . . . you . . . you mustn't repulse 'em, Mr. Milt."

"No, I won't, Ponny," he assured her with a solemn face.

He let himself into the street and closed the gate after him. As he did this, the looseness of the hinges, the broken palings, the gaunt outline of his rented house here on this back street in Florence, all combined to give him a twist of repulsion when connected with the thought of a "position."

Because, as a matter of fact, the Colonel had no position. Ever since the Civil War had lost him his place as an overseer on a cotton plantation, he had desired the post and circumstance of a country gentleman. Only nowadays there were no country gentlemen. Nowadays one reached gentility by other methods, but Colonel Vaiden, somehow, had not succeeded in fitting himself into those other methods.

For a long stretch the Colonel's failure had been a kind of standing riddle to persons who had known of his distinguished services during the war and his leadership of the Klan during the Reconstruction. But this riddle gradually lost point with time. So now, as the Colonel glanced back in the twilight and saw in the doorway the bulky outline of his wife, he knew that, besides himself, she was the only human being on earth who believed that upon him, eventually, would fall some great, noble, and extraordinary estate. She was constantly expecting it out of a persistent faith and admiration for her husband's ability.

As the Colonel stepped across a gully in the neglected street he rewarded her loyalty by thinking in a kind of annoyed fashion:

"I should have asked her to go with me . . . damn it . . . Ponny's a good girl. . . ."

Cherry Street, along which Colonel Vaiden moved, was bordered by bare weed-grown lots and an occasional stark

frame house with a chicken coop and a privy in the rear. Two
or three squares farther on the pedestrian turned westward
toward Market Street. Here the neighborhood began to
improve: dark masses of magnolias and live oaks screened
the houses. Opening on the sidewalks were double gates to
admit a horse and carriage, or perhaps a milk cow of mornings and evenings.

These were still ordinary middle-class homes, but this evening they stiffened a determination in Miltiades to reach
this stage of luxury. Yes, and, by gravy, he would do even
better than that! These frame houses with magnolias and live
oaks, he would have something better than that . . . he did
not know just what that better ménage would be, but a
quiver of impatience went through him to be at it. Whatever he did he must do quickly; whatever he gained he must
gain with speed; . . . he was forty-eight years old.

When Miltiades reached Market Street and turned southward toward the courthouse he abandoned his thoughts of
future wealth to decide whether or not he should stop by the
boarding house and ask his brother, Augustus Vaiden, to
go to the speaking with him.

He hesitated over this point, first because he did not approve of Augustus, who did nothing at all. Augustus' wife,
Rose Vaiden, ran a boarding house and Augustus puttered
about, helping with the cooking, talking to the boarders,
walking downtown for letters, and that was all Augustus
did. It annoyed Miltiades, such an ambitionless brother!

The second reason Miltiades had for not stopping by was
that Rose Vaiden did not like him. He liked Rose all right in
an unenthusiastic sort of way, but Rose did not like him in
any way whatsoever.

These pros and cons moved through the Colonel's mind
with more irony than definition, and now, after he, apparently, had raked together two good reasons for not stopping,
the Colonel mentally determined to drop in at the boarding
house and take Augustus with him to the speaking.

When this plan developed out of Colonel Vaiden's musings,

he had come in sight of the two-storied Vaiden boarding
house standing darkly against the sky. A light in the kitchen
window reminded Miltiades that Rose and Augustus kept a
servant, while his own wife, Ponny, always had had to do
her own work. This seemed incongruous. He, Colonel
Miltiades Vaiden, without a cook, while Augustus, his
younger brother, who had no more ambition than a cotton-
field negro, should have one . . .

At this point a movement of surprise, almost of shock,
went through the Colonel. In front of the boarding house
stood a carriage and horses. For a fantastic moment
Miltiades thought that somehow or other Rose had bought
them and there they were. Then he knew this could not be.

He walked on curiously, when from inside the half-seen
vehicle a man's voice said impersonally:

"Good-evening, Colonel Vaiden. My wife and I stopped
by to take Miss Rose and her husband to the speaking. Will
you ride down with us?"

Miltiades took off his hat to the woman he could not see
in the carriage.

"Thank you, Judge, but the air is so fine tonight I believe
I'll continue my walk, if you don't mind?"

The voice in the carriage completely acceded to this
request.

"It is a very fine night, Colonel."

And Miltiades went on alone with a vague relief that
someone else was taking his brother to the speaking.

Half an hour later, as Colonel Vaiden approached Court
house Square, a distant burst of cheering told him that the
speaking already had begun. As he drew nearer the lilt of
the voice of an orator came to his ears. Then he could see the
speaker, elevated on the portico of the courthouse in the
light of four oil lamps. The man on the platform was Governor Terry O'Shawn, a lawyer of Florence, who had risen
to the Governorship of Alabama. That was why Florence had
turned out en masse to honor the Governor. He was one of
their own townsmen.

Governor O'Shawn stood in the midst of the four lamps shaking a fist over the heads of his audience. He was demanding to know upon whose bosom battened the blood-sucking harpies of Yankee manufacturers!

"Look you, my fellow citizens," he inveighed, "Yankees buy up your cotton at five cents a pound; they manufacture it into shirts, sheets, socks, and what not, and send it back to you.

"But do you get it at five cents a pound? Not by a long chalk! No, they begin with a manufacturer's charge of six cents a yard on calico. The Yankee wholesaler adds two cents more; the Yankee jobber another cent. Yankee railroads tax the South one tenth of a cent per yard. All this is understandable. I agree to it. A manufacturer, even a Yankee manufacturer, must live, although God alone knows what for!"

Here laughter and cheers interrupted the orator. Dignitaries sitting in the shadow on the platform behind the Governor looked at one another in amusement. O'Shawn took a sip of water and then went on full tilt:

"But, ladies and gentlemen, that is not the damnable phase of this premeditated murder of the South. In addition to these onerous and excessive charges of manufacture and transportation, a Republican Congress, sired by Wall Street and dammed by the Yankee manufacturers, has placed a protective tariff of three cents a yard on calico; and today, every time your daughter buys a new dress or your boy gets the goods to make a shirt, some Northern octopus reaches his slimy tentacle into your pocket, Mr. Taxpayer, and mulcts you out of three cents a yard on everything you buy. That's what they call governmental protection!

"But is our raw cotton protected three cents a yard, or a mill a pound, or anything at all? It is not! Our raw products don't need protection! The South, that lovely vestal, whose form was bayoneted by war and ravished by Reconstruction —she doesn't require protection! Such is the even-handed justice of our Republican high protective tariff. What is

sauce for the goose is apparently not sauce for the wounded
Bird of Paradise. The plight of the South, thrust into the
undesired company of the other states of this Union, recalls
to my mind, ladies and gentlemen, that apt and searching
parable spoken by our Lord and Saviour, Jesus Christ,
when He described the fate of that traveler who fell among
thieves !"

An uproar of cheers stopped the speaker. Voices shouted:
"Go after 'em, Terry! Give 'em both barrels, Terry!"

Even Miltiades felt a grateful glow at this excoriation of
the traditional enemies of his country.

Governor O'Shawn called the crowd to order with an
uplifted hand. When the applause stopped, he began again
in a soft, round tone:

"Gentlemen, ladies, I can carry the parable even further
than that. There was, if I read my Bible aright, a Samaritan,
a good Samaritan, who picked up the hapless traveler,
poured oil on his wounds, placed him on his donkey, and
bore him to an inn.

"I appear before you this evening, ladies and gentlemen,
as a forerunner of that good Samaritan. I come as a herald
of a great Democrat and a great friend to the South. In
counsel he is a Solon; amid the corruptions of our national
politics he is a Cato; as a leader of reform against the high
tariff embattlements of the Northern plutocrats he is a
Richard of the Lion Heart. I refer, ladies and gentlemen,
to that peerless leader, that incorruptible patriot, that wise
and sagacious statesman, our next President of the United
States, Grover Cleveland!"

Shouts, cheers, pandemonium broke out in Courthouse
Square. Hats boiled up between Miltiades and the light.
Even the dignitaries on the portico clapped. Governor
O'Shawn stood by his table mopping his flushed conical fore-
head. In the midst of the uproar a rustic voice shouted:

"Say, Terry, who is Grover Cleveland, anyway, an' whar
does he come frum?"

This caused laughter, but it stilled the applause to await

the answer, because hardly a man had heard the name Cleveland before. The Governor smiled in sympathy with the general amusement.

"Mr. Cleveland is a member of the New York bar."

"Oh, jest another damned Yankee, is he?" drawled the voice.

"He's a nominee of the Democratic party for the Presidency of the United States!" snapped the Governor.

When the orator resumed his discourse, Miltiades Vaiden stopped listening with a restlessness that was natural to him. The Colonel did not enjoy listening to an effective speech from the crowd. If he had been on the platform with the dignitaries, if he were placed so that the speech would pick him out as a man worthy of consideration, a man of position and influence . . .

The mere suggestion of station and power set up a titillation along Miltiades' nerves. He drew a deep breath.

Here a hand touched his shoulder, and a voice behind him said:

"Hey-oh, Colonel, looks like you ort to be up on the stage with the rest of 'em."

Miltiades looked around, balanced between dislike of the hand on his shoulder and the slight gratification of being considered worthy to sit on the platform.

"I don't like to push myself forward," he said gravely.

"You haff to these days, Colonel. Honors used to seek men, but nowadays men seek honors."

"M-m . . . that's true." Then, after a moment, he added, "I was looking for Augustus and Rose, they're in a carriage, have you seen them?" With this Miltiades began moving slowly away from the hand on his shoulder so that its removal would appear unplanned.

The man took down his hand and began to look around.

"There's some buggies yander," he said in the flatted voice of a man whose friendly advances have been declined.

Miltiades walked away in the direction of the buggies on the opposite side of the Square. He was annoyed at himself

for treating the countryman in this fashion, but the hand
on his shoulder had been even more annoying . . . he put
the matter out of his thoughts.

The Colonel had no desire whatever to find Augustus and
Rose, but what he had said to the countryman set him going
on this errand with some vague idea of keeping his word
good. As he drew near the line of shadowy vehicles he began
looking for Judge Ashton's carriage, which would contain
his brother and his sister-in-law.

The occupants of these carriages usually sat staring
fixedly at the speaker. These carriage folk were, in the main,
members of the very oldest families in Florence. In the dim
illumination from the speaker's table across the Square,
Miltiades caught, here and there, the outline of a woman's
face. Even half seen, like this, some of them conveyed that
odd quality of inherited sensitiveness which is what is meant
by breeding.

As Miltiades passed a small single buggy with a pretty
bay mare between its shafts, he heard a lover's tiff going on
in undertones. A girl's voice was saying tautly:

"Lucius, I—I'll get out!"

A youth's voice replied hastily:

"No, don't get out, Miss Sydna. . . ."

"Then sit on your side and listen to the Governor," advised the girl in annoyance.

"I was listening to him, too," teased her companion.

Colonel Vaiden caught a glimpse of the girl's face, a
graceful face filled with the embarrassment of a young girl
who had not yet learned to deal with the small improprie-
ties of the admirers whom she attracted.

The Colonel would have walked on past in silence, but
the expression of the girl aroused in him a sharp disapproval
of the youth in the buggy. Without glancing around he said
in a curt undertone:

"Young man, in a lady's presence you should imitate a
gentleman, at least temporarily." And with that he walked
on.

The faint noises in the runabout hushed. In the silence, Miltiades could hear Governor O'Shawn's peroration:

"And you ladies who have graced this occasion with the bouquet of your faces and the music of your laughter, while you may not sully your fair hands with the ballot, it is yours to see that your husbands and sweethearts march to the polls in November and cast their votes for a white man's party in a white man's land. No true Southern lady would do more; none can do less. I thank you for the inspiration of your presence here tonight."

Here the speaker bowed and turned to men on the platform behind him. This ended his oration.

The usual clapping of hands broke forth. The dignitaries on the portico arose and began congratulating the speaker. The line of carriages near Miltiades started to move. Out of one of the vehicles Miltiades heard the hearty voice of his brother Augustus:

"Milt, wasn't that a speech? Didn't the Governor wade into Wall Street?"

Rose's contralto added something about Marcia . . . Marcia's boy . . . Miltiades did not quite get it. The carriage rolled on out of hearing.

The Colonel moved aimlessly along the street, a little embarrassed to be seen walking in the midst of the moving vehicles. He turned out of their line toward the old Florence Hotel on the corner of the Square.

As he went he thought over the Governor's peroration to the ladies . . . the honor in which Southern men held their women . . . how true were O'Shawn's words. Take, for example, his own action in rebuking the youth in the little hug-me-tight buggy. A Northern man would perhaps have laughed, or have listened and said nothing, but he, a Southern man, had reproved the misdemeanant with a phrase. . . . He continued slowly and aimlessly across the Square with no particular end in view save that, subconsciously, he was putting off as long as possible his return to his fat wife, Ponny.

CHAPTER TWO

Now that the speaking was over, the crowd flowed away in all directions. The first to get in motion were a small group of negroes who had been listening afar off from the front of the old Florence Hotel. To these negroes the Democratic speaking had been a vague demonstration against their liberty. They had, only a score of years before, been set free from slavery by the Republicans. Now all the group were uneasy lest, if a Democratic President be elected, they should be returned to their bonds. One of their number mumbled:

"We ort to been ovah to Mistuh Landahs' meetin'. He stan' by us; we ort to stan' by he."

"Mistah Landahs is sich a dried-up man," complained a second.

"He is a cu'is man," put in a third.

"All Republicans is cu'is if they's white men," opined the first negro philosophically.

"Not in St. Louis," put in a bullet-headed negro who had worked as roustabout on the steamboats. "In St. Louis, Republicans wears high hats an' smokes big seegars jess lak dey wuz somebody."

"St. Louis ain't Flaunts," put in a cautionary negro.

"Hit sho ain't," agreed the third.

The little group fell silent again, watching the white gathering disperse into the dimly lighted streets. Presently a wizened oldish negro feigned a yawn and said he guessed he'd better be moving off home.

The first negro gave a snort of laughter.

"You do, an' Gracie'll have you movin' back quicker'n you moved off. . . . Dis is Sad'day night."

10

The smallish gray-wooled old negro turned on his companions and warned them that they had better remember how the she-bears had come and et up forty little children who had mocked Elijah, a servant of God.

At this the other negroes became silent, for the oldish black man was a preacher of sorts. Presently they began to drift away, but the wizened negro who had said he was going home remained where he was on the hotel corner.

He stood for twenty or thirty minutes, then presently sat down on the iron grating which screened the kitchen window of the hotel in the basement. Then he lay down on the grating like a bundle of rags, pillowing his head on his arms. A faint warmth drifted up from the kitchen, alleviating the chill of the summer night. After a while he fell asleep.

Among the vehicles that rattled away from Courthouse Square a large family carriage went north up Market Street, and a block to the west a little runabout turned northward up Pine Street.

In the large carriage Judge Ashton was saying to his guest, Augustus Vaiden:

"Cleveland is a strong man, Augustus, he will carry New York, Pennsylvania, Indiana, Ohio, and, of course, the South."

Augustus, who never gave politics a thought, agreed to this and then added:

"Riding away from the speaking like this reminds me of fox-hunting. It would be almost cold enough to fox-hunt to-night. I wish I was out listening to the old Dalrymple pack."

Judge Ashton laughed a metallic, ringing laugh that was very friendly and pleasant.

"Miss Rose, when your husband gets to heaven, the first thing he's going to inquire about is the fox-hunting."

The two women in the carriage acknowledged this masculine interruption by laughing and reproaching the speaker for impiety; then Mrs. Rose picked up her conversation with Mrs. Polly Ashton where she had left off:

"I don't know whether Marcia will come or not. . . . I hope so."

"I do hope she will. . . . She was such a pretty girl."

"She looks just as she always did," assured Rose; "her eyes are just what they were when she was a girl."

"When is her boy to come down?" inquired Mrs. Ashton.

"In time to start to college this fall."

"What's his name?"

"Jerry. He's named for his father. He calls himself, Jerry Catlin the second."

The elders smiled at this.

"Marcia's boy would be original," opined the Judge, drawing down his horses near the Rose Vaiden boarding house to let his guests out.

"Send young Jerry over to see my Jefferson when he comes," invited the Judge.

"I will," assured Rose. "I've been thinking about some nice boys for him to associate with."

Mrs. Polly Ashton said she knew the boys would have a good time together, and then, as she drove away from the boarding house, she made a mental note that she would keep her son Jeff away from Jerry Catlin the second until she had time to see what sort of a boy *he* was. The amount of time this required was apparently only a few minutes, for presently she decided that Jerry Catlin the second was not the sort of boy she could let her son Jefferson associate with— and that was settled.

In the second buggy, the small rubber-tired runabout which moved up Pine Street, another conversation was struggling along with considerable bitterness.

"I suppose," said the young man driving the bay mare, "the reason the old codger 'tends to everybody else's business is because he hasn't got any of his own to attend to."

The girl compressed into the seat beside him retorted warmly:

"It was his business."

"Was his business?"

To this repetition the girl replied nothing.

The youth went on:

"If he wasn't such an old man I'd show him how to insult me before you, Sydna."

"Yes, I imagine you would, Lucius Handback!" satirized the girl in an access of distaste.

"I would!" declared the youth hotly. "I'd call him to account!"

"Did you know that Colonel Milt Vaiden was the man who led the Klan when they wiped out the Leatherwood gang?" inquired the girl drily.

"What of that? He had men behind him, ready to help him."

The girl pondered a moment and then said in quite a different voice:

"Besides that, Lucius, he had to correct you when you were bothering me back yonder."

The driver turned in the darkness.

"Had to correct me! What's old man Milt Vaiden got to do with me?"

"It isn't with you; it's with me," said the girl in a far-away voice.

"Why, Sydna—what in the world . . . ?" He paused a moment and became jealously speculative. "He—he's not in love with you, Sydna?"

"The idea! Colonel Milt is old enough to be my father . . . and he's a married man. . . . Lucius, you're the awfulest person!" She tried to pull herself away from him in the constricted space.

"Well, you won't tell anything! I ask you a question, and you won't tell me a thing!"

"No, I won't!"

"Then I have to guess," declared Mr. Handback doggedly, "and if you get mad at my guesses I can't help it."

"At least guess something respectable, if you're guessing about me," admonished the girl.

"Look here, what is between you and old man Vaiden, Sydna?" pleaded young Mr. Handback, almost distracted. "Look here—you—you don't love him, do you—or him you?"

At this repeated offense Miss Sydna Crowninshield became permanently silent. She rode on to her mother's home on Pine Street, disregarding as far as possible the pressure of her companion. She alighted without waiting for Lucius to help her to the ground. With a brief good-night she disappeared within her own gate and found her way alone up the fragrant box-lined path.

As the girl walked up this unseen curving path she presently forgot Lucius Handback, and against the darkness there floated a strange, romantic picture of Colonel Miltiades Vaiden and her dead father, whom she had never seen.

It was a battle picture, and it came to her in the likeness of a painting. The painting was all around her in the form of a cyclorama. On the vast canvas she saw regiments of painted soldiers charging across a landscape. The chief figures in this cyclorama were Colonel Vaiden and her dying father. It was, she thought, the battle of Shiloh, where her father had been killed.

All this elaborate mental arrangement had come to her years and years ago, when she was a small child. In Louisville, Kentucky, her mother had taken her to see a cyclorama of the battle of Gettysburg. When she and her mother had seen the picture, her mother had wept. Drusilla's weeping and the battle scene had filled the little girl's heart with pity and terror. And she believed it was a picture of the battle of Shiloh, where her father had been slain. The wounded man nearest her became her father, and a comrade bending above him became Colonel Miltiades Vaiden.

Her father, she imagined, was whispering to Colonel Vaiden, "Take care of my little girl, Sydna," and the comrade bending down was promising that he would.

Now, as Sydna walked up the graveled path to her door tears began trickling down her face that she should have appeared to belittle herself, even through no fault of her own, before her lifelong protector and ideal of chivalry, Colonel Miltiades Vaiden.

While Sydna was feeling these sharp misgivings, Colonel Vaiden himself moved slowly along a diagonal across Courthouse Square toward the old Florence Hotel. The windows of the hotel were alight, and even from his distance the Colonel could hear irregular outbursts of laughter from the lobby.

This laughter, the Colonel divined, came from traveling men who were matching yarns by way of entertainment for the evening. He walked on, listening to the hilarity with the dissympathy of a man harassed by his own affairs and to whom all jests were unpalatable.

A voice behind him calling out, "Mr. Bivins! Oh, Mr. Bivins, just a moment!" caused the Colonel to look around.

A middle-aged man came hurrying up.

"Mr. Bivins, add three rolls of plow lines and a dozen mule collars to my order. . . ."

When the man came closer, Colonel Vaiden saw who it was and felt a sharp impulse to turn and walk on without a word. His dignity, however, forbade that, so he said briefly:

"I am afraid you have made a mistake, Mr. Handback."

Then the merchant discovered his own error and began begging Miltiades' pardon. He explained, with considerable confusion, that in the dark he had mistaken Miltiades for a hardware drummer who was staying at the hotel.

"That's all right, Mr. Handback," interrupted the Colonel with an ancient resentment flatting his tones.

This disconcerted Mr. Handback even more.

"You're about his height. . . . Slim's thinner than you. . . . I oughtn't to holler at folks in the dark, anyway."

"That's all right," repeated Miltiades with distaste.

But Mr. Handback, once involved in conversation, could not disengage himself easily. He followed on to the hotel in the wake of his companion's contempt.

Miltiades presently began enjoying in a sardonic way the confusion into which the merchant had fallen. He thought to himself, "That's what comes of being a thief . . ." And here he was moved by a sharp physical desire to turn and kick J. Handback's rump clear around Courthouse Square . . . the damned apologetic crook!

The Colonel recalled clearly the offense which now reduced the merchant to such an embarrassed favor currier. Handback had accepted twenty-five hundred dollars' worth of the Vaiden cotton in his store on the very day he made an assignment in bankruptcy. It was all the cotton which Miltiades and Augustus and Cassandra and Marcia Vaiden had raised in a season; their whole year's work gone without a penny. That had been twenty years ago.

Now, with this ancient transaction in their thoughts, the two men would probably have walked to the hotel in silence, had not another group of men entering the Square created a diversion.

J. Handback pointed across the dimly lighted plaza.

"Look yonder, won't you? That damned Landers and his nigger meeting just now breaking up!"

Miltiades looked without enthusiasm and said nothing.

J. Handback began again, exaggerating his contempt to cover his own silently arraigned case.

"I swear I wouldn't affiliate with them black monkeys, not to be postmaster all the rest of my life. I wouldn't do it!"

"A man'll do most anything for money," observed Miltiades drily.

"Uh . . . m-m . . . yes, but I wouldn't do that," stammered the merchant. "It cuts a man off from the society of decent men and women. It's social suicide even to vote the Republican ticket here in Florence, much less bob-bashiely with niggers!"

By this time the Colonel really had become interested in the spectacle before him.

"Yes, I've often thought about Landers," he agreed with less animosity toward his companion: "mixes with niggers;

attends their stinking political gatherings; preaches social equality by his actions—all to keep a little two by four postmastership here in Florence, Alabama, that pays . . . what does it pay, do you suppose?"

"Oh . . . nine or ten hundred. . . ."

"There you are, nine or ten hundred dollars. . . ."

"And what he can steal out of letters. . . ."

"I never heard anybody accuse Landers of stealing anything."

"No, but I say a man who'll do what Landers does will steal!"

"M-m . . . yes . . . he might. . . ."

"Well, I for one can't stand to rub shoulders with a coon. In my store I keep 'em on the other side of the counter; in my fields I keep 'em at the business end of a plow."

"That's right." Miltiades admitted this reluctantly, because it condoned in a subtle way the merchant's theft of the cotton from his family.

"I just can't stand a nigger," repeated the merchant a little emptily.

At this juncture the two uncongenial companions paused before the hotel door. Bursts of laughter from the traveling men came quite loudly now. J. Handback noticed under his feet a bundle of rags that lay stretched out on the iron grating over the basement window. He gave the object a slight kick. It moved and grunted.

"Hey, what you lying here for?" demanded the merchant stepping back from the bundle.

A negro lifted a blinking face in the dim light of the street lamp on the corner.

"Gittin' a li'l' res'," he grunted.

"Is that you, Lump?" inquired the white man quickly.

"Yessuh," mumbled the negro glumly.

"This is a hell of a place to sleep on. . . . How long you been here?"

"Evah sence de white fo'ks' speakin'," answered the negro resentfully.

"Well . . . don't let me disturb your slumbers," said the merchant with an attempt at humor.

"You mean my slumbahs on dis gratin'?" asked Lump dourly.

"Of course I mean this grating. . . . Look here, nigger, don't get impudent with me!"

"I ain't gittin' impidunt." The small black man sat up slowly, blinking at the street lamp.

The merchant stood looking down on Lump when a burst of laughter from the hotel lobby seemed to turn his thoughts from the negro. He looked at Miltiades and asked tentatively:

"Colonel Vaiden . . . might I ask you to do me a favor?"

"What is it?" inquired the Colonel dubiously.

"Would you mind stepping in the lobby and telling Slim Bivins to add three rolls of plow lines and a dozen assorted mule collars to my order?"

"No-o. . . . I don't mind. . . . Why don't you do it yourself?"

"Because if I go in Slim'll sell me more collars and rope than I want; then I'll have to drink with him and listen to his jokes. I won't get away till midnight. He can't do you thatta way, because he don't know you."

"Well . . ." agreed the Colonel reluctantly, "what is it you want to order?"

"Three rolls of plow lines and a dozen assorted mule collars."

"We-ell . . . I'll give it in just as you said it to me."

"Thank you very much, Colonel—very much," said the merchant gratefully. "Good-night."

"Good-night," returned Miltiades, wondering a little to hear himself saying good-night to J. Handback. Then he gave an inaudible sniff of laughter through his nose as a man does when he is disgusted with himself.

J. Handback moved off toward Market Street, apparently going to his home in the northern end of town.

The small negro on the grating and the tall man on the step watched him in silence. Once the retreating merchant paused to look back over his shoulder. At last, when he became a dim blur against the walls of the opposite stores, Miltiades saw him change his course in the general direction of East Florence.

A vague speculation floated through the Colonel's mind as to why J. Handback should have turned toward East Florence, but he neither pressed the point, nor did he care. Any unconventionality which the merchant probably had in mind was no more in the Colonel's estimation than where some dog buried a bone. The fellow was a thief. . . .

At another burst of laughter from the lobby Colonel Vaiden turned into the hotel and left the small negro still sitting motionless on the grating, staring up at the street lamp, at a row of gnarled mulberries which began at the corner and extended southward along a line of offices called Intelligence Row, and at the remote indifference of the stars.

Inside the lobby of the Florence Hotel Colonel Vaiden found a group of five commercial travelers with cigars cocked at optimistic angles as they retold bawdy-house yarns and spat at dirty brass cuspidors. On the wall behind the clerk's desk a heroic-sized lithograph of Grover Cleveland stared solemnly down upon the guffawing yarn spinners.

For some minutes Colonel Miltiades Vaiden stood just inside the doorway listening to the lickerish and utterly impossible anecdotes. The Colonel was the sort of man at whom the tale tellers would glance now and then and allow to remain standing where he was. This slight discourtesy did not offend him, but it set him in a mood of ironic musing. Here was he, a man filled with an unavailing certainty of his own ability, and here were these gregarious drummers without a thought of anything beyond cards, whisky, and women; yet he had nothing to do, he was at a social and financial stalemate, while they moved along their grooves like oiled and prosperous automata.

He still thought wryly of this antithesis as he went forward and asked for a Mr. Bivins.

A slender red-headed man arose, introduced himself, and
offered his hand with a traveling man's affability. The
Colonel explained the extra items which J. Handback wanted
to add to his order. Mr. Bivins became businesslike at once.
He went to a desk in the lobby, drew out his order book, and
poised his pencil.

"What grade plow line does he want?"

The Colonel didn't know.

"Then I'll ship him my second grade. Handback is a man
who never buys the best grade of anything, but I understand
he sells the best grade of everything."

Laughter broke out in the lobby at this characterization.

"Was there anything else, Mr. Vaiden?" inquired Bivins,
laughing with the others at his own jest.

"No, that was all he told me to order," said the Colonel,
with half his attention on the drummer's great catalogue.

"No plows, horseshoes, nails, bolts . . . ?"

"No, that was all he said."

"Well, I appreciate your courtesy. Won't you sit down a
minute? Andy, bring two glasses of cracked ice. . . . You'll
take a snort with me, won't you, Mr. Vaiden?"

Miltiades agreed to the snort and sat down to wait for it.
As he did so a faint tentative design began to grow in his
thoughts. He began mentally taking stock of every avail-
able resource which he possibly might scrape together. He
thought over his own family, Rose and Augustus, his sister
Cassandra, his other sister Marcia, who lived up in Tennessee. He was considering borrowing some money. The sum
he had in mind was five hundred dollars. He wondered if he
could start a little business on a capital of five hundred
dollars, but then he knew he would never be able to raise that
amount among his brothers and sisters, and the notion faded
from his thoughts.

His conversation with Bivins had continued in the

mechanical fashion of unattended talk. He was asking the drummer how he found business over the country.

"Pretty good now," declared Bivins with a salesman's optimism, "but when we get him seated in the Presidential chair—" he nodded at the lithograph behind the clerk's desk—"you'll see business pick up sure enough. The minute the Democrats get hold of this country the South is bound to boom."

"That's right," put in a drummer with a harelip: "buy ever'thing low, sell ever'thing high, do a rushing trade all the year roun', that's the Democratic platform, Mr. Vaiden."

Miltiades suddenly set aside this irrelevant conversation.

"May I have a talk with you privately for a moment, Mr. Bivins?" he asked.

The drummer's manner changed.

"Certainly." He glanced about, led the way to a door that opened into a hall. He went to a hat tree, rested an elbow on it, and took his cigar from his mouth. "Now, what can I do for you, Mr. Vaiden?"

Miltiades knew almost to a certainty that his request would be refused, but he thought to himself, "It won't make any difference. I'll be as well off refused as I am now." He moistened his lips and said aloud:

"I was thinking of starting a business of my own, Mr. Bivins."

The drummer opened his eyes.

"A whole stock?"

Miltiades nodded.

"Going to run a hardware store, Major?" inquired the salesman, instinctively bestowing some title on his prospect.

"No, general merchandise."

"I see . . . have a hardware department . . . now . . . now, just wait here a moment. . . ."

Bivins went back into the lobby. Miltiades could see him through the open door moving with a kind of springiness in his thin legs to his catalogue on the writing desk.

The harelipped drummer called out in flapping tones:

"Slim, what you goin' to do with that?"

"Select a shotgun. Major Vaiden's ordering it through J. Handback."

The slim man came back alertly with his catalogue.

Miltiades' confidence was deserting him. He began a tentative:

"Now, Mr. Bivins, as to terms . . ."

"Terms no object," scouted the drummer, "when you hook up with the Black Diamond line, you'll get the goods, and the terms will take care of themselves. All right now . . . adzes, axes, axletrees, ax handles, Axminster carpets, ash trays, ash cans, awls. . . . Oh, Andy," he called to some noise in the lobby, "bring 'em right out here in the hall, will you?"

The lobby door opened, and the negro porter came out with tray and clinking glasses. Mr. Bivins closed his book, handed a whisky to Miltiades, took the other and lifted it to the level of his eyes.

"Here's to love, its joy and fret.
May this bring a solace and help you forget
The woman you want . . . and the woman you get."

Miltiades had no answering cliché. He touched his glass to that of Mr. Bivins, and the two drank solemnly.

The drummer put his glass back on the tray, thumped his catalogue.

"Now, Major, le's start," he urged briskly.

When Miltiades returned to the problem of stocking his store Mr. Bivins proved to be a man of endless memory. He rattled off lists of merchandise almost alphabetically. The Colonel himself had once been an overseer on a cotton plantation, and his memory of the commissary guided his purchases. All the time he was uneasy about really getting these goods from the drummer. Now and then he would interrupt the order in an effort to ascertain the terms on which he was to receive this stock, but Mr. Bivins shooed him down. He would do everything any other house would do.

In the midst of this brisk trading the lobby door opened, and the harelipped man entered the hall. He began, in his jocular voice, saying it took Bivins a hell of a time to sell a shotgun; then he ejaculated, "How the devil are you selling shotguns with your catalogue opened at slickers?"

Bivins began laughing and admitted that he was selling Mr. Vaiden a complete line of merchandise. The harelipped man was genially outraged.

"Don't you let Slim Bivins stock you up on that Black Diamond trash he sells. What you need is the genuine Bulldog Brand, Mr. Vaiden."

His noise brought other salesmen into the hallway, and for the next two hours Miltiades was deluged with prices and freight rates from Louisville, Cincinnati, St. Louis, and Evansville.

When the night was more than half gone Bivins nodded Miltiades aside and said, "Now, Major, I can ship you my goods in ten, twenty, or thirty days—any time you say."

Miltiades, who had grown dull during this prolonged buying, became alert again at this final adjustment of terms.

"When am I to pay for these things, Mr. Bivins?" he inquired, looking at the salesman.

Bivins came to a halt, a little surprised.

"Why . . . don't you want to pay for them now?"

"Well, no—that wouldn't be convenient," admitted the Colonel a little uneasily.

"Could you . . . pay me half down?" suggested Bivins uncertainly. "My firm would carry the rest for thirty, sixty, and ninety days."

Miltiades came to a halt in his mercantile career.

"Let me see . . . my bill comes to . . ."

"Nine hundred and sixteen dollars," supplied Bivins hopefully.

Miltiades was embarrassed. He thought swiftly that he might borrow two hundred dollars on the proposed stock of goods from his wife's father.

"Suppose I send you two hundred . . . three hundred when I receive the goods?"

"Three hundred?" repeated Bivins in amazement.

"And make payments every thirty days," added the Colonel.

"You can't pay half down now?" pressed Bivins in flatted tones.

"No-o . . ." admitted Miltiades, with a drying mouth, "at present my resources are tied up in a cotton plantation —near BeShears' Crossroads."

Mr. Bivins closed his order book.

"Ed," he said to the dry-goods drummer, who stood awaiting his turn, "Mr. Vaiden here tells me his assets are tied up in a cotton plantation out somewhere near BeShears' Crossroads."

"What's the idyah?" demanded the harelipped man brusquely. "Did he imagine he could buy a stock of general merchandise by giving a mortgage on a cotton crop?"

"I don't know what he thought," said Bivins.

"I told you in the beginning," stated the Colonel with a whitening face, "that we'd better discuss terms first!"

"Hell fire, I thought you wanted to know what discount I'd give for cash!" cried Bivins, and he snapped his rubber band on his order book.

The dry-goods man said querulously:

"Damn it, I've set up here nearly all night! A man never gets ahead by working at night."

The Colonel had a desire to punch their collective heads. A moment ago they were all so polite; now they were sarcastic and insulting. He looked at them inimically:

"Won't a one of you men sell me some goods on time and let me pay for them when I can?"

The dry-goods drummer turned to the porter and told him to lock up the sample room again and not to wake him till ten o'clock next morning.

To this by-play the Colonel made a stiff bow.

"All right, gentlemen. I'm going to do business here in

Florence, and one of these days you drummers are going to come begging me to let you open your sample cases in my store. . . . Good-evening."

Colonel Vaiden passed out of the hotel vibrating with anger and chagrin at what had happened. He was not, as he fatuously had forecast, as well off now as he had been before he was refused credit. He had felt all the time that he would be refused, but now that it had come to pass, he was morally wounded and deeply incensed.

He paused on the steps of the hotel damning the drummers to hell. One of these days they would beg him for an order . . . just as he had said.

A late moon had risen and cast a faint glimmer over the courthouse tower and the tops of the gnarled mulberries along Intelligence Row. Then the Colonel saw the small negro still curled on the basement grating. This annoyed him. He kicked the negro's legs.

"Get up! What do you want to hang around here for all night?" he demanded in brittle temper.

The black figure stirred.

"Got to hang roun' some'r's all night," it mumbled.

"Whyn't you get along home?"

"I git uhlong home I come back fasteh 'n I got."

The white man turned from the negro and started walking along the west side of the Square toward Market Street. Two lights, moonlight and lamplight, lay mingled in faint yellow and white spotulations along the thoroughfare. Miltiades began thinking what he should have said to the salesmen. He should have said:

"Gentlemen, I entered this hotel to do one of your number a slight favor; then I desired to ask him a simple question about the possibility of credit. He wouldn't hear my inquiry until he had run up a long bill of goods; then the group of you insult me about the matter. Do you call yourselves Southern gentlemen?"

Miltiades' lips took on a contemptuous smile as he

imagined how the drummers would have stood, quite taken
aback at his cold and scathing dignity. Presently this drifted
from his mind and left him thinking of the commissary he
had run before the war on the old Lacefield plantation down
in the Reserve. He had controlled two hundred negroes,
fifteen hundred acres of cotton, and the commissary. The
commissary itself had been a mere detail in those days, but
what he had learned about it would become important when
he finally obtained a store of his own.

The Colonel moved up Market Street with the faint moonlight persistently bringing back the old Lacefield plantation
days. He remembered old man Carruthers Lacefield and his
wife; A. Gray, the son, who was now editor of the Florence
paper, and the daughter of the family, Drusilla. . . .
Drusilla had been engaged to be married to him, and she had
eloped with another man, Emory Crowninshield, on the night
before their wedding. . . . Again he recalled very distinctly
his return home after the war, how he had engaged himself
to Drusilla once more and had seduced and jilted her. That
was a long time ago, yet Drusilla's gift of herself to him
still stood like a far-away light amid the foggy commonplaces of his succeeding love life.

However, it seemed to Miltiades that after all it was a good
thing that he had not married Drusilla. He had not made a
success, and their contemplated marriage always tacitly had
been founded on his becoming wealthy and successful. He
still believed he was going to be successful, but he would not
have liked to share with Drusilla this long flat stretch of
poverty. For Ponny—for his fat wife Ponny—it was all
right, but for Drusilla it would have been impossible.

The sound of footsteps filled the last of the night with a
far-reaching, uneven clacking and exorcised the ghost of
Drusilla. The Colonel stood looking down the milky blur of
Market Street with a faint curiosity as to who could be
walking away from town at such an hour. Presently a figure
defined itself against the gray pall of the morning, weaving
a little from side to side. The man came up within fifteen or

twenty yards of Miltiades, then stopped and stood with a hand on the palings, looking at him.

The identity of the befuddled man caused Miltiades not so much surprise as a sort of contemptuous recognition of something he should have guessed. He turned to walk away when the figure came on again as if touched off by a button.

"Why, it's my frien' Colonel Vaiden," it babbled. "Thought for a moment . . . might be somebody . . . wouldn't want to see me out . . . you know . . . late like this . . . but . . . but see I'm in han's of a frien' . . . eh, Colonel? . . . we're frien's, ain't we, Colonel?"

Miltiades stood with military erectness looking at the fellow.

"Well, yes," he agreed drily, "you might say we're friends, barring the fact that you stole twenty-five hundred dollars from me twenty years ago."

J. Handback came to a pause.

"Still think o' that?"

"Now and then."

"Uh-huh . . . now an' then," agreed the merchant, with wounded gravity, "but . . . but you never conshidered me, I . . . s'pose?"

"I don't know what there is to consider."

"Hol' on," protested the drunken man, "lots to conshider. . . . I . . . I had a big stock merchandise, Colonel . . . trem'lin' . . . trem'lin' on edge of bankrup'cy. I . . . I couldn't say to you that mornin' . . . 'No, can't receive your money, Colonel . . . not solvent.' Immejiately ever'-body would wanted theirs back. . . . They . . . they did . . . few hours later, anyway . . . but . . . but . . . didn't know that then."

Moisture had come out on the face of the merchant in his earnestness.

"Well," said the Colonel after a moment, "we won't stand here on Sunday morning and go into that."

"No . . . no . . . won't go into that. . . ." He stood for a moment or two, ill at ease; then, by way of changing the topic, "Didn't see nothin' more of that damn nigger-lovin' Landers, I s'pose?"

"No, and I hope I won't."

"Amen to that, Colonel. . . . Disgrace . . . 'filiatin' with a lot o' damn dirty niggers . . . ort to be drummed out o' town. . . ." Here he came to another conversational dead end and stood looking around in the graying morning. "Well . . . better be movin' 'long some'r's. . . ."

As the fellow lurched forward, the convention of seeing a drunken acquaintance safely home came upon Miltiades.

"Do you know where you're going, Mr. Handback?" he inquired without enthusiasm.

"Now . . . now, Colonel, I . . . I can't truthfully say I know where I'm goin'."

"Don't you know your way home?"

"Yesh . . . I know my way home, but . . . but I can't go there."

"What's the matter?"

"Muh . . . muh wife not expectin' me." He gave Miltiades a badly done wink. "I'm off . . . seein' 'bout one o' muh farms."

"I see. . . . Then what are you going to do?"

"Well, I . . . I b'lieve I'll jess walk home with you, Colonel . . . set aroun' an' . . . an' talk till church time."

"That's not practical," declared the Colonel at once. "Ponny would see your condition. She might mention it to somebody."

"Don't b'lieve she could tell it on me, Colonel. . . . Don't b'lieve a soul in the worl' have a spishion."

"She might. I wouldn't want to risk it," decided the Colonel.

Miltiades stood considering what was best to do. He disliked the man, but Handback had a very good reputation. He was a deacon in the Methodist church, and the Colonel did not have the petty spite to allow the fellow to waste his good name by wandering around on the streets drunk. So

now he took his arm and started thoughtfully back down
Market Street toward town.

Handback offered no objection, but began explaining himself more fully.

"Jess been to see a frien' o' mine, Colonel . . . lady
frien' . . . sh-she's damn near a lady . . . damn near
white, too, even if I do say it."

"M-m," said the Colonel, with the disapproval of one man
for another man's unconventionalities.

"Now . . . now . . . man needs a li'l' relaxation," defended the merchant, "relieves business strain. . . .
Whicherway we goin'?"

"To the hotel."

"By George . . . good idyah . . . forgot we had a
hotel." The merchant's steps depended more and more on the
Colonel. "But I should uh stayed out the night at Gracie's
. . . ver' nice woman, Colonel . . . kep' her for years . . .
Clean . . . discreet, an' . . . an' obligin'. . . ."

They were approaching Courthouse Square again. Some
of the lamps, which were gauged to extinguish themselves in
the morning, were out. Miltiades angled across the square
with his burden.

The single night light burning in the lobby had faded to a
small pale tongue of flame in the gray morning. The night
clerk dozed with his head on the register. Miltiades did not
waken the man but maneuvered his charge up the flight of
stairs into the first empty bedroom he found. He stood for a
moment breathing deeply from his exertion, then tiptoed
down again. The clerk was still asleep. Behind him and above
his head was a large lithograph of Cleveland bearing the
legend, "The man from Buffalo—the hope of Southern
Democracy."

When Miltiades walked out of the door again, the small
old negro, Lump Mowbray, had disappeared from the grating over the basement window.

CHAPTER THREE

THE small wizened negro who had slept on the hotel grating all night now shuffled along a road which led from old Florence to East Florence, Alabama.

When the black man had seen J. Handback, the merchant, enter the hotel, this automatically released Lump from his vigil on the grating. Now he mumbled to himself as he moved along the road:

"Bettah watch out, white man . . . road ob de sinnah leads to 'struction. . . . You gwi' cry, 'Lawd! Lawd!' but de Lawd won' know ye. . . ."

Here the distant intonation of a steamboat caught Lump's ear. He forgot his anathema to listen, and presently identified:

"'At's de *Rapidan* . . . comin' troo de shoals. . . ."

Then he moved on with his mumblings.

At the first shanghai cabin within the bounds of East Florence, Lump stopped at a rickety gate which was supported by two bare posts. It had no fence on either side; nevertheless, the small negro stopped just outside the gate as if he were excluded by it and called in a guarded voice:

"Sistah Tony! Oh, Sistah Tony!"

There was a movement inside the shack, and a middle-aged coffee-colored woman with a motherly face opened the door.

"Dat you, Brothah Lump?" she asked in her soft negro voice.

"Yes'm. . . . You kin let Toussaint go home now when he wakes up."

"Lawzee, Toussaint done gone home half hour ago."

Lump looked at the gathering silver in the sky and shook his head.

"Hits a mo'tal shame, Sistah Tony . . . hits a mo'tal sname fuh a woman to ack whicherway as Gracie do, huh wid a grown son."

"Yeh . . . but hit's been goin' on fuh a long time, Brothah Lump."

"Yeh, de Lawd's patient, but when He lay He han' on dat woman, He gwi' lay it on huh."

"Dat's a fack," agreed the coffee-colored woman with equal solemnity.

As she said this three children appeared in the doorway beside her, a black child, a brown child, and a small yellow child. The small one caught her mother's leg through her mother hubbard.

"How de Lawd lay He han' on Miss Gracie, Mammy?"

"You-all go back to yo' pallets." The mother pushed them away.

When they disappeared, the negro man shook his head.

"Chillun allus want to know somep'n."

"Hit's nachel—hit's nachel," said the woman, "evahthing what's bad is nachel."

The wizened man scratched his wool.

"I was jess wond'rin', Sistah Tony . . . you livin' heah lak you is, a single woman . . . jess wond'rin', if'n I come roun' to see you some eb'nin' when de chillun's asleep . . . would I be welcome?"

"Go 'long, Brothah Lump, hush yo' foolishness."

"It ain't foolishness. . . . I means hit, Sistah Tony."

"Co'se you means hit. When a man speaks to a woman like dat, he allus means hit." Then she added significantly, "I heard de *Rapidan* while ago. . . . Fo' Spot on de *Rapidan*."

"Well . . . nobody skeered o' Fo' Spot."

"Maybe not, but de *Rapidan* blowed while ago, jess a same. . . ." Then, of a sudden, she thought of something really important: "Lawzee me, Miss Rose ain't specktin' de *Rapidan* tull sometime dis eb'nin'!"

"Whut she speck'n hit fuh?"

"Specktin' huh nephew on hit. Gwi' meet him at de boat, but you know dat boat's whistle ain't gwi' wake no white folks up. . . ." She stood pondering what to do. "Look heah, I gotto git dese chillun somep'n t'eat, 'n'en I'll hurry ovah an' sta't breakfus' fuh Miss Rose an' tell huh de *Rapidan's* in hea'in'."

"Weil, if'n you change yo' min', lemme know."

And Lump moved from the isolated gate down the lane. His thoughts now came back to Gracie, Gracie, who was breaking the Lord's commandments and living in sin. And here was he, Lump Mowbray, a man of God, who wrestled with her in her wickedness, and she paid no heed at all. He shook his head. . . . "Lawd, tech dat Gracie's ha'd hea't."

A little later, with a sense of getting home, Lump entered a trim white cottage by the back door. A blond youth with blue eyes and the dried-looking blond hair of a negro was making coffee on a stove.

Lump stepped inside and asked in a lowered voice:

"Is yo' mammy asleep?"

"I thought I heard her while ago."

"I'll take a cup o' coffee to huh," offered Lump.

"Don't bother, I'll do it," said the son, with a touch of jealousy.

The black man became hortative at once.

"Look heah, Toussaint, what you wastin' yo' time makin' coffee fuh? Why'n't you take yo' blackin' box ovah to de co'thouse? Lot o' white folks wantin' to shine dey shoes full chu'ch dis mawnin'."

"I don't like to shine shoes," frowned the boy.

"Don't you like a nickel?"

"I don't like bendin' down, shinin' shoes," restated the white negro.

"You's a fool niggah. Don't want to ben' down an' shine shoes! Don't you know de Bible say dem as ben's low shall stan' high? Now, you take yo' breshes an' go on ovah to de co'thouse lak I tol' je."

The voice of a woman from the front room interrupted

the discussion by asking Toussaint to bring her coffee.

The white youth poured out a cup and hurried into the front room. It was a neat room with white counterpaned bed on which lay a creamy-faced woman. The woman stretched out her arm and took, not the coffee, but her son's hand. She patted his hand and held up her cheek for him to kiss.

"What were you and Lump arguing about?" she asked gently.

"He wanted me to go down and black shoes."

"Well . . . why don't you?"

"I don't like pickin' up nickels the white folks throw on the ground."

"Don't they . . . hand them to you?"

"No, they throw 'em on the ground . . . and I don't like blacking shoes."

The quadroon looked at her son with a disturbed face.

"Toussaint, you'll have to do something for white people. . . . You have to live."

"I'll work for myself some day," said the boy moodily.

"If we ever get money enough, I'll take you to school somewhere," said Gracie earnestly. "You can learn a profession, you ought to do anything you can now to help, Toussaint."

Lump entered the doorway with a sugar bowl.

"Whut I wuz tellin' him. You got a up-haided boy, Gracie. Them as hol's they haid high shall be brought low. At's whut de Bible say."

"I believe I'd go on, Toussaint," suggested the mother affectionately. "Everything you make is that much."

The white negro boy gave over his cup, kissed his mother again, and went back into the kitchen after his kit. When he was gone, Lump stood looking at the woman in bed with the bitterness of long abstention in his face. He knew who had been in the room that night.

"I 'clar', Gracie, de Lawd don' like yo' goin's-on. Sen'in' away yo' chile at night. Somep'n gwi' happen to you an' Toussaint one o' these days."

"You know a lot about the Lord," said the woman uneasily.

"I kin read de Bible," defended Lump with spirit.

This troubled Gracie. Her wizened hanger-on and his Bible always troubled the woman more or less. She had an unadmitted feeling that Lump was a kind of carping, fault-finding voice of God in her home.

"No, suh," concluded Lump, "de Lawd don' like no sich, an' he ain't gwi' bless no chile whut come frum sich doin's eithuh."

The woman pushed herself up on her elbow, her black eyes hardening at the man.

"You leave Toussaint out of this." After a few seconds she added, "You know he's better off as he is."

"You means . . . whut you means . . . better off as he is?"

"You know what I mean!"

"You means . . . high colored . . . lak his is?"

"I mean he's fine looking and high spirited and honorable and good and . . . white, and you know he wouldn't have been if——" She stopped passionately, ready to fling out, "—if his daddy had been a black scarecrow like you!"

It was Lump's misfortune to understand perfectly what she left out. A wave of wrath lifted his voice.

"Yes, if . . . if. . . . Do you know whut de Bible say? Hit say, Cuss be de seed ob de scarlet woman! Hit say she sins an' wipe huh lips an say, 'I have done nothin'.' Dat's you, Gracie Vaiden, sinnin' an' wipin' yo' lips an' sayin' you ain't done nothin'! But cuss shell be yo' seed, Gracie Vaiden! He shall be struck down an cas' in de fiah. . . . De Bible say hit!"

Gracie sat up and looked at her monitor in horror.

"It doesn't say it!" she cried.

"Hit do say hit! I'll show you. . . ."

He started toward the kitchen for the Bible. Renewed fear went over the quadroon.

"Let it alone! Let it alone!" she called after him. She got

out of bed, crossed to the door, and thumb-bolted it. "I hope your Bible chokes you!" she cried through the door— "always ramming it down other people's throats!"

She was on the verge of weeping. Her chronic fear that something might happen to Toussaint was reinforced by Lump's quotations. They tore at her heart. She stood by the door, her heavy bosom rising and falling.

As for herself, something might happen to her. She was a woman living in sin. Mr. Handback kept her. Here she led an isolated, apprehensive, and vaguely melancholy life. But Toussaint was innocent and honorable and truthful . . . and white. It would be terrible if anything, through her sins, befell Toussaint.

CHAPTER FOUR

AT SOMETHING near six o'clock that Sunday morning the organ tone of the *Rapidan* rolled out over Florence and the countryside, and in this wide scope its heavy musical note set off various reactions.

For example, Miss Tony, the coffee-colored single woman with so many children, hesitated as she was about to leave her shack and suddenly decided that she would not work that day. So she sent word to her white folks by Toussaint Vaiden, who was passing, that she had a misery in her side and couldn't come. Then she remained at her gate, where the whistle had caught her, waiting luxuriously in the early morning sunshine until Fo' Spot should appear down the lane.

On board the *Rapidan* itself, the thunder of the whistle above a certain stateroom caused young Jerry Catlin to roll out of his berth, peer through his cabin door, and see the long skinny bridge at Florence with its sixteen piers. He began a hurried packing of his suitcase lest the packet land and steam away again with him still on board. The freight elevator and the bridge which he could see coming closer and closer overwhelmed his imagination. He wondered how he would ever find his uncle Augustus in the great metropolis he was approaching. His father and mother and brothers and sisters, whom he had left down the river beyond the edge of this new universe, seemed not only to have been left behind, but to have vanished utterly from the world. He felt sick.

The same blast of the *Rapidan's* whistle which had aroused Jerry Catlin to homesickness and uncertainty

rattled at the window of room number seven in the old
Florence Hotel on Courthouse Square and startled from an
uneasy sleep Mr. J. Handback, Esq., senior partner of the
firm J. Handback & Son, General Merchandise.

Mr. Handback did not know what had awakened him.
He was conscious only of a pain in his temples when he lifted
his head and looked at the window.

The merchant did not recognize his sleeping quarters. He
got to a sitting posture, clenching his eyes shut at the pain
the movement cost him. When he opened them again he saw
the courthouse outside the window and decided slowly that
he was in one of the bedrooms of the old Florence Hotel.

He had no idea how he got there. As he sat pressing his
fingers to his temples he had a ghost of a memory of two
men weaving their way across Courthouse Square to this
hotel. And he had a residual impression that one of these
two men had been talking and talking to the other of the
most intimate and indiscreet matters. As to the identity of
the good Samaritan who had brought the talking man up
to this room, J. Handback had not the slightest clew. But
the other man, the talker, who had done the confiding, the
merchant suspected was himself.

So now he sat, poulticing his head with his hand, wondering apprehensively who that first helpful man could have
been. He hoped he was not a gossipy man. Suppose his wife
should get hold of the story, or his son Lucius, or the
deacons of the Methodist church! Suppose public talk
forced the other deacons to take official notice of the matter.
They might have to do something about it. By custom and
practice these deacons officially were unobserving, each one
of the others, but enough gossip could push even a Methodist
board of deacons to the wall and their eyes, albeit ever so
unwillingly, could be opened.

J. Handback arose painfully from his bed, swearing to
himself that he would never again visit the establishment
which he kept in East Florence. It was Sunday, he was
disheveled, and he could not very well go home to dress. He

got to the door, opened it, and called out with due regard
for his aching head:

"Andy! Oh, Andy, where the devil are you?"

A bulky black man, sweeping the lobby below, dropped
his broom and hurried upstairs as fast as his weight would
allow. When he saw Mr. Handback standing in the door of
number seven calling for ice water he wheeled down again
and in due time reappeared with a pitcher.

The porter had large, perfectly flat, noiseless feet,
encased in dilapidated canvas slippers which were run over
in both easterly and westerly directions. He entered number
seven as silently as the ghost of a hogshead. His rolling
black face, the manner in which he poured a glass of water,
all exuded sympathy. He offered the water to the man seated
on the bed and poured more into the bowl to bathe the
patient's face. The merchant drank, closed his eyes, opened
them again and said:

"Andy, could you press this suit?"

"No trouble a-tall, Mistah Han'back. . . . Ah'll set a
arn on de stove."

"Well, get it off of me."

The exertion of stooping and pulling the cuffs of the trousers over the shoe heels caused Andy to puff and perspire.

"Now, what else, Mistuh Han'back?"

The merchant looked at himself, fingered his collar.

"Listen. Go around to my store and yell for Love or
Stebbins to let you in. Bring me a white fifteen and a half
shirt, a black bow tie that's already tied, a pair of black
socks . . . and, Andy, there's no need to mention who you
want 'em for."

"Mistuh Han'back, I ain't potahed in dis hotel six year
gwine on seven fuh nothin'."

This pledge of silence brought back to the merchant's
mind the other man, who had helped him into the hotel on
the preceding night.

"And, Andy, did you happen to notice who it was came
into the hotel with me last night?"

The porter pondered.

"I didn' jess zactly notice who come in wid you, Mistuh Han'back."

"Did you see who went out?"

"No, suh, didn' see that neithah . . . mus' 'a' been asleep."

"Well, get my clothes and hurry back with 'em. I've got to be at the church by eleven. I'm an usher."

"Yessuh, yessuh, mighty pa'ticklah job, too. I knows. I'se a ushah at St. James."

The fat negro was hurrying out when he remembered something.

"Mistuh Han'back, ea'ly dis mawnin' when I steps outside to see if'n I could heah anything uv de *Rapidan*, I saw Col'l Milt Vaiden come out o' dis hotel. Don't reckon it could 'a' been he, do you?"

At the mention of the name a queer desolation of spirit spread over the merchant.

"Colonel Vaiden!"

Andy noted his patron's dismay and immediately shifted to the other foot.

"Oh, I don' reckon it was he. De Colonel was powwowin' wid de drummahs all night long. Guess he got th'ough wid 'em 'bout fo' o'clock dis mawn."

The merchant exhaled a long breath.

"No-o. . . . I don't suppose it was him."

But even as he said this, the fact stood before the merchant that it had been Colonel Miltiades Vaiden. The whole encounter came to him, still nebulously, but with complete certainty. He even remembered what he had said to the Colonel, his arguments for going to his quadroon mistress . . . of all men in Florence to pick out Miltiades Vaiden for such a confession! The most unforgiving enemy he had in the world!

In the midst of this shock and dismay at his own self-treachery, the porter returned with the clothes. Mr. Handback put them on, bathed his face again, and went down

into the Square. As he stepped out of the hotel door he saw
Governor O'Shawn, under a mulberry tree, having his shoes
shined. The boy who was doing this work seemed to be a
white boy. Now, it happened that J. Handback was looking
for a boy, but he wanted a colored boy. He wanted to send
a note, and he thought a white boy might read a note delivered to his care, but a colored boy would not. So now he
strolled down to the Governor, keeping an eye out for a
black lad.

Governor O'Shawn stroked a choppy, silvery mustache.

"Good-morning, John. Out early this morning."

The merchant explained he had come down to add some
items to an order he had given Slim Bivins, then added that
he was looking for a nigger boy to take a note.

The Governor nodded toward his bootblack and said that
was one.

"That boy a nigger!"

The Governor closed his eyes and nodded again.

"Yes, sir. Niggers are growing up here today, John, you
can't tell from white boys. They're a social danger. Now,
when that boy grows up, what's he going to do? Will he
stay black, or will he go off some place where he's not known
and pass himself off for a white man?"

Handback thought about this.

"That's a serious proposition."

"It's a problem the South has got to face," said the
Governor.

Here the merchant raised his voice and called out:

"Oh, boy, come back here, I can use you."

The octoroon, who had finished and was walking away
with his box, approached the two men again.

At the same moment, from the direction of the boat landing, a tall, thin boy came up Intelligence Row carrying a
dilapidated suitcase. As the newcomer drew near the group
cn the corner he angled across the Square to avoid passing
them.

J. Handback drew out a memorandum book, scribbled a

note, tore out the page, and asked the octoroon if he knew where Colonel Miltiades Vaiden lived. The bootblack said he did.

"Here's a dime and a note. Take the note to the Colonel before church time, or it'll be too late."

The octoroon put his shoe box in the hollow of a mulberry tree and set out with the note. The white boy with the suitcase was about the same size as the negro, and when it came to actual tint, much of a color too.

The white boy moved slowly up Market Street, shifting his suitcase from hand to hand at shorter and shorter intervals. He was evidently tired, so the colored boy with the note remained behind the white boy lest he be commandeered into the chore of carrying the white boy's grip.

But the white boy really was not thinking of his suitcase. When he had walked out of the business section of Florence, the old manors, half hidden by trees, charmed him. They were redolent of a poetry that had been poured into his eyes since babyhood.

This was Florence, the world about which his mother, Marcia Vaiden Catlin, had told him innumerable tales. At any moment, it seemed to the lad, some hero of a story might step out of one of these great old gates and accost him; some soldier, or lawyer, or orator, or great slave owner; people of that ancient and magnificent world which his mother had known!

The boy with the suitcase wished to inquire where his uncle Augustus and his aunt Rose lived when he saw a boy in knickerbockers jumping on a lawn.

Jerry Catlin had never before seen a boy of his own size wear knickers. He paused by the iron fence with his question in his mind, but was stopped from asking it by the unusualness of the strange boy's attire. He stood at the fence until the boy in the yard stopped jumping and called out:

"What you got in that box?"

"It's not a box," said Jerry, "it's a telescope."

The boy came running to the fence.

"Let me look through it."

"It's not that sort." Jerry put down the heavy pack. "It's a telescope suitcase to put my clo'es in."

The boy looked at the suitcase.

"You must keep your best clothes in that," he opined.

"No, I've got my best clo'es on," said Jerry innocently.

"I see," nodded the boy, "you have to carry the others in a box because if you put 'em on they'd fall off."

At this gratuitous insult a flush of wrath went through Jerry. He started to climb the fence and avenge this slur on his clothes, but just then a much subtler revenge suggested itself.

"I have things in there more important than clothes," he said stiffly.

The boy looked at the grip, and presently curiosity made him ask:

"What is it—a pistol?"

"No, a book," said Jerry.

"A book! . . . Say, I know who you are. You're Jerry Catlin. You're coming to your aunt Rose's to go to school. You've got school books in there, but they won't do up here in Florence."

"It's not school books at all!" replied Jerry tartly, "it is one book."

This captured the strange one's interest.

"Well, what book?"

"Ingersoll," said Jerry importantly.

The boy in knickers was at sea.

"What does it tell about, wicked women . . . or outlaws . . . or what?"

"Naw," ejaculated Jerry, disgusted, "it's an infidel book. It says there ain't no God. I'm an infidel. I don't believe in any God."

The boy on the lawn stared blankly and fixedly at this.

"Who do you believe made everything?" he asked in an incredulous voice.

"Don't know," admitted Jerry promptly.

"Well, there you are, God must have done it," declared the boy.

"Looky here," said Jerry, "did you know the Bible said in one place that the men who were with St. Paul on his way to Damascus heard a voice saying, 'Saul! Saul, why persecutest thou me!'? Then, in another place, it says the men who were with St. Paul saw a light but didn't hear any voice."

The boy stared at Jerry.

"Well . . . what of that?"

"Why, one account or the other is a lie. You know God wouldn't write a lie in the Bible . . . so there ain't no God."

The youth considered this in shocked silence.

"Looky here," went on Jerry, "did you know ever' time Ingersoll went to lecture he would stand perfectly still a whole minute before his audience and say, 'If there is a God, I'll wait here one minute for Him to strike me dead'? He actually done that. And I'm not afraid to do it myself. I'll do it now. . . ."

And Jerry drew out a new gold-plated watch which his father had given him, opened it, and stood watching the second hand go around.

Knickerbockers backed away from the fence.

"You haven't got the sense you were born with!" he cried in alarm. Then he added in a different tone:

"Here, stop that and grab up some rocks. Yonder comes the blamedest uppetiest nigger you ever saw!"

Jerry shut his watch and put it in his pocket.

"Where is he?"

"That boy coming up the street."

"Why, he looks white!"

"He is white. He's a white nigger, and as uppety as they make 'em!"

The two boys began looking for stones.

The octoroon in the street saw their hostile preparations and called:

"Now, look here, I haven't done nothin' to you-all."

"Why, no, you haven't," cried knickers, "but we thought we'd like to see you dodge a little, nigger."

"Let me alone," said the white negro. "I saw you pickin' up them rocks."

"Well, dodge a little."

"I'm not goin' to dodge!"

"Oh, you're not?" Knickers tossed a stone at Toussaint, not very hard, but it went close enough to cause the octoroon discomfort. The white negro simply looked at it and made no movement to avoid it.

"Oh-ho!" shouted knickers. "He thinks we can't make him dodge! Come on, pile the rocks to him!"

The messenger cried out in a defensive voice:

"Look here, if I throw at you-all, you'll say I done it for nothin'!"

A stone whizzing past cut off his sentence. The octoroon dodged involuntarily. The white boys shouted in triumph:

"We knew you'd dodge! Now run . . . run!"

They were throwing as fast as they could. The negro dodged another stone. Then, in the midst of the bombardment, he turned his back and continued deliberately walking amid the hurtling stones.

A thrill went through Jerry when he saw the octoroon would not look and therefore could not dodge.

"I got him!" cried knickers, but his missile just grazed the negro's leg. Another whizzed by his head. Jerry was throwing too. One of his stones went under the blond negro's arm. They knocked up dust all around him. Just then Jerry saw he was really going to hit the octoroon. He cringed within himself and yelled desperately:

"Dodge, boy!"

The missile struck the negro's elbow. A piece of paper fell from his hand. He stooped to pick it up when another stone hit him on the knee. He got the paper, straightened, and yelled back:

"I told you I wouldn't dodge! Kill me, but I won't dodge!"

The two white boys suddenly ceased throwing. The octoroon went limping with his paper up the middle of the street.

"Aw, the devil," said knickers, "that's the way with him . . . most despisable nigger in Florence."

"What's his name?" asked Jerry in a tone through which his heart beat.

"Toussaint . . . Toussaint Vaiden," said knickers, disgusted.

"Vaiden!" repeated Jerry with a blank face.

"Yes, his mammy was one of the Vaiden niggers."

Jerry stood looking after the octoroon with a long face. This was a disconcerting twist, to step into Florence and throw stones at the son of one of his mother's old slaves.

"I wonder if I hurt his arm?" he asked in concern.

"I hope I hurt his leg!" snapped knickers, who could not forgive the octoroon for braving down his stones.

Jerry climbed the fence and got into the street again.

"I've got to find where my uncle Augustus lives," he said rather lamely.

"It's right yonder, the first . . . second . . . third . . . fifth house on the right."

Jerry picked up his telescope again and set forth with his second-best clothes and Ingersoll's proof that the New Testament contained contradictions within itself and that, therefore, the deity was nonexistent.

CHAPTER FIVE

W HEN the limping octoroon boy approached the Vaiden
home on Cherry Street, Colonel Miltiades Vaiden had been
lying awake in bed for upwards of two hours.

It was the Colonel's habit to awaken at six o'clock every
morning, no matter when he went to sleep. Since that hour
he had lain awake beside his fat wife, giving himself over to
astringent reflections furnished by his two encounters with
J. Handback. He believed that if it had not been for the
blow inflicted on him by his ancient loss to Handback, he
would, at that moment, have by his side Drusilla Crowninshield, instead of the shapeless, almost non-sexual bulk of
Ponny.

It amazed the Colonel that the loss of twenty-five hundred
dollars two decades ago should have brought him down to
this bare rented house, which from his first glance depressed
him. If he had married Drusilla he would never have thought
of living in such a house; he would have lived in style somehow, possibly by sinking in debt.

The woman beside him breathed heavily. The sun slanted
through the window onto a bare ill-jointed floor. The Colonel
was living in an old Florence boom house which had been
flung together hastily and which had deteriorated in the
same way.

A faint tapping at his door broke the renter's reflections.
He thought it was a neighbor's child who had come to borrow
a bucket of water. He got out of bed and went to the door
in his nightshirt.

A boy, apparently white, stood outside. He had his
shoulder hitched up so that his arm rested against his side.
With his left hand he gave Miltiades a note.

46

The Colonel took it and asked aloud:

"How did you hurt your arm?"

"Run against a post," said the boy.

Miltiades looked a little curiously at the messenger. There was something almost familiar in his glum blond face. Then the Colonel decided the boy resembled someone he had known a long time ago. He began reading the note.

A pucker of surprise wrinkled his eyes. He stood looking at it for half a minute in silence. From the bed Ponny asked:

"Can't you read it, Mr. Milt?"

"Certainly." To the boy he said, "This doesn't require an answer."

As the boy moved away, Ponny called curiously:

"Who's it from?"

"Handback."

"Handback!"

Another interval of silence, then:

"Yes, it's from Handback."

"What in the world does he want?"

"Wants to see me after church today."

"Of all . . ." The woman sat up in bed. "What does *he* want to see *you* about?"

Miltiades looked at his wife in her nightgown, her breasts overflowing her stomach, her stomach overflowing her legs, her legs overflowing the bed. He looked but he did not see her. He smiled with contempt as he thought silently to himself, "Handback thinks I'm as unprincipled a rascal as he is!"

"Mr. Milt!" cried Ponny. "Is he going to offer you a partnership?"

"Hardly."

The wife studied her husband out of round china-blue eyes.

"Mr. Milt, you know what he's going to ast you."

"How could I know in advance, Ponny?"

"Well, you do."

"He is going to ask me not to do what you're going to ask me to do." Miltiades was rather pleased with the neatness of this sentence.

"What's that?"

"He doesn't want me to tell something I know, and of course you do."

Ponny opened her eyes in advance umbrage.

"Well, I hope you're not going to keep a secret from your wife just to please a thief who has robbed you and your folks. You wouldn't do me thatta way on account of his feelings!"

"No, on account of my own feelings."

"Your own feelings?"

"Yes, as a gentleman."

Ponny looked at her husband with a desolate face.

"Mr. Milt, you don't treat me right! You let me set here in the house . . . never take me out nowhere. Now you won't even tell . . ."

"Oh, he gets drunk," capitulated the Colonel, "he doesn't want me to tell, and now I'm asking you not to tell."

"Well, I know if a man had stole from me I wouldn't feel called on to keep a secret like that for him."

"Can you imagine a gentleman spreading a report that he saw another man intoxicated?"

"What difference does that make to you?"

"Being a gentleman?"

"Yes. You're not rich."

"Ponny!" snapped the man, "you breathe a word of what I told you . . ."

"Oh, don't bother! I'll keep the old hypocrite's secret for him. I never see anybody to tell it to, anyway."

In his heart Miltiades stormed at Ponny's grossness; aloud he said:

"It was my fault, I shouldn't have mentioned it to you."

The woman recovered from her fright and sat thinking.

"Mr. Milt, why couldn't you make him take you in as a

partner now? If he won't do it, tell him you'll tell all you
know."

The husband stared at his fat wife aghast.

"My God, Ponny, do you want me to turn blackmailer?"

"Would that be blackmail—making him take you in as
partner?"

"Of course! A partnership would be one sort of pay!"

The woman blinked her eyes.

"I thought blackmail was where you made somebody leave
money in a hollow stump."

The man thought in silent disgust:

"What a fathead I have to live with!" He put the note
in his pocket. "By the way," he recalled, "Rose shouted
something to me last night about Marcia."

"Whyn't you stop by and ask what she said?" inquired
Ponny in annoyance.

"She was passing in the Ashton carriage."

"Going to the speaking?"

"No, coming from it."

"Mr. Milt," complained Ponny, "you told me there wasn't
going to be no ladies at the speaking last night."

To the husband's dismay tears began to form in Ponny's
eyes.

"Why—why, Ponny, I didn't think there were going to
be."

"And I may not be able to get out no more in the future,"
repined the fat woman.

"What makes you say that?" asked Miltiades incuriously.

"I think I'm in a fam'ly way," said the woman in a far-off
voice.

The man looked at her.

"You're always thinking that."

"Well, I've missed this month completely," she said in
melancholy argument, "and I don't feel good."

"Well—maybe you are," returned the husband with more
skepticism than hope.

For a long time when Ponny announced her belief that

she was with child, Miltiades would become hopeful and excited, but her symptoms had turned out false so many times that he had ceased to credit them. He wished he had a son. It would break the loneliness of just him and Ponny in this bare house. A baby at least would clutter things up a bit.

And then he wanted a son to pick up life and go on with the Vaiden name after he had laid it down. When Miltiades thought of this he always imagined a youth carrying a banner inscribed with the name "Vaiden." It was a high name, a noble name.

The queer part of this was that, so far as Miltiades knew, no Vaiden had ever been high or noble. They were all very ordinary folk. But this affected not in the slightest degree the glory of the Vaiden name. His father, his brothers, his forbears had not lived up to that name. So far, neither had he. But one of these days, God willing, he, Miltiades Vaiden, would live up to it. And, if his own strength failed, and Ponny's symptoms proved valid, then this seed of the Vaidens, sleeping in the womb of his fat wife, his son and heir, would march on with the name in dignity and glory which no number of individual failures could impair.

He went to the large woman, put an arm around her bulky back and tenderly kissed the plateau of her cheek.

Somewhat later, Miltiades and his wife set forth for church. On Sundays the Colonel felt more complacent toward Ponny than he did on weekdays. A spiritual calm caused the man, not only to accept the heavy woman with equanimity, but even to feel a sympathy for her flesh. He was genuinely solicitous about getting her to church.

When the two came in sight of Mrs. Rose Vaiden's boarding house they were just in time to see the accommodating Ashton carriage stop for Rose and Augustus.

Mrs. Ashton was calling out:

"Jerry, there's room for you! Mr. Sandusky, tell Jerry there's room for him."

Rose, who was entering the carriage, said, somewhat perturbed:

"He says he doesn't want to go to church."

"Doesn't want to go," repeated Mrs. Ashton, surprised that Jerry's wants had anything to do with it.

"He was on the boat last night and is very tired," excused Rose.

"When I was a young rooster," recalled Augustus in a hearty voice, "I'd have ridden all night to get to a meeting, much less offer that as an excuse for not going."

"Won't you take his place, Mr. Sandusky?" suggested Mrs. Ashton.

Mr. Sandusky, who was Mrs. Rose's boarder, came out of the door at this proffer, but just then the group saw Miltiades and Ponny coming down the street.

"Oh, yonder comes Ponny!" exclaimed both ladies at once. "Ponny will have to ride!"

Augustus, who was already in the carriage, began climbing out, but Rose caught her husband's arm and put him back.

"I'll walk with Miltiades," she decided briskly. "I don't want you walking through the hot sun, Augustus."

Judge Ashton's eyes twinkled at Rose's coddling of her husband. Mr. Sandusky, who was coming down the path to the gate, now stopped and was thought of no more by anyone, including himself.

All who could reach Ponny helped push or pull, and finally she was seated in the carriage, breathing heavily, but triumphant.

Judge Ashton flicked his horses, and away they went with much clatter and little speed. Mrs. Rose, who had chosen to walk, dropped in beside Miltiades. She began walking quickly, partly because she was the song leader in her church and must be there on time, and partly because she did not like Miltiades and wanted to be rid of him as soon as possible. She was unconscious, however, of this last reason as the basis of her rapid walking.

As for Miltiades, he kept alongside his sister-in-law, accepting her silence and quick motion as characteristic of her. When he was with her like this, he wondered, rather amused, why she had ever married Augustus.

"Rose," he said aloud, "is it your intention ever to admit Augustus to good health again?"

"I knew you were thinking about Augustus," said the wife drily.

"Well, that's permissible—to think about one's brother."

"And there is one thing I can say about Augustus," went on Rose pointedly, "he really does work."

This reflection on his own idleness brought the Colonel's badinage to the earth.

"Well, I'm always thinking and planning and trying to do something, Rose," defended Miltiades seriously.

"Why don't you farm? You can farm," pointed out the brother's wife with discomforting precision.

"Money's not in planting any more."

"There's a living in it."

"Yes, but who wants just a living? . . . My goodness, with everything just beginning to open up in the South— Cleveland going to be elected—if a man could just get in the current he'd be made."

Rose listened inattentively.

"Where do you think the money is if it's not in planting?"

"Where it has always been—in niggers," returned the Colonel.

"I don't see that—they're not slaves any longer."

"M-m. Some men make it out of them anyway." This recalled J. Handback to the Colonel, and he told his sister-in-law about the note.

Rose looked her astonishment.

"You don't suppose he is going to pay back the money he stole from us right after the war?" she ejaculated.

The Colonel laughed sardonically at the idea.

"What does he want, then?"

"Well, I don't know . . . he wants me to meet him after church. . . . What church does he attend?"

"I'm sure that has never interested me. And don't meet him anywhere, Milt; let him come to your church, if he wants to see you!"

After a moment the Colonel agreed to this, and then Mrs. Rose cast about to furnish Miltiades the information he had first asked. At that moment, across the thoroughfare, a slender girl with glinting hair came up a transverse street into Market, evidently on her way to church. The sister-in-law raised her voice:

"Sydna! Oh, Sydna, good-morning. Do you know what church Mr. Handback goes to?"

"Good-morning, Miss Rose. Why, the Methodist, I suppose. I heard he gave a lot to the new church they're putting up."

"Thank you, Sydna." Then to Miltiades, "I wouldn't go a step out of my way to see him."

"No, I won't," decided Miltiades, irritated at the thought of the thief Handback giving away a lot of money to help build a church.

Mrs. Rose Vaiden's question, all unknowing, had thrown Miss Alberta Sydna Crowninshield into considerable perturbation. The girl looked across the street and speculated almost in a panic why Colonel Vaiden wanted to know what church Mr. Handback attended. She wondered if the Colonel intended to speak to Mr. Handback about the conduct of his son, Lucius, on the preceding evening. It would be very noble of the Colonel, certainly, but it would be sure to get her talked about. She had an impulse to run and catch up with the Colonel and plead with him not to vindicate her honor. Because in Florence, when a girl's honor was vindicated, she was just about ruined. It made so much talk. She went on to her own church, the Episcopal, in trepidation.

Still farther up the street, behind Miss Crowninshield, two persons stood in the gate of the Rose Vaiden boarding house. These were Jerry Catlin and Sandusky, the boarder.

Sandusky was a small, fully grown man of the sort who had never been young. He listened while Jerry talked with vehemence.

"The trouble with people is," denounced Jerry, "they don't think for themselves!"

"You think for yourself?" inquired Sandusky in the nasal drawl of the country.

"Of course I do, and I can't conscientiously go to any of their churches."

"Why kain't ye?"

"You know why, Sandusky . . . I don't believe in God."

"You ain't thinking for yourself now," drawled Sandusky; "you got that idee out of a book."

Jerry blinked at this twist, but after a moment fell back on the aristocratic argument:

"At least I don't follow the crowd. I don't believe what everybody believes."

"That's ag'inst you," observed Sandusky. "In law we figger the more witnesses you got the more li'ble you are to be right."

This irritated young Jerry. Sandusky never argued fairly. He always oozed around the main question of whether or not there was a God and brought up secondary matters which were not at all important.

At this point young Jerry had heard his aunt calling across the street and a girl's voice answering her. He looked down the street, forget all about his atheistic argument, and after several seconds asked in a completely changed tone:

"Who is that, Sandusky?"

"Her name's Crowninshield," stated Sandusky as impersonally as the city directory.

"Well . . . that isn't all of it, is it? What's the rest of her name?"

The boarder pulled at his chin.

"There are sev'rul men trying to go with Miss Sydna Crowninshield already," he advised in a detached tone, "and all of 'em is rich. So, personally, when I see Miss **Sydna** Crowninshield walkin' off frum me, I jest let her walk off."

"Sandusky," said Jerry, embarrassed, "do you know what would happen to you if the fool killer should come along now?"

"Sure, I'd be left stan'in' here by myse'f."

A few minutes later young Jerry decided that, after all, he believed he would go to church, and he set out walking rapidly down the street after a vanishing blue dress. He had supposed that Miss Sydna Crowninshield would go to his aunt's church, but when the girl turned into the Episcopal church, it left the young man with an odd emptiness to his spiritual enthusiasm. He continued mechanically to the Christian or Campbellite church where his uncles and aunts had gone with a feeling that he had been duped.

The Campbellite church, some six blocks farther down the street, was a box-like frame building unrelieved by the slightest architectural concession. Jerry found the interior as rigorously plain as the outside. Its windows were square cut and of clear glass. It had no aisle or nave or transept or pipe organ. At the far end was a wooden platform with a small square pulpit. The front of this pulpit was a marble slab with this text carved in it:

"PROVE ALL THINGS AND HOLD FAST TO THAT WHICH IS GOOD."

The preacher stood beside the pulpit with his hand on a large Bible.

As Jerry entered, an usher in a sad black Sunday suit took him in tow, but Mrs. Rose looked around, saw who it was, and with a smile of gratification beckoned Jerry to sit beside her. While Jerry gained his seat, the minister stopped his discourse because his sermon was a precise geometrical analysis of the will of God, and if his congregation lost a single minor premise his whole demonstration would be thrown away.

The preacher was a weather-beaten, round-headed man with a flat, thin-lipped mouth who smacked his lips after each sentence as if savoring his own syllogisms. He used various texts of the Bible as major and minor premises and moved infallibly toward a Q. E. D. which would land his congregation, after death, in an Oriental Jewish city, built of gold and elaborately decorated with jewels, which was the exact antithesis of the church in which they sat. The congregation evidently expected their taste in architecture to change sharply in the next life.

The minister, in his sermon, described this heaven so solidly and in such a matter of fact way that a whim passed through Jerry Catlin's mind. He had always supposed heaven to be located in a rather diaphanous place, say on clouds. But this minister was building it so heavy and square cut that Jerry decided the place would presently cave in, and there would be a lot of broken wings and harps up there in the wreck if the preacher didn't take care.

The youth smiled faintly and glanced at his aunt. He wanted to whisper his sacrilegious fancy in her ear, but did not quite dare to do it.

Sitting by Jerry's side Mrs. Rose Vaiden was likewise not listening to the sermon. From time to time she hummed inaudibly to herself middle C, for she led the singing, and no pipe organ was allowed in the Christian church. Thus she had to freshen her keynote now and then to have it when she wanted it.

By Rose's side sat Augustus, her husband, who watched a fly on one of the clear glass panes flirting with a spider's web. At intervals, as he followed the fortunes of the fly, he wondered if he had taken the hog its slop that morning. Then he thought he would get Buck Mosely, the negro who cultivated the old Vaiden place, to haul him a load of stove wood. He stared past the fly through the window at a summer cloud and presently was embarrassed to straighten up his head from a nod. He batted his eyes and looked around to see if anyone had observed his lapse. The preacher's demonstration smacked on with arithmetical precision. Then Augustus began a desperate struggle to stay awake. He stretched his eyes and bit his lips. Presently he thought he was fox-hunting and could hear the hounds belling down the frozen dale . . . the pack was a flying symphony beneath the crystal stars. . . . Rose's hand plucked his sleeve for him to stand up. The congregation had arisen and were singing the doxology.

To this singing Miltiades Vaiden contributed a passable baritone. As he sang he was mentally uneasy about J. Handback. He wondered if he should have gone to the Methodist church and seen him. Not that anything would have come of it. . . .

All through the sermon he had thought of J. Handback and suffered the exquisite uncertainty of a man who does not quite know whether or not he wants to do a certain thing. Well, at any rate, the die was cast, he would not get to see his man, and that ended it.

A few minutes later, as Miltiades walked out of the plain door of the Christian church, Mrs. Rose turned and said to him in a disapproving but gratified tone:

"There's Handback now, Milt, waiting to see you."

Then Miltiades saw the merchant, and a penetrating relief went through him. He left his own group and joined the storekeeper, who said it was a beautiful day, and then added in an explanatory tone that he was an usher in the Methodist church and had slipped away before the congregation was dismissed.

"You got my note, did you?" he asked.

"Yes, I got it," returned Miltiades in a noncommittal tone.

"Well, I didn't know . . . niggers are getting so unreliable nowadays."

"That's a fact," agreed the Colonel absently.

The merchant coughed slightly.

"I thought I would like to talk things over with you, Colonel," he began. "I used to do a good business with your family. I—I was a great admirer of your sister Cassandra, a brainy woman if there ever was one. . . . I hope her health is still good."

"Very good, thank you," said Miltiades, who had not seen Cassandra for months.

"And your brother Polycarp . . . a fine boy, Colonel. The county certainly lost one of its coming men when he was killed."

"I don't know," said Miltiades meditatively, "he probably wouldn't have been a money maker. The Vaidens never have been, somehow."

"Well . . . he may not have been," conceded the merchant.

The two men walked along, a little at loss to get at the point that interested them. Now that he was with Handback the Colonel was not at all sure of what he wanted or what he hoped to get. He began at random again:

"Lot of money going to be made these coming four years, Mr. Handback."

"Hope so," said the merchant absently. "You mean the election?"

"Yes, when the Democrats win, the South ought to come in for an era of wonderful prosperity."

"So the Governor seemed to think. . . . By the way, last night, after the speaking, I—I met you, didn't I?" inquired Handback carefully.

"Why, yes, that order for mule collars . . ."

"I mean after that?"

"Yes, you met me again . . . just before day," nodded Miltiades impassively.

The merchant drew a breath.

"We . . . talked about . . . a good many things, didn't we?"

"About drinking . . . and colored prostitutes," said the Colonel.

"I . . . see," said Handback in a bleak voice.

"You mentioned how they cleared a man's head," continued Miltiades with a faint acrid amusement.

"M-m . . ." mumbled the merchant, looking back at the crowd they had left behind them.

The Colonel suddenly took a philosophic turn, for no conscious reason.

"You know, Mr. Handback, I don't know that you are so far wrong about that. Look at our fathers: they drank when they wanted to; they took their slave women when they wanted to; they led a natural life, and they lived longer than folks do nowadays."

The merchant looked at the Colonel in surprise and began smiling faintly in relief.

"Well, now, it does look that way, doesn't it?"

"Certainly, certainly." The Colonel dismissed the topic roundly and after a moment went back to his former subject: "Yes, we're going to have a period of fine business, Mr. Handback, and incidentally, I think you ought to begin to make preparations for it."

The tradesman's thoughts still hovered over the idea of secrecy.

"I've been adding to my stock a little."

"I didn't mean so much your stock, I meant . . . new ideas in your firm," explained the Colonel, in a tone that was casual.

"New ideas," repeated Handback, a little at sea.

"M-m . . . another clerk . . . perhaps a mature man who would be of assistance in working out plans to get your share of the trade."

Handback began to perceive whither this conversation tended.

"The trade I get has to come to me anyway," he said.

"That's true, but even at that you'll need more help in your store," persisted the Colonel earnestly. "Why not have a grown man instead of a boy? Business experience is a good thing in a store." The Colonel moistened his lips. "Look at me, I ran one of the biggest plantations in the Reserve before the war and made it pay. I'd be bound to have ideas if I were in your store, Handback!"

The merchant walked along staring at the Colonel in amazement.

"You are not suggesting that I . . . take you in as— as a clerk, Colonel?"

"I want to get into business," nodded the Colonel. "It's all right for me to live on my income in ordinary times, but when you see a boom right on you . . ."

Handback began to shake his head.

"You don't want to come to me, Colonel. What you need is experience in a show-window store."

"What's that?"

"I mean the fancy stores for fashionable trade."

"No, I want just an ordinary store," assured the Colonel.

"M-huh . . . well, all right," agreed Handback diplomatically, "when this rush you are talking about comes to pass I'll bear you in mind, Colonel." He scratched his jaw and looked at Miltiades. "Is—is that all right?"

The two were now approaching the Episcopal church, out of which the congregation was beginning to emerge.

"It seems to me," said Miltiades slowly, "if you are going to take on any help you ought to take it on in time, and . . . you ought to have a grown man who understands and sympathizes with your way of looking at life, instead of some young jackanapes who doesn't comprehend you and goes about gossiping about everything that he sees and hears."

Mr. Handback looked at the outflowing congregation and moistened his lips.

"As I say, if I need a man, I'll certainly take you, Colonel."

Miltiades frowned and appeared to study.

"I'll have a time explaining this to Ponny," he said at length.

"Why to Miss Ponny?" asked Handback apprehensively.

"Well, she saw your note and thought you were going to offer me a position."

Mr. Handback drew a little away from the church crowd.

"Look here, Miss Ponny has no idyah of anything, has she?"

"Oh, no, certainly not. If I should get a position she would think that was what you wanted with me. Besides, you are going to need a man."

"Look here," began the merchant, with a damp face, "if I should take on another man . . . I couldn't afford to pay anything much . . . a new clerk isn't worth anything in a store, Colonel . . . more trouble than they come to . . . asking prices and where everything is . . ."

"Oh, I'd expect to start with a small salary," agreed Miltiades quickly, "say . . . fifteen dollars a week."

"Why, Colonel!" cried the merchant, "the very best clerks in the show-window stores don't get but twenty-five a week . . . and they think they're drawing the earth!"

"What would be your idea?" asked Miltiades, a little taken aback.

"Why, you really won't be worth five dollars a week for a long time, Colonel," said the merchant uncomfortably.

"Suppose we compromise on seven and a half," suggested Miltiades, "after all, it's the experience I'm after, not the wages."

"Well . . . all right . . . you're welcome to what you learn from me. . . . You're right sure Miss Ponny don't know anything about anything?"

"Why should she? There's nothing unusual in you wanting a clerk."

Mr. Handback was reassured.

"All right, then, seven and a half."

He breathed audibly, drew out a handkerchief, and wiped his face.

"Well . . . I believe I'll drop back down to the store," he said. "Good-day."

And he joined that part of the church crowd who were moving toward town along Market Street.

CHAPTER SIX

COLONEL MILTIADES VAIDEN took the opposite direction from his new employer and went up Market Street. He entered the crowd just in time to be a great handicap to a young man who was walking immediately behind a girl in a blue dress. Miltiades did not observe who the young man was, but young Jerry Catlin knew that his uncle Milt was behind him, and so he was estopped from dropping in beside the girl and entering into conversation with her, as he devoutly desired to do.

The hobbledehoy moved along in the crowd, pondering some way of speaking to the girl ahead of him, when a red-headed man brushed past Jerry, walked up beside the girl, took her parasol out of her hands, and said:

"I've been looking for this blue sunshade everywhere."

The girl began laughing.

"What were you doing at church, Mr. Bivins?"

"Came to hear you sing, of course."

Sydna rippled into laughter.

"Mr. Bivins, you're the silliest thing."

"They tell me there's a lot of other fellows here in Florence just as silly as I am."

"Oh, the idea! Who's been telling you that?"

"A little bird."

The conversation depressed Jerry Catlin. It was so inane. He thought if he could have walked with Sydna Crowninshield, he would have struck off on some profound, fascinating subject. He did not know exactly what it would have been, but whatever it was, he could feel that it would have absorbed them both, utterly.

So great an impression did the girl in blue make on young

62

Mr. Catlin that for a number of days she almost completely occupied his thoughts.

From his aunt Rose Jerry learned all about the Crowninshields. Sydna's mother had been a Lacefield. The Lacefields were once the wealthiest family in the Reserve. Sydna's father, a Confederate colonel, had been a very brilliant man. She, Rose, had never seen Colonel Crowninshield, but from all she had heard he must have been a very brilliant man.

"I heard Mother speak of Colonel Crowninshield once," said Jerry.

"You did!" ejaculated Mrs. Rose, pausing in kneading her pie dough and looking at Jerry with surprised and reminiscent eyes.

This did not arouse any suspicion in young Jerry. He would never have dreamed that his mother could have been in love with anyone besides his father. He was about to ask more questions when Mrs. Rose exclaimed:

"There's your uncle packing stove wood in that hot sun! Jerry, don't allow him to wag a load like that!"

Mrs. Rose's concern about Augustus' health was contagious. Jerry dashed out into the yard and began taking the sticks out of his uncle's arms. Augustus protested loudly, but he was really very pleased at the fuss Jerry and Rose made over him. When he was in the kitchen, seated, Mrs. Rose thought she would reward Jerry for his help.

"Gussie," she said as she scolloped her pie, "tell Jerry something about Colonel Crowninshield."

"He was a stuck-up little coxcomb," announced Augustus promptly, "he wouldn't take me and Carp in his regiment."

"Why, your father wouldn't let him!" defended Mrs. Rose.

"I was as much a man at fourteen as I ever have been since!" boomed out Augustus under the impression that he was extolling his self-reliance at fourteen.

"You know he was a very fine orator," suggested Mrs. Rose.

"Windy," ejaculated Augustus.

"He died like a hero at Shiloh!" cried Mrs. Rose.

"Got his whole regiment cut to pieces . . . that was poor generalship," declared Augustus.

No admission of a good point in Sydna's father could be got out of Augustus. Mrs. Rose had made several pies, and by way of doing a favor to Jerry, for she saw which way his thoughts tended, she did one of the pies up in a buttered paper and wrote a note which read:

> DEAR DRUSILLA: The bearer of this little gift is Jerry Catlin, Marcia's oldest boy.
>
> ROSE.

She dispatched Jerry with it to her neighbor's.

The Crowninshield home to which young Catlin wended his way lay on Pine Street, west of Market and three blocks farther south in the direction of town.

Traffic from the north did not pass along Pine Street, so it displayed a sort of woodsy smoothness, scattered with leaves and twigs from the live oaks that rose above it. Here and there an impression of buggy tracks showed that it really was a street. The birds liked Pine Street and kept up a continuous chirping and carolling in the trees. Jerry Catlin, with his pie, did not think to listen to them, but the fragrances of the thoroughfare were more conspicuous. Virginia creepers waylaid the passer-by, and magnolias, from their porcelain bowls, spilled an intangible honey. As Jerry entered the Crowninshield gate, rows of box hedges lining the curved walks exhaled a musky greeting.

The portico of the old Crowninshield home had square wooden columns, and the interior of the hallway presented a faintly museum-like appearance with its ancient furniture. Jerry, armed with note and pie, pulled at an old brass lion's foot, which only rattled feebly and did not ring.

The boy stood in a trance amid this almost remembered loveliness in which his mother once had lived. Before the war all the South, Jerry thought, was like this Pine Street, a dreaming beauty, a leisurely paradise in which Time eddied round and round and did not flow anywhere. He drew a breath of homesickness for something he never quite had known.

Footsteps from the interior drew him out of his reverie. He straightened himself to withstand the charms of Miss Sydna Crowninshield when a middle-aged colored woman, with her lips full of pins, stepped into the hallway from an inner door.

She produced no impression on Jerry beyond the fact that she was a negro woman.

The quadroon took the pins from her mouth.

"Won't you come in?" she asked. "Did you try to ring the bell?"

"Yes, it didn't do anything," said Jerry.

"No, it doesn't ring. At this house you walk in and keep knocking at doors until somebody answers you. Who shall I say is calling?"

"I'm Jerry Catlin. Here's a note and a pie."

As Jerry delivered these valuables the quadroon looked at him with a dawning face.

"Are you Miss Marcia's boy?" she asked in excitement. "Why, of course you are. You've got your mammy's eyes made over! Well, I declare!"

The colored woman stared at the caller a moment longer, then turned and went hurrying into an inner room, calling,

"Miss Dru! Miss Sydna! Here's little Missy's boy Jerry come to see you!"

"Who is it, Gracie?" called a voice.

"Little Missy's boy."

When she had delivered her valuables she came back to Jerry, dabbing at her dramatic black eyes with a tiny handkerchief.

"Who are you?" asked Jerry, bewildered and vaguely moved.

"I'm Gracie. I belonged to your grandpa, ol' Pap. I was your mammy's body servant."

The use of the term "body servant" instead of maid was the last touch to transform the present into the past. Jerry followed his mother's old body servant into the rooms.

Through a doorway, two apartments distant, Jerry glimpsed a quick slipping of graceful limbs into a garment of silk and a warning cry of "Don't bring him in here, Gracie!" and the slamming of an intervening door.

"Lordy!" gasped the quadroon. "Scuse me, Miss Sydna! Scuse me, Mr. Jerry!" and the cream-colored woman hurried out of sight to ascertain the amount of damage she had wrought.

To Jerry, left in the room, the momentary glimpse he had caught of Sydna developed like a photographic plate. He saw more and more of what he had seen, the graceful length of the girl's legs, the slenderness of her compressed waist, her bosom cupped up and made prominent by her corset. He was utterly out of countenance. He felt impelled to steal out of the house and go back to his aunt's. In the midst of this embarrassment Mrs. Drusilla came out, followed by Gracie.

"Well, Mr. Catlin," smiled Drusilla, "I'll have to call you Jerry. You must excuse us, Sydna is having a dress made. Gracie, doesn't he look like his mother?"

"The spirit and image," agreed the quadroon.

"It was nice of Miss Rose to send over the pie. How did you leave your mother?"

Here Mrs. Drusilla called aloud to Sydna to put on her dress and come in and see Jerry Catlin.

"Will your mother come down to see you while you are here?" she asked of the caller.

"I don't suppose she will make such a long trip," said Jerry. "It's fifty miles by road and a hundred by water."

"Dear me, it's clear away. Marcia shouldn't have settled down so far from her old friends."

Here an inner door opened, and Sydna entered the room. At the sight of her dark eyes, her blonde hair, her demure dress now safely concealing any disturbing charms, Jerry's face turned a dusky red.

All three of the women began talking rapidly to rescue him from his embarrassment.

"My Toussaint told me one of Mr. Augustus' nephews had come," said Gracie.

"I saw you last Sunday coming from church," recalled Sydna, smiling at him.

"Yes, I saw you," said Jerry. "I was fixing to speak to you when that fellow came up and began talking to you."

"Oh, Alex Bivins. He's such a nuisance," said Sydna.

Jerry felt much better.

"Are you going to stay with your uncle Augustus or your uncle Miltiades?" inquired Mrs. Drusilla.

"Oh, my uncle Augustus," said Jerry.

"Mr. Milt won't be at home much now," said Gracie.

"Why?" asked Sydna curiously.

"He's working in J. Handback's store."

Drusilla turned on the colored woman.

"Working where?"

"In J. Handback's store."

"Doing what?"

"Why . . . clerking, I suppose. He sold a pound of bacon to Toussaint."

Sydna caught at the back of an ancient Phyfe chair.

"Colonel Milt isn't . . . clerking in a store!" she gasped.

"I—I suppose he is. . . ." Gracie began to realize the enormity of her own news.

Jerry stood in the middle of the floor with his brows puckered.

"You don't mean my uncle Miltiades is a clerk!" he gasped.

"He sold my Toussaint a pound of bacon," repeated Gracie in an empty monotone.

CHAPTER SEVEN

THE report that Colonel Miltiades Vaiden was a clerk in J. Handback's store affected a number of persons, each in a different manner.

To Mrs. Drusilla Crowninshield it brought an empty conclusion to a sort of half sad triumph that her old lover's marriage with Ponny BeShears for her money had gained him, in the end, nothing at all.

The daughter Sydna fell into a vague wonderment if, by any possibility, Colonel Vaiden were entering the Handback store to scrutinize more carefully the character of Lucius Handback. Such extreme knight errantry Sydna felt possible in Miltiades. The girl had never spoken a word to the Colonel that she remembered. Her mother's attitude toward Colonel Vaiden had impressed a reticence upon the daughter. At times Sydna thought of what she would say if she should speak to him; she would try to thank him for his care over her, for being a kind of invisible guardian over her . . . here her thoughts lost the form of words and became a feeling of sweetness and gratitude.

When Jerry Catlin brought the news to his aunt's boarding house he had to repeat it several times before its degrading content really sank into the understanding of Augustus Vaiden and Mrs. Rose.

"Clerking! For Handback? You don't mean he's a clerk in Handback's store!"

"He sold a pound of bacon to Gracie's boy, Toussaint," repeated Jerry as bewildered as his hearers.

"He must have just happened to be in there," hazarded Mrs. Rose, "and thought he'd help 'em out in a rush trade. . . ."

Augustus shook his head indignantly.

"Rose, you know he never would have happened to be in
J. Handback's store!"

This news, which Gracie, the seamstress, let drop so casually in the Crowninshield manor held some disturbing overtones for the quadroon herself.

She had dispatched Toussaint several days before to go to
town and get a pound of bacon.

When she gave him this commission her almost white son
had asked in an intent, even voice:

"Am I going to stand up for a whole pound, Mammy?"

Gracie became at once uneasy about her restive, unadjust-
able son.

"No," she cried sharply, then tempered her voice to a
persuasive tone: "No, Toussaint, don't say anything about
the pound. . . . If it looks too little, you might say, 'I
wanted a pound . . .' no, I wouldn't say anything at all
about it."

Old Parson Lump Mowbray, who sat moistening his
thumb, turning through his Bible, grunted out:

"If'n dey shawt-weight you too much, Toussaint, wras'le
wid de Lawd about hit in prayah."

"Looks like a man ought to have the right to say what he
thinks."

"Ye-es," drawled the preacher, "oncet I stood up an' said
whut I thinks, an' dat white man nea'ly busted my runnet."

"There ain't no white man going to bust my runnet," declared the white negro with equal soberness.

"Toussaint, don't talk like that!" begged Gracie in distress. "Just go ahead and take what they give you and don't
say anything!"

Her whole body felt jumpy lest her son should speak his
bitter thoughts before white folk. She would get him North
as soon as possible. A romantic notion of installing herself in
some Northern city as a Mexican woman continually dwelt
in Gracie's mind. Toussaint would go through college; he

would become a professional man, and he would marry . . .
the rest Gracie never really put into words, but she always
saw her white son married to a white woman and the long
stain of negrohood in her line brought to an end.

Toussaint set off toward old Florence on the mission,
hazardous for precisely him, of buying a pound of bacon.
As he walked along he planned how he could show the grocer
that he knew he was being short-weighted and yet not be so
overt as to cause trouble. It was a ticklish enterprise.

When he reached town he walked past a number of stores
with plate-glass windows, but finally turned down a side
street, where a crowd of negroes were collected. He went inside and found himself in a large, gloomy building with one
brightly lighted spot near the far end which lay under a
skylight. At a high bookkeeping desk, under this bright
light, stood Mr. Handback, the proprietor. Negro customers
moved in silhouette between this illuminated spot and Toussaint.

Toussaint glanced around among the clerks with an idea
of choosing one with whom he might safely remonstrate for
a sixteen-ounce pound. Two of these clerks were country
boys. At the front end of the store Lucius Handback sold
goods with the expertness of a youth who had been in his
father's business all his life. Toward the rear of the store a
number of negroes were waiting for somebody in their midst.
Toussaint went closer and saw a middle-aged man writing on
the back of a negro's due bill.

As Toussaint recognized this clerk a queer sensation went
over him. It was Colonel Miltiades Vaiden. He stared, hardly
crediting the enormity. Moreover, it had a very personal
bearing on himself. He knew that Colonel Vaiden's family
once had owned his mother and his grandmother, Hannah,
before her. From these Vaidens, he had derived, through his
mother, whatever education he possessed. Now to see the
former owner of his family weighing goods out to a bunch of
cotton-field negroes, it pinched something in Toussaint's
chest.

The Colonel looked up at the octoroon's steady gaze and moved toward him. He was extremely weary from his unaccustomed work.

"What can I sell you, son?" he began, with the courtesy of a white man to a white boy, when he recognized the light-colored negro who had brought him the note; then he changed to:

"What do you want, boy?"

"A pound of bacon, Colonel Milt."

"Let me have your due bill."

"I haven't got any due bill."

"How you going to pay for it?"

"I have the money."

"Oh . . . I see. Stebbins!" he called to one of the country boys, "what's the price of bacon?"

"Sixteen cents," called back Stebbins.

Miltiades went behind a counter, took a knife, and cut off a strip of bacon. A dozen negroes watched the operation, evidently eager to engage the Colonel the moment Toussaint had finished. The dignified white man laid the bacon on the scales and pushed the pea along the beam, then he wrapped the meat in a brown paper and handed it to the boy.

It suddenly occurred to Toussaint that in the shock of seeing the Colonel behind the counter he had forgot to look at the scales. Now, when he took his bacon, the words and actions which he had been reviewing since he left his mother's cottage sprang automatically into action.

"Uh . . . Colonel . . ." he ejaculated, "did you give me a pound?"

"Yes."

"Uh . . . may I see it on the scales . . . if you don't mind, Colonel?" asked Toussaint beginning to tremble inside of himself.

"Don't you think I know a pound?" asked the Colonel with the easy incense of a man nearing fifty, who is tired.

Toussaint was so nervous he could think of nothing but the truth.

"Y—yes, I think you know," he stammered. "I—I wanted to see if—if it was a pound."

His manner more than his words penetrated the Colonel's fatigue.

"See if it's a pound!"

"Y—yes, sir. . . ."

"Why, you damned gingerbread nigger! Insinuating I'd short-weight . . ."

The next thing Toussaint knew a terrific force whirled him around. The store spun about him. The next instant terrific shocks went through his spine as the Colonel kicked him toward the door. The door itself made a flying leap at him. He flung out his arms and crashed down on his hands and knees. Before he could scramble up another kick mashed his face down in the tobacco spittle on the floor. The prostrate boy heard a voice shouting:

"Colonel, what you doing?"

And the Colonel's enraged answer:

"This damned gingerbread bastard insinuated I short-weighted him!"

"Well . . . let him go."

The store was full of negroes looking on in silence. Toussaint got to his feet. His spine and buttocks were so numb he could hardly walk. He hobbled to the door and eased himself down the steps by holding to the door facing. He got across the sidewalk to a hitching post and leaned against it, nauseated.

Some of the negroes around the door began laughing with the loud clacking of field hands. Presently a middle-aged black man came out of the store bringing Toussaint's hat and his pound of bacon.

"Yellow boy," he said, as he handed these to the octoroon, "you sho' is a fool. You got yo' poun' o' bacon. De reason all dem niggahs was stan'in' roun' waitin' fuh de Col'l to trade wid 'em was 'cause he nevah shawt-weights nobody. When he weighs you a poun' you gotta poun'. An' lissen to me, yellow boy, it is much mo' dangerous to accuse a white man of shawt-weightin' you when he ain't 'an when he is."

That Saturday night, the two clerks, Stebbins and Love, swept out the store. As they swept they would slyly thrust out their broom handles and try to trip each other up. Then the sweeping would turn into a wrestling match.

Miltiades Vaiden was tired, and the persistent scuffling of the two clerks annoyed him. Lucius Handback snapped irritably:

"Damn it, Stebbins, you and Love stop that!"

From his high desk the elder Handback remonstrated:

"Boys, go on with your sweeping, we want to get away from here."

The brooms started swishing again.

Mr. Handback was not particularly annoyed at the animal spirits of his clerks. He always hired inexperienced country boys at a wage of three dollars a week, and he expected them to be boys. These two clerks boarded at the merchant's home and roomed in the upper story of the store. They were in no rush with their sweeping, because they would have to stand and wait till the bookkeepers had finished their work.

Every Saturday evening Lucius Handback helped his father with the books. He assorted the tickets of the day's sales, made them into little bundles, and gave the amount of each bundle to his father to put on the ledger, and then filed away the bundles as reference against a day of settlement with the negro purchasers.

Lucius did this work automatically and with a persistent dissatisfaction in his heart for the grimy merchandise store in which he worked.

The youth's ambition was to own a fashionable shoe store on Market Street. He could imagine himself in a bemirrored shoe store with a double row of chairs and footstools. He fancied himself on the ladies' side continually concerned with the fitting of suède shoes on pretty calves and ankles. His clerks would work on the men's side.

On this particular evening, besides his general dissatisfaction with his father's business, he wanted to get through
with his posting and walk up Pine Street to see if there was
a light in the parlor of the Crowninshield residence.

Lucius had sent Sydna Crowninshield a note asking that
he might call and had received an answer that she was
otherwise engaged that evening. Lucius wanted to know, did
she really have an engagement, or was she keeping her threat,
made two weeks before, that she would not see him again.

No matter what Lucius found in the Crowninshield window, darkness or light, it would upset him. If light, he
would be jealous, if darkness he would be angry and miserable. So he was on needles and pins to go and see which it
was.

But he was talking about his projected shoe store. He
could not approach his father directly on the point because
his father disapproved of it, so he flanked the topic through
Miltiades. He said to the middle-aged clerk in a low tone,
apparently not to disturb his father:

"Saw Bradley today."

"What did he have to say?" asked Miltiades, who had no
interest in Bradley.

"Tried to sell me that lot on Market Street, said it would
be a wonderful location for a shoe store."

The elder Handback grunted from his posting:

"You get a real-estate man after you, and he won't give
you any peace. He's as bad as a life-insurance agent."

"He agreed with me it would make a good stand."

"He'd agreed that black was white if he could make a
sale."

Lucius argued hopelessly with Miltiades:

"One of these days somebody's going to put up a first-
class shoe store in this town. If Daddy would step in and
do it, that would end it: it would be him."

After some moments of silence Mr. Handback grunted:

"No outcome in a shoe store."

"People wear shoes!"

"The whole shoe trade of Florence wouldn't reach twenty thousand a year; no, by grabs, it wouldn't go fifteen."

"But, Dad . . . that would be fifteen!"

The father continued his posting a moment longer and then asked drily:

"What would you do if a nigger woman come in and wanted shoes?"

"Do like they do everywhere else: let her look at 'em and buy 'em. If they didn't fit her when she put 'em on, that would be her lookout."

This of course was true. Mr. Handback had asked the question merely to remind Lucius that all of his customers would not be pretty white women.

The merchant dropped his part of the conversation and allowed Lucius to continue talking at him through Miltiades. The older Handback began thinking about Gracie; whether or not he should go to Gracie when he had finished posting his ledger. He wondered uneasily what Gracie would think about the Colonel having kicked Toussaint. She might very well be angry and difficult to propitiate. Gracie was not like Handback's wife. When Mrs. Handback became angry she began to rehearse an endless list of offenses and grew angrier and angrier until finally, by dint of sheer numbers, the charges grew to such a bulk the passion of the wife could stretch around them no longer, so they all escaped. Among the general exodus, J. Handback's last offense went with the others, and there was peace again.

But the yellow woman did not work that way. She might say, "You let one of your clerks kick Toussaint." That one specific thing would lie between them, and it might cost him five, ten, or even twenty dollars.

He decided that he would not go to Gracie's that Saturday night. He did not care much about it anyway. He was tired. They had had a rushing trade. It would do him good to go home and sleep. Then he wondered what Gracie would say to a shoe store. He would never have mentioned such a thing to his wife, but the quadroon seemed interested in anything he had to say. She was bright for a nigger.

Once, long ago, the Yankee governor of Alabama had kept her in Montgomery, and she had got in the way to talking quite sensibly about all sorts of things. It interested Handback to think that a carpet-bag governor once had kept Gracie. When he thought of it he always added the mental note: "She must have been damned good-looking then."

His thoughts wandered on and on as he posted his ledger. The Colonel, sitting near Lucius, was idle while everyone else in the store was busy. On the desk was an envelope containing seven dollars and a half which was the Colonel's wage for the week. This irritated Handback. That envelope would have paid off both Love and Stebbins, with a dollar and a half left over. But all this went to the Colonel, who really wasn't worth as much as either of the boys.

Now, as the merchant posted his books, he began wondering how he could make the Colonel worth seven dollars and a half a week.

Some days before Miltiades had offered to help the boys sweep and dust, but Handback had said:

"No, let them do it, it's their job."

His actual reason was, if he allowed a seven-and-a-half-dollar man to do a three-dollar job, he would lose on Miltiades exactly four dollars and a half every week. Therefore he kept Miltiades free until he could think of something more profitable for him to do.

Somewhere near midnight the sweeping and bookkeeping came to an end. Stebbins and Love went upstairs, and ostensibly to bed, but when the others had gone away they came down again, went to a pool room and played pool.

J. Handback, once out of the store, halted irresolutely. He really wanted to talk to Gracie about the shoe business. Lucius would keep ding-donging about a shoe store, and he wanted to talk about it to some disinterested person. Not that he expected any directing wisdom in the quadroon's replies, but it clarified his own ideas to talk them over.

The merchant was conscious of this liberating effect the colored woman had upon his ponderings, and he reflected that, since he had paid for her services anyway, it was nothing but good business for him to go down and collect.

So he turned his steps toward East Florence.

When Lucius Handback set out for the Crowninshield residence on Pine Street he was possibly less subject to the influence of the store than any of the other employees.

First his thoughts hovered over the possibility of another store. If he had a shoe store he thought he would not run after Sydna Crowninshield as he was now doing. He would likely be intimate with a dozen girls prettier than she. They would not only be prettier, they would be more amenable to the suggestion of his narrow-seated buggy; girls acquiescent on occasions.

Then, as the younger Handback approached the Crowninshield residence, these supposititious women faded from his mind and his heart began to beat. He peered through the dark street for a gleam of light. Presently he caught a bare glimmer of a lighted window. It was almost obscured by foliage. It looked as if the light were turned very low.

The storekeeper's son held his breath as he moved along the opposite side of the street. A furious mental condemnation filled him that a girl like Sydna Crowninshield should sit up at all hours with a low light with any caller whatsoever. Whoever it was would get Sydna talked about! If he—the beau inside—had a spark of gentility about him, he would not compromise a beautiful girl like Sydna Crowninshield!

Here Lucius almost walked into a dim gangling figure who leaned against the fence and gazed, apparently in a trance, into the Crowninshield yard.

The clerk came to a halt and considered the silent figure with a faint hostility mingled with curiosity.

"What are you looking at, friend?" he asked.

The figure gave a little start and became aware of Lucius.

"That light yonder," it said uninformingly.

"What are you looking at the light for?"

The boy hesitated, then said:

"In the dark you always look at a light if there is one."

"Yes . . . that's a fact," agreed Lucius thinking over this odd reply. "Is that the only reason you're looking at it?"

"I was reading about lights in the library today," said the figure.

"Yes, what did you read?"

"Why, that there were lights around people. It said you could see 'em in the dark if you were sensitive enough."

"What sort of lights?"

"It said pure thoughts made a blue light and a sincere love made a pink light; a lustful love made a red light. There were a lot of other sorts. Of course I don't believe in anything like that, but I was just standing here thinking about it."

The youth's extraordinary maunderings kept Lucius' mind from too painful a concentration on the fact that Sydna Crowninshield had a caller.

"I wonder what color I'd have?" he asked with amusement.

"I don't know . . . and besides, I don't believe in it."

"May I ask your name?" inquired the clerk.

"Catlin . . . what's yours?"

"Handback."

The hobbledehoy straightened himself somewhat.

"I didn't know who you were, or I wouldn't have gone on like that."

"Why?"

Jerry hesitated, but finally came out frankly:

"Well, you go to see Miss Sydna, and you drink and gamble. That's no way to do when you're going to associate with a pure woman."

"Just what's that to you?" inquired the clerk, not amused at all.

"Nothin'. I was just telling you why I wouldn't have

ᵣₑ.lked to you if I'd known who you were. You asked me, and I'm telling you."

"I see," said Handback. He pondered a moment, and then asked, "How did you learn so much about me?"

"Why, ever'body knows it. I was talking to Miss Sydna, and she told me."

"Oh, then you enter her presence sometimes, do you?" asked the clerk mimicking the boy.

"I go over to see the fam'ly sometimes. My mother and Miss Drusilla were old friends."

"Well . . . haven't you got any faults, Mr. Catlin?" inquired the clerk.

The boy shifted his position against the fence and nodded at the lighted window.

"I confessed my faults. . . . I—I told her I didn't believe in God."

"Didn't believe in——" Lucius looked at his vis-à-vis with a little shock; then this changed into mere grotesqueness. "You don't seem to believe in much of anything," he said.

Jerry remained silent at this.

After a few moments Handback continued:

"Look here, if there isn't any God, how can it be a fault not to believe in Him?"

Jerry was disconcerted at this question. He pondered on the lighted window.

"Now, that is a question," he admitted finally. "Now, looky here, I'll tell you how it is. Religion helps a person to do right, and ever'body needs all the help they can get. So it's a kind of fault for a person not to believe in God, no matter whether there is one or not."

A tingle of satisfaction went through Jerry at having successfully stated one of those vague paradoxes which often hovered around him, but which usually faded when he essayed the nice business of pinning them down with words.

"Well," said Lucius in a different tone, "you're getting too deep for me. Only I think it would be damned hard luck to die and go to hell for not believing in something that never did exist."

At this moment the discussion was interrupted by the opening of the Crowninshield front door.

This door was not behind any foliage. It stood in dim illumination, and silhouetted against it appeared a man and a girl. Jerry's heart almost stopped beating as the two figures coalesced in the embrace of parting lovers.

As Jerry stared, the blood beat in his ears. The glimpse he had once had of Sydna half disrobed in the sewing room rushed back upon him in painful voluptuousness. He moved away toward his aunt's boarding house, still staring back at the dim door. The caresses of the lovers filled his own body with tremors of induced desire. But behind this contagious eroticism lay a shock, a feeling of profanation that Sydna Crowninshield could or would be kissed. He felt somehow as if she had betrayed him. He came to another halt, shivering and staring at the sight.

After endless minutes the lovers in the dim doorway parted, and the man disappeared into the darkness. The hobbledehoy heard his steps coming down the graveled path. The girl in the doorway waved a hand into the darkness and then closed the door. Jerry could imagine her going back into her room, disrobing with the man's caresses still burning her body. He was as moved as if he himself had had her in his arms, only this was painful instead of ecstatic.

At this point Jerry's attention was caught by Lucius Handback's voice saying in a tense undertone:

"Is that you, Thorndyke?"

The steps of Sydna's lover halted, and his voice replied:
"No, this is Bivins."

"I don't care who you are, it's damned ungentlemanly, staying in a girl's parlor until after midnight!"

"Who the hell are you?"

"Makes no difference who I am," trembled Lucius' voice; "you'll get the girl talked about . . . staying all night with her!"

By this time Bivins recognized the clerk, for he said in a different tone:

"Look here, Handback, I don't want any trouble with you."

"The hell you don't . . . come fooling around my girl . . . trying to get next to her . . . then don't want any trouble with me!"

"I never had any such intentions!" snapped the drummer.

"That's a damned lie, I saw you in the door. . . ."

"Look here, Handback," quivered Bivins' voice, "I sell goods to your daddy. . . ."

"By God, you won't any more, and you're a damned liar and a woman chaser, and you know it!"

To Jerry's ears came the crack of a blow. The next instant the boy heard blows, grunts, the tramping of feet in the graveled walk.

Jerry listened, vibrating with induced wrath. Lucius Handback was fighting for the good name of Sydna Crowninshield. The boy started running to help him. He'd lend a hand against Bivins.

At that moment he heard footsteps running under the trees, and then the blackness was shattered by the flashes and roars of two pistol shots.

Jerry stopped. Horror swirled through him. He listened with mouth open but heard nothing more except the complaint of some bird in the trees. He thought to himself:

"My God, somebody's killed! One of 'em's killed!"

Fear seized Jerry. He started up the street again, taking long silent steps. He breathed through his mouth and listened with all his ears. When he felt out of danger he stopped again, breathing heavily and listening.

Then he heard someone coming up the street after him. The boy scuttled over the fence and hid to see which of the rivals was still alive. His heart beat so loudly he was afraid the man could hear it.

The walker passed within three feet of Jerry. It was his uncle Miltiades.

CHAPTER EIGHT

THE two revolver shots had come to Colonel Miltiades Vaiden's ears, but he had not heard them. He was indeed unaware of any of the outward world about him. His mind was on the store. He was walking through the night amazed and sardonically indignant at the huge amount of business that flowed through the store.

Revelation of this had come to Miltiades because J. Handback, at last, had thought of an evening chore for the Colonel which would be worth seven dollars and a half a week. This was, posting the sales tickets in the ledger while he, J. Handback, filed them away. The middle-aged Colonel wrote a clerkly hand and was honest, so the merchant had made him a kind of assistant bookkeeper.

His very first evening at this work showed the Colonel the huge volume of his employer's business. Grist mills, saw mills, cotton gins, lumber yards, cross-tie yards, and of course cotton plantations, marched through page after page.

At first Miltiades was simply astonished, but now, as he walked home, he began to think that the money of the Vaidens was part of the original capital of the store. The nest egg he should have had lay embedded in the base of this vast complex of enterprises. And now here he was, a clerk, in the system of properties which he had helped to fund, drawing from it, by dint of endless labor, seven dollars and a half a week! This was the cause of his ironic amusement and indignation. He laughed aloud and became aware of his surroundings. He was approaching his own jerry-built house on Cherry Street.

When Miltiades entered his bedroom, Ponny was asleep. Her bulk was covered by a sheet, and on the floor beside

82

her bed lay a sadiron wrapped in rags. Evidently she had
been in some sort of pain before she went to sleep and had
applied the heated iron to her shapeless body. Miltiades
meant to ask her, when she awoke next morning, what was
the matter, but he overslept himself, and when he finally did
awaken, Ponny had removed the iron.

The fat woman had an exciting subject to talk about. She
said to the man in bed:

"You awake, Mr. Milt? I heard there was trouble downtown last night."

The Colonel blinked his eyes at his wife and said:

"Yes, I'm awake."

"There was a fight downtown last night."

The Colonel became completely awake.

"Who was it?"

"Mr. Han'back's boy and a drummer. They were fightin'
over Sydna Crowninshield."

"That's funny. I left the store right after Lucius. Anybody get hurt?"

"I don't think they did. A nigger told Mrs. Klem that
Rose Vaiden's nephew come out with a pistol and shot a
couple o' times in the air and chased 'em both away."

Miltiades sat up in bed.

"You don't mean it! Well, I be John Brown!" He gave
a grunt of laughter. "Well, young Jerry is a Vaiden, after
all, isn't he?" Then he reflected that the object of Jerry's
knight errantry was Drusilla Lacefield's daughter, and he
ejaculated with an odd feeling, "Well, well, well. . . ."

Ponny sensed what these "wells" meant and disparaged:

"I don't see what they wanted to fight about her for—a
girl settin' up in the parlor till a way after midnight!"

At that moment Miltiades became sure that the girl whose
escort he had reproved on Courthouse Square weeks before
had been Sydna Crowninshield, and he wondered uneasily if
anything had happened to her.

"What are you thinking about?" asked Ponny suspiciously.

"About Handback. . . . I got a new job last night."

"What was it?" inquired Ponny, knowing that was not what he had been thinking.

"I helped with the ledger. Handback has accounts on top of accounts. He must be worth one or two hundred thousand, maybe more."

"Don't see why you should draw such a long breath over that!"

Miltiades thought how absurd it was for a great non-sexual bulk like Ponny to be jealous; then he conjured up a reason for drawing a long breath,

"Because with all Handback's money, the fellow really gets nothing out of it. He slaves just like Love and Stebbins . . . or me. His home isn't anything to look at, and his store's a hole." After a moment he added, "The first thing I'll get when things come my way is a home . . . a place where a man can live."

"I wish we could have a better house now," said Ponny, reaching past the overhang of her body to put the plates on the table; then she tacked on, "I feel bad this morning. I have a bad taste in my mouth."

"What did you heat that iron for last night?"

"How did you know I heated an iron?"

"I saw it wrapped up by the bed."

"Why, I was cold, and sick at my stomick. . . . Mrs. Klem thinks I'm three months gone."

"Yes . . . what Mrs. Klem thinks," echoed the Colonel ironically.

Ponny finished putting the things on the table, then said in a wounded voice:

"There's your breakfast, Mr. Milt."

"Aren't you going to eat?"

"I'm not hongry."

But her tone told Miltiades that her feelings had been hurt and she was denying herself breakfast to punish him.

"Oh, Ponny," ejaculated the husband, "sit down and eat your breakfast and don't act so silly!"

He himself put his napkin in his lap, bowed his head, and murmured in a monotone:

"Father, sanctify this food to our bodies, and our lives to thy use. Amen."

The Colonel lifted his head, and Ponny, who had bowed where she stood obstinately in the middle of the kitchen, lifted her head also. She put two sticks of wood in the kitchen step stove.

Miltiades began thinking again of Jerry Catlin; how his nephew had chased away the rivals fighting for Miss Sydna's hand. It was exactly like a Vaiden, he thought. He could imagine Polycarp Vaiden doing precisely that sort of thing. It might have been a Quixoticism out of his dead brother's gay, brief life.

A great many other persons in Florence besides Miltiades sat in judgment that morning on the supposed exploit of young Jerry Catlin. Some of the oldsters attributed it to the boy's maternal grandsire, old man Jimmie Vaiden, who had been quick tempered, unaccountable, and quite as likely to do one thing as another. Others shook their heads and said that young Jerry was well on his way toward getting himself shot, and thus following the footsteps of his uncle Polycarp, who had been a wild drinking man. Judge Ashton recalled that Jerry's paternal grandfather, old man Philo Catlin, had, single handed, put to flight a gang of rascally horse thieves during the war.

Mrs. Drusilla Crowninshield got the current report through her cook, Pammy Lee. Pammy Lee was fifteen years old and was the second oldest daughter of Miss Tony's brood. Miss Tony had hired Pammy Lee to Miss Drusilla at fifty cents a week, with the unilateral understanding on Miss Tony's part that when the daughter, under Miss Drusilla's tutelage, really learned to cook, then she, Miss Tony, would hire Pammy Lee to some other housewife who paid more and oftener.

Pammy Lee was very black, because at the time of her

conception the taste of Miss Tony was less corrupted by color prejudice than latterly it became. The daughter's wool was tied up in strings and stood out in all directions, thus giving Pammy Lee a perpetual air of excitement.

When the black girl rushed in to tell how Mr. Jerry Catlin had shot a pistol and chased two of Miss Sydna's beaux from the front gate, Pammy Lee appeared very excited indeed.

Mrs. Drusilla opened her dark eyes in astonishment and dismay.

"Lucius Handback and Mr. Bivins?"

"Yes'm . . . fightin' each other!" cried Pammy Lee.

Mrs. Drusilla sensed in advance the indefinite disgrace this would bring upon Sydna.

"How did you find all this out?"

Pammy Lee nodded quickly with white eyes.

"Pahson Mowbray tol' Mammy dis mawnin', an' Newt Hixon tol' Pahson Mowbray, an' Jute Wilkes tol' Newt."

Mrs. Drusilla stopped this linked hearsay with a wave of her hand. Besides, it was true. She had heard the two shots herself. She left Pammy Lee in the kitchen and went to the living room.

"Sydna," she asked in a tense tone, "did you know Lucius Handback and Mr. Bivins had a fight last night?"

"Mother! What about?"

"Why, you . . . of course!"

"Me! Oh, Mother!"

"Yes, yes, it's 'Oh, Mother' now! I told you I never liked that Mr. Bivins, but you kept letting him come!"

The daughter stared at her mother with big eyes.

"Did anybody . . . get hurt?"

"They would have . . . killed each other, perhaps, but Jerry Catlin rushed over with a pistol and chased them both away."

At this news Sydna uncurled the foot she sat on and put it on the floor.

"Jerry did that! What for?"

"What does any of the Vaiden blood do anything for? Next time he's likely to turn right around and do the opposite." Then she added more cogently, "I suppose he realized how people would talk about you and thought he would stop it."

"He's awfully young to think about that."

"Then apt as not he just wanted to be in the fight. I don't know. You can't tell anything about a Vaiden!"

Sydna sat completely at sea. She did not know what to do. On the preceding night she had engaged herself to marry the hardware salesman and now here he had walked out and had a fist fight at her gate and had been chased away by a boy. She could have wept.

And she was disappointed on several counts. Hers was such a poor sort of romance. It would not compare with her mother's drama of eloping with her father on the very eve of her wedding with Colonel Milt Vaiden.

For Mr. Bivins and Lucius to start fighting like niggers in her front yard! What a come-down!

Here she began thinking about Jerry rushing over with his pistol under pretense of protecting her good name. She knew it was jealousy. He was always asking her about Mr. Bivins and Lucius, their characters, what sort of men they were; and then he would become moody and dejected. She thought that was the basis of Jerry's disbelief in God, because she let Lucius and Mr. Bivins come to see her.

The first inkling that Jerry Catlin had of his own heroism in the exciting scene of the night before came from Sandusky.

He and Sandusky roomed together, and the boarder read Governor O'Shawn's law books till all hours of the night. Jerry didn't like this. Sandusky's lamp, and his mere presence in the room, frustrated a certain design, a sweet luxury, in which young Jerry wanted to indulge. The hobbledehoy wanted to lie in bed in the dark and think about Sydna Crowninshield. He would think about her in the light of his discovery that she kissed men. If she kissed Bivins, why shouldn't she kiss him, too? Lucius Handback had suggested that she went even further than kisses with Bivins. This angered Jerry and at the same time set his heart to beating. If she went further with Bivins, why might not he, Jerry . . .

A thought came to Jerry that some day he might frighten Sydna into the rapture of letting him hold her in his arms. He would accuse her of an intimacy with Alex Bivins, and then he would extort a similar favor or he would tell on her.

But all this imaginary and lascivious blackmail could not go on with the lamp lighted and Sandusky up reading a law book.

So one night, in desperation, young Jerry sat up in bed and cried out:

"Sandusky, are you going to read all night long?"

The boarder came out of his reading and asked irrelevantly:

"Jerry, did you use my pistol?"

Jerry blinked with a suspicion that Sandusky had gone to sleep over his book.

"Your pistol? Hey, Sandusky, wake up and go to bed."

"I'm awake. You haven't got a pistol of your own, have you?"

Jerry decided to answer this question, meaningless though it be.

"No, you know I haven't got any pistol."

"Then you must have used mine."

"When?" inquired Jerry, becoming wider awake himself.

"Why, last night, when you shot and skeered Alex and Lucius in front of the Crowninshield place."

Jerry was amazed at this extraordinary version of his inglorious flight.

"Who told you that?"

"Governor O'Shawn told me. It was the question he ast me."

Jerry was astonished and quite taken aback.

"How came Governor O'Shawn asking about me?"

"Why, when anything like that comes up, the Governor asks me what offense has been committed and makes me write out an indictment. I've been writing out your indictment for about an hour. You were guilty of carrying concealed weapons, of intimidation, of assault, of impersonating an officer, of . . . there's another one . . . there's one more." Sandusky began pawing through his papers, shutting and opening his small reddened eyes.

Jerry's mouth went dry.

"What you going to do with that indictment when you get it fixed?"

"Show it to the Gov'nor in the morning."

"What'll he do with it?"

"Correct it."

"Oh . . . I see," breathed Jerry, who perceived the indictment was an academic exercise. Then he recalled the actual rôle he had played in the episode.

"I didn't use your pistol, Sandusky."

"Whose did you use?"

Jerry decided he would not tell Sandusky what really had happened.

"I have friends who have pistols," he said evasively.

Sandusky thought this over.

"Well, your friend, whoever he is, has committed a few offenses, too. He has furnished a deadly weapon for felonious purposes; he furnished a deadly weapon to a minor; he furnished a deadly weapon . . ." Sandusky went on and on.

CHAPTER NINE

Where young Jerry Catlin had been put to these transitory qualms about the fight on Pine Street, his uncle Miltiades Vaiden was wondering if the incident might disturb his own personal relation with the store. He walked down the next morning planning to mention the matter casually to Handback and say that he was not in any way Jerry's guardian.

When he entered the store he saw the merchant in the brightly lighted bookkeeper's pen, talking to a negro who stood just outside the rail.

Handback seemed to be putting the black man through some sort of catechism, asking him could he read, could he figure, could he write his name. The negro could not do any of these things.

"All right, Loob," said the merchant finally, "you can tend twelve acres on the old Mowbray place. Your cabin will be across the field from Dudley's." Handback called one of his clerks: "Stebbins, let this nigger have six dollars' worth of anything he wants." Then he turned to Miltiades. "I wonder if you would do a little errand for me this morning, Colonel?"

Miltiades was slightly offended that he had been kept waiting on Loob, but he was glad no mention had been made of Jerry's chasing Lucius with a pistol. He asked what was wanted.

Handback picked up a yellow order sheet from his desk.

"I wish you'd take this to Alex Bivins at the Florence Hotel and tell him I cancel it . . . damn red-headed shikepoke!"

The Colonel saw that Handback was taking up the incident, not against his nephew, but against Bivins, where the blame properly belonged. He smiled:

"Shall I add that?"

"Can if you want to," returned the merchant humorlessly. He pondered a moment and added, "Stop by the post office as you come back; and if you see Lucius anywhere—he's prob'ly talking to that pest Bradley—tell him to come on back to the store, ever'thing's all right."

Miltiades nodded. He did not realize his errand was an overture of peace from the merchant to his son. The two had fallen out because Lucius had wanted to cancel the Bivins order and his father had not wanted to cancel it.

Handback cleared his throat and continued looking at the Colonel. He had a criticism which he wanted to make of the Colonel's work but which he had kept putting off from time to time. Now that he was out of temper he could make it.

"Another thing, Colonel . . . you noticed that nigger, Loob Snipes, I was talking to?"

"Yes, I had to wait till you had finished talking to him."

Such a delicate reproof passed over Handback's head.

"You noticed the fool answers he made to my questions?"

"Yes."

"Well, ever' nigger I got on my plantations is just about like Snipes. They can't read, write, figger, or spell their names. I'm dang careful not to hire any other kind."

"M-m . . . just how do I come into that?"

"Easy enough," explained the merchant bluntly. "Here in the store, when you trade with 'em, knock off ten per cent of the weight and add on ten per cent of the price. They never know it. It ain't enough to hurt 'em, and it's a big help to the store. I mention this because you've just about got the niggers so they won't trade with anybody but you. It over-works you, for one thing. You'll break down."

Miltiades gave the storekeeper a level look.

"You expect me to short-weight the niggers who trade with me?"

"Now, now," protested the tradesman, "*is* it short-weightin' 'em? Ain't it well understood a nigger pound is about twelve ounces? Why, it's a kind of unwritten law. They expect it. And to have one clerk, like you, weighin' out sixteen-ounce pounds throws ever'thing out of whack. It disorganizes business."

A number of thoughts went through the Colonel's head. He spoke only one:

"I don't want to have to knock down and kick out every nigger who accuses me of short-weighting him."

"Well, there's no need to do that either," said the merchant in a disappointed tone; "don't be so touchy. And think over what I've said to you."

The interview was over, and Miltiades walked out of the store, disgusted with his employer.

Outside, the first tang of autumn was in the air. People in the street moved more briskly to the turn of the year. Miltiades stopped by the post office and took the Handback mail out of an oversized box. Inside the postmaster's private office, the Colonel saw Landers working at his desk. The Republican postmaster produced an odd impression of isolation on the Colonel. Outside the office once more, this was forgotten.

At the Florence Hotel, Andrew the porter told Miltiades that Mr. Bivins had been writing letters all morning and finally had taken them and gone out with them: "One was to he gal, an' one to de post office, an' one to de newspapah office," explained the black man. "He gib 'em to me once to delivah fuh him, 'n'en change his min' an' took 'em hese'f."

With these three ports of call in view, Miltiades set out after the salesman and caught up with him as he entered the office of the *Florence Index*. As Bivins evidently had delicate business to attend to, the Colonel waited outside a few minutes, but presently his patience gave out, and he went in.

The red-headed youth stood beside a desk in conversation with the editor. The editor, a small sharp-featured man, lifted a hand at Miltiades and went on talking to the drummer.

"Why not give me an ad to run for your firm?" he suggested.

Bivins glanced uneasily at Miltiades.

"My firm don't advertise in papers, Mr. Lacefield, they just stick posters up in stores."

"In a case like that, I can't put the interest of your firm ahead of my subscribers. They pay for the news, and I have to give it to 'em."

"I see; but if we took advertising it would be different?"

"Certainly, a paper has got to protect its advertisers."

The drummer hemmed and frowned.

"Well, now, how little could we take and still be protected?"

"M—well, a page is worth ten dollars."

"Oh, my God, they wouldn't stand for a page!"

"Then a half page?"

"Why not a quarter of a page? That would be two and a half."

"That would be three," said Lacefield.

"Now, how the hell come that?" cried Bivins.

"Now, now, Mr. Bivins. You a traveling man. You know if you buy anything in large amounts you get it cheaper."

"Well, all right: shoot a quarter at three."

"Fine. Now, what sort of ad do you want run in your space?"

The salesman pondered a moment.

"Just say, 'Black Diamond Hardware is the Best and the Cheapest. Beware of Imitations.' "

"Pretty good ad. Straight and to the point."

The editor made a note of the wording on a pad of paper.

As the salesman turned to go, Miltiades intercepted him at the door.

"Mr. Bivins, Mr. Handback wants you to cancel that order he placed with your house."

The red-headed man shot a glance at the elderly clerk.

"I imagine it does you a damn lot o' good to tell me that."

He drew out his order book and tore out two sheets.

As Bivins walked out, Lacefield turned to Miltiades with a puzzled face.

"Milt, what the hell did that young fellow do?"

"Don't you know?" ejaculated the Colonel in surprise.

"Haven't the ghost of an idea. He blew in here and asked me not to print it in my paper. I told him I wouldn't if he would give me a year's subscription and take some advertising. He did that. Now, what in the devil have I promised not to print?"

While Colonel Vaiden explained to A. Gray Lacefield the nature of the open secret which the *Index* had pledged itself to observe, Mr. Alexander Bivins walked out into the early autumn sunshine thinking what to do next.

The greatest anxiety filled the drummer. He wondered if Sydna Crowninshield would hold against him what had happened. He thought not. She was such a sweet, sensible girl. And on the preceding evening she had promised to marry him. She surely wouldn't discard him for a difficulty that was no fault of his own.

Then another quandary seized on Bivins. He wondered whether or not he should report this trouble to headquarters in Louisville? If he did not how would he explain the loss of the Handback trade? If he did, would he hold his job?

The irony of the thing, the steel that gyved him, was that he had always supposed eventually that some woman would ruin him. Everybody warned him that women would be his ruination. But he had thought it would be bad women. He supposed he would get stabbed in a brothel or be shot entering the wrong room in some hotel. He never dreamed he would get in such a mess as this over a sweet religious girl for whom he felt the utmost respect and tenderness. It was fantastic the way women really had undone him. To visit a virgin was more dangerous than to chase a punk.

Mr. Bivins continued chewing on this bitter paradox as he walked up Pine Street toward the Crowninshield home. As he drew near the place he drew a note from his pocket and reread it. It said:

My DARLING FUTURE WIFE, no matter what you hear about me, I want you to know that it wasn't my fault. When I came out of your home last night, I met Lucius Handback, who accused me of things which I cannot even write to a lady like you. I at first tried to pacify him, but he kept saying harder and harder things until we got into a fight. I didn't want to hurt him, so I pulled out the pistol which my firm has me carry because I sometimes collect money for them, and fired it twice in the air. It scared him, and he ran off and let me alone.

Darling, I do not care if I lose the Handback trade. My firm will stand behind me. They would hardly turn off their finest salesman just for one account. I have written a complete statement of the matter to my firm, and if you hear Lucius Handback threatening to report me to my boss, you can tell him I've already done it.

Honey, I love you more than anything in this world.

> *A glance from your eye*
> *Makes me sigh.*
> *A smile from your lips*
> *Makes me*

With eternal devotion, your future husband, ALEX.

The poetry in the letter Mr. Bivins had composed himself. He had not been able to finish the last line. So now, under the trees, he tried to think up some appropriate word with an "ips" sound. He still thought of nothing that would do, but he did add a postscript:

Since writing the above old man Handback has canceled his order. It will be a cold day in August before he finds another line of hardware equal to **Black Diamond** Brand either in quality or price. A.

He sealed the envelope, entered the gate, and walked up the graveled path to the Crowninshield front door. He knew the futility of the lion's foot and knocked.

Presently Pammy Lee came out and told him that Miss Sydna's mammy said that Miss Sydna was indisposed.

"Her mammy said that?" noted Bivins.

"Yes, suh, dat's whut huh mammy said."

"Look here," said the drummer in an undertone, drawing out his note and a dime, "give this to Miss Sydna herself, and tell her I'll wait for her answer down at the end of the block. You bring it down, and I'll give you another dime. Understand?"

The little negress took the note and disappeared. Before the salesman had time to get off the porch she was back again and handed Bivins his envelope unopened.

"Huh mammy say they ain't gwi' be no ansah," she announced.

The drummer felt empty and unnerved. He got down the steps and moved along the box-lined path to the gate.

Inside the living room Mrs. Drusilla was commenting viciously:

"Calls himself a gentleman and then tries to communicate with you clandestinely . . ."

The mother, who had eloped with Sydna's father on the eve of her wedding night a score of years before, was very wroth at such base subterfuges.

With the going of Mr. Bivins, Sydna Crowninshield at least felt that relief which comes with settling a quandary. She would not marry the hardware salesman. She watched him walk away, and realized, as she stood beside the window in the quiet old room, that she was twenty-two years old, unmarried, and unengaged.

She was getting frightfully old.

She drew a long breath and looked through the small panes at the trees in her yard. They sent down squadrons of autumn leaves, some whirling over and over, some sailing around and around, until they stranded on hollyhocks and zinnias and grass below. The girl felt restless and vaguely angry at both Lucius Handback and Mr. Bivins. Between the two of them they had treated her meanly.

She could stay cooped up indoors no longer. She picked up a book and started outside. She was going to a hammock and a set of willow furniture in her yard which was screened by a parterre of box.

As she walked around a lilac bush into view of her garden set, she was a little surprised at a gangling figure in the hammock.

"How long have you been here?" she asked with a faint mechanical smile.

"A little before Bivins came."

"No, keep the hammock, I'll sit in the chair."

"Well . . . all right. . . ." The youth was grateful for a place to lounge. After a moment he added with a faint question in his voice, "He left quick?"

"Yes, but he'll stay gone for a long time," said Sydna in an odd tone.

A squeeze of relief went through Jerry's chest.

"You mean . . . he's gone for good?"

Sydna came up to him and swung the hammock a trifle.

"I understand you had something to do with this. I don't know whether I have you to thank or blame."

Jerry moved his slim body a little to one side in the hammock in unconscious invitation for Sydna to sit beside him.

"Was it . . . serious?" Sympathy and concern were now in Jerry's gray eyes.

"We were engaged," said the girl in a monotone.

"To be married?" asked the boy in a low voice.

"Of course, foolish."

A pang of undoing went through Jerry. If she and Bivins were engaged, then they had had a right to kiss in the doorway; and now he reddened at the thoughts he had entertained of extorting kisses from her. Then a magnificent renunciation popped into Jerry's head. He raised up in the hammock.

"Miss Sydna, if—if you're sorry, would you like for me to—to approach Mr. Bivins in a diplomatic way and—and tell him you changed your mind?"

"Why, Jerry, you know I wouldn't. . . . I shouldn't think you'd want to!" she ejaculated on the impulse.

"W-well," stammered Jerry, "I thought . . ." He was reduced to silence by a confused desire to sacrifice himself for her happiness. He wished she could walk on his body to some great happiness for herself. This reminded him of what he had been reading in the school library, and presently he said, "You know there are men like that in the world, Miss Sydna: they call 'em adepts."

There was something comforting to the girl about Jerry. He was such an awkward, blushing boy. He was like a poultice after the possessive rivalry of the older men.

"Like what, Jerry?" she asked, going back to his sentence.

"Why, holy men who go about the world doing good . . . er . . . sacrificing themselves."

"They are adepts?"

"Yes."

"I'm afraid I never heard of adepts."

"You prob'ly didn't," agreed Jerry: "they are a kind of brotherhood. They live mainly in India and travel around the world doing good, but they keep themselves unknown to anybody except other adepts. But if an outsider grows spiritually until he is ready to be initiated, then this brotherhood knows it. And no matter where you are, in America, in England, in Russia, one of these adepts comes to you . . . unknown to you, mind you, just an old man walking by, and he tests you; he puts questions to you that test you . . . and you don't know you're being tested."

"Tests you how?" inquired the girl curiously at this rig-marole.

"Why, to find out whether you are really pure and holy and fit to enter the brotherhood."

"What would the test be like?"

"Oh, most anything. He might ask you for something to eat . . . or ask you to do something that would show you had a good heart. It is always something that will really test you."

The girl sat looking at him, finding an odd comfort in his whimsicality.

"Jerry, where did you find out all this?"

"In a yogi book in the library."

"A yogi book?"

"Uh huh."

"Well . . . you don't believe it, do you?"

The adolescent blinked his eyes and looked at her.

"Why-y . . . no . . . no, of course I don't believe it."

"Yes, you do, you halfway believe it."

"Oh, no, I don't any such thing," he denied stoutly.

"Well, anyway, it's sweet of you to believe it," she said, smiling tenderly at him.

Jerry colored for no understood reason. He was about to protest more strongly his complete skepticism when the clacking of a horse's hoofs and the murmur of a rubber-tired buggy drew their attention. A flush of annoyance went through the girl.

"Now, there," she ejaculated, "I wish you had a pistol to run him off again."

"Who . . . what?" asked the boy.

"Oh, that buggy . . . you know who's coming."

Jerry utilized his supine position to peer down under the box shrubs. He reached back a warning hand to Sydna.

"You keep hid," he directed, "and Pammy Lee won't know where you are."

The girl caught his hand to hold him and keep him from rolling out of the hammock. At her touch an amazing sweet tingling flowed up Jerry's arm and into his chest and throat. It was so unknown, strange, and surprising that the adolescent was conscious of nothing beyond the rapturous fingers.

"Is it Lucius?" whispered the girl, staring at Jerry as if he were her eyes.

The youth saw nothing at all. He made a great effort to look and see who it was.

"It's . . . it's . . . it's Uncle Miltiades in a buggy," he identified at last.

"Your uncle Miltiades!" ejaculated the girl in surprise. "Wonder how came him in a buggy?"

There was no need of concealment any longer. They both stood up and looked.

"Well, that is queer," observed Sydna in surprise, "he's in Lucius Handback's little hug-me-tight. . . ."

The two stood looking after the Colonel as he drove on up the street wondering the reason for this. And their fingers dropped loose.

The passing of his uncle Miltiades in the Handback buggy ended the first movement of love between young Jerry Catlin and Sydna Crowninshield. It was not to be resumed consciously, like an accustomed garment. The girl stood smiling faintly at the boy.

"I wonder why Colonel Milt went by in Lucius's buggy?" she repeated, and with the question turned toward the manor as if the answer lay somewhere in the house.

Jerry was shaken at the intangible thing that had happened to him.

"I got to go," he said, and moved bemazed among the box borders toward the gate.

Sydna went into the house without looking back. She found her mother in the kitchen and told her that Colonel Milt Vaiden had gone up the street in Lucius Handback's buggy.

Mrs. Drusilla paused with flour on her hands.

"That's odd. I wonder why he was in the Handback buggy. . . ." She stood thinking over possible reasons for this anomaly. "Was he driving fast or slow?" she queried.

"Pretty fast." Sydna began to perceive that the Colonel's driving at all was a significant thing. Suddenly an explanation came to her:

"I'll tell you what it is, I'll bet Miss Ponny . . ." she paused with a catch of her breath.

Mrs. Drusilla stared. "Why, certainly, that must be why he was sent for!"

"And Miss Ponny's size and everything!" cried Sydna.

Mrs. Drusilla began pulling off her floury apron.

"That's all it could be! The Handbacks wouldn't lend their horse and buggy for any other reason in the world!"

"Mamma, what are you going to do?" asked Sydna.

"Why, Ponny's up there by herself. They haven't any money for trained nurses or anything like that!"

"But you're not going!"

"Of course I am. Ponny is an old friend."

Mrs. Drusilla untied and threw her apron on a chair, then hurried out of the house to get Rose Vaiden. As she rushed up Pine Street she was thankful that she had borne Sydna in her own flexible girlhood. Ponny must be thirty-eight . . . thirty-seven at least.

As she neared the Vaidens' she saw young Jerry in the front yard. She called urgently for him to run tell his aunt to come to the gate quick. Jerry vanished in the house, and in a few seconds Mrs. Rose came hurrying out the door. Drusilla motioned her to the gate and explained in a low voice.

"Oh! Oh!" cried Mrs. Rose, *sotto voce*, "I heard she was expecting it but I didn't know anybod/ else was!"

"We ought to go up there!"

"Of course, of course! Jerry! Oh, Jerry, run over to Mrs. Ashton's and borrow their horse and buggy, quick!"

"What'll I say?" cried Jerry, dashing across the lawn and vaulting the fence.

"Tell her we've got to go see Ponny!"

Jerry sprinted away to deliver this message. He was no sooner out of sight than they began to say, "Why doesn't he come back? What's keeping him?"

Presently the carriage appeared coming up the street. The two women climbed in, dismissed Jerry, and clucked and whipped their way toward the Vaiden home in the north end of town.

"I wonder if it'll be a boy or girl?" hazarded Rose.

"Oh, a boy!" cried Drusilla, who could not imagine Miltiades becoming the father of a girl.

Their talk broke off as they came in sight of the Colonel's home. Only the Handback buggy was hitched at the gate.

A spasm went through Rose's breast.

"Oh, they haven't even got a doctor!"

Just then they saw the bulk of Ponny fill the kitchen door and wring out a dish rag. The fat woman saw who was in the buggy and stared in amazement.

"Rose! Drusilla!" cried Ponny in bewildered hospitality. "Come in!"

"Why, no," began Rose in the utmost confusion, "no, we were just driving out this way . . ."

"Won't you come in?" cried Ponny in a wounded tone. "When I saw who it was I thought you-all was a-comin' to see me at last."

The two women looked at each other, then prepared to get out. Miltiades came and hitched the horses and assisted the ladies to the ground in the grand manner.

They made quite a strange call: Drusilla sitting in the shabby tenement of her old lover; Rose amused and quite at sea; Ponny flustered, ashamed of her house, and wondering why the two women had come. When the visit came to an end the humor of the situation struck the two ladies.

"Drusilla!" cried Rose, as they drove away, "what geese we are! Rush off and borrow a buggy to help at Ponny's childbirth just because we saw Milt Vaiden drive by your home!"

The two fell into helpless laughter as the Ashton bays ambled back toward town. After a while Mrs. Rose composed herself and asked curiously:

"Drusilla, why do you suppose Milt Vaiden *was* driving the Handback buggy?"

CHAPTER TEN

THE coming of their visitors was just as mysterious to Ponny and Miltiades as the buggy had been to Drusilla and Rose. When the Colonel resumed his delayed lunch his wife said heavily that she wished she had a nicer home.

"You may get one before long," said the Colonel, who, during Drusilla's visit, also had wished for a better house.

"What do you mean, Mr. Milt?"

"Handback has raised my salary to ten dollars a week."

"How come him to do that?"

"He wants me to go out and see about the niggers on his places."

"Well, I hope you're not going to. I thought you was going to work in the store!"

The Colonel frowned.

"To tell you the truth, Ponny, I don't get along so well in the store. My way of clerking doesn't suit Handback."

"Don't you do enough work?"

Miltiades gave a short laugh.

"That's the trouble, I do it nearly all. The niggers flock to me because I give 'em a square deal."

"Huh," said Ponny, who hardly knew what to say to this. Then she repeated that she hoped they could get a better house.

The horse and buggy which had so excited Drusilla was the first earnest of Miltiades' new position as overseer. The Colonel had driven by his home for twelve o'clock dinner while on his way to one of the Handback plantations. After he had eaten and was driving once more, he kept an eye out for Bradley the real-estate man.

One always found Bradley by keeping an eye out for him,

because the fellow had no office. He was, however, the kind of man who was always just coming in sight when one looked out in the street.

As luck would have it, just before the Colonel turned off into Waterloo Road on his way to one of the Handback holdings, he saw Bradley. He stopped his horse and waited. The real-estate man immediately hurried his steps, calling out cheerfully:

"Good-evening, Colonel. Well, it looks like we're going to have a Democratic President at last."

Bradley was a tall, well set-up man with curly black hair and a big reddened, blue-eyed face that was molded into a permanent optimistic smile.

"Bradley," said the Colonel, "I've been thinking about another house, something nicer than I've got. I can pay about twenty-five dollars a month for it." The Colonel really had in mind fifteen dollars a month, but he hoped to settle on a twenty-five-dollar house and jew Bradley down.

The real-estate man drew a cheroot out of his vest pocket and slipped it into Miltiades' vest pocket. As he did so he said:

"Know the very house you want. Some folks living in it now, but I think I can turn 'em out and let you have it. Le's drive around and look at it."

"I won't want to change for about a month," said Miltiades, "and I haven't got time to drive around now."

"All right, see you tomorrow and show you the house." He took his foot off the buggy step and jotted a memo on the back of an envelope as Miltiades started his horse.

As the Colonel drove on, he drew out Bradley's cheroot and smoked it. Under the spell of the tobacco he thought of J. Handback turning him out of the store and making him an overseer again because he dealt honestly with the negroes. A crinkle of satire went through Miltiades' thoughts. If he ever got a store of his own he was going to deal with black folk with strict fairness. Why, he'd have a trade . . . he'd have a big trade. . . .

Now and then, on the road, the Colonel passed wagons of seed cotton rattling toward Florence. As his thoughts drifted here and there these wagons presently reminded him of the cotton which he had hauled into Florence years before and which J. Handback had stolen from him.

And now here was he, Miltiades Vaiden, setting out to oversee the Handback farms and teach pin-headed negroes how to grow more cotton for the benefit of J. Handback, Esq. That was a droll but brackish idea.

Here the Colonel reached in his pocket and drew out a list of the tenants he was to see. After each name was marked "white" or "colored," as the case might be. Nearly all of the tenants were negroes.

Presently he turned down a side road to visit the first name on his list. He drew up his buggy on the chips of a woodpile in front of a shanghai cabin. He lifted his voice and called out:

"Meggs! Oh, Luster Meggs!"

A negro man appeared in the door with his hat in his hand. The Colonel explained he was from Mr. Handback, and the negro asked apprehensively:

"Does I owe you-all somp'n, Colonel?"

"I imagine so, but that's not what I'm here for. What do you do with the manure in your stable, Luster?"

"What do I *do* wid hit? Why, Col'l, mainly, I scrapes hit off'n my foot."

"Well, from now on spread it over your fields. That's one of the things I came down to tell you to do."

"Yussuh!" ejaculated Luster blankly.

"Let's go down and have a look at your stable," suggested the Colonel.

Luster put a hand over his mouth to conceal his laughter.

"Col'l . . . you driv frum Flaunts to see my manu'?"

"Not just to see it, to tell you where to put it, and I'll be around every week or so to see that you put it there, Luster."

"M-huh . . ." said Luster, suddenly sobering.

Farther along on the same plantation the Colonel stopped

at the shack of a white tenant named Dalrymple. When Miltiades drove up, the share cropper was amazed and delighted.

"Why, howdy, Colonel! Git out an' come in. Here, lemme rest your hat. How's Cousin Dal makin' it at the store?"

"What store?" inquired Miltiades, a little curious.

"Why, Han'back's store, of course," ejaculated Dalrymple; "he clerks there."

The Colonel recalled that he had heard Love called "Dal."

"Oh, Dal's getting on fine," praised Miltiades. "Is Love a cousin of yours?"

The tenant took out his pipe and broke into incredulous laughter.

"Why, Colonel, you know he is. Sam Love come up from Winston County and married Paw's sister. . . . Of course, you don't know who my paw wuz?" The tenant winked at the silliness of his own jest.

"I wouldn't be likely to forget him," agreed the Colonel.

"Of course you wouldn't. . . . Who was he?"

"Have you forgot your dad's name?" laughed the Colonel.

"No, I haven't, have you?"

"Of course not."

"Then who was he?"

The Colonel felt an acute discomfort at not knowing all about the family of his companion which the hill man expected. He made a flying guess.

"My gracious, boy, as much as I bobbashieled with Sheriff Dalrymple, not to remember him!"

The tenant stared in amazement.

"Why, he's not my pappy, he was my gran'paw. My pappy was yore orderly in the Confederate army at Corinth. He used to tote letters and dispatches to yore tent. He fit with you at Shiloh!"

Miltiades was genuinely moved.

"Well, I be damned! That boy, your father!"

"Yes, sir, he's my pap. I tell my boys about it. I tell 'em to hand it down to their boys when they grow up, that their

grandpappy was orderly to Colonel Milt Vaiden an' fit by
his side at Shiloh."

The Colonel smoked his cheroot, compressing his lips
around the tobacco and staring out over the lean and jaded
fields, hard ridden for cotton, decade after decade and
spurred by many a plow.

In Dalrymple's company he felt himself to be of some
immemorial age. The tenant farmers were like weeds which
sprang up on the thin soil and died down in swift generations.

It was only after several minutes that his mind came back
to the fattening of these lank acres around the shack. He
began a tentative suggestion of fertilization and rotation of
crops. Dalrymple shook his head.

"What's the use, Colonel? Year before last, I made eight
bale o' cotton. Last year I made four. Well, I come out jest
the same both year . . . broke even, that's all." Dalrymple
scratched his stubbly chin, a little puzzled.

A wave of wrath passed through Miltiades that J. Handback should cheat the son of an old comrade in the war
as he did an ordinary negro.

"It seems to me," said the Colonel diplomatically, "that
you should have got more for your part when you made
eight bales."

"Seems like that to me too, but I didn't. Ol' man Han'-
back showed me the figgers. An' another thing, the ol' man
keeps puttin' in niggers wherever he can. They tell me he has
turned off Arthur Lay for next year to put in a nigger
named Loob Snipes. . . .

"And besides that, down in the Reserve a yeller gal has
set up teachin' a nigger school. Lucy Lacefiel' is her name.
Well, she's boun' to do more harm than good. It's the ruination of a nigger to go to school. They immejiately git too
edjercated to work. If there's anything that gits my dander
up, it's to see a edjercated nigger ridin' aroun', or a passel
of black nigger young 'uns packin' off to school when they
ort to be in the fiel' pickin' cotton."

"You certainly are right there," agreed the Colonel wholeheartedly.

From across the field came a faded woman, a half-grown boy, two girls, and a smaller child, all in rags.

"Colonel, stay and have dinner with us," invited Dalrymple as his family came in from cotton picking.

Miltiades aroused himself.

"No, I've got to be going. I had a snack before I left home. I'll tell Dal you asked about him when I get back to the store."

"Do, an' tell him, if he ain't too stuck up, he might come out some day and see his country jake cousin."

Here the tenant laughed at the absurdity of calling himself a country jake.

Through the following days J. Handback's treatment of Gibeon Dalrymple stuck in the Colonel's thoughts with a kind of chronic irritation. To do a white man like that! To cheat and degrade the son of a soldier who had marched by his side in the gray columns of the Confederacy!

There were a few other white tenants on the Handback plantations, and the Colonel probed them on this point. All of them had grievances. They suspected they were being systematically swindled but were unable to check up their accounts and discover the fraud. Most of them depended on their memories. A few brought up some lead-penciled figures in a yellowed sweat-soaked memorandum book. When they tried to check this version with the orderly array of the store ledger, they were immediately lost in a maze of figures. They always wound up by accepting Handback's statement, grumbling that something was wrong, and putting their own books unhappily back in their pockets.

The white tenants, too, had a feeling that back of their plight stood the negroes. The whites were likely to lose their cabins and land at any time, and a negro family be installed in their stead. When this exchange was once made, the cabin

became permanently a negro dwelling, because no white
family would live in it after negroes had occupied it.

One of these white tenants was named Cady. He lived on
the Lacefield place and was particularly vicious toward a
negro family who lived a half mile farther down the Reserve
road. He complained that the daughter of this negro family
taught a negro school and wore shoes and stockings on her
yaller legs and ribbons in her hair, "better'n I can dress my
own gal!" declared Cady angrily.

"Dalrymple was telling me about her," sympathized the
Colonel with answering distaste. "Her name's Lucy Lacefield."

"That's hit," nodded Cady, "she puts on like she was
white, an' totes a han'kerchief."

The Colonel shook his head.

"Niggers are getting out of their places," he agreed.

"Somebody's goin' to haff to take 'em down," opined
Cady.

The tenant sat in his cabin cutting lumps from a stick
which was wrapped in a greasy red paper.

"What's that you're haggling at?" inquired the Colonel
after a space.

"Dinnymite," grunted Cady, putting his whole weight
on his knife.

The Colonel backed away.

"What the devil are you hacking at it like that for?"

Cady began to laugh.

"Going to the creek and dinnymite me a mess o' fish."
Then, by way of tomfoolery, he tossed one of the small pieces
among the live coals in his fireplace.

Miltiades scuttled into the yard, and Cady followed him,
doubled up with laughter.

"Colonel, don't you know if you set far to dinnymite it
won't do nothin' but burn?"

"I know I'm not so cold I have to warm over a dynamite
fire," said Miltiades.

This jest completely overcame Cady. He pulled off his

flop hat and beat the ground with it while he wheezed with laughter.

"I God, beatenes' man I ever heard talk. . . . They ain't but jest one Colonel!"

Wiping his eyes, he proceeded to a wagon loaded with cotton in front of his cabin.

"My ol' womern an' gal picked that," nodded Cady, "an' they's more in the fiel', an' they're still a-pickin' all day an' ever'day."

His voice had the pride of ownership in it.

"Let's get this to gin," suggested Miltiades, "and be ready for the rest when they get it out."

"Suits me from the groun' up!" cried Cady, and he set out to hitch his mules to the wagon.

Miltiades did nothing but stand by and watch, but this cheered Cady to work with great energy. If the tenant had been left to himself for a moment he would have gone hunting or fishing. He was always working energetically at something, but seldom at anything that was necessary to be done.

In a little while the Colonel and his tenant were in the wagon headed for the gin. As they jounced along in the soft cotton they saw other wagons moving in the same direction.

It was almost a wonder where all the cotton came from. The acres about them were so thin and impoverished by decades of cotton planting. Still, the combined harvest of a whole section yielded a rich return.

The thing that gyved the Colonel was the use to which all this yield would be put. J. Handback would take it all, use a negligible fraction on his family and quadroon mistress, and with the rest he would buy more gins, more plantations, increase the stock in his store, and none of it would ever come to anything more than that. The ironic part of it was that he, Miltiades Vaiden, was one of the units in Handback's pointless accumulation.

At a turn of the road they saw the gin with rapid puffs of steam rising above its roof. Lines of wagons stood in the gin yard awaiting their turn at unloading. From a platform at the height of the second floor, negroes slewed the bales onto an inclined plane, and rolled them down into the gin yard below. A little distance out in the yard, other negroes with a tripod and scales weighed the bales and daubed their weights on their ends with black paint. The seed of the cotton was carted out of the gin yard and left to decay in a great pile.

As the Colonel got out of the wagon and went about the building he had an odd feeling that the bales which rolled down in the yard were the self-same cotton which he and his sister Cassandra had picked and delivered to the Handback store twenty years before.

He and his family had grown five bales of cotton . . . the Colonel continued thinking about it. At that time cotton was worth a dollar a pound. Every bale he had lost to Handback was worth five of these modern bales. It was as if he had delivered to the merchant twenty-five present-day bales.

From the gin loft Miltiades looked down in the yard and began counting twenty-five bales. They made a big pile of cotton. On the end of each bale were its weight and the initials, "J. H."

An outbreak of oaths and shouts in the yard brushed away the Colonel's thoughts. He ran out on the platform and saw the small furious figure of Cady striking a big clay-colored negro. The big man pushed him off, and Cady was frantic with anger. He spewed out vile names and leaped ineffectively at his antagonist. The negro grumbled out:

"Bettah leave me uhlone, white man! Bettah git on away now."

Miltiades hurried down the incline.

"Here, Cady, what's the matter? Nigger, what have you done to him?"

"Nothin', Col'l Milt."

As the yellow man glanced around, Cady snatched up a boom pole and brought it down with a crash on the negro's head. The yellow man staggered, then jumped forward, wrenched the pole from Cady, and threw it on the ground.

"Look heah," cried the negro, "if'n some o' you white men don' stop dis man . . ."

Cady went crazy with anger. He reached in his pocket and came out with a big half-breed bowie knife whose blade flipped open with a spring.

At this Miltiades leaped in behind the little Berserker and caught him by both arms. Cady whirled on the Colonel and struck with his knife. Miltiades felt a sting in his arm.

"Mus' I grab him?" yelled the clay-colored man.

"No . . . you white boys run here!"

The onlookers, whom the Colonel called, suddenly came to life, rushed in, and fastened Cady's knife arm. The little man frothed and struggled and kicked; his rage was astonishing.

"Cady, what in the hell did he do to you?" cried the Colonel, shaking the small man.

"Cut his waggin in ahead o' mine! Damn his yeller hide!"

"Did you cut in ahead of Cady?" asked Miltiades, feeling his wounded arm.

"Col'l, I been heah thutty minutes 'fo' Mistuh Cady driv up," defended the yellow man.

"Luke was here first," corroborated two or three other teamsters.

"Cady, what are you making trouble like this for?" demanded Miltiades.

"He wasn't in line!" cried the little man.

"How in the hell could he have got your place if he wasn't in line?"

"He's jest a damn stuck-up nigger!" cried Cady.

"You niggers and white men let each other alone," ordered the Colonel. "This gin'll handle all your cotton without you fighting about places."

"No nigger can drive up an' take my place," repeated Cady.

"Hush, hush, that's all right. The wagon that gets in first, gets ginned first."

The Colonel was annoyed at getting his arm cut and his sleeve stained. He made a poultice of lubricating oil and lint and bound that to his arm. That would make it fester, and the Colonel believed festering was the first step toward a cure. Some of the negroes recommended fresh cow dung for the purpose, but the engineer said the oil was just as good.

When the dressing was over, the Colonel discovered a plan of action had precipitated itself in his head. He gave the teamsters their orders as he drew his shirt over his padded arm.

"I want you boys to haul some of this cotton to the railroad yard in Florence, and I want some of it laid down at Connors' Landing. I'm going to ship it by boat," he directed. Then he added, "River rates are cheaper than railroad rates."

"Yes, suh," agreed a negro, "I bet it 'ud take a fo'chune to move dat cotton eidah by train aw boat."

One of the men asked in a matter-of-fact way how many bales went to Florence and how many to Connors' Landing.

The Colonel hesitated with an odd feeling.

"Lemme see, I believe I'll have . . . twenty-five bales hauled to Connors'," he directed.

As Miltiades drove home that evening he went over in his mind all sorts of explanations to an imaginary J. Handback why he had dispatched twenty-five bales of cotton to Connors' Landing.

He tried out in his soliloquy a casual reference:

"I had twenty-five bales hauled to Connors' Landing to-day. . . ."

After a space he tested a fuller explanation:

"I sent twenty-five bales to Connors' Landing today; freight rates are so much cheaper by boat than by train."

As Miltiades thought these words, the merchant's answer sounded from nowhere in his ears:

"How came you to take it on yourself to say how my cotton should be shipped?"

This disconcerted Miltiades.

"Well . . . the gin yard was getting full. . . ." After a moment he revamped this reply for another: "I knew it would be money in your pocket. If you don't want it there, we can bring it back."

The dialogue in the Colonel's mind lapsed into a mental silence, and a sort of gloom fell over the thinker. He wondered what Handback actually would say.

When Miltiades drove up Market Street and turned the corner for the store, nobody was in the building except Love and Stebbins. Both the Handbacks were at supper. The Colonel was oddly worried. He told Stebbins he did not know whether to drive the buggy out to his own home for the night or leave it there at the store and walk home. It seemed to Miltiades this was the cause of his worry—what to do with the buggy.

"What's the matter with your arm?" asked Love.

"I got it hurt at the gin—nothing of any consequence. . . I believe I will drive the buggy."

"Sure, take it on!"

Miltiades went to the bookkeeper's pen, fiddled about a minute or two with paper and pen, then said:

"I'll make out the bales and weights after supper."

"Sure, no rush," agreed Love.

When Miltiades went out the door, Stebbins said to Love:

"Dal, that's the honestest old man that ever drew a breath."

"He lost his place here in the store on account of it," said Love meditatively.

"Yes, but he's drawin' more money now than he was ther," pointed out Stebbins.

The two youths were moved at the manner in which Providence recompensed righteousness.

That evening, as Miltiades ate supper, a curiosity crossed his mind as to what Ponny would think about the matter if she knew of it.

The fat woman herself asked him:

"See Mr. Bradley today?"

"Yes, I saw him."

"Did you mention a house?"

"Yes, I mentioned it." Miltiades began smiling.

"What's funny about that?"

"Nothing. . . . Bradley gave me a cheroot . . . just stuck it in my pocket."

"Well, are you going to get another house?"

"I . . . don't know. . . ." Miltiades forgot to eat and sat holding his cup, looking at Ponny.

"What's the matter with you, Mr. Milt?" The fat woman's curiosity was vaguely tipped with apprehension.

"Why, nothing . . . not a thing in the world. . . . I had the hands haul twenty-five bales of cotton to Connors' Landing today."

"Well . . . what of that?"

"I'm going to ship 'em by boat instead of rail. I'll save some freight that way."

"Now, think of that. I declare old Handback ought to pay you more, Mr. Milt. Now, maybe you saved him a hundred dollars in just one day!" She exhaled a long breath which might have been a sigh except it was too loud.

"Well, maybe he will some day. . . . I've got to feed Handback's mare. I'm keeping her for the night. I've got to get some corn somewhere."

"Borrow it from the Klems. Goodness knows they've got watter enough out of our well."

Miltiades went over to the Klems' and got the corn. Mr. Klem refused any pay, and Miltiades gave a dime to the smallest Klem, which the mother vainly tried to make the dirty little girl return.

The Colonel went home with his corn and in a queer ebullience of spirits. He fed the mare and went back into the house.

Ponny was getting into bed. The springs creaked under her weight. Miltiades undressed, drew on his nightshirt, put

out the light, and got in beside his wife. In the darkness such
causeless excitement filled the man that the pressure of
Ponny's thick soft arm against his own moved the Colonel.
He caressed her shoulder and heavy bosom. A little tremor
went through the Colonel's nerves. His odd stimulation gave
him a feeling as if it were his wedding night.

Ponny moved herself slowly in bed and asked with drowsy
curiosity:

"Mr. Milt . . . what in the world did happen to you today?"

The actual breaking of the news to J. Handback that his
cotton had been hauled to Connors' Landing fell out quite
otherwise than Miltiades had anticipated. The next morning, as he called off the names of the tenants and the weights
of their cotton to the merchant, the Colonel observed that
Handback was deducting a certain amount from the weight
of each bale. After some observation the overseer asked why
he was doing it. Handback said the negroes were accustomed
to having fifteen percent deducted for "tare." When Alex
Cady's weights were called, Handback began the usual calculation.

"Look here," interrupted Miltiades, "you're not figuring
your tare off of Cady's crop, are you?"

Handback said he was.

"But he's white," objected the Colonel.

"But I could have a nigger in his place if I wanted one,"
protested the tradesman.

"But the point is you haven't got a nigger in his place.
You've got a white man."

"I don't see why you should hold out for Cady," argued
Handback. "He gave you some trouble at the gin yesterday. Besides that, if I failed to charge tare against Cady
he'd go blowin' about it among the niggers, and they'd get
stirred up. No, I've got to treat 'em all equal."

There was enough truth in this argument to pass muster,
and Miltiades thought to himself that this implication of

equality was bound up in any hiring of negroes whatever. "They ought to be owned," he thought gloomily, "if this is going to be a white man's country." Then he struck off on another tack:

"Look here, you can afford to ease up on Alex Cady and Gibeon Dalrymple, I've already saved you more money than the tare on their cotton will come to."

"How's that?" inquired the merchant, losing his antagonistic tone.

"Why, the freight on your cotton. I delivered twenty-five bales at Connors' Landing to go by boat. That'll save a dollar and a half on the bale."

The merchant came to a pause.

"Did you do that?"

"Yes," said Miltiades, a trifle defensively, "it was the only sensible thing to do."

"I know it! I know it!" agreed Handback. "I've had it in mind to do that very thing every fall, but one reason or another I never did do it. Last fall I was all fixed, but the L. and N. freight agent come around and talked me out of it. Man ought never to listen to a plague-taked freight agent!"

"I suppose not," agreed the Colonel, in relief.

"Why, the devil, if they have to talk you into using their blame' line, there must be some drawback to it or you'd use it anyway. How many bales did you say you sent down?"

"Twenty-five."

"How come you to start with just twenty-five?"

"Well . . . I had to start with some number."

"I mean, whyn't you send more?"

"I thought maybe you needed some quick cotton on the market. I didn't know how your finances were."

"M—m, I do need some quick cotton, and my finances are dern low," admitted the merchant, frowning; "that's one of the things that always stopped me—that and the freight agent." He picked up a pencil and began figuring on the back of an old envelope. "Put five hundred more bales down there," he directed finally.

"Well . . . all right," agreed the Colonel.

"And, Colonel," began the merchant with appreciative eyes.

"Yes?"

"Nothing," said Handback.

Miltiades divined that his employer had had an impulse to raise his salary but had controlled himself in time.

This sudden determination of the merchant to bank five hundred bales of cotton at Connors' Landing had a queerly depressing effect upon Miltiades. He set out for his round of the plantations with a feeling that some ill thing had befallen him. Exactly why, he could not say. Still, somewhere in the Colonel's heart he had had a feeling that the twenty-five bales at Connors' Landing in some vague way belonged to him, and that the new cotton which presently would be hauled and cover up the twenty-five bales would lose him some sort of intangible property rights in them. It was, of course, a purely nonsensical fancy, but still, it was enough to depress the Colonel for several days.

CHAPTER ELEVEN

T HOSE original twenty-five bales of cotton, after they had
become lost among the five hundred J. Handback had piled
down at Connors' Landing, became a kind of obsession with
Colonel Vaiden. With no intention of doing so, he was continually thinking of ways to repossess this cotton, although,
as a matter of fact, he never had possessed it.

With a wagon and team he might haul the twenty-five
bales to the old Vaiden place and store them in the shed of
the forge which his father had built long before the war.

Sometimes he calculated the twenty-five bales would bring
in twenty-five hundred dollars. That amount in cash ought
to mean a seven-thousand-dollar credit with some wholesale
house. With this he could start a small mercantile business.

Then he began thinking over the negroes he might possibly get to haul the cotton for him. He had helped Luke
Anders in his fight with Cady, but Anders was a yellow
negro and not without brains and penetration. Then there
was Loob Snipes, who was dull enough but clumsy. . . . A
notion popped into the Colonel's head to use Gracie's boy.
The Colonel held a sort of authority over Gracie and her
son—an authority undefined on the one hand and un-
acknowledged on the other: it was a vague relation that persisted between ex-master and ex-slave. There was something
between them. They were not just a white man and two
negroes.

One afternoon, in the shortening autumn day, Mr. Klem
called out in neighborly fashion as Miltiades passed the
Klem home:

"I believe we're goin' to have a break in our dry spell, Colonel," and he quoted the adage, "Evening gray and morning red bring down rain upon his head."

Miltiades considered the sky.

"We may get some out of the south."

Klem was delicately flattered to be talking to a clerk and an overseer.

"Hope it doesn't raise the river. I waded Mr. Boggus' cattle over to the island to graze yestiddy. I added two yearlings of my own for luck."

"Is it as low as that?"

"Why, there hasn't been a steamboat up for weeks. . . . Er—I understand there's going to be something doing up your way, soon, Colonel."

This observation startled Miltiades. He thought for an instant Klem meant something about cotton.

"What sort of doings, Mr. Klem?" he asked soberly.

"My wife says your troubles are going to be little ones purty soon." He gave a respectful laugh.

"Oh . . . well, I don't know," said the Colonel, not much relishing the subject with Klem.

Miltiades walked on to his own home with his thoughts divided by the prospects of autumnal rains and the possibility that Ponny was pregnant. Both these topics bore somewhat on the matter of cotton. When the river rose Handback would ship his cotton on the first steamboat that came up over the shoals. If his wife should have a child it would make the repossession of his cotton all the more imperative.

However, Miltiades did not really believe in his wife's pregnancy. He had been married to her for twenty years, and if she ever intended to have a child . . . His thoughts moved on in vague negation.

On this point, however, Ponny herself was in quite a different mind. When Miltiades reached home she told him she had rested very well that day. The Colonel said he was glad to hear it and began thinking again of the rain and the cotton.

"I've already et," said Ponny. "I laid your supper on the table."

Miltiades went into the kitchen, thinking it was Ponny's imagination that caused her to shift her meals to all hours. As he ate he called out:

"Ponny, are you going to want any hot water or anything tonight?"

The fat woman enjoyed fancying herself pregnant. She sat in her chair, listless and voluptuous with a feeling of being coddled. She always had been too huge to be coddled physically, but now, under the stress of a possible baby, Miltiades coddled her with unusual attentions.

"I . . . don't know," she called back flabbily. "I may want something to eat."

"What do you suppose it will be?" inquired the Colonel a little anxiously.

"Well . . . I don't know . . ." The fat woman sat thinking. "A hot baked sweet potaty with butter on it, Mr. Milt."

"Why, Ponny, I can't bake you a potato."

"You can heat one up . . . don't eat that fat one in the dish."

"No, I won't."

"And a glass of hot milk with the white of an egg beat up in it."

Miltiades finished his supper of cold vegetables and cold pork, most of which had come from the old Vaiden homestead. Then he began laying a fire in the kitchen stove to heat up the potato if it were required. As he worked his thoughts went back to the cotton. His shrift there, he felt, was growing brief. If it should set in raining and raise the river and a steamboat should come along . . .

As he placed the paper and kindling in the stove a faint indefinite murmur set up through the house. He paused in his fire building and listened. From the front room Ponny called:

"Mr. Milt, there's somebody at the door."

"That's the rain, Ponny," called back the husband.

Ponny insisted:

"No, Mr. Milt, that's somebody knocking. Go see who it is."

"It's the rain," repeated the Colonel, and he thought, "What if the river rises and Handback gets away with his stolen cotton again!"

Nevertheless, he started for the door. As he passed through the living room Ponny made a gesture for him to keep the visitor out if he were a man, as she was in no condition to be seen by a man.

A touch of amusement went through the husband.

"You look exactly like you've always looked," he whispered.

Ponny was piqued.

"Luly Klem says I don't."

"Oh, I'll keep him out," whispered Miltiades, making a patting gesture with his hand. He walked on to the front door.

It was dark outside, and it really was raining. In the doorway he saw a man. A moment later he recognized his brother Augustus.

Since it was Augustus, Miltiades took the visitor into the sitting room. As Augustus entered he inquired after Ponny, knowing her dubious condition.

"I feel sorter peaky," said the fat woman, turning her large face from the fire. "I'm hungry of nights. I just had Mr. Milt to fix the stove to heat me up a sweet potaty tonight. . . . How's Rose?"

She enjoyed enumerating what she considered to be symptoms of her condition. She enjoyed the faint malaise that caused her mountain of flesh to feel like butter about to melt and run. She enjoyed talking in a weak voice.

Augustus sat down before the fireplace in which a bright fire was burning to keep the dampness away from Ponny. The elder brother was wondering what could have brought Augustus to his home. He said in the voice of one making conversation that he thought the fall rains had set in.

"That's not a point of faith," said Augustus soberly, "it's actually doing it outside." The younger brother then began talking to Ponny about some late pears Rose was preserving.

Miltiades continued intermittently to ponder what Augustus could have come for and to listen to the increasing murmur of the rain. He wished his brother would go away so he could plan undisturbed about his cotton. Not that his plans would amount to anything, but at least he wanted to think about it.

A faint mirth passed through Miltiades at the consternation that would seize Augustus if his brother knew what was going on in his head.

Here he was interrupted by Augustus, beginning to explain his visit:

"I'm thinking about getting a job, Brother Milt. Rose throws cold water on the idyah, of course."

Both Miltiades and Ponny stared at their visitor.

"Getting a job!"

"Yes. How did you land your place? Did you just walk up and ask for it?"

Miltiades suspected that Augustus had found out how he really did get his place and had come to make sport of it. He replied soberly:

"Certainly, I met Handback that Sunday, and he said he needed a clerk."

Augustus sat gazing into the fire and shaking his head at this riddle.

"Anyway, Brother Milt, I thought I'd come and see what you thought about it. I thought maybe you might know of an opening." He arose to go.

"I'll inquire around."

Miltiades got up at once in order not to delay his brother's departure. The two men walked out into the dark hallway. The wind, pushing at the front door, made it creak intermittently. Miltiades opened it, and a chill rain blew inside.

"Brother Milt," said Augustus in a different tone, now that they were out of Ponny's hearing, "I came over here to advise with you about Jerry."

Miltiades suddenly perceived that the job had been mentioned to throw Ponny off the scent.

"What about Jerry?" asked the older brother, with a sudden fear that his nephew had stolen something.

"Well," began Augustus uncomfortably, "the little nincompoop has got himself into a lot of trouble at school."

The term "nincompoop" told Miltiades that Jerry had not done anything very serious.

"What's he been up to at school?" he inquired.

"Well . . . he refuses to attend chapel."

"Why?" ejaculated Miltiades, quite at sea.

"Well . . ." Augustus was really embarrassed over how to put it, "the little idiot says he doesn't believe in God."

Both men stood silent in the dark hallway with the mist blowing in on them. To both this was the oddest, the most uncalled for and pointless difficulty a boy could get into.

"I think," offered Augustus tentatively, "he does it to show out."

"Says there's not any God . . . what's that got to do with going to chapel?"

"Well, there is generally supposed to be some connection between religious services and the deity. At any rate, that's Jerry's point as I understand it. He refuses to go on with one without the other."

"Well, this isn't much of a time for a joke, Augustus," said the older brother, "if this is serious."

"It's serious enough all right," replied Augustus soberly. "Jerry is on the edge of getting himself kicked out of college."

The Colonel promised Augustus to do what he could in the matter at some future date, and the younger brother went back home through the rain alone. When Miltiades returned to the living room, Ponny immediately wormed out of him what he and Augustus had been talking about, and she grew excited. She thought Miltiades ought to go at once. The Colonel wanted to know what was the hurry.

"Why, suppose Jerry was to die tonight, not believing in God," cried Ponny, "his soul would be lost!"

"That may be," agreed the Colonel, "but Augustus was worrying about how to keep him in school. He has not been expelled, but he has been suspended."

"That's terrible!" cried Ponny.

"They're making a bugbear out of it," frowned the Colonel beginning to get ready for bed.

"Well, now, looky here, Mr. Milt," said Ponny seriously, "if Rose let Augustus come out on a night like this, I think you ort to go on now and do whatever you can about Jerry. Good gracious, Rose must be terrible worried!"

"What can I do tonight?" asked the Colonel uncomfortably.

"I don't know. You can go see. Rose sent Augustus. Now, please go on, Mr. Milt."

"Well, of all silly things!" cried Miltiades, "wanting me to go out in the rain because my nephew is a fool!"

But Ponny kept on heavily at her husband, and after a while he got himself ready to go out.

Now, as a matter of fact, Ponny's deduction that Rose had sent Augustus out into the rain was incorrect. The rain had come up several minutes after Augustus had left the boarding house for his brother's home. He had set forth, however, protesting:

"Rose, I don't believe I'd better go now, I'm afraid I'll get rained on."

"Augustus," Rose had replied, almost beside herself with anxiety, "don't you know it won't rain with you going on such a mission as you're on?"

This sentence referred to the religious nature of Augustus' errand. His trip was meant to restore Jerry to the orthodox faith, and Rose did not believe God would let it rain on a man engaged in such a pious work.

"I believe it's going to rain," repeated Augustus skeptically.

And sure enough, he hadn't gone two blocks before it began to rain. In a way Augustus was glad of it. It would teach Rose to take better care of him in the future. As for Jerry, he was a fool, and it made no particular difference whether a boy like that went to school or not. Getting himself suspended for not going to chapel!

Drops began to trickle down his face, and his clothes felt damp. He supposed he was in for a serious cold.

While this disaster of getting wet overtook her husband, Mrs. Rose was working in the kitchen of the boarding house. When she heard the rain on the roof and at the windows she could hardly believe her ears. She stopped work and gasped at her coffee-colored cook:

"Tony, is Gussie back yet?"

"Don' guess he is, Miss Rose. He lef' jess a while ago."

Mrs. Rose was so upset she could not go on with the dishes.

"Tony," she said, "you'll have to finish the things."

"Law, yes'm, Ah'll finish 'em," agreed Tony, seeing her mistress so disturbed.

The white woman wiped her hands on a dish towel and took off her apron. She hesitated, taut with the need of action. Then she walked rapidly out of the kitchen to the staircase in the front hallway. She climbed the steps and saw a light shining under a door. She knocked peremptorily. Sandusky's hill twang called out, "Come in."

"Is Jerry in there, Mr. Sandusky?"

"Yes, he's in here."

Rose opened the door and stepped inside.

"Now, Jerry," she said tensely, "you see what you've done with—with your paganism!"

Jerry sat on the bed, and Sandusky was at a table piled with books.

"Why? What have I done?" ejaculated Jerry defensively.

"You caused your uncle Gussie to be out in this cold driving rain!"

"Is he out in the rain?" cried Jerry, amazed.

"Yes, and you did it!" accused Mrs. Rose.

"How did I do it?" asked the boy, conscience struck.

"He went up to Cherry Street to get Miltiades to come here and talk to you about what you claim not to believe in!"

"Well . . . I didn't send him!"

"Your unbelief did!"

Jerry simply sat and looked at his aunt, unable to debate so obvious a truth.

"If . . . your . . . uncle . . . Augustus . . . takes pneumonia . . . and dies," intoned Mrs. Rose in solemn wrath, "then you'll realize . . . there is . . . a God, Jerry Catlin!"

Jerry looked at his aunt's strained face, but the realist in him bobbed up even under such a tragic hypothesis.

"How would that make me know there was a God, Aunt Rose?"

The woman was amazed at such perversity.

"Why, Jerry," she quavered, "don't you know God strikes down those who are nearest and dearest to touch an unbelieving heart?" Mrs. Rose began weeping in silence, the tears trickling down her cheeks in the lamplight.

"Y-yes," wavered Jerry, "I'd heard that . . . but look here, Aunt Rose, if—if there ain't no God, d'reckon he'll keep his health?"

The woman put up a hand on the door facing. For anyone to reason, unemotionally, about God made her feel sick. Then, to Jerry's dismay, she lifted her palm in the rain-haunted room as if she were giving him her blessing and said in a shaken tone:

"God have mercy on Jerry Catlin, my poor little pinhead of a nephew, questioning You!"

She went weeping out of the door into the dark upper hallway, and a few moments later Jerry heard her going down the stairs.

Young Jerry Catlin and oldish Mr. Sandusky sat in silence for several moments after Mrs. Rose left the room. The monody of the rain swelled and diminished and filled the upper story of the boarding house with its melancholy note.

Jerry was conscience struck that his uncle Augustus was out in this rain on his account. He went to the window, cupped his hands against the pane, and tried to peer out.

"I bet this does make Uncle Augustus sick," he said in the lowest spirits.

"Why?" asked Sandusky from the book-piled table.

"Getting wet," ejaculated Jerry in surprise.

"He'll get dry again," opined the boarder.

Jerry looked to see if this were some sort of monstrous jest . . . that if his uncle Augustus got wet he would simply dry off like an ordinary person. The boarder was perusing a sheet of legal cap.

"Why do you let those teachers at college suspend you simply because you don't want to go to chapel?"

"Why do I let 'em?"

"Yes, why do you?"

"Because I can't he'p myself, of course."

"Why, you certainly could. They can't suspend you on account of any religious conviction you've got."

"They have done it."

"Not legally. The Constitution forbids the mixing of civil and religious matters. The way you'd go about getting your rights back is to file a bill in chancery enjoining the trustees of the college from suspending you."

"The trustees didn't do it, the faculty did it."

"The faculty operates through the trustees. Here, look here—" he held up the paper in his hand—"I've been writing a brief of your case. Governor O'Shawn looked it over this morning and corrected it. It tickled him. He said he believed it would hold water."

As Jerry pondered this information, there gathered in the boy's mind the gloomy grandeur of forcing himself upon the faculty by cold process of law. He could imagine how

the girls would look at him, a strong, somber man wringing
an education from a cowed but hostile faculty.

"I haven't got any money to start a lawsuit with," he
said aloud to Sandusky.

"Don't have to have any, you could plead *in forma
pauperis,*" planned the law student promptly.

"But I couldn't pay the lawyer, either."

"That wouldn't be necessary. I'd take your case as your
amicus optimus."

"Look here," said Jerry suspiciously, "ain't that Latin?"

"Yep."

"Thought you had a hard time with Latin in college;
now here you are talking it."

"Well, the Latin I read at college I can't remember, but
the Latin I read in the Governor's law books I can't forget.
. . . I'm funny that way."

This peculiarity of Sandusky's did not interest Jerry.
He began thinking again about enjoining the trustees. It
held out austere blandishments. Then it occurred to Jerry
that the same reason that had kept him from going to
chapel would also prevent him from using any force to put
himself back in school. Only a few days before he had
adopted as the rule of his life a policy of passiveness, of
nonresistance. He did this because his occult books had told
him that love was more powerful than force, and humility
overcame pride. Now, if he were to begin a lawsuit, that
would be a contradiction of the principle which was to rule
his life.

"No, Sandusky," he said slowly, "I can't go to law about
this matter."

"Why?" ejaculated Sandusky annoyed.

Jerry shook his head with a smile which he believed to
be faint and sad.

"I'm afraid I couldn't explain it to you, Sandusky, I'm
afraid you wouldn't understand."

Sandusky looked at the hobbledehoy through the lamplight.

"It'll be a hard frost in August when you can explain anything I can't understand."

Jerry continued looking at Sandusky, thinking contemptuously:

"You dried-up self-centered hill billy, you are going to be a failure compared to the charity and humility that are going to rule my life." But he said nothing, because the sort of man he was going to be would not mention the sort of thing he was thinking.

As a matter of fact, there was no one in the boarding house Jerry really could talk to. None of them understood him; none of them could understand what he had set his heart upon.

Following his resolution, Jerry meant to give up all thought of worldly goods, of honor, of place, of the desire for women, everything. According to the book he had read in the library, he could, by a series of austere exercises, develop strange powers within himself. And, if he faithfully followed the path, one day a guru, a holy man, would come to him and initiate him into the higher mysteries.

When that happened, he could lift himself up in the air by sheer power of his will. He could make a sack of gold come to him. Of if a little child were sick he could touch it, and it would become well and laughing again. . . . All this would happen when he became an initiate.

A desire seized Jerry for some person who could comprehend and sympathize with his aim. Sandusky would not do. Sandusky was worse than nobody at all.

The youth got out of bed with a long sigh.

"I think I'll take a walk," he said.

"In the rain?"

"If you think it won't hurt you, it won't," said Jerry.

The boy walked out of the room and tiptoed downstairs. The door of the sitting room was ajar, and he saw his aunt Rose soaking the feet of his uncle Augustus in hot water and handing him a hot toddy. She was thwarting, as best

she could, the Lord's probable intention of piercing Jerry
Catlin's skeptical heart with the death of his uncle.

Jerry walked out the door to the front gate. The rain
almost had stopped. A chill mist blew in his face, and he
heard drops falling from the trees. Across the sky moved
torn wracks of cloud vaguely visible in the night. Through
a rift he saw for a moment or two a vaporous new moon. The
thin crescent was tipped far over. It was a wet moon.

"No wonder it rained," thought Jerry.

He let himself out the gate and moved down Market Street
in the mist. Presently he crossed over to Pine and walked
among the dripping trees and the thin fragrance of
chrysanthemums, and so on down to the undefined mass of
the Crowninshield home.

Some window was visible as a dim quadrangle of light.
Jerry stood looking at it, thinking perhaps Sydna might be
reading in the room. He wanted to explain himself to Sydna.
He wanted to tell her that he had made a vow of utter truthfulness and abstinence. A feeling of dramatic loneliness filled
him as he opened the gate and walked up the wet, curving
walk.

He reached the portico, and knowing the condition of the
lion's foot, tapped on the door. The hall was dark. The light
he had seen from the walk was invisible from the door. A
feeling of dismay went through the boy. He was afraid that
Sydna had quit reading, put out her light, and gone to bed.

He knocked again, more loudly; then, after a pause,
moved across the porch to where he could see the window.
It was still illuminated. When he returned to the door a
voice said:

"Is that you, Jerry?"

"Yes, this is me."

"Has it stopped raining?"

"It's still drizzling a little."

Sydna hesitated and then said:

"Lucius Handback is in here. . . . Won't you join us?"

Jerry felt a sinking sensation, as if he suddenly had been betrayed.

"Oh, no, I—I've got to get back home. I—just came over for a book."

Sydna herself became concerned for the youth's embarrassment.

"What sort of book? . . . Come on, let's look."

"No, I don't reckon you've got it. . . . I'll have to go." He began backing away in the darkness.

Sydna took a step after him.

"Wait a minute, Jerry, I wanted to see you. What happened over at college? What did you get into?"

"Why, nothing, they just . . ."

"Have they expelled you?" asked Sydna, touching his hand and trying to see his face.

"No . . . just suspended me."

"Because you wouldn't say your prayers?"

"No, because I wouldn't go to chapel. . . . Who said I wouldn't say my prayers?"

"Pammy Lee."

"Well, plague take that little nigger!"

"Jerry, why won't you go to chapel?"

Jerry became more embarrassed.

"Why . . . Sydna . . . I—I made a pledge to—to be absolutely truthful."

"What's that got to do with chapel?"

"Well, I don't believe in it, and I can't go through the motions."

Sydna veered away from this sore spot.

"Jerry, whom did you make your promise to?" she asked gently.

The youth became embarrassed anew.

"Nun-nobody . . . Well, myself . . . I mean my—my soul."

"Your . . . what?"

"I—I've been reading about souls in a book. . . . I've changed my mind about 'em. The book says that it's been through all sorts of things . . . bugs and beasts and birds, and finally it'll get pooled with a lot of other souls, and ever'thing'll come to a stop." He was backing off the porch.

Sydna was distraught.

"But, Jerry, the faculty can't suspend you for that! . . . Wait, stop, don't go. . . . For believing in souls and wanting to tell the truth."

"Well, you see they're not strong for either—I—I mean in any special way."

"Jerry, do you really have to go?"

"Oh, yes, I promised my aunt Rose I'd be right back."

The girl stood on the portico and watched him melt into the night. She felt sick about him. She could have shaken the faculty of the Florence college for not understanding and appreciating Jerry. The idea of suspending such a— such a sweet boy!

She turned slowly back to the parlor and to Lucius Handback, whom she had deserted.

Young Jerry Catlin walked back to his aunt's boarding house under a peculiar depression. He had not got to talk to Sydna about his occultism, how love and desire had been exorcised from his life, how women meant nothing to him, and he was practising concentration on the sacred word "Om" until he should become one with the universal. It was raining dismally again, and Jerry screwed up his shoulders against the chill downfall. He tried to remove his mind from this discomfort, and also from the sharper and more penetrating pain that Sydna Crowninshield was sitting in her parlor with Lucius Handback. He repeated the magic syllable a number of times, and between repetitions he thought dolefully, "Well—what difference does it make if he is there? . . . Women are nothing to me . . . any more. . . ."

A lantern approaching Jerry on Market Street caught the adolescent's attention. Its beams discovered a slanting maze of rain falling out of blackness, through the light and into blackness again. Then he noticed the fantastic lights and shadows playing on the lantern carrier's legs. A fancy came through Jerry's head that the person with the lantern might be a holy man come to tell him that he had been adjudged worthy of initiation into the mystic and supernatural order of adepts. . . .

As the man was about to pass he lifted his lantern and said:

"Hello, is that you, Jerry?"

The boy's fantasy vanished, and he answered with a shiver:

"Y-yes, Uncle Milt. . . . B-bad night, isn't it?"

The uncle hesitated.

"You cold?"

"Nun-no . . . I—I'm not cold. . . ."

"I came down to see you, Jerry. Both of us are wet already. Suppose we walk on a little way and talk, if you don't mind."

"No, I—I don't mind."

He turned and went plashing along through the water on the sidewalk, waiting for his uncle to begin.

Miltiades Vaiden's own situation was even less agreeable than that of the nephew. Jerry was an inscrutable repetition of the Colonel's sister Marcia. The only difference was, where Marcia went off on a tangent, Jerry, apparently, stayed off on one.

"I hear you've been having trouble at college, Jerry," approached Miltiades carefully.

"A little," admitted the boy unencouragingly.

"Augustus told me that you—er—that is he came up to my home a moment ago to tell me. . . ." The Colonel came to a halt. Disbelief in God was such an irrational idea that he could not go on.

"I—I know what Uncle Augustus told you," shivered Jerry.

"Well, Jerry, that's a strange notion of yours. . . . I don't see how you can possibly think . . . you know, when everything around us . . . the sun, the moon, people, animals . . . and the Bible itself telling how it was all made. . . ." Miltiades grasped at his subject, trying to get an intellectual hand-hold on the smooth perfection of its sides. But it was so obviously and simply true that there was nothing more to say about it than simply to state it. He gave the matter up and turned to a more human mode of persuasion.

"Look here, Jerry," he said, "we Vaidens are an old and a naturally religious family. Your grandfather was a Hardshell Baptist. Your great-grandfather, Simeon Vaiden, who lived in South Carolina, was a shouting Methodist who got converted under John Wesley himself. I'm a Christian; people call me a Campbellite. Now, I didn't really expect you to become a Campbellite. I sort of thought the new generation would take up its own church just as we Vaidens always have done. But I didn't believe you'd quit. I can't believe any Vaiden actually would quit."

For some reason Jerry was deeply and painfully moved.

"Uncle Milt," he shivered, "you nee'n' feel so bad about me. I know the Vaidens are a fine fam'ly. S-so are the Catlins. P-Papa told me that our name used to be Coerling, or Kerling, and—and it m-meant noblemen. C-Catlin is a corruption. P-Papa told me that."

"There you are," said Miltiades, "you ought to believe in God."

"Well . . . I—I really do," shook Jerry.

"I thought you said you didn't."

"Well, I—I don't believe in their s-sort of God, exactly."

"Oh, that's all right," agreed Miltiades, "that's natural. You are a Vaiden. But couldn't you go to chapel and not cause all this disturbance about it?"

"T-to tell you the t-truth, Uncle Milt, there's n-no sincerity in the chapel exercises. They d-don't mean what they s-say. They're not exercises at all."

"You don't mean the professors and pupils are hypocrites, Jerry?"

"N-no, they're just not interested. T-they don't think

about their s-souls at all. Why l-look, they t-take only th-thirty minutes a day for chapel, and nun-nobody concentrates on anything. Th-they don't really c-care anything about it. I think it's a s-s-sacrilege myself, and I'm not going to d-do it."

Miltiades came to a long pause.

"So that's your objection to chapel? It occupies too short a time and is not sincere?"

"Y-yes, sir, th-that's as near as I can tell you."

For a moment Miltiades suspected Jerry was inventing an amazing lie to let himself out of a close place, but that was nonsense. The boy would have lied to the professors and remained in school.

The uncle did not understand his nephew. To the Colonel religion was a mass of verbal truths, a kind of indisputable emptiness which he had never thought of questioning. However, he thought he had learned enough of the situation to go to the dean of the college and have Jerry readmitted to his classes.

"What have you been doing with yourself while you've been out of school?" inquired Miltiades in the tone of one whose mission is concluded and who makes conversation.

"Oh, knocking around town, talking to people."

"Meet any interesting folks?" inquired Miltiades, stopping and turning back to the Rose Vaiden boarding house.

"I guess Cap'n D-Dargan was as interestin' as I met."

"What did he do that was interesting?"

"Well, f-for one thing, he run the *Zebulon D.* up Buffalo River after a l-load of goober peas."

"The *Zebulon D.* was his boat?"

"Yes, sir; and as he was going up, he c-come to a bridge that was t-too low for the *Zebulon D.* to p-pass under. So the C-Cap'n sent out his roustabout with dynamite and blew it up."

Miltiades checked his rapid walk.

"Blew up the bridge!"

"Y-yes, sir."

"Where is Buffalo River?"

"It's a little river that runs into the Tennessee below where I live."

"Did steamboats run up that river?"

"N-not till Cap'n Dargan went up with the *Zebulon D.* T-that's what the lawsuit was about. The sheriff and the j-justices of the peace s-said Cap'n Dargan h-had no right to blow up th-their bridge, but the C-Cap'n said they had obstructed a n-navigable stream with their b-bridge, an' he had a right to b-b-blow her up. The j-justices claimed the B-Buffalo was not navigable because s-steamboats didn't go up it, b-but the Cap'n claimed it was b-because he went up her in the *Z-Zebulon D.* And—and the supreme court d-decided in his f-favor."

Jerry began laughing and shaking with cold at the oddity of the suit.

Miltiades was smiling and thinking that his nephew was much livelier company than he had anticipated.

"When did you hear this tale?"

"This afternoon, down at the landing, on the *Zebulon D.*"

"Did the boat come up over the shoals?" inquired the uncle, more interested.

"I—guess so, I d-don't know."

"Is the boat down there now?"

"I reckon so. It's tied up for the night, I think."

"That was an interesting tale," said Miltiades; "it really was."

They were at the boarding-house gate now. Miltiades lingered a moment with the passing thought that his nephew's relations with God were reëstablished and his mission was fruitful.

"Well, good-night," he said. "I believe I'll walk back to town and look in at the store."

"G-good-night," chattered Jerry, thinking that his uncle Miltiades was the brainiest of the Vaidens. . . . Not that he was disparaging his uncle Augustus.

CHAPTER TWELVE

W HEN Colonel Miltiades Vaiden was well away from the boarding house he extinguished his lantern and moved through the darkness amid the gusty patter of the rain. He wondered if the boat at the landing were going up the river or down? If up, was it feasible to ship cotton by way of Chattanooga?

Now that he was in actual motion, endless details of his enterprise passed through his mind. To whom should he consign his cotton? Where would he cash his return draft? Then should he leave Florence or stay where he was? His future stretched before him indistinctly, like a road with many prongs, any one of which he might choose. It was as vitalizing as marching against an enemy on a battlefield.

The distant lights of Courthouse Square striped Miltiades' path with reflections and gave him pause. He turned south to Tombigbee Street to avoid the illumination, and walked behind the hotel and past the jail to the river.

The last half mile of the Colonel's path led through muddier and muddier footing. There were no sidewalks, and the road itself was cut up by freight wagons. The way grew so bad it stopped the Colonel's planning and forced him to put all his attention on how to get over the road.

Somewhat later the sibilance of the river reached his ears, and he saw the red and green lights of a steamer in the darkness. Miltiades approached the bank carefully, his feet slipping and sinking in the mud. As he descended the bank, other lights appeared, a dim illumination on the cabin deck, a faint reddening from the furnace, a lantern on the iron guard of the stern wheel, and two more lights far ahead and close to the water.

The Colonel began shouting Captain Dargan's name. A negro's voice on the boiler deck called back to know who wanted Captain Dargan. Miltiades replied, "A shipper!"

At that moment a foggy voice boomed from the cabin deck:

"Who wants to see Cap'n Dargan, and what you want to see him about?"

"Damn it," snapped Miltiades, "I'll state my business when I'm aboard!"

"Black Jack," said the foggy voice, "show him the gangplank!"

The black man produced a lantern, and Miltiades saw the faintest possible reflection in the slippery gangplank. It looked like a shimmer stretched over nothing. He risked himself upon it and groped carefully aboard.

On the cabin deck stood an abdominous man who possessed the foggy voice. He preceded the Colonel to the cabin door, which was outlined in a faint rectangle of light.

Inside the cabin four men sat playing seven up. On the corners of the table were little piles of small change and glasses of whisky. The quartet squinted their eyes against the smoke of their cigars and studied their cards with the greatest concentration.

The Colonel's fat escort said:

"Man to see you, Cap'n Dargan."

One of the players, with a long purple-veined face, twisted about in his chair.

"What you want to see me about?" he asked in a voice that discouraged business irrelevancies during the ritual of seven up.

"About shipping cotton."

Captain Dargan got up from his chair.

"Take my hand, Windy." He drank the last of his whisky and pocketed his coins. "How much cotton you got?" he asked.

Miltiades gave a swift thought as to how much cotton he did have. He glanced around the cramped boat.

"How much can you carry?"

"Hell, I guess I can carry all you got. . . . How much you got?"

"Let me see you by yourself a moment," said Miltiades.

The two men went into a little office boxed off in front of the cabin. As Miltiades entered this cubicle he had in mind to say twenty-five bales, but with a little stir in his diaphragm he really said:

"I've got five hundred bales."

The skipper looked at the wet clothes and muddied legs of his visitor.

"Where is it?" he inquired.

"Connors' Landing."

Dargan poked his head out of his little office.

"Pilot, where's Connors' Landing?"

"About sixteen miles below here, Cap," said the pilot, around his cigar.

"Five hundred bales. . . . Where's it going?" asked the Captain.

"To New Orleans. What you going to charge me to take it there?"

Dargan frowned.

"I'm not in the New Orleans trade. I work around Cairo usually. When I saw from the river reports that the Tennessee was so low nothing but small boats could get up it, I loaded out of Padooky and come to Florence."

"Look here," said the Colonel, growing impatient, "I want to get this cotton to New Orleans without transshipment. Can you put it there for me?"

The man studied a moment.

"Now, let me see . . . New Orleans . . . tell you what I'll do. Make you a flat rate of five dollars a bale."

Miltiades gave a brief smile.

"Now, just because you're down South, don't jump at the idea that everybody you meet is a fool. It's a mistake a lot o' you Yankees make."

"Why, hell," cried Dargan, "I'm quoting you a fair price!"

"Seventy-five cents higher per bale than railroad rates from Florence to New Orleans."

"Look here, I'm not competing with railroads. I've got to get so much money out of my boat ever' day to keep her a going concern."

"What'll you charter me your boat for?" suggested the Colonel, taking another turn.

"Well . . . I have chartered her for two hundred a day."

"Isn't that a stiff price?"

"Yes, but I paid a stiff price for the old scow, and this crew don't exactly work for nothing, either."

"Two hundred a day . . . how long will the trip take you?"

"Now, lemme see . . . three days to Padooky . . . ten hours to Cairo . . . an' five days more to New Orleans."

"Nine days?"

" 'Bout that."

"You'll take it down for eighteen hundred dollars?"

"It may take me longer."

"Look here," suggested Miltiades crisply, "let's figure on a nine-day trip at eighteen hundred. Now, for every day it takes you longer than that, you forfeit two hundred dollars of your pay; for every day less than that, I'll add a bonus of three hundred dollars. How's that?"

Dargan scratched his head.

"You want to get it down there right quick, don't you?"

"Yes, cotton's going down."

"I imagine it's the election doing that."

"I suppose so. When we get a Democrat in the White House prices will pick up again."

"Well, I'm a Republican myself," said the Captain. "I believe if the Democrats git in they'll bust the country wide open; but I don't believe they're going to git in."

"That's a point on which we will have to disagree until

after the election. Now, Cap'n, when can you get started with this cotton?"

"Why, I'll drop down in the morning."

"You couldn't start now?"

"My God, you are in a rush!"

"What do you think I'm offering you a bonus for? With the amount of cotton I've got, hours may mean dollars, and a day will run into sure enough money."

Captain Dargan looked at Miltiades with the shrewd reddened eyes of a man who had drunk for so long a time that he was most completely sober when he was about a third full of whisky.

"I suppose we could start now. . . . I'll have to hustle up some rousters."

"You haven't got a crew aboard?"

"No, I pick up my labor wherever I am."

"You mean you've got to get niggers from around here in town?" inquired Miltiades with concern.

"M-huh." The Captain took his pencil and began figuring again.

"How'll you get 'em?"

"Whistle 'em up." He stuck his head out the office door. "Pilot, we're going to start tonight. Blow up a crew of niggers right away."

The group at the table instantly broke up, draining the last of their whiskies. Windy Bickle, the fat mate, propelled himself through the front door of the cabin and began booming:

"Black Jack, stoke her up . . . we're gittin' under way!"

A thin man, who was the pilot, went into his stateroom for a coat. The engineer started below. Miltiades watched these preparations.

"I don't see how you're going to get the niggers. . . ."

At that moment an ear-shaking roar broke out right above the roof of the cabin. Dargan mutely pointed upward and stopped trying to talk. The enormous noise disconcerted Miltiades. It was as if a stentor were announcing to the world

that he was making away with J. Handback's cotton. The
sound hurt him. Then it stopped as abruptly as it began,
and the patter of rain reasserted itself on the cabin roof.

"What was that for?" asked Miltiades.

"Calling up the niggers."

"Will they know what it means?"

"Hell, ever' river nigger in Florence is tumbling out of
his bed this minute. There'll be plenty of niggers."

Captain Dargan turned to his desk and began drawing up
a contract, setting forth the bonuses and penalties for less
or more than nine days. As he wrote, the whistle blared out
again. When it stopped, Miltiades observed the rising hiss
of steam in the boilers below.

All these sounds were grouped for Miltiades around the
central fact that Florence negroes would load the Handback
cotton onto the *Zebulon D*. Every laborer who handled the
cotton would know what went with it. A kind of sick anxiety
invaded the Colonel as he watched Captain Dargan make
out the contract for the freight. Then a rather hazardous
idea came into his head.

"Captain," he interrupted uneasily.

"M-m." The skipper paused, keeping his eyes on his writing.

"These niggers that are going to load the cotton?"

"Yes . . . what about them?"

Miltiades cleared his throat.

"How about taking them along with you—to—to unload
in New Orleans?"

Dargan looked up in amazement.

"Take 'em with me!"

"Yes," repeated the Colonel, stiffening himself. "Take 'em
with you . . . sign 'em up for the whole trip."

"Why, hell fire," ejaculated the Captain, "that would
cost——" He broke off, looking at the Colonel intently.
"This is a funny sort of thing," he observed, "you paying
a bonus of three hundred dollars a day for quick delivery,
but still shipping by barge instid of by railroad."

"It saves hauling by wagon from the gin to Florence," said the Colonel.

"Your gin on the river?"

"Within a mile of the river."

"And now you want the niggers who load the barge taken to New Orleans with the cotton?" Dargan narrowed his whisky-reddened eyes.

"You'll need 'em to unload."

"I understand that. There ain't no longshoresmen in New Orleans." The Captain tore his contract in two. "I'm going to have three thousand dollars flat for this trip, mister."

"Look here," cried Miltiades, "that was a trade! I can explain this thing. I—I'm in debt. My cotton's liable to be levied on any minute. I don't want my creditors to know where it went or what boat it went on. I want to get it to New Orleans on the Q. T."

Dargan nodded all through this explanation.

"That's all right with me, what you want it there for, but it's going to cost you three thousand flat if I put this cotton in New Orleans."

"God damn it, your first offer was twenty-five hundred!"

"Listen, I'm doing you a big favor. Besides, my boat is li'ble to be tied up in a Federal suit."

"Now, don't act like a Yankee and take advantage of my necessity. We made a fair-and-square trade."

"Listen," pointed out the man who had blown up a bridge for a load of peanuts, "you have to use my boat or none at all. You were a damn fool for showin' your hand like you did. I got to play my cards the best I can. Three thousand is letting you off light."

The Colonel stood looking at Dargan's long chin and purple-veined nose.

"All right, now we understand each other," he agreed, "will you run at nights, put out your lights, shut off steam, and float past big towns until you get out of the Tennessee River?"

"Listen," said Dargan, thumping the desk with his open

palm, "you can risk me gettin' to New Orleans with your cotton if my three thousand is wrapped up in it."

"All right, that's settled," agreed Miltiades, in profound relief.

"I'll write a new agreement." He stepped out of the office and opened the cabin door.

"Windy! Windy!" he called.

He must have heard a reply above the steam and the rain, for he gave out his instructions:

"Windy, tell ever' damn nigger that rolls cotton tonight he's got to sign up for a trip clear down to New Orleans. Don't slip up on a single damn one of 'em, Windy."

CHAPTER THIRTEEN

I N THE rainy morning the *Zebulon D.* steamed away from Connors' Landing. From where he stood on the bank, Miltiades Vaiden watched the whitened water flung up by her stern wheel and the black rolls of smoke from her chimneys beaten down to the surface of the river by the rain. Ahead of the boat he had just a glimpse of the barge piled high with cotton bales.

The roustabouts, as the towboat moved away on her voyage to New Orleans, fell into the melancholy chanting of their race:

> *"Ohio boun', Ohio boun',*
> *Oh Lawd, yes, Ah'm Ohio boun'."*

Their song mingled with the exhaust of the engine, the rapid tat-tat-tat of the paddlewheel, and the *basso profondo* of Colbert Shoals, into which the *Zebulon D.* was steaming.

On the bank Colonel Vaiden stood speculating on how long before the roustabouts would get back to Florence from New Orleans. He would have just that length of time to receive and dispose of the returns for the cotton he was shipping. Even with the boat and barge still in sight, he felt pressed for time. The cotton would be missed, he believed, within twenty-four hours. The bank of the river was trampled into a loblolly by the night-long labor of the roustabouts. . . . The Colonel glanced about him in the gray descending curtain. No one, he supposed, would be abroad on such a morning. Then he planned, if he were seen, if the loss of the cotton should be attributed to him, to claim that he was attempting to collect an old debt. In reality he stood within his rights. When it came right down to the justice of it, no grand jury would say he had committed a theft. He could look any man in the face and—— A sudden plashing in the edge of the river gave Miltiades a violent start. He whirled with a feeling as if a cold wind were blowing through his chest. Then he saw a cow adrift, trying to paw her way out of the river through a fringe of willows onto the bank. As his sensation subsided, the Colonel thought that this might be one of the cows that Klem, his neighbor, had waded across to an island to graze. The rising river had no doubt set her adrift. He started down to help the cow ashore, but the urgency of the bill of lading in his pocket for five hundred bales of cotton stopped him. He turned and started walking up the road that led away from the landing.

The Colonel followed an odd route. He stepped in the wagon ruts which were now runnels of water and which washed out his tracks immediately. He followed the water to the top of the bank, then proceeded along the side of the road, keeping to the moss and grass. A mile farther on he deserted the road for the woods, where there was no probability of being seen. He found himself in a monotony of desolate scrub oak which he remembered from his fox-hunting days. About a mile from where he stood was a fox den, and ten miles farther westward, toward Waterloo, was another den, the old Johnson Bluff Hole. Near that hole, twenty years ago, his brother Polycarp had been waylaid and killed.

Miltiades followed a course toward the old Vaiden place. As he plashed along in the perfect sameness of the oaks he thought intently about the details of getting the money for his cotton. Then presently he began to wonder what his people would think of him. What would Marcia say, and Augustus and Cassandra? A kind of heaviness filled him that he was doing something contrary to the practice of his brothers and sisters. Then he began thinking out an argument for himself as he walked toward the old Vaiden homestead, the beginning of all their wide-flung family.

He and his brothers and sisters had been cheated out of
their cotton crop by Handback. He, Miltiades Vaiden, had
collected five hundred bales of cotton for an original five.
But cotton just after the war was worth a dollar a pound,
while now it was worth only twenty cents a pound. Handback had had the money for twenty years. At ten per cent
that would double twice . . . twenty-five bales would be,
fifty . . . a hundred bales. But he had collected five hundred bales. That would be fifty per cent, doubled twice.

These figures moved through Miltiades' head with the
repetition of things heard in a fever. He walked on through
the woods thinking five . . . five hundred . . . fifty per
cent, when a wheezing laugh startled him out of this mental
repetend.

He turned, and after looking around for a moment saw
a gray squirrel giving its wheezy bark with an absurd jerking of its tail. He stood for a moment looking at the little
furry jester when he heard a human voice say, *sotto voce:*

"Mister! Mister! Keep still a moment . . . please don'
move!"

Then Miltiades saw a little black boy struggling with a
preternaturally long musket, trying to level it at the squirrel by resting it in the fork of a bush.

The white man remained quiet for upward of half a minute when a disconcerting thought entered his head. He
looked at the little negro, wondering if he knew the child.
That was impossible to say. All negroes looked alike to
Miltiades until they were old enough to work. He came
around the bush to the young hunter.

"You tu'ned him," mumbled the child, still looking up
the black jack.

"Boy," asked Miltiades in an odd voice, "do you know
who I am?"

The urchin batted its eyes at the tone and gave a tiny
nod.

"Who am I?"

"Col'l Milt," whispered the child.

"And where do I work?"

Something about him terrified the child. Tears formed in its black eyes.

"At de gin," it whispered.

"Whose gin?"

"Mistuh Han'back's."

The Colonel looked silently at the little negro with a strange necessity driving down upon him. The pickaninny stood perfectly still now, not looking at Miltiades, but with its face turned, staring at nothing, swallowing its tears.

"Is your gun loaded?" asked the Colonel.

The child remained motionless and silent.

Miltiades took the gun and looked at it.

"It has no cap on the tube," he said in a gray voice.

"Muh-muh daddy . . . tol' me . . . not to . . . put on . . . de cap . . . tull—tull Ah got ready to . . . to shoot," trembled the little negro.

The Colonel reached down and took the musket cap from the small black hand. As he did so he thought with a kind of sick disgust:

"God Almighty, a white boy would have thrown away the cap . . . would have run . . . would have threatened me with the gun." The little negro remained paralyzed with fright. He wondered why he had ever spoken to it, why had he impressed his identity on its mind by talking to it?

"Who is your father?" he asked.

"Buck."

"Buck who?"

"Buck Mosely."

Miltiades did not recognize the name.

"What is your name?" he asked in a monotone.

"Milt."

"Is that all?"

The little black boy whispered:

"Milti'des Vaiden Mosely."

The Colonel batted his eyes, lifted his brows up and down, looked around him. He was on the old Vaiden place. Near him was a decaying rail fence. Inside the fence he could see a scattering of thin, blackened cotton stalks and beyond this patch on a gentle knoll stood a grove of pines. Amid the yellow sedge that carpeted the profound green of the grove stood a little huddle of weathered marble slabs. It was the Vaiden burial ground. Over the black jacks where Miltiades stood, over the pine-crowned hillock, the rain whispered its elegy.

"Come on," he said to the child, with a shiver, "let's get to the house. We can hunt squirrels on a brighter day."

The Moselys were the negro family living on the old Vaiden place with Miss Cassandra. In his abstraction the Colonel had come up on his old home unobserved. This was the point where he had planned to reappear in the world after the hiatus of his voyage on the *Zebulon D.*

Presently he came in sight of the somber story and a half log house where his sister Cassandra lived. Near by stood the smaller cabin of the Moselys.

Originally there had been two slave cabins on the Vaiden place: one belonging to old Aunt Creasy, the other to Columbus and Robinet; but the men's cabin had fallen into disrepair, and the Moselys had surreptitiously used its clapboards and some of its rafters for fire wood. Then they asked if they could burn the rest of the cabin for fuel, and Cassandra had let them do it. They needed only one cabin on the place, the thin soil could not possibly have supported two families.

As Miltiades and the child came down the muddy path in the rain, a negro's voice called from the stable:

"Well, Li'l' Col'l, did je git any?"

And the child called back in its high voice:

"No, Poppy, I didn't git none. I seen one, but I didn't git none."

Then the voice in the stable ejaculated:

"Lawzee, I di'n' know you was wid him, Col'l Milt. I wouldn't spoke his name like dat."

"It's all right," said Miltiades, looking at the stable, whose logs had decayed and sagged at one end.

"Altreen named him fuh you, Milti'des Vaiden," explained the father, climbing out of the crib into the soggy manure in the hallway between the stalls. "We calls him Li'l' Col'l, an' dat's why he's boun' to take dat gun an' go huntin'." Buck broke out laughing at his little boy. He checked his mirth almost at once and said:

"Milti'des, run quick an' tell you mammy Col'l Milt is come an' fuh huh to put on a fresh breakfus'."

Miltiades carried the musket, and the child broke into a run toward the big house, splashing in the muddy road.

"How's everything getting along, Buck?" inquired Miltiades, glancing at the rail fences that were toppling down.

"Why, fine, Col'l Milt, evahthing jess gittin' 'long fine."

"How's Sister Cassandra's health?"

"Spry as a kitten an' gittin' youngah evah day she libs. We wuzn't speckin' you dis soon, Col'l Milt."

"I rode from Florence with a drummer going to Waterloo," explained Miltiades. "I dropped off at the Crossroads and walked over."

"Yas, suh," nodded Buck. He scratched his head a moment and then added quickly, "Yas, suh, yas, suh."

"I'd like to have Altreen clean my shoes and dry them while I'm here."

"Yas, suh, Altreen'll do that. If'n you could stir up some mo' pants somewhere, Altreen would clean yo' pants, too."

Miltiades looked down at his clothing. He was dubious about appearing before Cassandra in such a plight.

"I've got to get something done to these clothes before I go back to town," he agreed to Buck.

He walked on down the road to the ancient big house. It recalled to the Colonel his father's large family, and yet, in the same breath, it looked as if it always had stood as empty and melancholy as it did now.

One of the old black oaks in the front yard had been

struck by lightning and mutely held up a huge dead splinter to the capricious sky.

Miltiades pushed his way into the yard by pulling the top of the big gate away from its post and stepping over its immovable bottom. A negro's rabbit dog gave a wail at seeing a white man and fled in terror.

There was quite a stir when Miltiades entered the big house. Altreen and her half-grown daughter were busy with home-made brooms and dust cloths. They were not so much tidying up the house as they were trying to make it look less deserted.

A tall white woman with thin gray hair parted severely in the middle and done up in a small knot at the back of her head came out in the rain-splashed open hallway.

"Why, Miltiades, what in the world!" ejaculated Miss Cassandra, looking at her brother. "How came you down here at this time of day?"

The Colonel drew a breath. He detested lying to anybody, not because he had any scruples against it, but because it appeared cowardly.

"I found a good way to come down. I thought I could get back to the gin in time for a day's work."

"How did you come?"

"A drummer was going to Waterloo."

"And you walked from the Crossroads?"

"Yes."

"What drummer was it?"

Miltiades had forgot the endless curiosity of a woman isolated on a farm.

"Why, I don't suppose you know him. His name was Wilson."

"I wonder if he is any kin to the Arkansas Wilsons?"

"What Arkansas Wilsons?"

"Why, the ones who sued Sylvester."

"I didn't think to ask him," said Miltiades, faintly amused.

"Well, you are absent-minded. I wonder if you can wear

one of my skirts while Altreen cleans your trousers. Did you specially pick out the muddy places to wade in?"

The habitual Vaiden irony toward all situations almost reëstablished for Miltiades his father's home of twenty years ago.

"You don't have to pick the muddy places between here and the Crossroads, they've already been gathered for you."

Miss Cassandra smiled faintly. She thought silently how queer it was that Miltiades had never made a great success in life. She considered him a sort of success because he contrived somehow to exist in Florence, but he had not distinguished himself.

Once, soon after the war, she had thought Miltiades would become the Governor of Alabama one day. She never quite knew why he had ebbed away from his brief prominence—and neither did Miltiades.

The two went into the ancient living room with its whitewashed logs and high, narrow windows. Miss Cassandra got out a wrapper which she thought Miltiades might put on while Altreen cleaned his clothes. The only trousers on the place were those which had been worn by Buck, and they wouldn't do. Miltiades finally went into the company room and put on the wrapper.

Changing his clothes in the silent room recalled Drusilla Lacefield. In this room he had spent the night on which he was to have married Drusilla. From here he had gone out to feed his horse at the stable, and there he had found the slave girl, Gracie, and forcibly possessed her body. This was something he did not think of once in ten years. Now it moved soberly through his memory without compunction or shame or any reminiscence of pleasure in the long past act.

Presently he returned to the living room in his sister's wrapper.

Miss Cassandra said soberly:

"You look funny, Miltiades."

The Colonel sat down before a fire over which hung an oven on a crane. One of Altreen's half-grown girls came for the clothes and retired precipitately, biting her thick black lips to restrain her giggles.

"That was Cassandra," said Miss Cassandra drily.

The Colonel looked at his sister questioningly.

"I met a very small Miltiades lugging a musket he could hardly hold up," he said.

"Yes. You see I once said to Altreen jokingly why didn't she name some of her babies after the people who had lived on the place. I didn't really think about her doing it. I wish now I never had mentioned it."

"It must be disagreeable," reflected Miltiades.

"It is, but I can't very well unname them. I hear them playing and shouting, 'Ulysses! Augustus! Miltiades! Marcia!' in their nigger talk. A kind of travesty on our family. I've half a mind to turn them off and get another family."

"Well . . . Altreen's a good cook . . . and she's clean," said the Colonel.

"All of them are clean when they live with me," stated Miss Cassandra concisely. After a moment she went on, "Now, that little Miltiades you saw: he can already spell in words of one syllable."

"Oh . . . you're teaching him?"

"Well, yes, it won't hurt any of them to learn how to read and cipher, and it gives me something to do."

"Everybody says that an education ruins a nigger," suggested Miltiades tentatively.

Miss Cassandra clicked her tongue.

"That girl Cassandra who took your clothes can read in my old Chautauqua books right now—when I make her—and what harm does it do her? She's still a nigger and will never be anything else."

"I suppose that's true," agreed Miltiades, looking at the coals with the oven hanging over them. "I suppose they are like parrots—just memorize what you teach them and never really learn anything at all."

"Little Miltiades understands a soldier has to have a gun," defended Miss Cassandra distantly.

A touch of humor visited Miltiades at his sister condemning negroes as a whole as imbeciles but making exceptions of the pickaninnies she taught.

They changed the subject, Miss Cassandra asking Miltiades when he had heard from Marcia.

"The last thing I heard from her," added Cassandra, "she was thinking about sending Jerry to Augustus's to go to school. I suppose she gave that up."

A qualm seized Miltiades.

"Why, Cassandra, Jerry has been with Augustus and Rose ever since late last summer!"

It shocked Miltiades that no one had thought to write and tell Cassandra that young Jerry was in Florence.

"Well, I declare!" ejaculated Miss Cassandra, perturbed. "Some of you-all could die up there, and I'd never find it out."

"I really ought to come down here oftener," said Miltiades, conscience struck. "Augustus ought to come. He's got nothing to do."

"It wouldn't be any use for Augustus to come," said Miss Cassandra, "he has no administrative ability. How is young Jerry getting along at school? Slow, I imagine, if he takes after his mammy."

Miltiades looked into the coals over which his breakfast baked. He hardly knew whether he was amused or anxious.

After a pause he said:

"Jerry has been suspended."

"What?"

"M-huh."

"What for?"

"Well . . . they suspended him for not believing in God."

Miss Cassandra put up a thin hand and wiped her mouth

"Then he's a Vaiden," she said. "His name may be Catlin, but he's a Vaiden. I'll warrant that boy amounts to something one of these days."

What this meant, Miltiades did not know, whether or not

it meant that Miss Cassandra agreed with Jerry's atheism the Colonel could not tell. None of the Vaiden brothers and sisters ever talked to one another of their religious beliefs, or indeed of any other of their genuine emotions. All of the Vaidens lived in solitary confinement, until death, perhaps, broke the heavy bars of their souls.

The little black Miltiades finally brought Miltiades's breakfast. As the white man took the tray from the little black hands, Altreen, the child's mother, urged from the doorway:

"Tell Col'l Milt, Milti'des, tell him."

The child was whispering something.

Miltiades bent down to hear.

"What is it, Milt?" he asked.

The little boy was whispering:

"I can write my name."

CHAPTER FOURTEEN

W HEN Colonel Miltiades Vaiden finished his visit, Buck
Mosely hitched up the wagon and mules and drove him to
the Handback gin. As Miltiades jounced along the road
on a sack of straw laid across the wagon hounds, the cotton and the bill of lading seized his thoughts again. He reviewed his calculation about the *Zebulon D.* and her barges;
how long it would take them to reach New Orleans, and
then how many more days it would require for the draft
to return to Florence.

In the midst of this preoccupation a faint impression of
the negro child, Miltiades Vaiden Mosely, flickered through
his head. When he considered what almost happened, a
shadow of horror drifted across his thoughts and then was
gone.

When the Colonel and Buck arrived at the Handback gin,
the negro hung around the place until Miltiades found a
way to go on to Florence, and then Buck went home.

The man who took the Colonel to Florence was a
Northrup. He knew the Colonel, and the Colonel knew
Northrup's father and mother. Miltiades remembered when
Heck Northrup had married Daisy Miller before the war.
The family lived down toward Waterloo.

Young Mr. Northrup asked the Colonel what he thought
about the coming election. Miltiades thought Cleveland
would be elected by a large majority.

"I wonder if we'll get a Democratic Congress to stand by
our President?" questioned Northrup with the gravity of a
young man engaging an old man in conversation.

"I believe the Democrats will have a majority in the
house, but probably not in the Senate," said the Colonel

abstractedly "By the way, did you hear a boat go down last night?"

"Go down where?"

"Why, the river," said the Colonel, feeling that Northrup was a dull young man.

"What boat?"

"Just any boat."

"Hasn't the water been too low for boats?"

"I was wondering if this rain let the boats over the shoals," said Miltiades.

"I don't imagine it has yet," said Northrup judicially.

It occurred to the Colonel that he ought not to have introduced the subject of steamboats. He should have stuck to Congress. He tried to think of some other neutral topic, and he came very near asking how long it would take the mail to come from New Orleans to Florence, but he censored that question, too.

As the buggy neared Florence, Northrup asked where the Colonel would get out. The Colonel said he wanted to go home, but the young man could put him out at Handback's store.

"No, I'll take you straight on home," said Northrup. "It won't put me out much."

"I left a baked sweet potato for Ponny to eat last night," said the Colonel, troubled, "and I was wondering if she ever fixed it up and ate it."

"You wasn't at home last night?"

"No . . . I went down to my farm. Got a mighty no-count nigger on my place . . . everything run down."

"Who took you down to your farm?" inquired Northrup.

"Why, a drummer."

"A drummer. . . . Where was he going to?"

"Waterloo."

"Why, that's funny," reflected Northrup with curiosity.

"What's funny about that?" inquired the Colonel, looking at his host intently.

"I imagine my telephone's out of order."

"What's that got to do with drummers?"

"Why, Mammy runs a boarding house in Waterloo. Most of the drummers patronize her because she's a widow woman. When one comes in she rattles the cigar-box telephone I put up between our places, and I go over and tend to their horses."

"Maybe this drummer didn't stop with your mother," suggested the Colonel.

"I guess he did. They nearly all do. What was his name?"

"Wilson."

"Wilson . . . What house did he travel for?"

"Some hardware house."

"Why, they ain't any Wilson traveling for any hardware house. . . ." Suddenly Mr. Northrup turned to Miltiades excitedly:

"I'll bet you six bits you didn't come down with any drummer at all!"

"What do you mean?" inquired the Colonel, resentment in his voice.

"Exactly what I say," cried Northrup with excitement. "I'll bet a dollar to a doughnut that you come down the road with a thief!"

Miltiades looked at his companion intently.

"Who has lost anything?" he asked in a changed tone, "and what's he lost?"

"Some people up about Huntsville. I don't know what they lost."

This location calmed Miltiades in some degree.

"I hadn't heard about it," he said.

"Yes, some burglars went through Huntsville a few days ago, and I'll bet this man Wilson telling you he was a hardware drummer . . . did he have a gun or a revolver for samples?"

"No, he just said he was a hardware drummer," repeated Miltiades, wishing he had not picked on exactly this imaginary person to bring him to the Crossroads.

"Now, he might have been a detective," hazarded North-rup. "When we get to Florence I'll look him up."

"How look him up?" frowned the Colonel.

"Look on the hotel registers."

"You probably won't find him. He brought me down late last night."

Northrup pondered this.

"Then he wasn't a drummer," he decided.

"Why?"

"Why, because drummers travel on expense accounts. They always get to a hotel before supper and start out after breakfast. No, he wasn't a drummer. Now, he could have been a cattleman or a cross-tie buyer or a goober-pea man —they don't have expense accounts and are li'ble to drive day or night, but a drummer . . . no, the man you saw wasn't a drummer. . . ."

By this time Mr. Northrup had reached the spindling iron bridge across Cypress Creek on the western edge of Florence.

Across the bridge Northrup took an old grass road north-ward instead of the main road going straight into town. This led him around through some woods into Cherry Street. He talked of the robbers all the way and finally delivered Miltiades at his home.

The Colonel asked him what he was really going to do about the man Wilson.

The young man said he was going to report it to the *Index*.

"I don't believe he was a thief," said Miltiades, "and if you put anything like that in the paper and he sees it, he may start a libel suit against you. And if you do put it in the paper, please take particular care not to mention my name. He did me a favor, and I'd hate to make him a poor return for it."

"All right," agreed Northrup, "how about me saying, *I* rode down with a man calling himself Wilson who was a thief? You see I've got to tell A. Gray Lacefield, the editor, somebody rode down with Wilson, or nobody would have known anything about his going down."

"Suit yourself," agreed Miltiades drily, "but keep me out of it."

CHAPTER FIFTEEN

W HEN Miltiades entered his house again, Mrs. Ponny Vaiden went through the perturbed and suspicious catechism of any wife to any husband who, unexplained, has stayed abroad all night.

The Colonel repeated his story about the drummer.

"What in the world did you want to go with a drummer that time of night for? And it a-raining!"

"Well . . . I wanted to see how Cassandra was getting along, and I didn't want to use any time belonging to Handback."

"Handback! Handback! You minding that he gets every minute coming to him after what he's done to you!"

The Colonel felt an impulse to tell his wife what he really had done. He wanted to talk about it. He was on the verge of saying that he had got back everything Handback had stolen from him with fifty per cent interest . . . fifty per cent . . . he would like to laugh with somebody over an interest rate of fifty per cent per annum.

"Did you ever eat that potato I fixed for you last night?"

This switch to a potato when she could see clearly he was thinking of other things reawakened Ponny's suspicions.

"Mr. Milt . . . have you . . . been . . . to . . . see . . . anybody . . . last . . . night?"

The Colonel had to stare at Ponny for several seconds before he realized that she was talking about Drusilla. Her conjecture filled him with the disgust a man feels for the misplaced jealousy of his wife.

"Ponny! Tchk! You are so ridiculous!"

The fat woman was somewhat abashed to have accused him falsely, but at the same time she was relieved.

The Colonel stood looking at her, thinking how trivial was a woman's mind, always running on love and kisses and gallantries . . . to make sure that none of these things got out of pocket. He glanced down at himself.

"I'm going to have to change these clothes."

"What'll you wear?"

"All I've got left is my Sunday suit."

"Now, Mr. Milt, you know you're not going to wear your Sunday suit to that store!"

"I can't walk the streets like this!"

"That old gray suit's good enough for the store."

"I won't be seen downtown wearing patched pants!"

"Wear your Sunday suit and carry your gray ones, then change after you get in the store."

Such palaver over a suit annoyed Miltiades. His brain twitched to get at the complicated problem of the cotton, and here was Ponny going on about his clothes.

"I'll have all the clothes I need . . . both of us will . . . before long."

"What makes you say that?" began Ponny; then she divined he was talking about the success he always had intended to make and in which she always had believed; so she added:

"Yes, that's so, but this Sunday suit may have to do till then."

Miltiades went to the closet, got out his best suit, and began getting into it.

Ponny watched him with a wife's continued anxiety about his clothes.

"Suppose it rains?"

"I'll take the umbrella."

"Well, but an umbrella doesn't really keep a person's clothes dry, and it never has rained on that suit since you got it."

"We ought to see if it will draw up," said Miltiades; "it may be a better suit than we think."

"You say the silliest things," said Ponny.

He took his old greened umbrella and went out of the house.

The sky was still a murk, but it was not raining.

Miltiades began picking his way among the succession of pools in Cherry Street with a feeling that this day was but a continuation of yesterday. He had had no sleep to divide the one twelve hours from the other. This confusion of the days permeated all his thoughts.

Suddenly he wondered if he had changed the bill of lading from his everyday suit to his Sunday suit. He clapped his hand to his inner pocket and felt the official paper. It soothed him as abruptly as the fear of forgetting it had startled him.

Now that he was alone he began calculating once more how soon he could get returns from his cotton. He went over the same figures again, adding them up, getting the same result which he had got a hundred times already. He was going down now to mail his bill of lading to Carter & Company in New Orleans. Then he meant to rent a post-office box.

The post-office box was important. There were some Vardens living in Florence, and once one of these Vardens had opened a letter of his that had come to the general delivery. If a Varden should open a letter and see a check in it for thousands of dollars . . . Miltiades unconsciously quickened his gait, although he knew the draft for the cotton could not arrive under eleven and a half days.

The Colonel did not turn off at the store, but continued to Courthouse Square and the post office. When he stepped into the building he had an irrational feeling that he had won a very close race. He went to the general delivery and asked for his mail.

The clerk, a blanched youth named Crowe, flipped through the "V" box and handed out a letter. It was post-marked Imboden, Arkansas. Miltiades knew it was from his brother Sylvester, and this surprised him. He heard from his brother in Arkansas only once in two or three years. He put the letter in his pocket and told the clerk he wanted to rent a post-office box.

Crowe moved over to the tiers of glass boxes, put his hand in one and thumped on the pane.

"This 'un about right, Colonel? Can you see into it all right?"

The Colonel went up and tried the box, standing erect and looking into it. He felt vaguely as if he were being fitted for a suit of clothes. He tried on several boxes, the clerk thumping inside, and the Colonel standing erect and looking in as if he could not possibly bend an inch.

"I'll take this one," decided Miltiades.

"Number sixty-two. That will be twenty cents the quarter. You look mighty dressed up today, Colonel. Going somewhere?"

Miltiades ignored this question.

"Be sure and put all my mail in that box."

"Certainly, certainly."

"Look here, I wanted a box with a key to it."

"Oh, you wanted a lock box."

"Yes, I might want my mail on Sundays."

"They're thirty-five cents a quarter. But all our lock boxes are taken. I can put your name down, and if anybody gives up a lock box you can have it."

"No, that'll do." He got two dimes out of his pocket and laid them on the shelf of the general delivery window. "Be sure and put all my mail in it."

He went out of the post office into the gloomy street again. He had nowhere to go except the store. He did not want to go to the store. He did not want to see Handback again.

The toleration, the almost friendliness which his ᴗᴗsociation with the merchant had aroused was quite gone. He felt a renewal of anger at Handback for ever having swindled him, and a harsh humor which colors the satisfaction of a person playing even with an enemy.

As he walked back to the store, his lack of sleep caused

Market Street to seem a little strange. He tried to keep his wits about him. He shook his head a bit to set the street back where it belonged. A countryman stood on the curb eating cheese and crackers with the help of a long-bladed knife.

Miltiades thought if this man knew what he had done, how he would stare, and then rush and tell.

Across the street, in the door of Simpson's drug store, Miltiades saw Alfred Thorndyke talking to Frierson the jailer. They were discussing the weather. He could tell by the way they looked up at the clouds. The clock in the court-house tower began striking twelve. The wet air brought the notes close to his ear. The clock seemed to lean forward and strike in his ear privately and secretively.

A dash of rain came pattering down on the watery street, and after half a minute stopped as abruptly as it began. It reminded the Colonel of the first brief burst of firing at Shiloh.

A short, compact man came running around the corner from the direction of the store. He turned into Market Street and saw the Colonel. He came running toward him waving his hands.

"Milt Vaiden! Miltiades Vaiden! Hold on a minute! Wait!"

A shock of resistance and antagonism went through the Colonel. It aroused him completely and suddenly put the whole street right.

"What do you want, Handback?" he asked, and awaited his approach.

"My God, man!" gasped the merchant. "You've ruined me! You've broken me up!"

Miltiades stared at the fellow's clay-colored face. His heart began beating in his heavy chest. He wondered swiftly if there were a possibility of instituting a lawsuit to hold the cotton he had seized upon.

"What you talking about?" The Colonel wetted his lips.

"You've cost me ever' damned bale of cotton I've got!"

Miltiades wondered how Handback came to know so

quickly. He drew in his breath to say, "And you cost me every bale I had once." He was interrupted by the merchant rushing on:

"It's all gone. . . . Ever' bale we had down there's washed away. . . . It's scattered from here to Padooky!"

The merchant was staring at his clerk in the utmost anguish of soul. A sharp, almost painful twist went through Miltiades as he reoriented his thoughts to Handback's point of view.

"They're washed away!" he echoed in amazement.

"Ever' damn bale!"

"Who told you?"

"Loob Snipes. He just got in. He was out possumhunting last night and come by the landing this morning. . . . He says ever' bale's floated off."

"My God! . . . the water couldn't have got to your cotton that quick . . . this rain isn't enough."

"Oh, hell, it's above . . . it's been raining above for a week . . . it's just got here. The river's jumpin'."

Handback caught Miltiades' arm and began propelling him back up the street toward the courthouse.

"What you going to do?"

"Telephone! Telegraph! Set guards out below and save what we can! God damn it! Hell fire! That was what the freight agent said would happen. He warned me. A man's a damn fool not to listen to somebody with sense!"

"Mr. Handback," cried the Colonel in spontaneous sympathy, "I'm awfully sorry I got you to put your cotton——"

"Oh, hell . . . my cotton . . . I had it done . . . it was my fault!"

They hurried on to one of those little doorways between stores. They entered this and went clattering up a flight of narrow, dusty steps. At the top were two unpainted doors. An osteopath's card hung from one. On the other was painted in uneven black letters, "Telephone office."

Inside, a girl sat at a tiny switchboard.

"Look here, Margaret," cried the merchant, "what places can we get down the river?"

The operator became excited at the merchant's manner.

"What places do you want, Mr. Handback?"

"Why, any places! My cotton's washed away . . . five hundred bales. I've got to post men to fish 'em out."

Margaret began a frantic twisting of a handle.

"Riverton's the first place I can get, Mr. Handback."

"All right, Riverton!"

"Who do you want to speak to at Riverton?"

"Why-y . . . the steamboat agent."

"The ferryman," interrupted Miltiades sharply.

Handback turned and blinked at his clerk.

"You say the ferryman?"

"Sure, down at the river all day long . . . he may have caught some already."

Margaret was now saying:

"Corinth, I want Riverton . . . ring back on Riverton . . . yes . . . you say when . . . now . . ." And Margaret renewed her frantic ringing. "Riverton! Riverton! Riverton!" she screamed.

"They'll all wash past," groaned Handback, "while I'm getting the place. What's the next place after Riverton that's got a phone?"

"Savannah, Tennessee."

"Skips away down there?"

"Yes, sir, that's the next one on the river, there's plenty among the inland towns, along the railroads."

"Colonel, write out a message to Savannah. We'll leave it here. Let's go down to the landing and send a couple of nigger oarsmen to look along the drifts. Maybe some hung up in the drifts."

Miltiades went to a desk and scribbled a message to the ferryman at Savannah saying five hundred bales of Handback cotton washed away . . . hold . . . reward. J. Handback & Son, Florence, Ala.

He handed it to the merchant. Handback read it.

"Put down ten dollars' reward for each bale," he dictated.

Miltiades added the figures. The merchant looked at it again and passed it on to Margaret.

"Let's go," he said.

As the two men started out the door Handback turned back inside.

"You dropped something, Colonel," he said.

He went back and picked up an envelope on the desk where Miltiades had written the message. He handed it to his clerk, and they hurried on down the steps. The envelope contained the bill of lading which Captain Dargan had given to Miltiades at Connors' Landing.

CHAPTER SIXTEEN

THE helping of Handback with his telephone messages did an odd thing to the Colonel. It showed him that he was not collecting a debt. It defined him, even to himself, as a man who was making a grab.

The two men had gone down to the river landing and hired a couple of negroes to row down the river. The oarsmen were to search the banks and log drifts and willow brakes for the vanished cotton. The black boys were regular skiff men who would make good mileage and had river eyes. They were to pull down as far as Cerro Gordo and then come back with their skiff on the first up-river boat. They were to cost Handback three dollars a day and their return fare.

This useless expenditure irked the Colonel. It would be fifteen or twenty dollars thrown away.

As the white men picked their way back up the muddy road to town the Colonel said interrogatively:

"Mr. Handback, you won't need me to handle your nigger tenants any more, will you?"

Handback looked at him in surprise:

"Why won't I?"

"Your cotton's in . . . and I don't fit into the store very well."

"You're not thinking about quitting, Colonel?"

"I don't want to take your pay for nothing."

Handback looked at his clerk and shook his head.

"Well—" he paused with the inexplicableness of the Colonel's character passing through his head—"Well, I hate to see you go. We got along a lot better than I thought we were going to, Colonel. . . . Of course, this is a hard blow to me. . . . I don't quite see how . . ." He moved

171

along the muddy road taking irregular steps. "Of course, I'll be glad to save every penny I can," he concluded.

A kind of relief went through Miltiades. If he had acted upon his impulse he would have taken some other direction and walked away from the merchant.

"I hope," said Handback after a prolonged pause, "I'm not put down and out like I was right after the war. I don't believe I could climb back up another time, Miltiades."

The two men had come to a seldom used road which branched off toward East Florence. Handback paused.

"I believe I'll walk up this way, Colonel. It's not so muddy, and walking's better . . . if you don't mind."

For a moment Miltiades thought Handback was inviting him to go with him; then he saw the merchant was saying he would like to go on by himself.

Miltiades touched his hat and continued into old Florence. After he had walked for five or six minutes it came to him that Handback was going by Gracie's cottage. He drew down his lips, not at the merchant's morals, but at his taste.

And so it came about that the Colonel quit the store.

When he was home again and told of his action to Ponny, his explanation to his wife, why he had done it, was of a most unsatisfactory character.

The fat woman could see in the step only blank irrationality.

"Why, Mr. Milt, what did you make him take you for if you was goin' to quit all of a sudden like that?"

"Well . . . he's in a tight, Ponny . . . and he doesn't really need me."

"He needs you as much now as he ever did, don't he?"

"But his cotton's gone. His whole year's work is wrapped up in that cotton. He might not be able to pay me."

"You could at least have stayed on at the store until he failed to pay you," said Ponny practically.

"Ye-es, but I didn't like to push myself on him. Then I really caused him to store his cotton at the landing. . . ."

The Colonel paused once more on the very edge of telling

Ponny the whole matter. She really ought to know. She was involved in the uncertainty of the situation as completely as he himself. It would be better that he told her rather than someone else.

"You are going to haff to hire a nigger to come and cook for me, Mr. Milt," said Ponny apropos of nothing.

"Well, all right, I'll do that."

The eleven and a half days which Miltiades calculated he would have to wait before he received any returns for his cotton stretched out into a subjective eternity.

Twice a day he went to the post office to look in his call box. When he saw it was empty he became apprehensive lest his draft had come and had been misplaced in the office. Each time he found it impossible to go away until he asked Crowe to search and make sure. For two or three days the assistant said very cheerfully as he riffled through the "V" box:

"I don't think I missed you, Colonel. Got you on my mind. Won't let anything slip through into the general delivery." But after the eighth or ninth morning he shortened it to, "Nothing. If you get anything it'll be in your box."

The Colonel became a nuisance at the post office. He was falling into the class of those seedy men who, having nothing better to do, continually inquire for their mail.

To Miltiades the days became panicky. At any moment, now, some of the negroes who shipped on the *Zebulon D.* might drift back into Florence. Then a minor fear assailed him. He thought one of the younger roustabouts might read in the paper of the supposed loss of Handback's cotton. And these younger, literate negroes might write home what had become of the cotton.

A kind of revulsion went through the Colonel at the multiplication of negro schools and the increasing literacy of the black folk. It would come to no good.

He walked about the streets looking at every negro, wondering if this one or that knew anything of the cotton.

Early Sunday morning he was awakened out of his sleep

by either a dream or an impression that his draft had come. He sat up in bed and blinked his eyes. His heart beat. A kind of agonized near possession of the draft tingled through him. He felt he almost had got it and yet somehow had missed it. He looked around his bare bedroom, with its incidental beauty of an old spool bedstead and a hand-pieced quilt, filled with the lingering distress of the nightmare.

He had an impulse to get up immediately and hurry down to the post office and look in his box. But it was Sunday, and there would be nobody in the office to hand out his mail.

He moved his legs from under the cover carefully and sat up on the side of the bed. It was a cold morning; the loosely built room was as chill as the out of doors.

Ponny groaned and moved her bulk a little, then lay still, but evidently was awake. After a while she asked in a saggy monotone what time it was.

Miltiades' watch, in a large worn gold case, lay on a chair on top of his clothes. Miltiades reached out, looked at the time, then wound the watch with a little gold key, as he always did when he first picked it up in the morning.

"Twelve minutes past eight."

"I'm goin' to church," said Ponny in her sleepy voice.

"I wouldn't if I were you, Ponny."

"I'm goin' . . . it may be the last Sunday I'll be able to git to church."

She lay still several minutes longer, then began moving herself, flinging away the bedclothes with the illy coördinated movements of the very obese. When the open yoke of her nightgown discovered the rolling masses of her breasts, Miltiades saw a drop or two of milk on one of her nipples. It gave him a sharp surprise. It suggested the actuality of his wife's pregnancy.

The Colonel tried again to get her to stay at home, but she got out of bed with much effort and moved across the floor in her bare feet. The boards squeaked and groaned. She went to her great chair, where her clothes were laid out, sat down, and began panting and drawing on her huge stockings.

Miltiades suddenly felt sorry for her.

"Ponny," he said, "we'll have a much better home than this—we'll have a nigger here all the time to make fires and do everything."

"Yes, and you've throwed up your job," puffed the fat wife ironically.

Miltiades smiled drily.

"That won't have much to do with it. I couldn't keep a nigger making ten a week."

He began drawing on his ordinary suit.

She looked at him.

"Ain't you goin' to church?"

"Not this Sunday."

"Why?"

"I don't feel like it. . . . You know it was a funny thing that young Jerry said to me the other night."

"What was that?"

"He said the reason he didn't go to chapel was because the people were not sincere about it."

"You don't mean to say that you believe . . ."

"No, talking about the church reminds me of what Jerry said."

Ponny got to her feet, did up her hair before a mirror that hung on the wall, and moved ponderously into the kitchen about breakfast.

"Listen," advised the Colonel, "if you are bound to go, I'll walk down and tell Rose. I imagine she will get a way for you."

"The Ashtons will."

"Yes, I imagine so."

"I can't understand why you don't want to go to church yourself?"

"Well . . . I . . ." He drew a long breath and said nothing more.

"Don't understand it. . . ." She looked at him over the oilcloth tablecover.

At a little before ten o'clock Miltiades started for the post office and stopped by Rose Vaiden's boarding house to be-speak a conveyance for Ponny.

This commission was not grateful to Miltiades. He felt it a kind of let-down to obtain a ride for Ponny through Augustus and his wife. It was, of course, Rose who was popular enough to commandeer a horse and buggy for Ponny, but Miltiades didn't want to be beholden to anybody.

Augustus had married well. If he himself had married Drusilla, he fancied . . . but if he had married Drusilla the Handback cotton theft would have been impossible; his whole mode of life and thought would have been impossible; perhaps the real truth of the business was that Drusilla was the impossible one, and marrying Ponny was the only way he, Miltiades Vaiden, could ever have acted.

When Miltiades called Rose Vaiden to the door of the boarding house, Rose, for once in her life, was pleased to see her brother-in-law.

"You had a good influence on Jerry," she said grate-fully: "he's back in school again, and everything's all right."

"That's good. . . . I wonder what I said to him?"

"Well, he said he was proud to be a Vaiden, that he looked up to you and would take your advice."

"I'm glad he took it that way."

"Yes, he said he expected somebody would come to him and give him good advice and inspire him, but he said he never dreamed it would be his kin folks."

"Why not?" inquired the Colonel curiously.

"I haven't the slightest idyah. He's a queer boy."

"He goes to chapel all right now?"

"Yes. He told me it would train him to concentrate on higher things under adverse conditions."

Miltiades began laughing.

"I think I know what he meant."

"There was another thing I wanted to see you about," said Rose. "What do you think about Augustus taking a job?"

"You mean about his health?"

"Yes, I don't believe he could stand the confinement."

"What sort of a job is it?"

"Down at the Barham Second-Hand Furniture Store. He's got an offer to be a clerk. Old Mr. Barham sits there all day long, and he says it's telling on him. He wants Augustus to come sit in the store while he gets out a little."

"Well . . . I believe Augustus could do that," said Miltiades soberly.

"Well, I don't believe he could stand the confinement. And a second-hand furniture store isn't cheerful. If Augustus could find something to do in a cheerful place . . ."

"I don't imagine he will stay down there any longer than he enjoys it," said the Colonel in quiet satire.

"That's just where you're wrong," responded Rose tartly. "Augustus is a steady worker once he gets started."

Miltiades saw that it was time for him to go. Rose had lost her smoothness with him. He mentioned Ponny's desire to go to church, and Rose said she would get the Ashtons or somebody to drive up and get her. The Colonel told his sister-in-law good-bye and went on downtown.

Miltiades' brief pleasure in jibing at Augustus vanished at once in his renewed expectation that his draft would be in the post office.

On his way downtown the Colonel met a number of persons on their way to church. In comparison with the draft he was expecting the whole to-do about churches seemed insignificant. Several persons invited him to come with them. He declined their offers courteously and hurried on to the post office in Courthouse Square.

As he drew near the musty building his heart began beating. He entered the door and tried to look across the lobby at once into his box. The lobby itself was empty. He walked across to his call box with his eyes fixed on his number. The narrow tallish box was empty.

A trembling set up in Miltiades. He could scarcely believe his eyes. He looked at the empty box for several seconds

when suddenly he knew that the clerk had put his letter into
the general delivery. He began peering through the dim
glass boxes trying to see one of the postal employees inside
the mail department.

He saw nobody.

"Damn the careless clerk," thought Miltiades, blowing
out a breath, "after I've bought and paid for a box . . ."
and he rattled on the call boxes. "Hey, inside!" he called. "I
want my mail!"

He listened. He could not see very well through the dusty
glass. He went to a letter drop and peered through the narrow opening.

"Somebody inside!" he called. "I want my mail!"

He could see tables and chairs and mail sacks and a cold
stove.

"Damn such clerks!" growled Miltiades. "Never at their
posts!"

A negro's voice behind him said:

"Is you lookin' fuh a postmaster, Col'l Milt?"

"I'm looking for a clerk."

"Who, Mistuh Waltah Crowe?"

"Him or Landers."

"Mistuh Waltah gone ridin' wid he gal."

"Well, I be damned. . . . Wonder where Landers is?"

The negro stood blinking his eyes as if he were responsible.
The Colonel studied the black man.

"Does Landers go to the nigger church?"

"Oh, no, suh."

"Where do you s'pose I'd find him?"

"Well, Ah do' know zackly, Col'l Milt. Mist' Landahs, he
walk out on de creek nea'ly evah Sunday mawn'n'."

"What direction?" asked the Colonel.

"Up by de bridge on de Watahloo Road."

"D'reckon he's there now?"

"I'se seed him dis Sunday an' dat. Speck he is."

"Well, I know damn well he won't be there," growled the
Colonel, "and if he is there he won't come to the office and

see if I've got any mail . . . such a damn set of unaccommodating Republican post-office employees. . . ."

The Colonel strode out of the office already in a dudgeon
at Landers for being about to refuse to come and look for
his mail.

The Colonel's way lay along Pine Street, which was continued out of town as Waterloo Road. At the end of the
street it turned left down a wooded hillside, then led through
a scattering of negro cabins and so to the creek. When
Miltiades reached the bank of the stream Landers was not
to be seen.

The creek itself tumbled down wide rapids in the November sunshine. A solitary kingfisher sat as sentinel over one
of the pools. Colonel Vaiden's wrath at the post-office officials
subsided under the trance of the autumn morning. He wondered if his feeling about the draft had been false. An uneasiness came over him that Captain Dargan had misappro-
priated the cotton, but this passed away, because the towboat and its barges would stand good for the loss. Then he
simply wondered if the draft had come? He began counting
up the days again. Then he thought how undependable New
Orleans people were. They drank coffee in bed before they
got up in the mornings. They danced all night. They were
a frivolous folk. Miltiades damned them for their general
inefficiency.

A thin man of medium height, wearing the baggy clothes
of a post-office employee, appeared walking along the opposite side of the creek.

Miltiades moved toward the edge of the creek, waving a
hand with an irrational feeling that the man might vanish
as unexpectedly as he had appeared.

"Mr. Landers! Oh, Mr. Landers!" he called above the
watery baritone of the stream.

The postmaster walked with head down and hands behind
him.

Now he looked up and around.

"Yes," he said, "what is it?"

He stood looking across the creek at Miltiades, as if he were completely at sea why anyone had called him.

"Will you let me in the post office?"

Landers collected himself.

"Do you want in right now?"

"Well . . . before long."

"I'm going to walk down the creek a way," said Landers; "I'll be there in about half an hour."

"Well . . . all right," called back Miltiades.

But when Landers resumed his musing posture and started forward once more, the habitual loneliness of the man impressed the Colonel.

What Landers had said about meeting him at the post office in half an hour was a lonely phrase. It implied that of course the Colonel would not want to walk back to town in Landers' company. Yet the fellow was granting him a favor. Suddenly it seemed boorish to accept it in such a fashion. The Colonel quickened his gait, paralleling the postmaster.

"Mr. Landers," he called, "you are going to the post office and so am I. . . . Wait there a minute. . . ."

The thin man stopped walking and sat down on a stone. The Colonel turned back to the bridge at a quick pace. As he went he reflected that never in his life had he seen a white man walk the streets with Landers. He half regretted his rashness. He would think up some good reason for separating from Landers when they reached the edge of town.

He joined the postmaster, commenting on the beauty of the day.

"They told me at the office you walked out here," explained the Colonel.

"I come out Sundays when the weather's good," said Landers, using a Northernism.

The Colonel really had very little to say to Landers.

"By yourself?" he inquired, and immediately hoped that Landers would not think that he meant nobody in Florence would walk with him, which was the truth.

The postmaster walked on for a space as if he had not heard the question, but finally gave the odd reply:

"I don't know."

The Colonel looked at him, rather surprised.

"You don't know whether you walk by yourself or not?"

Landers glanced at his companion and then said in a hesitant manner:

"Not with anybody on this side, of course."

"This side?"

"Yes . . . this side," nodded the postmaster in a very simple way.

"This side of . . . of . . . do you mean the creek?"

"Why, no, I mean . . . this side of the grave. . . . I'm glad you came along. I've often wanted to talk about it with somebody."

The Colonel walked for several moments in silence at being shifted so abruptly to this unusual mental plane. He felt the utter loneliness of this man who moved about imagining such extraordinary communications with never a person to mention them to.

"Don't you ever talk about it to . . ." the Colonel almost said "niggers" but changed it to "your friends?"

"No, they would just get nervous about it."

"Yes, I fancy they would," agreed Miltiades, and a wrinkle of mirth passed through his mind.

"So I hope," added Landers, "that you'll consider anything we talk about confidential."

"Certainly, certainly," agreed the Colonel, becoming interested in the postmaster's vagaries. "You say sometimes you are not alone?"

"No, I'm not," repeated Landers in matter-of-fact tones.

"Do you think—er—some particular person is with you?"

"My sister," nodded Landers.

"You have a feeling your sister is with you?"

"Well, she said she would be," explained the postmaster.

"She said she would . . . do you mean before she died?"

"No, afterwards . . . about a year ago."

"How did you know it was your sister?"

"I didn't. One day an old gentleman came to me in the post office and asked for his mail. I looked, and he didn't have any. Then he said, 'A woman wants to speak to you.' I said, 'Where is she?' He said, 'In the back part of your post office, where we can be by ourselves for a few minutes.' I looked around and didn't see anybody and asked what woman it was. The old man said her name used to be Ora Landers. Well, I looked at him for about a minute; then I said, 'Ora Landers was my sister. She is dead'; and the old man said, 'I know it.'

"I had the queerest feelings, of course. I said to him, 'I think you must be a humbug . . . or crazy'; but I opened the door and let him in."

"And what did he do?" asked Miltiades.

"Why, he said my sister wanted to tell me I was not by myself all the time like I thought I was, that she was with me whenever she could be, and I wouldn't be lonesome long."

Miltiades pondered this.

"Isn't that about the sort of thing those fellows always say?"

"I—I imagine so," agreed Landers vaguely; "nobody ever came up to me like that before."

"How much did he ask you for?" inquired the Colonel.

"Nothing. When we were through he walked out, and I never saw him again."

"Didn't get a cent out of you?"

"No."

Miltiades pondered a moment.

"Did he mention anything about politics?"

"No, just what I told you."

"It may have been a practical joker," hazarded the Colonel, "seeing you are so much alone."

"Ye-es . . ." hesitated the postmaster, "but he would have had to find out the name of my sister and that she was dead. Nobody in Florence knows I ever had a sister, or where I came from, or anything at all about me."

"M-m . . ." nodded the Colonel.

"What do you suppose he meant by my not being lonesome long?" asked the postmaster.

"Have you been . . . since?"

"Why, of course," said Landers.

"Then I suppose," said the Colonel with a skepticism which he did not altogether feel, "I suppose that was about like all the rest of it, and it didn't mean anything at all."

The postmaster was a little perturbed.

"You may be right. I suppose you are. You know when you first asked me if I walked here by myself I said I didn't know. I suppose I really am by myself, after all." He walked along frowning and pulling at his narrow chin.

"What did you think he meant?" inquired the Colonel, vaguely touched at the man's uncertainty and instant dejection.

"Why-y I . . . didn't know. I thought for a while maybe she meant I was going to meet some woman and get married; then I thought maybe she meant I was going to die."

The Colonel cheered him up briskly:

"Now, look here, a man of your age is a lot more likely to marry than he is to die. Then you lead such a retired, sober life, nothing's going to happen to you. . . . What made you think it was really your sister, anyway? . . . Did you take the whole thing on the old man's say-so?"

"Why . . . not exactly. . . ." The postmaster seemed a little uncertain and ill at ease. "I—I believe I'll tell you just what did happen. . . . I'd like to have your opinion on it. I've thought about it a good deal . . . if you don't mind?"

"Certainly," nodded Miltiades, wondering what was coming next.

"Well, I said, 'How do I know you are Ora?'"

"And she sort of laughed and said, 'Do you remember old Marth Killicut?' "

"Did she laugh and say this or did the old man do it?" probed the Colonel.

"Why, really, the old man, but I was considering him as Ora."

"I see. . . . Go ahead."

"I said, yes, I remember Marth Killicut.

"And she said, 'Yes, and you ought to be ashamed, Manuel, you gave her a little son.'

"Well, that sort of got me. I said, 'What do you mean, Ora—a little son?'

"And she said:

" 'It died before it was born. I've seen the little thing several times since.' "

Landers stopped and stood looking at the Colonel with a strained face.

"What do you make out of that?"

Miltiades shook his head blankly.

"Nothing at all. . . . Who was Marth Killicut?"

"A street walker I knew a long time ago. I had forgot all about her until the old man said I had given her a son."

"And he told you this son died before he was born?"

"That's what the old man said."

"He may have known Marth Killicut. She may have told him."

"How would she have known whose son it was? Why would she have picked out me?"

The Colonel stood faintly shaking his head.

"And he didn't ask you for any money?"

"No, when we got through, he walked out, just like I told you, and I've never seen him again."

The Colonel stood nodding faintly and looking at the postmaster.

"If he'd only tried to hold you up for some money . . . but he didn't do that. . . ."

CHAPTER SEVENTEEN

W̲HEN Miltiades and Landers reached the deep cut in the wooded hillside where the Waterloo road entered Pine Street, the Colonel said he had to stop by and see the Crowninshields a moment and so let the postmaster go on to the office alone.

Colonel Vaiden made a polite pretense of walking a little way toward the Crowninshield residence, but crossed to Market Street and went to the office paralleling Landers.

The odd story which Landers had told him continued to weave about the Colonel an aura of some other world than this which he could feel and touch and see. In the sunlight before him intangible beings might be moving and thinking and performing non-human errands of which the Colonel knew nothing.

A sudden outbreak of church bells burst on the Colonel's attention. The Episcopal, the Methodist, the Baptist, the Christian bells began ringing in different keys and timbres far and near. Within twenty or thirty minutes sermons would be preached about all sorts of things in these churches, and the Colonel thought, what if Landers should rise up and repeat his story to these congregations, what would they think of it? The Colonel smiled to fancy what they would think of it.

As Miltiades hurried on to the post office, he recalled a number of incidents of somewhat the same tenor that had happened in his own life. An old Methodist minister used to visit his father's house who had a gift of clairvoyance. This old preacher, Parson Mulry, had foretold the fall of Fort Sumter on the day the battle occurred. After the war, his own mother had waked up from a noonday nap weeping and saying that his brother Polycarp had been shot and killed, and sure enough he had. Now here was Landers with his strange tale.

The people on their way to church would not credit any such stories as these, but they would sit under their bells, and sing and pray and listen to ancient wonder tales with the greatest reverence. It was odd and rather droll.

Miltiades turned the corner at Courthouse Square in time to see Landers enter the post-office door. A few moments later, when the Colonel went into the lobby, he spoke to the postmaster as if he had not seen him before.

"Will you look in the general delivery, Mr. Landers, and see if any of my mail was put in there by mistake?"

Landers glanced at Miltiades' empty box, then turned to the general delivery and asked if Miltiades were expecting some special letter.

"Yes, I am," said the Colonel; "it ought to be here."

"When was it mailed?" inquired Landers, going through the "V" box and finding nothing in it.

"It should have been mailed day before yesterday," said Miltiades, looking at the empty box with a sudden desolation upon him.

Landers watched his patron's face with concern.

"Maybe Crowe knows something about it. . . . He came in to make up the northbound mail. . . . Crowe! Oh, Crowe! Do you know anything about a letter for Colonel Vaiden?"

From among the mail bags in the rear of the office Crowe called back:

"Yeh, he got one. I put it in the Handback lock box. The Colonel didn't have anything but a call box, and I knew he got the Handback mail, so I just put it in there over Sunday."

Miltiades leaned against the general delivery window. His mouth went dry.

"So . . . it's been taken out," he said in a low tone.

"Why, I suppose so." The postmaster moved out of sight of the Colonel.

Miltiades stood perfectly still with an internal trembling. His nerves tautened. Handback had his letter. He had probably opened it by mistake. If he noticed his name, he would surely see the New Orleans postmark and see the cotton broker's return address. He would have to suspect something. It would be before him like a signboard.

A sudden line of action came to the Colonel. He would go to Handback, get the draft, or kill the merchant. His heart beat. He was turning toward the lobby door, when Landers appeared at the general delivery window again. He pushed through a long envelope.

"Here it is," he said. "Nobody has come for the Handback mail."

As Miltiades took the envelope a curious wrath filled him.

"Will you tell your goddamned clerk," he snapped savagely, "that the reason I rented a box was to put my mail in."

Crowe's voice arose, explaining his act:

"Colonel, I knew you wanted your letter and we would all be out of the office Sunday morning."

"But, damn it, I told you every day for two weeks to put my mail in my box. I told you that a thousand times, and now . . . by God, I'll report such a damned fool . . . I'll report you to the Post Office Department."

"Colonel, he thought he was doing you a favor," mollified Landers.

"I don't give a whoop in hell what he thought! Why can't he follow instructions? The damned long-eared Republican jackass!"

He walked out of the door vibrating with a desire to commit mayhem on Crowe. For the idiot clerk to jeopardize the very thing he had been guarding and fending and protecting . . . damn such a fool!

The Colonel put the letter in his pocket and kept his hand over the pocket. He walked across the street, past the Florence Hotel, and stopped under one of the twisted, misshapen mulberry trees in front of Intelligence Row.

He stood behind a bole which had decayed into a wide, warped half shell with a bunch of mulberry sprouts growing out of it.

He opened the envelope with fingers that trembled lest they tear the enclosure.

Inside was a bill of sale and a draft for forty-eight thousand, seven hundred and fifty-one dollars and thirty-seven cents.

The draft was light blue. The figures and letters were a deeper blue and written in a clerkly hand. The Colonel stood looking and looking at it, breathing rapidly through his open mouth. Forty-eight thousand. . . .

The blood beat in his temples and throat.

The draft could not be cashed on Sunday. How much time Miltiades would have to cash it, he did not know. If Handback got a hint of it he might have the payment stopped in New Orleans. He, Miltiades, could not hope to draw such a sum from one of the Florence banks without investigation.

All these conditions flickered through Miltiades' head as marginal notes to the trembling, central satisfaction of his possession of the draft.

Then he began thinking more connectedly where he could possibly cash the draft and what he could say to the banker. He wished he had not cursed Walter Crowe for putting his envelope into the Handback box. It might cause Crowe to wonder what the letter contained.

The Colonel's reflections were disturbed by some negroes loitering up Intelligence Row, talking, guffawing, and slapping each other on the back.

When the black men saw Miltiades under the mulberry, they abruptly dropped their horseplay and moved past him in decorum.

The manner of the negroes caught the attention of the ex-overseer. He wondered why their sudden change. Was it something about him, or did they think that he knew something about them? Some knowledge somewhere had caused the black men to quiet down like that. Normally they would have exaggerated their horseplay in an effort to amuse a white onlooker. A suspicion went through the Colonel.

"Where have you boys started?" he asked casually.

"Jess gon' up de street, Col'l," said one of them, still moving past.

"Well, where have you been?"

"Jess down street. . . ."

"Did you come up from the landing?" he inquired more narrowly.

"Oh, no, suh," denied the spokesman at once.

"Did you come from the depot?"

"Col'l, we ain't come f'um anywha," explained another negro earnestly; "we is wha we allis is."

By this time they had drawn up to a gingery standstill before the Colonel because his manner and continued questioning forbade that they pass on by.

A suspicion that was blood brother to a certainty came over the Colonel.

"Look here, did any of you niggers ship on a towboat a week or so ago?"

"Which boat—de *Zebulon D.?*" asked a black man quickly.

"Yes, I believe that's her name," nodded the Colonel.

"No, suh!"

"No, suh, Col'l!"

"No, we din' ship on no *Zeb'lon D.*, Col'l Milt, we's reg'la' steamboat niggahs, we is!"

"Yes, suh, we all of us ship on de *Zeb'lon D.*," stated a brown man with a faint touch of antagonism in his voice.

An odd feeling as if Intelligence Row were sinking beneath him caught the Colonel.

"Weren't you hired for the whole trip down?" demanded Miltiades, looking at the black men in frustration.

"Oh, yes, suh," nodded a black man, eager to propitiate him.

"Well, how did you get back here so quick? Did you come today?"

"Yes, suh. . . ."

"No, suh. . . ."

"Yes, suh . . . we ain't come today."

"Well, damn it, when did you get here?"

"We been back heah 'bout a week, Col'l Milt."

"A week!"

"Isn't we been back 'bout a week, Fo' Spot?"

" 'Bout uh week. We come in Saddy night on de *Rapidan* . . . dat's 'bout uh week."

"How in the hell did you get back so quick?"

"Why . . . uh . . . we jump de *Zeb'lon D.* at Padjo, Col'l Milt," explained a black man unhappily.

"What made you jump her? How did you get paid off?"

Fo' Spot fumbled with his rag of a hat.

"W-well . . . de wh-whole crew, white an' black, got to shootin' craps at Padjo. An' us niggahs got broke an' needed some money. So Cap'n Dargan jess paid us off fuh de whole trip and busted us ag'in. 'N'en, of cose, us niggahs jump de boat an' come home."

"Craps! Craps!" said Miltiades shivering violently, "of all goddamned immoral games . . ."

"Yes, suh . . . craps," returned the black man sympathetically; "but, Col'l Milt, even if we is back, we still 'membahs what white man weighed us out a whole poun' of sugah un' coffee fuh ouah money an' what did'n'."

And with this vague encouragement the group shuffled on toward the hotel corner.

The discovery that every negro in town knew the facts about the Handback cotton dismayed the Colonel. And now, suddenly, he realized that in their eyes he was an arch thief. The way they quieted before him and gave him side glances showed that. All the negroes knew it, and hanging immediately over his head, like a knife just ready to drop, was the time when every soul in Florence, white and black, would know it, and then what was he to do?

The Colonel put his envelope into an inner pocket and straightened his shoulders.

"Well," he thought with a tang of defiance, "I have collected an old debt, and the niggers can look wall-eyed about it if they want to, and if anybody else wants to follow their —er—example, they can . . . start."

CHAPTER EIGHTEEN

Eᴀʀʟʏ Monday morning Colonel Miltiades Vaiden walked from his home on Cherry Street through the heart of town to the railroad station. He did not know the exact schedule of the train crossing the river to Sheffield and Tuscumbia. He had not ridden on a train since he had been to Arkansas fourteen years before to visit his brother Sylvester.

At that time he had considered settling in Arkansas, but he had not liked the water or the mosquitoes, or the buffalo gnats, or the bottomless mud, or the people, or the flatlands, so he had come back to Alabama.

Now, a journey of five or six miles on a train to Tuscumbia gave him a sense of novelty, and it shifted him to a place where he was not so well known.

The long spindling bridge across Tennessee River clacked its length beneath the car wheels. Midway the bridge the Colonel saw a flock of ducks high up against the sky, winging their way South against the coming winter. Miltiades watched their migrant "V," thinking whether he should get off in Tuscumbia or take a train on to New Orleans.

The New Orleans trip had popped into his head during the night. His draft was on a New Orleans bank. At this bank, all that would be necessary for the Colonel to do would be to identify himself and receive the money. From New Orleans he could travel on into Texas and lose himself.

But the mere connotation of Texas brought a wave of repugnance to Miltiades. Cattle, cowboys, Indians, bad men, ranchers, round-ups, gambling halls . . . he had no moral objection to any of these, but he had an objection of taste to them all. They were undignified. They had nothing in them of the grand manner which he admired and to which he was born. The very thought of Texas brought him a fore-shadowing of nostalgia for this rolling, wooded, historic land which unwound before the window of his car.

Ahead of him the locomotive shrieked, rattled through an outskirt of negro cabins, and presently drew up at the Shef-field station.

The Colonel was only four miles from his home but he had not seen Sheffield in such a long time the depot seemed strange to him. As the engine panted at the station a thought came to Miltiades that the Colbert county sheriff might possibly be waiting to step on the train. He looked out on the platform. The conductor stood talking to the station agent, and the crowd who had got off the cars moved on uptown. The conductor called all aboard, signaled the engineer, and swung up on the last car. The train jerked forward.

The Colonel settled into the tentative security of flight and addressed his thoughts once more to his probable fu-ture. What most disturbed him was the impulse he felt to run, to fly the country. He decided within himself that this was something he would not do.

Two miles farther on, the train slowed down for Tus-cumbia. Here is where he would have to buy his ticket for New Orleans if he went to New Orleans. He stepped off his car onto the platform with a kind of tightening of his nerves. He glanced at the ticket window with its notices to pas-sengers plastered up around it. And he turned away from it, thinking he would be damned if he ran away from his own country because he had collected an old debt.

There was an aged man standing on the platform tap-ping his cane against the boards. Miltiades went up to him.

"My name is Vaiden," he said. "Which is the best bank in Tuscumbia?"

The old man seemed not surprised.

"The Planters'," he said. "My name is Sully. I have heard of the Vaidens over about Florence."

"That's where I come from," said Miltiades.

Old man Sully blinked eyes that were faded with age.

"Are you any relation of old man Jimmie Vaiden?" he inquired.

"A son," said Miltiades.

"Well, well, I've heard a lot about old man Jimmie Vaiden . . . a great Baptist . . . and he'd pay you what he owed you. . . . How is your father?"

"He's dead," said Miltiades. "He's been dead twenty years."

"Is that so?" ejaculated old man Sully in a shocked tone. "Twenty years . . . I declare. . . . Well, he was an older man than I was." The old man came out of his reminiscing:

"Young man, what do you want with a bank, and can I help you anyway?"

The Colonel suddenly cast his die on the Planters' Bank in Tuscumbia.

"If you wanted to walk around and introduce me to the banker I'd appreciate it," he suggested tentatively.

"With pleasure! With pleasure. I've heard of the Vaidens all my life—which one are you?"

"Miltiades Vaiden."

"Oh! Oh, yes, I've heard of you. You are a power in the Klan."

"I was," said Miltiades, "when there was a Klan."

"Yes, yes, of course. . . . Well, Mr. Vaiden, I'll be very glad to do anything I can for you."

Old Mr. Sully turned about and started with the Colonel uptown. He extended the genial good-will of one old Alabama family for another, although between the two clans no personal friendship had ever existed.

They knew much of each other, however. Miltiades recalled that a nephew of this old man had been killed in the first battle of Manassas. And old Mr. Sully told how a Vaiden back in South Carolina had married a Sully, one of his own great-uncles. And so, before the two had reached the Planters' Bank they were kinsmen, as nearly always happens when two Southerners meet and talk for fifteen minutes.

The president and acting cashier of the Planters' Bank was a Mr. Knoblett, a Northern man. As Miltiades and old Mr. Sully entered they met Mr. Knoblett escorting a woman in black out the door. He was saying:

"Now, you are sure you don't mind parting with the canteen, Mrs. Jason?"

"Oh, no, we don't use it for anything around home . . . it leaks."

"Well, that doesn't matter for my purposes. Good-afternoon. Gentlemen, what can I do for you?"

Old man Sully cleared his throat.

"Mr. Knoblett," he quavered genially, "this is Mr. Miltiades Vaiden. He asked me for the best bank in town, so I brought him here."

"That's correct," agreed Knoblett in his clipped Northern voice.

"I told him you was a damned Yankee, but us Tuscumbia folks didn't hold that against you when you were lending us money, but we sure did when you come to try to collect."

Knoblett and old man Sully fell to laughing.

"That's natural, that's perfectly natural. Mr. Sully. Was Mr. Vaiden considering a loan?"

"No," said Miltiades, beginning to feel his heart against his ribs, "I came by to cash a draft."

"Oh, I see," nodded Knoblett, going back to his cage.

Old man Sully turned toward the door.

"And, Mr. Vaiden," he called by way of adieu, "if you've got an old uniform, or scabbard, or bayonet, anything at all left over from our late unpleasantness, don't let Knoblett find it out, or he'll talk you out of it."

"A uniform or bayonet," repeated Miltiades in a puzzled tone.

"It's just old man Sully taking a shot at my collection," said Knoblett. "I'm a bachelor. I live in a big house and I have to fill it full of something."

"Confederate bayonets and uniforms?" queried Miltiades.

"And letters and discharges and shoes and haversacks—anything the Confederate soldiers used."

"What are you making your collection for?"

"Don't ask me why men collect things. Trying to make today big enough to include our yesterdays, I suppose. If that isn't the reason, then only the Lord knows why I collect."

"You remind me a little bit of a Kentuckian I knew in the army," said Miltiades; "his name was Bloodgood."

Knoblett laughed.

"By the time men get to be of our age, Mr. Vaiden, about all any new acquaintance can do is to remind them of somebody else. You know at times I have thought that is why we die. We become more and more intricately linked with the past, until finally we drift completely into it . . . and we are dead."

Miltiades regarded the Northern man with one of those sudden inexplicable sympathies.

"You should have married," he smiled: "it would have given you much better reasons for death."

The banker laughed.

"That doesn't sound like Southern gallantry. . . . How much is your draft for?"

Miltiades hesitated for a moment, and then said:

"Forty-eight thousand dollars . . . and a few cents."

Mr. Knoblett, who was behind his cage and had pulled his cash drawer open, let his hands rest on the till.

"Let me see your draft."

Miltiades drew it out with fingers that tingled.

Knoblett looked at it.

"I'll have to telegraph for an acceptance of that amount."

"Where to?"

"To the bank it's drawn on."

"Well . . . that's all right."

His relief that the telegram was to go to New Orleans and not to Florence was in his voice.

"How are you going to want it?"

"In as big bills as you've got."

"We haven't any very big bills . . . never use them. . . . I might get you a few at the other bank. . . . You will have to pay for the telegram."

"Oh that's all right," agreed Miltiades with a flicker of amusement at this Yankeeish penny-counting.

The Colonel was inexpressibly relieved that the investigation was directed toward the paying end of the draft and not its origin.

Knoblett came out of his cage.

"It'll be an hour or so before we hear from our telegram, why not come around to my house? I'd like to show you the silver cup General Robert E. Lee used during his last campaign around Richmond."

The banker's collection of Confederate relics brought about a subtle disturbance in Miltiades' thoughts. The old canteens and muskets and swords, a stand of battle-torn colors, restated to him the dignity, good faith, and honor of that cause for which once he had fought. The collection made a silent commentary on the enterprise in which the Colonel now was engaged.

The two men spent over an hour and a half in the museum. Knoblett, with a Yankee's inquisitiveness, had learned the personal history of each piece he possessed. A belt had been worn by a private soldier named Henry Jones through the Shenandoah campaign. These colors were borne by General Wilder's brigade at Chickamauga. Here was Lemuel Peters' discharge at Appomattox. A simple collection attended by simple histories.

An odd thing was, the mute reproach of the collection did not in the faintest degree move Miltiades to alter his design. It was as if some second person in the Colonel stood shocked and dismayed at the height from which he had fallen; but these emotions were entirely cut off from his actions.

Later, in the vault of the Planters' Bank, when Knoblett

actually was packing bills into a valise which the Colonel had bought, all these feelings vanished.

"You have had a very successful year," observed the banker, fitting the packages into the leather bag with a cashier's carefulness.

"The most successful of my life," nodded Miltiades with an inward touch of humor.

"I congratulate you," said Knoblett.

The answers Miltiades made to the banker's commonplaces seemed spoken by another person. He himself stood looking at the money in a kind of concentration. Presently he would take the valise to the station. Then how he would dispose of the wealth disturbed him.

"I particularly wanted it like this," said Miltiades. "I want to offer actual bills to a man for his plantation."

"Excellent psychology," said the banker, handing the Colonel the valise, "you should have been a Yankee, Mr. Vaiden."

The valise was heavier than Miltiades had expected it to be. Knoblett drove the Colonel almost down to the station and then suggested that Miltiades walk around the street corner onto the platform in order not to appear as having come from a bank with a new valise.

"I don't believe anybody can get it away from me," said the Colonel.

The thing that reached Miltiades even through the mist of greenbacks was Knoblett's concern about the money. The banker wished strongly for the Colonel to have the money and keep it. Miltiades felt he could be friends with the Yankee.

There were two trains out of Tuscumbia within the hour: a train going south and a local going back to Florence. Miltiades walked up and down the track, well away from the group on the platform, after the manner of nervous travelers. He was thinking how to safeguard his money. It was a completely new problem to him. What to do with a valise full of illegal bills?

Several dispositions passed through his head: burying them in the earth; depositing them in some bank under an assumed name; going to Texas, where all men were lost in anonymity. These plans flickered before his mind as he walked up and down the track at the far end of the platform away from the crowd. He shifted the valise from one hand to the other.

The train appeared, a spot, far down the rails. The Colonel glimpsed a tongue of white; thirty seconds later came the blast of a passenger train. The train rushed up to the station with a clashing rhythm, a smell of smoke and heated oil. Miltiades knew it was the southbound for Birmingham. He went over to a brakeman and asked:

"Is this the Birmingham train?"

The brakeman said:

"Yes, you've just got time to get your ticket."

Miltiades stood looking at the train, thinking he could buy a ticket and go south on it. The brakeman gave him a half amused second look and then forgot him. He was accustomed to travelers acting in an imbecile manner when the train arrived at a station.

Some decision within the Colonel, which he did not recognize, kept him looking at the train and thinking that if he wanted to he could now go south.

Slim Bivins came off the train, handed his grip and sample case to a negro porter, and started uptown. The express pulled out of the station, and presently the local backed in, looking very small and rusty after the roar and glitter of the southbound. Miltiades stepped automatically aboard with his valise and after a few moments was rattling home again.

As he rode back with puffs of coal smoke eddying through the car window he began inventing reasons for his return. If he were arrested and jailed, he would make better wages in jail than he had ever made before in his life. The sentence could not be longer than two or three years, that would be sixteen thousand dollars a year. Then it would be all over;

he could spend the rest of his life in peace. He was going back because he had a legitimate claim against Handback and would not fly the country because he had collected it. He was going back because he would not leave Ponny in her condition. He thought of reason after reason for his return.

When the train crossed the river and drew up at the depot, the necessity of doing something with the fortune became imperious. The valise in his hands must be put down somewhere. But everywhere he could think seemed an impossible hiding place. The moment a breath of his coup leaked out, Handback would overrun Florence with search warrants. He, Miltiades, would be landed in jail, and then the trial would begin.

A hotel bus in front of the station garnered in a few travelers at twenty-five cents a head. The driver did not flag Miltiades. He was a home-town man, and home-town men knew the station was not as far away from the business section of Florence as the bus driver shouted.

Miltiades did not even see the bus. He was remembering that during the Yankee invasion the Southern whites entrusted their valuables to their black slaves. No white man ever found what a negro hid; the white psychology of finding never paralleled the black psychology of hiding. The thousandth twinge of anger and frustration went through Miltiades that the negroes were ever set free; that the peculiar services which the black folk could render their white masters were lost.

As Miltiades walked along the road with his valise he saw free negroes, as useless as free horses, walking to and fro, and him with forty-eight thousand dollars to safeguard somehow. The irony of the situation bit at the Colonel's nerves.

The road from the depot led at first eastward to the Florence–Sheffield road, then northward into Market Street. Miltiades walked to the main thoroughfare, but instead of turning north he continued straight along a secondary road that led to East Florence. He walked for some distance in complete concentration. After he had gone for perhaps a quarter of a mile he stopped before a gate hung between two gateposts but with no other sign of a fence. He called to whomever lived in the shack behind the gate. A negro woman began complaining:

"Who is dat callin'? Hello, what you want?"

A coffee-colored woman came to the door and then gasped out:

"Oh, is dat you, Col'l Milt! Scuse me, Col'l Milt!"

"Where does Gracie live?" asked the Colonel in a taut voice.

"Rat on up dat way!" Miss Tony pointed hurriedly. A number of small heads, kinky or curly, peered past the woman's skirts. The dark woman shoved their faces backwards with concealed violence.

"You fool young 'uns," she whispered furiously, "does you want to git killed?"

The Colonel suddenly had become the most terrible being a negro woman knows—a white outlaw.

CHAPTER NINETEEN

WHEN Colonel Vaiden reached Gracie's cottage its whiteness and neatness touched the visitor with the ironic fact that his family's former slave lived in a better house than his own.

He rapped on the panel; then, without giving time for an answer, opened the door, entered the hallway, and knocked again peremptorily. His impulse was to storm into the cottage, jerk open closed doors, and shout, "Gracie! Where the devil are you!" But in reality he stood inside, reaching back and rapping on the shutter impatiently.

An inner door opened, and Gracie came out. Her eyes were full of one kind of questioning which changed to another kind when she saw who it was.

"Why, Colonel Milt!" she gasped. "What's happened?"

She saw the new leather case and knew this had something to do with her. A fear went through her mind that it contained pistols and ammunition; that the Colonel was fleeing from officers and had come for her to hide him.

"Gracie, I've got this thing." He swung the valise a bit. "I want you to take care of it for me."

His tone took instant and unquestioning possession of her.

"Till you come for it?" She looked apprehensively at the bag.

"Yes. . . . Here it is—where you going to hide it?"

"I . . . don't know . . . up in the loft I suppose . . . Nobody ever goes up in the loft."

"I want it kept safe," said the Colonel, "it's important . . . it's money!"

"Law, Col'l Milt!" The cream-colored woman began to tremble.

"Can you put it up in the loft? . . . It's heavy."

"I don't know. . . ."

Gracie came forward to take the bag, but she was so shaken she could hardly lift it. She knew perfectly well that the money belonged to Handback, that Miltiades had stolen it.

"Oh, my Jesus," thought the quadroon, "here he comes again, knocking me out of my place." As she took the bag and carried it into the kitchen she thought, "This'll get me into terrible trouble! I know it'll do it! In the kitchen I'll tell him I can't do it!"

She walked into the kitchen, trying to hold the bag away from her as if it were venomous. Every moment she planned to turn around and tell him she couldn't hide his bag.

The Colonel's rush pushed them both hurriedly into the kitchen.

There was a little square manhole through the ceiling, above the stove. Gracie seized her broom and began knocking it open with the handle. The Colonel watched her.

"I don't believe anybody will think to look up there," he said, staring at the manhole.

"I reckon not," said Gracie, in despair at what she was doing.

"If anybody asks you, tell 'em you don't know anything about it."

"Mr. Milt!" cried Gracie, "what do you want with so much for, anyway?"

"There, it's giving," said the Colonel. "Put your broom handle through the crack and prize . . . that's right . . . now get up on the stove and the table and put it through."

Gracie touched the heater.

"The stove's still hot."

"Lay a paper on it. . . . You won't stand there long."

Gracie did this, then lifted the bag from the floor to the table, and got up on the table and the stove.

Miltiades helped push up the bag with the straw end of the broom, while Gracie strained to lift it in the manhole.

The stove heated the sole of her shoe and began to burn her foot. She toppled the bag up into the ceiling.

"Away from the stovepipe! Away from it!" prompted the Colonel sharply.

Gracie worked at the bag so it would fall over the rafter away from the stovepipe. She jerked her foot off the stove and made shift to stand on the table.

"Put the cover back on the manhole."

"Lay something else on the stove, Col'l Milt, I can't put my foot on it any more."

"Here's a stick of stove wood."

The cream-colored woman put her foot on the stick and then readjusted the cover, working it down tightly with the blade of a case knife.

"Now, that'll do," said Miltiades, drawing a long breath and scrutinizing the ceiling.

Gracie got down awkwardly, trying to keep her weight off of her burned foot.

"Col'l Milt," she said, looking terrified at the ceiling, "won't that get you into lots of trouble?"

"I don't know," said Miltiades. "I suppose I'll find out."

"Col'l Milt, whatever made you do it to begin with?" she asked, overwhelmed by the magnitude of her former master's swindle.

"Do what?" asked Miltiades, with a faint, sardonic sense of humor.

Gracie could insinuate what she knew, but she could not speak of it openly.

"Well . . . you having so much money," replied the quadroon vaguely. She thought a moment and then asked, "What will I say you come here for, Col'l Milt?"

"If anybody saw me, they can guess what they want to."

Miltiades spent another minute in the kitchen, estimating the probability of fire from the pipe. Now that the manhole was closed it seemed as if the bag lay immediately against the stovepipe.

"Now, Gracie," he directed, "I am depending upon you to keep absolutely quiet about this."

"You know I'm not going to say anything," said Gracie gloomily.

"I mean inadvertently—by accident," impressed Miltiades.

He walked slowly to the kitchen door, opened it, and let himself out the back way.

Gracie watched him go with her heart beating heavily in her chest. She felt sick. Her foot, she believed, was blistered. She limped to a chair, sat down, and took off her shoe. The bottom of her foot had become filmed and glazed from the heat, but it was not blistered. It stung, but it would amount to nothing.

She made these observations while the body of her thought forecast unhappily what the future would bring and what had happened to her in the past through Miltiades.

It was Miltiades, long ago, who had forced her child upon her and this child finally had broken off her concubinage with General Beekman. She had persisted in keeping Toussaint, so Beekman had sent her away from Montgomery back to Florence. Now she had found an even, unemotional haven in this cottage which Handback had given her, and Miltiades had caught her up again and was using her under compulsion.

She had tried not to let him use her, long ago, in the stable loft, but she had been his slave. Today, in her cottage, she had become his servant again. She could not prevent him. His entrance and exit had been as brusque and matter of course as ever they had been on the old Vaiden place, when she was a slave girl in her white father's family.

She put some vinegar and soda on her foot, and the pain went away.

CHAPTER TWENTY

Wɪᴛʜ Miltiades the thought of Gracie lingered a bare moment after he stepped out of her door. She lived in a better house than he did: that was ludicrous. The heart of his thought was his money. Was it safe? Suppose some un-foreseen thing happened to him; suppose he did not get back for his money for a term of years, how safe was Gracie's stewardship?

The phrase, "a term of years," banished the quadroon woman completely from the Colonel's mind. He walked along the road from East Florence to Old Florence with a pre-monition of a dolorous journey that might be ahead of him.

He imagined himself walking like this in a shameful garb at shameful toil. Very well, suppose he allowed that he might be imprisoned . . . that he would be imprisoned. Would that change anything in him? Would he not retain his integrity as a Vaiden through a penal sentence? Fortune, luck, could not minify the deep reality of himself.

The Colonel admitted the possibility of being sent to the coal mines. He began dividing forty-eight thousand dollars by three, four, five, six. If they sentenced him for five years, he would be drawing nine thousand dollars a year during his imprisonment. He had never earned that much in his life.

But this wage depended upon Gracie. If she should appro-priate the money while he was under restraint . . . he put the idea out of his mind by saying aloud, "She's a Vaiden."

He did not mean by this that she was of the actual white Vaiden blood. He did not know that this was true. He meant that she was a unit of the old Vaiden ménage; that through the past the Vaiden blacks had always helped the Vaiden whites. They had helped them wring a living from the reluctant hills; they had helped them resist the assaults and imprisonments and thieveries of the Yankee invasion. Now, in this final stroke to reëstablish the Vaiden fortune, he felt sure that Gracie Vaiden would remain loyal to him. She was a Vaiden.

A band playing in the distance brought the Colonel out of his planning. He was entering Old Florence. The drums and brasses of the far-off music came to him not as sound but as a rhythmic pressure in his ears out of which arose the incomplete cadenzas of the trumpets. For a moment the Colonel wondered the occasion of the music, then relapsed into his own meditations again.

Where the East Florence road merged into Market Street, the makings of a crowd were moving with the Colonel toward Courthouse Square.

Presently someone clapped the Colonel's shoulder and called in blustery humor:

"Colonel, I was just looking for you. I went around to the store, and they told me you had flew the coop."

Miltiades blinked his eyes and reëntered the world about him.

"Yes, I've quit the store."

"When am I going to rent you that house you was talking about?"

Miltiades thought of his improved but precarious circumstances.

"You probably won't rent it."

Bradley closed an eye against his cigar smoke.

"Oh, come now, don't say that, unless you mean I'm going to sell it to you instead of rent it."

"When I'm out of a job it isn't much of a time to talk selling to me."

Bradley was an astute man. Now, when the Colonel alluded to his loss of a job and pleaded poverty, the real-estate agent immediately scented money somewhere. Bradley was astonished at this, and not absolutely certain, but it did sound as if the Colonel, somehow or other, had come into some money.

"Now, see here," he began earnestly, "if you should want to buy, I can put you in connection with any piece of property you take a fancy to. I'll make you a figger on any damn house in town you want."

"I don't want any house," repeated Miltiades with less patience.

"If you do want a house," said Bradley.

The real-estate man felt in his pocket among an assortment of cheroots, cheap cigars, and ordinary cigars. He offered the Colonel a cigar.

"Smoke this and make up your mind what you want."

The Colonel bit the end off it, and Bradley lighted it for him.

"What's the band playing for?" asked Miltiades.

The real-estate man stared as if the Colonel had taken leave of his senses.

"For the Democratic rally, of course. . . . Tomorrow's election day."

"Oh . . . yes . . . of course." Miltiades had a doped feeling as if election day had happened a long time ago.

"We're bound to win," pæaned Bradley. "Wall Street's betting five to three on Cleveland. When a Democrat steps in the White House, I expect to get my share of the flush times that are bound to follow."

"I imagine all of us will," said Miltiades.

"Sure. And they're already on the way. Do you know what I've been doing?"

"No, I don't."

"Been to East Florence to see about a site for a fertilizer factory. Got a commission out of the mail this morning to pick out a factory site. Think of that, a big thing like a fertilizer factory! I say Hurray for Cleveland, by God!"

Bradley waved his hat and fell to laughing.

The ebullience of Bradley caught Miltiades up, and the Colonel walked on home elated over the coming political rebirth of the South. This would be the first Democratic President since the war. It seemed a miracle that a man representing the sentiments of the Southern people should ascend to the control of the whole country. It was as if the gray armies of the confederacy had arisen from lost fields to march on to an ultimate victory. The final answer to illiterate black voters who, a few years ago, had swarmed to the polls and forced the white men to stand aside; the final answer was, a Democratic President!

The autumn day caught up the splendor of the Colonel's mood. The oaks on the college campus flung crimson leaves down the wind.

At the very moment that he walked along Market Street, fortune beckoned from every house and vacant lot. All one had to do now was to buy something and float to wealth on the swelling prices of a coming prosperity.

And he, Colonel Miltiades Vaiden, had maneuvered himself into position to found a great family fortune. If only he could proceed freely to use the money in his hands. But the moment the negroes let loose the secret of the towboat, the Handbacks would give him a lot of trouble. They would surely seize any property he might purchase.

The Colonel thought of buying property in his wife's name, but that would be too transparent. The courts would set that aside.

As Miltiades turned off toward Cherry Street, a very extraordinary idea struck him: to go to Handback and have it out with him. Settle it one way or the other. The plan was as imprudent as a jump in the dark, but the simple belligerence of the idea appealed to the Colonel. To go to Handback and have it out! He kept turning the notion over and over, looking at it with a kind of quiver of anticipation.

When the Colonel reached home, Ponny had the twelve o'clock meal ready. She was curious to know where he had been, and he said Tuscumbia.

His fat wife looked at him blankly.

"Did somebody give you a ride over there?"

"No, I went on the train."

"You went on the—— Why, Mr. Milt, what on earth did you want to go to Tuscumbia for?"

The Colonel began telling her about Knoblett and his collection of relics.

Ponny hadn't the slightest interest in the collection.

"The idyah of you just going over to Tuscumbia!" Ponny couldn't understand it. "Dinner's ready. . . . Mr. Milt, you're goin' to haff to get me a nigger. Cookin' gets my breath. . . . How much did it cost you?"

"The round trip was thirty-eight cents."

"Well . . . I don't see . . ." She stopped talking and moved heavily into the kitchen.

"Ponny, I think I can promise you a nigger to help you in the near future," said Miltiades.

"Well . . . I'm going to haff to have one. . . . I got some turnups this mornin'."

"Who from?"

"Buck Mosely brought 'em. . . . I was wonderin' if we couldn't get one of Buck's girls to do our work. Maybe we wouldn't have to pay her anything, coming off your own place . . . jest feed and clothe her."

"I could take that up with Cassandra."

"I know Cassandra wouldn't care. I kain't see what in the world made you go to Tuscumbia."

An impulse to tell Ponny the whole story came to the Colonel. He cast about for words to begin, but what he had done suddenly appeared as untellable. He could not start.

The fat woman had studied her husband's face for twenty years.

"Mr. Milt, what's the matter?" she asked uneasily.

He drew in a breath to say:

"I'm going down to Handback's to have it out with him," but he changed it to:

"Nothing, nothing at all, Ponny. . . . I've got to go - owntown again after dinner. I may not be back till late."

"How late?"

"I don't know. I'll be back as soon as I can."

He thought again:

"Damn it, I ought to tell her. . . . Suppose somebody else should tell her. . . ." He broke off his own thought with a disturbed feeling.

He finished his dinner, entertaining the fat woman with an account of how Bradley had tried to sell him a house.

"And he may do it some day, sooner than you imagine, perhaps," nodded the Colonel.

"Well, he could be pretty slow and do that," said Ponny.

That afternoon, when the Colonel started for town again, a countryman in a dilapidated buggy picked him up on Market Street.

Immediately he regretted getting into the buggy. The Colonel wanted to think about what he was going to say to Handback, but the countryman talked all the way downtown. He said he had picked Miltiades up because the Vaidens were country folks just like he was. He said he wouldn't pull a derned stuck-up little town johnny out of a mud hole. He said he was coming in town the day before the election because, by Gad, he didn't intend to come to the election itself tomorrow. He said the thievish Republicans was shore to steal the election anyway, and he didn't want to give them the satisfaction of killing his vote. The old man's talk creaked on like a water mill.

All Miltiades could think of was Handback . . . Handback . . . but he could plan nothing at all of what he was about to do.

Downtown, the Colonel climbed out of the buggy on Market Street and turned off for the store.

A larger crowd of negroes than usual stood before the entrance of the Handback store. The nearness of the election had brought them to town. They kept up the usual stir of black folk, some jigging, some talking loudly, some preternaturally grave.

The crowd recalled to Miltiades' mind the first day he had

ever come to the store as a clerk, and now here he was, after many fortuities, walking in for a final accounting.

As he moved through the crowd, one old negro thrust a bucket into his hand and said:

"Col'l, I been waitin' fuh you. . . . I want some lard."

"I've quit the store," said Miltiades without glancing around. "I don't work here any more."

The black man dropped behind him, mumbling:

"Sho' is sorry to heah dat. . . . Now dey ain't no *way* to git nothin' out o' dis sto'."

The dark interior of the store was swarming with black customers. Love and Stebbins were wrapping up goods and computing the balances on due bills.

At the notion counter a negro was blowing a melancholy tune on a mouth harmonica to see if he wanted to buy it. He played a wailing melody with a queer snoring accompaniment. Even in the midst of the milling negroes the music somehow suggested night and a morass and some lost traveler calling for help.

The tune harassed the Colonel's keyed-up mood. He was about to speak to the black boy when Lucius Handback said:

"Damn it, nigger, buy the harp or put it back."

The negro reluctantly put it back in the box.

The railed-off bookkeeper's pen in the rear of the store was unoccupied. When Miltiades saw this a surge of relief went through his nerves, and only then did he realize how much he dreaded his interview with J. Handback. He thought to himself:

"I'll go home. I don't know when he'll be in. I can't be waiting here indefinitely."

He had an impulse to walk quickly to the door, but he did not do it. He moved back deliberately, he had no reason to hurry.

Dalrymple Love caught sight of him and called genially:

"Hello, Colonel, come back to help us out?"

"No, just dropped in to see Mr. Handback a minute."

"He's out," said Love.

"Drop around another time. . . . You boys getting on all right?"

"We set up at night," laughed Love.

"What do you mean . . . sit up at night?" The Colonel was really curious.

"Watching for burglars."

"What burglars?"

"Well, they're in the papers. Me and Stebbins figger if they come to Florence we'll ketch 'em an' git the reward."

A negro standing near began laughing.

"Settin' up to ketch bu'glahs, white boy, yo' *re*ward gwi' be a coffin."

"There's Mr. Handback now," said Love; then he raised his voice:

"Mr. Handback, here's the Colonel come to see you."

"Well . . . well," said the merchant in an odd tone, advancing toward Miltiades through his black customers, "I was just wanting to see you, Colonel."

"That's good," said Miltiades, hoping the merchant had not heard about the cotton.

"Let's go back to the desk," said the merchant.

Handback had changed in the weeks since Miltiades had left him. His face was whiter, his eyes were not so full, his features were drawn, and he seemed grayer about the temples.

When the two were safely behind the rail, the merchant looked at his former clerk intently.

"Bradley tells me you have come into a lot of money," he said in a queer tone.

"Bradley!" echoed Miltiades, trying to think of some negro named Bradley. "What's Bradley?"

"Why, the real-estate man!" snapped Handback. "You know Bill Bradley!"

"Why does he say I have a lot of money?" demanded the Colonel, who did not even recall talking to Bradley.

"I don't know, but he thinks you have."

"How come him to mention me at all?" demanded Miltiades, excited and puzzled.

"He was after me about that damned shoe store. I told him I didn't have the money, and he said, 'Why don't you borrow the money from your old clerk?'"

Of a sudden Miltiades guessed that Handback somehow had got wind that he had money and now he wanted to borrow it. A twitch of irony went through the Colonel's mood.

"I haven't any money," he said, "and if I had, I would remember the money I let you have once, Mr. Handback."

"I am not wanting to *borrow* it," stressed Handback elaborately. "I was thinking about you last night. I was wondering how I could pay even part of my debts and keep my business going, and you popped into my head. The way you left me down at the river, so damned careful of my feelings . . . then today Bradley saying you had come into some money . . ."

Handback paused, looking intently at the Colonel.

"Is that why you wanted to see me," snapped the Colonel. "because you thought of me last night, and Bradley mentioned me this morning?"

"Not by a long shot. I went out among the niggers and begun inquiring about my cotton. Nobody knew anything about it till I struck Fo' Spot. He said maybe it was washed away and maybe a towboat took it. I said, 'What makes you think a towboat took it?' He said, 'Well, one thing, I he'p load it on the *Zeb'lon D.*'" The merchant began a sort of laugh. "That was one thing that made him think it."

A quiver of the pleasure and the power of anger swept through the Colonel.

"That's exactly what I came here to tell you," he nodded crisply. "I'm damned glad Fo' Spot saved me the trouble."

"To tell me!"

"Hell, yes, what else would I want to see you for?"

There was a silence. Handback began trembling.

"Where is the money, Milt?"

The Colonel leaned across and tapped the smaller man on the chest.

"It's . . . paying . . . for . . . the cotton . . . you
. . . stole . . . from . . . me . . . right . . . after
. . . the . . . war."

The shorter man swore an oath and jerked open a drawer
in his desk. Miltiades jammed an arm into the open drawer
and felt a pistol. At that moment the drawer rammed shut
on his hand, and Handback struck him, full swing, on the
head.

A gong-like ring and flames of fire filled the Colonel's
ears and eyes. With his free hand he caught the smaller
man's throat.

An odd fight ensued: Handback pounding at Miltiades'
face and jamming the drawer shut on his hand; Miltiades
jerking at the pistol in the drawer and sinking his fingers
into the merchant's throat.

At the fight under the bright illumination the whole store
fell into an uproar. Negroes yelled. A voice shouted:

"Colonel's got a gun!"

And black men scrambled and fought to get to the door.

Behind the notion counter Lucius Handback jerked open
the cash drawer and got another revolver. Miltiades saw
the son running toward his father with the weapon. He
swung Handback around and succeeded in jerking his hand
out of the drawer, but left the pistol in it.

He began backing Handback to the gate in the railing.
Lucius was right on them, watching for a shot. He pushed
his revolver past his father's body. . . . At that moment
a large negro caught the youth from behind. The pistol fired
through the skylight. Lucius was now cursing and trying
to shoot the negro who had him in his arms.

The colored man, frightened in his turn, was yelling:

"Hol' on! Hol' on, Mistuh Lucius! Don' shoot me! Don'
shoot de Col'l!"

Miltiades jounced Handback before him toward the door.

A man with a policeman's star forced his way through
the pandemonium. He made toward Miltiades and Handback.

"Here, you're under arrest," he shouted. "Stop that! What in the hell are you two old men fighting about?"

"He's a thief!" yelled Handback. "That cotton that washed away! He stole ever' bale of it!"

"Stole it!" cried the officer, coming up and stopping the men.

"Shipped it out on a towboat!"

"The Colonel did! Why, Mr. Handback, you're bound to be wrong!"

"I collected a debt he's been owing me ever since he bankrupted twenty years ago!" quivered Miltiades.

"Well, well, gentlemen!" cried the officer, amazed. "I'll have to arrest you both."

He noticed the negro still holding desperately to Lucius and the pistol.

"What the hell are you doing, nigger?" he shouted.

The officer strode over and struck the negro on the head with his billy.

"You black hound, fighting a white man! Come on with me!"

Lucius wheeled to fire, but the policeman grabbed his arm.

"Don't kill him! He deserves it, but don't kill him!"

The policeman took the negro and marched him toward the door.

"I'll have to ask you gentlemen to come along with me," he said to the two white men.

"I came here to tell Handback I had collected the debt he owed me," panted the Colonel; "he got mad and tried to shoot me!"

"You're the damnedest liar that ever spoke!" cried the merchant.

The Colonel struck at the merchant again, but the policeman stopped him.

CHAPTER TWENTY-ONE

WHEN the officer and his three prisoners arrived at the police court, the crowd which followed them reached around two blocks. Stragglers in the tail of the procession inquired of those farther up what all the disturbance was about. The man addressed would fling back some such exciting information as:

"J. Handback shot Colonel Vaiden!"

"Caught him stealin'!"

"My God, you don't mean to say *he* was the burglars!"

"Must have been! We got to hurry if we get a seat in the courtroom!"

This last statement was correct. There were no seats left in the courtroom. Men already had hurried and filled up the benches. They lined the walls like a regiment. Countrymen with the habits of the field hunkered down on their toes in the aisles as if they were there for the day.

When the policeman and his prisoners entered the courtroom it was full. The officer was vaguely embarrassed to have to bring in Colonel Vaiden and J. Handback, the wealthiest man in town.

"I've sent for the mayor," he said; "he'll be here in a minute."

The Colonel looked around the room at the faces. Outside the door he could see them piled on top of each other, peering inside. He could sense how amazed everyone was that he was in trouble. He had never been arraigned in court before. The only trial in which he had ever had a part was that of his dead brother Polycarp. Now the thought of Polycarp's trial came back to him and then faded away again, leaving him in the police court facing his own.

217

A queer, disagreeable satisfaction filled Miltiades at this violent outcome of his project. It was the satisfaction of a man who will at last have a question settled one way or the other. He did not look at J. Handback, but could feel the merchant looking at him.

Presently there was a pushing in the crowded doorway. Voices called out, "Here's the mayor! Make way for Mayor Dibble!" There was a great pushing near the door to let him through.

The mayor was a tall thin man with an emaciated face and reddish eyes. Now he entered the courtroom looking at the prisoners with concern and astonishment in his lined face.

When the policeman saw him the officer ordered the squatters to clear the aisle and let the mayor through.

Mayor Dibble got to the magisterial chair on the platform and looked at the negro.

"What's the nigger doing in this case?" demanded Dibble.

"Why, he was scuffling with Lucius Handback," charged the officer.

"What's your name?" asked the mayor of the negro.

"Loob Snipes," said the negro in a quick voice.

"Whose nigger are you?"

"I works fuh Mistah Han'back," said Loob.

"And you were scuffling with Mr. Lucius Handback!" cried the judge in surprise.

"Well, looky heah, Jedge, dish here was de way hit was. . . ."

The whole courtroom was already weary of the negro's case; they wanted to get on with the white men's cases.

"Look here, nigger, who's going to pay your fine," inquired the judge, "if you were fighting Lucius Handback and you're a Handback nigger?"

Miltiades spoke up.

"I'll pay his fine. That nigger kept Lucius Handback from shooting me with a pistol. That's all he was doing, Mayor, keeping Lucius Handback from killing me."

"Let him off with five dollars and the cost," said the

mayor. "Now, what's the charge against these gentlemen?"

The negro was straightway forgotten.

"They were fightin'," said the officer; "they were 'ras'lin' with each other when I come in the store and settled 'em."

"What was the cause?" asked the mayor, addressing both men at once.

"Vaiden, there, stole all that cotton I thought had washed away two or three weeks ago!" cried the merchant, shaking a finger at his former clerk.

"I simply collected an old debt he owed me!" declared Miltiades.

"That's an outrageous falsehood. I didn't owe him. . . ."

The Colonel whirled to strike at Handback again, but the policeman caught him.

"Put 'em on opposite sides of the courtroom," directed the mayor.

When the men were separated, the judge of the court asked:

"Did you attack Colonel Vaiden, Mr. Handback?"

"I don't know whether I did or not," said Handback angrily; "he was reaching in the drawer of my desk for my pistol."

"Your pistol!" ejaculated Dibble. "Do you mean to say the Colonel entered your store and tried to draw your own pistol on you because he had shipped cotton which you allege belonged to you?"

"I don't know what he came to my store for!" cried Handback angrily.

"I went there to tell him his debt to me was paid," said Miltiades crisply.

"And you both got mad and got into a fight over it?" suggested the mayor.

"Well, I wasn't mad," said the Colonel, "but when he hit me, I choked him and made him stop."

"I see, you remonstrated with him by choking him," nodded the mayor.

Some laughter broke out in the courtroom at this remark.

"Look here!" cried Handback, "the point is he's got between forty and fifty thousand dollars of my money."

"Were you trying to get that back by mauling him?" inquired Dibble.

"I was mad. . . . No, I knew I wasn't going to get my money back that way, of course."

"Well, gentlemen," said the judge, "this is simply another case of disorderly conduct. You both admit it. Mr. Handback was trying to collect money by hammering the Colonel in the face, and the Colonel was resisting collection by choking Mr. Handback. I'll fine you both five dollars and the costs."

"But, look here!" cried Handback, jumping to his feet, "that man has stolen forty or fifty thousand dollars of my money! Is this all the satisfaction I get?"

"Mr. Handback! You know you don't try a charge like that in a police court!" snapped the mayor. "And you don't bring such an action *viva voce*. You must seek your remedy for that offense elsewhere. Both you men were fighting, and I'm fining each of you five dollars and the cost. That's all."

CHAPTER TWENTY-TWO

As MILTIADES VAIDEN walked out of the police court, the thought that filled his mind was, "Now everybody in Florence knows what became of the Handback cotton." This knowledge blew like a wind through his nerves. It was said to him in a hundred different ways. The crowd, as he walked out of the courtroom, gave him more than enough space. They set him in the middle and looked at him. It was in a hundred curious and incredulous faces. It was in the voices of the few who spoke to him.

The Colonel moved along the street toward his home in the midst of a crowd, yet in a little physical pool of isolation. He reminded himself a little of Landers, but this spiritual discomfort seemed temporary because all the discomforts he had ever known eventually had passed away.

As the Colonel walked along he could feel the news of his theft spreading through Florence, out into the country, everywhere. It would go to Cassandra, to his sister Marcia up in Tennessee, to Augustus and Rose and Sylvester and Lycurgus; he could feel the shock of dismay in his absent brothers and sisters when they heard the news.

He put his family forcibly out of his mind and made himself think what steps he should take next. He would, he supposed, presently be taken with a warrant. The thought of being arrested in the street was disagreeable to him, and he hurried his steps toward home.

As he did so he became aware that somebody just behind him was adjusting his pace to his own.

A suspicion that it was Mayhew, the sheriff, disturbed the Colonel. He would not look around. He would not speed up his gait; he slackened it; the person behind him slacked off too. Out of the corner of his eye Miltiades could see the other man's shadow.

The Colonel had meant to go up Market Street, but now, to test the shadow and see if it were following him, the Colonel turned a block west and turned into Pine. At the corner the man behind him quickened his pace and came up to Miltiades.

"May I have a word with you, Colonel?" said a hill voice.

The Colonel stopped and looked around in considerable surprise. The smallish and rather oldish man who had followed him appeared vaguely familiar. He was dressed cheaply but neatly, after the fashion of country folk when they come to town.

"What can I do for you?" asked the Colonel.

"I was just wondering," hesitated the man with a touch of embarrassment, "I was wondering if you had thought of putting Mr. Handback and his boy under a peace warrant—" the fellow moistened his lips with his tongue—"not that it's any of my business."

Such a suggestion from such a person confounded the Colonel.

"What would I put them under a warrant for?"

"Because they lit into you without cause. Lucius Handback even shot at you. If it hadn't been for that nigger, Loob Snipes, he'd 'a' hit you."

"Do you imagine I'm afraid of the Handbacks?"

"There, I knew you'd say that," nodded the rustic, gathering courage. "It isn't a question of being afraid at all. Of course, they won't try to do you any more physical harm. You know that, and so do I."

"Then why place them under a peace warrant?" inquired Miltiades.

"Why, to get them on the run," explained the rustic earnestly, "occupy their attention by having them make out a peace bond to keep out of jail. It'll make the people think that you have been mistreated."

Such partisanship in his own behalf bewildered Miltiades.

"Look here," said the Colonel, "your face seems familiar, but just at this moment I can't recall . . ."

As he said this a small boy's derisive yodel broke out across the street:

"Hey, look at Jaky Sandusky, trying to be a lawyer! Look at Sandusky trying to get a case!"

The oldish youth glanced across at the small boys with the intense despisal of the countryman for the town dweller.

"You damn little brats!" he said.

A this point Miltiades identified the boarder at Mrs. Rose's boarding house. It also explained why the fellow had taken such a complete Vaiden view of the case. He had no doubt heard Augustus talk about the cotton. It comforted Miltiades intimately to know that Augustus had taken a pro-Vaiden view.

"No," said the Colonel to Sandusky in a different tone, "I won't swear out a peace warrant, Mr. Sandusky. How came you to think about it?"

"Well, I asked Governor O'Shawn what he would do about your case, and he said he believed he would make the Handbacks scratch their way out."

"Why did you ask Governor O'Shawn about the matter?" inquired the Colonel curiously.

"I read law in his office. When anything comes up, I ask him about it."

"Well, tha—that's commendable," hesitated Miltiades, rather embarrassed to know that Terry O'Shawn already knew of his peculation; "but I don't think I'll swear out the peace warrant, after all."

"The Handbacks will do something," warned Sandusky.

"I imagine they will," agreed the Colonel seriously.

"If they do, you'll need a lawyer . . . why don't you take the Governor?" inquired Sandusky gingerly.

"I will have to have one," admitted Miltiades.

"Then I'll sort of watch out for you, if it's all right?" suggested Sandusky.

"I won't have any trouble hiring a lawyer," replied the Colonel unencouragingly.

"Well . . . all right. . . ." And the boarder touched his hat awkwardly and turned back toward town.

Across the street the small boys who had been listening to this set up a clamor:

"Sandusky lost out! Oh-oh! Jaky Sandusky lost out! Ho! Ho!"

And a shrill falsetto shrieking:

"Jaky Sandusky's stuck on Sydna Crowninshield! Hay! Hay! What ye know about that!"

The shrilling of the youngsters lingered in Miltiades' ears for a moment or two and presently gave way to his constant concern as to what the Handbacks were likely to do.

Sandusky's advice about making the first move might be good. O'Shawn, apparently, had suggested it.

The fact that he had voluntarily gone to the Handbacks' store and entered into conversation about the cotton would be a point in his favor before a jury. A gratification went through Miltiades that he had acted just as he did. It might very well change any action that was brought against him from a criminal suit to a civil suit.

The Colonel's ponderings were a little disturbed by the small boys who had deserted Sandusky and who were now following him tentatively along Pine Street, saying something in undertones and breaking into loud laughter at whatever it was. Once the Colonel looked around at them, and the laughter lost its morale and was reduced to a tittering.

The urchins dropped off eventually, and the Colonel walked on up Pine Street, thinking again about the Handbacks and then about Gracie. From Gracie he went to Drusilla.

He hurried his steps to be past Drusilla's home. He wondered in annoyance why he had ever come past the Crowninshield residence; then he remembered Sandusky had caused this choice of route.

At the end of Pine Street Miltiades turned over toward Market. A browned man in a broadish hat sat on a horse where the cross street entered the main thoroughfare. A queer feeling went through Miltiades as he recognized the motionless figure of the horseman waiting for him in the afternoon sunshine. He had an impulse to turn and walk back the way he had come, but he continued forward.

"Hey-oh, Mayhew," he said, as he started to pass by.

"Hello, Colonel," said the horseman in a careful tone. "I just rode up to your house, Colonel. You wa'n't at home. I figgered out you'd took a side street, so I rode back and waited here where I knowed you'd have to come."

A kind of repulsion went through the Colonel at the sheriff's miserable English when arresting him.

"Did you want me?"

"Yes, ol' man Han'back swore out a state's warrant for you while ago. I'll read it to you."

Miltiades stopped beside the sheriff and stood looking up at him.

"You needn't read it."

"Well . . . all right : . . it's a warrant for ye, Colonel."

Miltiades nodded. He paused a moment and then asked: "Where do we go now?"

"Why, I'm afraid I'm goin' to haff to take you back downtown with me . . . I mean till you make your bond."

He got off his horse to lead the animal and walk back beside the Colonel.

"We might go down Pine Street," suggested Mayhew; "not much passing on it."

Miltiades agreed to this mutely. He felt Mayhew's consideration. They turned to walk back down Pine Street with the horse behind them.

The thoroughfare was almost deserted. A gray-wooled negro raked up leaves on a lawn.

To the Colonel the windows of the houses which they passed had the effect of the eyes of a multitude. The whole street seemed silently noting his arrest. He felt as if he were moving beside the sheriff on a high elevated ridge, a kind of prolonged pedestal which held him up to every eye.

As the two men walked along the Colonel heard behind him the subdued call of "Cotton," and a tittering. For a moment or two it did not occur to Miltiades that the call had any reference to him. It arose a little louder, "Steamboat Cotton!" More giggling, then a cry of "Barge Cotton! Towboat Cotton!"

Sheriff Mayhew whirled around.

"Here, you little devils!" he threatened; "shut that up and get on home, or I'll take you to jail too!"

The gang of little boys retreated a way, then broke into a shrill chanting:

"There goes Colonel Towboat Cotton and the sher'f! There goes Colonel Towboat Cotton and the sher'f!"

They shrieked with laughter at their song.

Miltiades clenched his fingers with desire to choke their scrawny throats. Suddenly he observed that he was in front of the Crowninshield home.

"Come on," he said to Mayhew with a dry mouth, "let's move on!"

The sheriff was as furious as his prisoner.

"I'll pick the little rascals up. . . ."

At that moment a slender girl came running out of the Crowninshield gate. She dashed across the road into the gang.

"You bad little boys!" she cried. "You are mean! You are outrageous! I'll tell your mothers on you! I'll tell your mothers on every single one of you!"

She was crying. She spread her arms and bore down on them as if she would physically stop their advance.

The gang fell back shouting:

"Oh, we ain't skeered of you! You can't do nothing to us! Miss Jerry Catlin! Miss Jerry Catlin!"

They went trooping back up the street hooting this new jest and were gone.

The two men looked after the vanishing children still vibrating with detestation.

"Wasn't that Miss Sydna Crowninshield?" asked the sheriff.

"Yes," said the Colonel.

"I didn't know she was a particular friend of yours."

"Neither did I," said the Colonel, in the tone of a man who could not understand the incident himself.

CHAPTER TWENTY-THREE

Tʜᴇ jail put an end to the riddle of Sydna Crowninshield's partisanship in Colonel Vaiden's thoughts. The small iron-barred windows in the brick wall dismayed him. When he entered the door the place had a smell reminiscent of an animal cage.

Frierson, the jailer, came to the front door, blinking a little because he had just got up from a game of checkers with Biggars, the fireman. The jailer put on an unusual gravity when he saw who was the prisoner.

"I suppose Colonel Vaiden will stay here till he makes bond," he suggested to Mayhew.

"Of course I want to make bond," said the Colonel. "How much is it?"

"It isn't set," said the sheriff. "We haven't had any pre-liminary trial yet to set the bond." He pulled a silver watch out of his pocket. "It's too late for a preliminary now."

"But, my God!" ejaculated Frierson, "the Colonel's not going to have to stay here all night, I hope!"

"If we can't get a preliminary trial to set his bond," said Mayhew, "I don't see as there's anything else to do."

The Colonel looked at Mayhew with rising anger.

"Why in the hell didn't you arrest me sooner?"

"I couldn't arrest you without a warrant," flung out Mayhew, with an officer's readiness to take offense. "I didn't get your warrant till a little while ago."

"Look here," put in the jailer, trying to arrange the matter, "you didn't have any trouble ketching him, did you, Mayhew?"

"Of course he didn't," said the Colonel.

"Besides that, he went to the Handbacks' store and told

'em what he had done. That shows he's not trying to get away. Why not turn him loose under his own recognizance?"

Mayhew stood shaking his head slowly.

"Frierson, a little case, I'd say yes, of course, but one running up into the forty thousands of dollars . . ." the sheriff shook his head more positively, "no, I'm not wanting my bondsmen to be out scratching up forty thousand dollars to pay over to the Handbacks. They've got enough money already."

Lancy Biggars, the fireman who had been playing checkers with Frierson, came out of the jailer's office.

"Mayhew, I'll go on Colonel Milt's bond," he offered.

The sheriff pulled down his mouth in a laugh.

"Lancy, did you ever stop to figger how many fellers like you it 'ud take to make good a forty-thousand-dollar bond? Damn if it wouldn't take forty thousand dollars' worth of legal cap for you boys to sign your names to."

"But, look here, tomorrow's election day," pointed out the jailer earnestly, "you know you're not going to get no trial held on election day."

"Frierson, why in the hell didn't the Colonel think of all these details when he took the cotton?" demanded the sheriff.

"Well, I tell you what I'm going to do," stated Frierson, "I'm going to turn the Colonel loose and tell him to report to me in the morning. I let half my niggers go home at night, and I never see 'em except at meal times."

"Look here, Frierson, the Lauderdale County jail is supposed to be a place of safe keeping. If you're going to act thatta way, I'll take him over to Tuscumbia and lodge him there."

"No, don't do that," interposed Frierson. "I get twenty cents a day for lodging prisoners, and I might as well have it as the Tuscumbia jailer."

The two officers stood pondering how to keep the Colonel in jail and at the same time let him go free.

"I have it," said Mayhew at last, "why not let the Colonel put up a cash bond with you, Joe, and go home?"

"Cash bond!"

"How much?" asked Miltiades.

"Oh, about fifteen hundred dollars—that's about what your bond would be. Could you put that up, Colonel?"

"Why-y, no-o," said Miltiades doubtfully, "I couldn't put up that much."

"Why, that's out of all reason!" cried the jailer.

"Well, damn it, anything," cried the sheriff, "a thousand, five hundred . . . name the figger yourself. I want a little assurance my prisoner will come back here tomorrow. I'm responsible for him, ain't I?"

"What makes you think he can make a cash bond?"

"I said, if he could."

In the midst of this endless and unprogressive talk the jail door opened and a smallish, cheaply clad youth entered. This time, within half a minute, Miltiades recognized the undistinguished features of Sandusky.

"I heard you were down here," said Mrs. Rose's boarder rather breathlessly, as if he had been running.

"Yes, I'm here," said the Colonel, who was unaware that he had any connection with Sandusky.

"Well, I got a couple of men to go on your bond—Mr. Augustus Vaiden and Mr. Landers, the postmaster."

"There ain't no bond," said Mayhew; "we haven't had no hearing yet, and they ain't none set."

Sandusky stared blankly at this.

"You're not going to keep him in jail all night, are you?"

The sheriff looked at Sandusky with distaste.

"Colonel, let me have a little private talk with you," suggested that youth.

Miltiades had no desire to have a private talk with Sandusky.

"What have you got to do with this, anyway?" asked Mayhew of Mrs. Rose's boarder.

"I could be the Colonel's counsel," said Sandusky.

"Are you a lawyer?"

"No, but I'm Governor O'Shawn's clerk."

"What in the hell's the Governor got to do with this?"

"Hell, go on and talk," interposed Frierson, "I've no objections, and you're both in my jail. You can use my office right in there."

"Don't muss up that checker game we left on the table," put in Biggars.

"Hell, muss it up if you need the table," said the jailer.

Inside the office, Sandusky closed the door on the men in the hallway.

"Look here, Colonel," began Sandusky in a quick undertone, "the Governor thinks it would be a good thing for you to sit tight jest like you are and let 'em put you in jail!"

"How came the Governor to think anything at all about me?" ejaculated Miltiades.

"I ast him."

"Well . . . why should I stay in jail if I can get 'ut?"

"Because he says Handback ain't really got nothing but a civil suit against you, and you'll have an action against him for false arrest and damages to character and reputation."

Sandusky was sharply excited. His fingers picked up and put down the checker men.

"When did the Governor tell you all this?" queried Miltiades.

"Why, since I left you," hurried Sandusky. "You see the Handbacks are the richest firm in Florence. No jury will like them putting you in jail. They'll give you a lot o' damage."

"Well . . . all right . . ." agreed Miltiades slowly. And he went back in the hall and told the men that he would not try to make bond.

When the other men had gone, Frierson, the jailer, stood in the hallway with his prisoner and said in perplexity:

"Now, by jiggers, I don't understand Mayhew at all. What earthly dif'runce does it make to him if I keep you in jail tonight or let you go home so long as I've got you to show in the morning?"

"I don't know," said Miltiades absently, overlooking the question in the gray fact that he was in jail.

"Me neither," said Frierson, "I never thought Mayhew was a spiteful man. He hasn't got a grudge against you, has he?"

"Not that I know of." Then the Colonel thought of the little boys mocking him in Pine Street. He knew that the malice of children was usually based on the dislike of the parents, so he added, "I really don't know who likes me and who dislikes me. I never have paid much attention to it."

"No, you——" The jailer broke off whatever it was he was about to say and substituted: "Well, if you don't mind, Colonel . . ."

There was a melancholy slope of steps leading from the hall into the upper story. Frierson indicated these steps.

"This jail is really rigged up for niggers," he said apologetically as the two started up. "I try to keep the corner cell with two winders in it for white men . . . and usually I do."

The Colonel preceded the jailer upstairs and entered the iron-barred simplicity of the upper story. It smelled of black men.

Frierson produced a key and unlocked the corner cell.

"I'm to go in here?" asked the Colonel in a queer voice.

"I'll send up my wife to change the cover on your bunk," suggested Frierson.

Miltiades went inside and felt the blankets. They were stiff with dirt.

"Be right back," said the jailer, "you can jest—er—set down, Colonel—an' make yourself at home."

Frierson did not turn the key in the lock, but went hurrying back downstairs to send up his wife with clean bedclothes. There was nothing for the Colonel to do except sit on the bunk.

The last rays of the sun fell through a narrow window and painted the black shadow of its bars on the sienna-lit bars of the cell. The Colonel sat looking at this complexity of color and design without thinking of it.

Just one physical fact gripped his mind: he was in jail. He felt slimy, as if he had been dropped into a cesspool. The flesh of his buttocks twisted away from the blankets he sat on, and presently he stood up.

He thought of a man who owned forty-eight thousand dollars spending the night in such a place!

But the forty-eight thousand which had got him into jail now did an odd thing. It stiffened the Colonel's feeling of superiority, of being untouched by his surroundings. He wondered if Gracie would betray her trust?

Following his thought of Gracie came the image of Drusilla, as if the quadroon and the aristocratic woman were linked by some obscure mental chain. He thought of Drusilla blankly, then of her daughter Sydna; how Sydna had run out into the street to defend him against the urchins. Then he realized that nobody had told Ponny where he was. He supposed the Klems would tell her first. He could imagine his wife's amazement, her incredulity, her shock. It occurred to him that if his marriage with Ponny had brought him the money he had expected he would never have been where he was now.

The door to the steps opened, and a light entered the upper story. Then Frierson appeared, followed by his wife with an armful of bedclothes. The jailer entered and held the lamp while his wife whisked off the offensive covers.

"We don't try to keep these beds clean any more," explained the woman. "We did for a while, but the drunks act so bad. . . . I'll bring you up a new pot, too, when I go down again."

The Colonel almost said, "Don't put yourself to any trouble"; but if he were to get any manner of rest in the noisome cell she would have to put herself to some trouble.

As the jailer's wife worked briskly, flinging out the clean

linen in the air and letting it settle smoothly on the mattress, she said without looking around:

"I guess you don't know me, Colonel?"

"You are Mrs. Frierson?"

"Oh, yes. I mean before I was married."

"Well . . . no-o . . . I'm afraid I don't know your maiden name."

"Don't you remember the little girl who used to come to the old Lacefield place once in a while with Eliza Ham?"

Miltiades recalled Eliza Ham but not the child.

"Are you that little girl?"

"Yes, I was Eliza Ham's niece," nodded the woman, with the back of her head toward the Colonel. "I tell Joe, there's never a bit of telling who we'll be called on next to entertain. A year or so ago Martha Killicut was here—did you know Martha?"

"No . . . I don't believe I did."

"She killed her baby when it was born," explained Mrs. Frierson, faintly embarrassed.

A glimmering notion that he had heard of Martha Killicut before passed through Miltiades.

"Martha Killicut . . . Martha Killicut . . ." he repeated, trying to capture the memory.

"Folks called her old Marth," prompted Mrs. Frierson, "although she wasn't so very old."

This tag of "Old Marth" completed the Colonel's recognition.

"I remember the name . . . I heard something about her, somewhere. . . ."

Both the jailer and his wife were disappointed not to learn what the Colonel almost recalled. The woman had finished the bed.

"Joe," she said, "you might leave the lamp up here. It'll be comp'ny for Colonel Milt, and it'll help keep the bugs away."

Joe glanced about and set the lamp on the sheet-iron floor. The two wished the Colonel good-night. This time, Joe locked

the door as silently and inconspicuously as possible. The
two disappeared down the iron-barred aisle and were gone.

Miltiades sat on the clean bedding and looked at the light.
Well, here he was, in jail. He stared at the lamp flame, which
burned motionless. The pot, which Mrs. Frierson after all
had forgot to exchange, scented the cell.

Presently these material data faded from the Colonel's
mind. He began going over and over the incidents leading
to this imprisonment as an animal walks back and forth
behind its bars. He did not know how long he kept this up.
After some length of time someone snored in a near-by cell.
A negro's voice said in an undertone to someone else:

"Punch dat niggah, don' let him 'sturb de Col'l wid he
snorin'."

The other cells were full of negroes who had quieted to
complete silence with the entrance of the Colonel. But they
fell asleep at last, and the jail was filled with the sounds of
noisy breathings. Then, out of the treadmill of his thoughts,
there popped into Miltiades' head the recollection of old
Martha Killicut.

She was the prostitute Landers the postmaster had mentioned at the creek. It was old Marth's dead baby of which
Landers' dead sister had spoken to the postmaster through
a wandering medium. The strangeness, the uncanniness of
this corroboration stumbled upon by accident, here in jail,
went through the Colonel with a breath of the outré and the
incredible.

It produced a strange effect. It created, for a moment,
an illusion as if the cell, the lamp, these negro prisoners
snoring around him were an insubstantial figment behind
which lay an unknown but a profound reality. This fantasy
propounded to the Colonel an ironic query. It asked him
why he had maneuvered Handback's cotton down the river,
and why he was sitting thus in the filth of this cell to hold the
money he had obtained by fraud?

The man in the lamplit cell could not answer this question.
He did not know. He did not know why he suffered this

ignominy to hold the fortune. He did not know whar he would do with the money. He sat pondering for a long time.

After a long while a grayness formed outside the window of the jail, and the bars stood out against the dawn. As it grew lighter, the Colonel got up, extinguished his lamp, and looked out the window. He could see downward into a little alley that led past the jail into Intelligence Row.

At first he saw only the narrow slice between the two buildings. In line with this slice were a column and the clock tower of the courthouse. Then, as the shadows in the alley clarified, he saw a tall boy leaning against the wall of a house and staring fixedly at the jail window.

The way the youth leaned against the wall and shifted his weight from foot to foot suggested to Miltiades that the watcher had been standing there for a long time.

After a few more minutes, as the illumination increased, the Colonel recognized Jerry Catlin, the son of Marcia, his sister. The boy stood watching the prison window that held his uncle.

CHAPTER TWENTY-FOUR

Voices in Courthouse Square were shouting, "Hurrah for Cleveland!" and somewhere farther away somebody yelled back, "Hurrah for Blaine!" and then broke into laughter after the fashion of a person who utters a ridiculous sentiment out of jest.

To Miltiades, the fact that it was election day lent a peculiar barb to his imprisonment. He sat on his bunk thinking that the men with whom he had fought through the war were making another effort to regain control of national affairs, and he was like this, sitting impotent in the county jail!

If only he had thought of this contretemps he would not have gone to Handback until after election day.

However, barring the election, Miltiades was glad he had pushed on into this final scene of his seizure of the cotton. Whatever was going to happen to him was now in process of being worked out. His waiting was over.

Two cells distant from his own a negro's voice asked humbly and apprehensively:

"Col'l, if'n de Democrats gits 'lected, will us niggahs haff to go back lak we wuz befo' de wah?"

"Of course not," said the Colonel, "that's foolish."

"Whut de Democrats gwi' do, then?"

"They'll run the country to suit the South. We'll have prosperity. You niggers will get higher wages, for one thing."

"Lawzee," ejaculated the negro, "dat's a ve'y dif'unt tune to what Mistah Landers sings."

"Naturally. He's got an ax to grind. He wants you to vote the Republican ticket to help him hold his job."

The Colonel said this with some sarcasm for the shoddy principle of Landers, trying to scare the negroes into voting the Republican ticket.

The door of the second story creaked open, and the Colonel paused in his silent condemnation of Landers. He listened for scuffling or staggering footsteps. As none came, a qualm seized upon Miltiades lest it was young Jerry Catlin.

The Colonel tried to get himself into a dignified attitude. He straightened his tie, then he saw the visitor coming quickly through the corridor toward his cell. Miltiades' embarrassment went away. It was nobody but Sandusky.

Mrs. Rose's boarder seemed to labor under some excitement.

"Colonel," he said, "I've been to the Handback store . . . been talking to Mr. Handback."

"Well, what did you say?" asked the Colonel indifferently.

"Why, I just told Mr. Handback how it was . . ." Sandusky paused and looked speculatively through the bars. "What would you give to get out of this, Colonel Vaiden?"

"Out of jail?"

"No, out of the whole thing. Old man Handback swears he's going to send you to the coal mines. I told him he couldn't do it. I told him he appointed you as his agent and let you handle his cotton; and I told him when you took advantage of your position to collect an old debt he owed you, he simply didn't have any criminal action against you. That's what I handed him."

The Colonel thought this over.

"That's about what I had in my head all the time," he admitted, impressed with Sandusky's analysis.

Sandusky nodded.

"Yes, of course, but now, by Jiggs, the court may not hold that. It could mighty easy say it was a simple case of appropriating goods, and it might accidentally turn out like Mr. Handback says."

"Look here, which side are you on?" asked the Colonel, looking uncertainly at the youth.

"Neither one nor the other," said Sandusky. "I'm trying to show Handback it might turn out to be a civil suit, and I'm trying to show you it might just as easily turn out to be a criminal suit. What I'm trying to do is to work up a compromise."

"Oh!" ejaculated the Colonel. "That's your idyah!"

"Yes, that's why I ast how much would you give to get shed of this whole business."

"I see . . . I see . . . you mean refund Handback some of the money."

"That's my idyah. How would you be willing to split the money if it settled off ever'thing?"

"Did Handback talk favorably to that?"

"Well . . . I talked to him a long time, and he fin'ly said he wouldn't mind paying you what he once owed you."

"How much did he figure that was?" inquired the Colonel.

"He said it was five hundred dollars," said Sandusky.

"Five hundred!" Miltiades really was amazed at the merchant's effrontery.

Sandusky nodded, a little at sea himself.

"Yes, he said you had five bales of cotton, and as cotton is worth a hundred dollars a bale, that would be five hundred dollars."

"Why, the damned scoundrel!" cried the Colonel. "He knows as well as I do cotton was selling for a dollar a pound right after the war. My cotton came to twenty-five hundred dollars."

Sandusky held to the bars, thinking over this angle of the settlement.

"Look here," he suggested, "suppose I bring Mr. Handback in to see you. Maybe you two can reach some agreement. After all, you are both honest men, and you want to do each other right."

"When can you bring him?"

"Well, as a matter of fact, he's downstairs. I persuaded him to come down here with me."

"All right, bring him up," agreed the Colonel, and Sandusky went hurrying off down the corridor again.

In a few minutes the short compact merchant followed Sandusky into the upper story of the jail.

Mrs. Rose's boarder, who had stage-managed the affair very well up to this point, became very nervous now that he actually had his men together.

"I—I wanted you two g-gentlemen to g-get together and talk this over," he said, wetting his lips.

"Well, I say I don't owe Colonel Vaiden anything at all," stated the merchant impersonally, talking to Sandusky, "but, as I told you, I am willing to make a reasonable allowance for what I did owe him before I was forced into bankruptcy. I told you I'd do that, and now I'll stick to it."

"So the question is, what is a reasonable amount?" suggested Sandusky.

"A reasonable amount," said Miltiades from his cell, "is what the cotton would have brought plus interest."

"Interest! Interest!" cried Handback. "You can't charge me interest after my assignment in bankruptcy! This is a gift I'm giving you. I don't owe you anything. You can't charge me interest on a debt I don't owe!"

"Well, by God, I am doing it, am I not?" demanded the Colonel crisply.

"No, you're not!" cried Handback. "You come such a tune as that, and I'll send you to the coal mines as sure as you're a foot high!" Handback was turning back toward the steps.

"Wait! Wait!" cried Sandusky. "Don't run off, Mr. Handback, before you get a single figger. . . . All right, Colonel Vaiden, how much do you figger your principal and interest comes to?"

"Fifty thousand dollars, to a dot!" snapped Miltiades. "I've figured it up a thousand times."

"Fifty thou . . . you mean that's what my cotton come

to!" cried Handback. He stared at the Colonel and began to laugh.

"How did you get that figger, Colonel?" inquired Sandusky.

"I charged him fifty per cent per annum," said Miltiades flatly.

"The legal rate's eight per cent," reminded Sandusky.

"When a man takes your money knowing he is going to make an assignment in three hours and never pay it back, he's a thief and puts himself outside the law. I feel justified in collecting anything I can lay my hands on."

"You call me a thief!" cried Handback, staring in amazement at the Colonel. "You sneaking scoundrel, asking me for a job as a clerk and pretending to be my friend. . . ."

"Mr. Handback! Colonel!" begged Sandusky desperately. "Won't you make each other some reasonable offer? Five hundred dollars is no offer! To say you are going to charge fifty per cent and keep it all is no offer! Be reasonable!"

Both men stood silent, Miltiades holding to his bars; Handback arrested on his way to the door. The Colonel really tried to think of some reasonable thing.

"Well, now, listen to this," growled the Colonel at last, "if the worst comes to the worst, I won't be sent to the coal mines for more than five years. Well, I'd give two thousand dollars a year to keep out of the mines. That's ever' cent I'd give back for a quit-claim deed to what I've got; ten thousand dollars. Handback can take it or leave it."

"Hell, I'll leave it!" snapped the merchant. "I'd give more than that to see you wear stripes for one year."

Sandusky stood in the corridor and watched one of his near clients walk out the door and the other go back to his bunk and sit down. The young man began a half-hearted argument with Miltiades to raise the price he would pay for his assured freedom.

"Look here," he contended, "if Handback and Mayhew get their fingers on the money, they'll take every cent of it, and you'll get nothing at all, Colonel."

"Get their hands on it?" queried the Colonel suspiciously.

"Sure, get their hands on it. . . . Why do you suppose Mayhew was so bound you should stay in jail all night last night and all day today?"

"Why . . . to keep me safe, I suppose," said Miltiades looking curiously at the young man.

"Well . . . you suppose wrong," said Sandusky.

"Then what did they keep me here for?" demanded Miltiades.

"I'm in their confidence," said Sandusky, "and that's all I can say. But I'll add this. If you'd ever been in the coal mines you'd give more than two thousand a year to keep out."

Sandusky took himself off, greatly disappointed at the outcome of his meeting, and left Miltiades alone.

Outside the jail the election was getting under way. Shouts and hurrahs came through the barred windows. The music of a distant band grew in loudness as it came marching through Courthouse Square. When it stopped there broke out a many-voiced shouting for Cleveland. Some voices struck up a drunken song:

"*See the boat go round the bend.*
Good-bye, James G., good-bye.
Loaded down with Cleveland men.
Good-bye, James G., good-bye."

When the voting was well under way, Frierson began bringing up drunk men and putting them in the cells. That meant the town calaboose was full, and the jail was receiving the overflow.

The Colonel listened to the growing confusion with his thoughts partly on the election and partly on Sandusky. He wondered what Sandusky had hinted at. He wondered what Handback and Mayhew were doing? It made him uneasy.

Now and then the notion of penal labor in the state coal

mines flickered in and out of his head. . . . It would be worth, Sandusky had said, more than two thousand a year to keep out of them. How did Sandusky know? Had he ever worked in one?

There was a newly imprisoned drunk in the cell next to the Colonel's. The fellow was very sick. He lay groaning on his bed, vomiting occasionally on his blanket and on the steel floor of the cell. His hair was wet from perspiration and appeared combed the wrong way.

The sour smell of his ejecta filled the Colonel's cubicle. In the midst of his groaning the fellow opened his eyes and stared without focus at Miltiades.

"You . . . Col'l . . . Vaiden?" he asked thickly.

"Yes," said the Colonel.

"Y-you got d-drunk, too?"

"No."

"Y-you di-didn'?"

"No."

"Well i-it's uh—uh climinal shame, anyway."

"What—me not getting drunk?"

"N-no. . . . Th-the woman."

"What woman?"

"Wh-why, th-th' woman 'at got k-killed . . ." The drunk man wobbled his head vaguely to indicate the direction.

At that moment Sandusky came up the corridor again. He was in a greater hurry than ever.

"Colonel," he panted, "they've . . . taken you up!"

"What do you mean?" inquired Miltiades. "Taken me up how?"

"Why, the Handbacks! They've agreed to settle for the ten thousand dollars. . . . I talked 'em into it."

CHAPTER TWENTY-FIVE

SANDUSKY had drawn up an agreement between the two parties. He handed it to the Colonel through the bars. It was a long paper in rather awkward legal style and abounded in the endless repetitions of such instruments.

It began:

"Know all men by these presents, that whereas John Handback of the firm of J. Handback & Son, doing business in the town of Florence, county of Lauderdale, state of Alabama, hereby acknowledges in behalf of himself and of his firm the following state of facts, viz., to wit, namely,

"First that the firm of J. Handback & Son is and was justly indebted to Colonel Miltiades Vaiden, residing in Florence, in the county of Lauderdale, state of Alabama, for a certain sum of money for cotton delivered to said firm by Miltiades Vaiden before a certain assignment in bankruptcy made by the firm J. Handback & Company in the year 1865. That the said money nor any part of said money has ever been paid and still constitutes a good legal debt against the firm J. Handback & Son, which is the successor of the firm J. Handback & Company.

"Secondly the said J. Handback engaged Colonel Miltiades Vaiden in the present year and entrusted to him the picking, ginning, shipping and selling of all the cotton raised on the plantations of the firm J. Handback & Son, for the purpose of repaying the said Miltiades Vaiden for the aforesaid outstanding debt. And whereas said cotton has been gathered, shipped and sold by the said Miltiades Vaiden, the aforesaid firm of J. Handback & Son agree to accept the sum of ten thousand dollars as their full and legal residue in the proceeds of said cotton.

"Witness our hands and seals, this the 4th day of November 1884."

Miltiades read this extraordinary document in amazement. "Will they really sign this?"

Sandusky nodded with pride.

"Yes, they'll stick their fists to her. What do you think about how it's written?"

"What's written?"

"The agreement. Don't it sound pretty good? I made it up myself, some of it, and some I got out of the *Legal Guide and Advisor*."

The Colonel paid no attention to the pride of the author. "You are sure Handback is willing to sign that?"

"He'll sign when you pay over the money."

"How will I know he'll do it?"

"I've arranged to let Frierson hold the paper and the money. He'll hand the paper to you and the money to Handback."

Miltiades looked again at the extraordinary concession. "I don't believe he'll do it. I believe there's some trick to it."

"Oh, no, he'll do it," assured Sandusky excitedly. "You say the word and I'll go down and have Frierson come up and turn you out now."

"Go ahead," agreed the Colonel, "and tell 'em if there is a trick to this, two can play at that game."

"It's no trick," insisted Sandusky; "they'll settle for ten thousand."

Mrs. Rose's boarder turned and went almost running down the corridor, and Miltiades heard him clattering down the steps to the lower floor.

Miltiades, in his cell, puzzled his head as to what sort of

trap the Handbacks were setting. Finally, a possible motive occurred to the Colonel. Handback might intend to follow him and seize the rest of the money by force.

The Colonel was still thinking about this when Frierson came leisurely up the corridor, jingling his keys, and opened the cell door.

As Miltiades stepped out the jailer said:

"This county's going to poll fifteen thousand for Cleveland. Everybody's come to town to vote. You never saw such a jam."

"Frierson," said Miltiades, "have you any idyah in the world what Handback is up to, making such an offer?"

"Well," said the jailer, "I think he is really afraid of a personal damage suit. I imagine he has been to see a lawyer, and the lawyer put the fear of God in his heart."

"You believe the offer's on the square?"

"Oh, yeh," nodded the jailer; "he's in as big a lather to take you up as you are to take him up. They want to call ever'thing off."

Miltiades walked to the door and down the steps with the jailer.

"Maybe I oughtn't to sign after all," he said half to himself and half to Frierson.

J. Handback himself was in the office of the jail. As Miltiades started out, he held up a paper and called out:

"Did you agree to sign this document, Colonel Vaiden?"

"What's in it?" asked the Colonel.

"You agree to hold us free from all personal damages. Sandusky said you had agreed to sign it."

"Yes, that was what I agreed to," said the Colonel.

"Well, that's what we want," said Handback.

The two principals sat down at a desk in the office and with evident distrust of each other signed their respective papers. The jailer took each paper after it was subscribed and filed it away in a small iron box, showing ostentatiously that it did not fall untimely into the possession of the adverse party.

"I'll be right here to hand you your paper when you come back with the coin, Colonel," assured Frierson.

The Colonel nodded, and then said casually:

"By the way, Joe, could you let me have a pistol to drop in my pocket? I don't want to be walking around with ten thousand dollars in a crowd like we have to-day."

"Why, certainly, certainly, Colonel," agreed the jailer. He went to the same iron box, drew out a six-shooter, broke it down to see that it was loaded, snapped it shut again, and handed it to Miltiades.

The gesture was intended more for Handback than for anyone else. Miltiades dropped the weapon in his pocket, bade the group good-day. As he walked out on the street with his shoulders back Frierson said:

"I declare, no matter what kind of scrape one of them Vaiden boys gets into, he acts just like a Vaiden!"

The back street on which the jail sat was filled with a back-street crowd. More or less sober men steered more or less drunken companions into this back street to quiet them. On the other hand, drunken men dragged more or less sober men into the back street to give them a drink and enliven them. The thoroughfare was a sort of alcoholic clearing house where intoxicated men were added to and withdrawn from circulation.

In a corner behind some barrels a small boy stood winking his eyes to keep from crying as he kept watch over a stupefied father. Further along two men were cursing and pummeling each other over a disagreement as to what majority New York would return for Cleveland.

This yelling and fighting and swearing did not divert Colonel Vaiden's mind from the astounding turn of fortune in the Handback matter. He glanced backwards now and then to see if he were being followed. He could not be sure, owing to the number of men in the street.

An idea came to him to go and vote and lose himself completely in the crowd around the polls. He walked through an alley that led into Courthouse Square and came out into a stream of men that flowed under the gnarled mulberries along Intelligence Row.

A band was playing. A great picture of Cleveland was painted on a banner and stretched between two poles. The Florence Fencibles were on parade in the Square east of the courthouse. They had a cannon to fire when they heard the returns that Cleveland really was elected. A number of ex-Confederate soldiers had put on their old uniforms and had come to town to vote for Cleveland.

The polling place was in the west room of the courthouse. Everywhere in the crowd, on the courthouse steps, in the polling booths, men were distributing Democratic ballots to prospective voters. These politicians questioned everyone as to whether he had voted or not.

"Use this for gun wadding to blow hell out of the Republicans," they would say as they thrust a ballot into the voter's hand.

On the table, where the election judges sat, was a pile of Republican ballots. Landers had put them there. The postmaster stood near the ballot box watching his pile of ballots, seeing that they were not thrown away. At long intervals a white man from the hills would edge in toward Landers, consult with him. The postmaster would get a Republican ballot and give to the man. The hill voter usually accepted Landers' word for the kind of ballot he was voting. He seldom knew how to read.

As Miltiades came up to the table the judges were questioning a young white boy.

"Have you paid any poll tax?" queried one of the officials.

"No, I came twenty-one since the poll tax fell due," said the youth doggedly.

"Where do you live?"

"In East Florence."

"What's your name?"

"Toussaint Vaiden."

From the crowd the voice of another boy called out:

"He's a nigger."

The spokesman of the judges straightened in his chair.

"No, you can't vote," and he waved the boy away.

Landers protested:

"Why can't he vote?"

"You know damn well why he can't vote," snapped the judge, "the grandfather of this boy was not a free man."

"How would that boy have blue eyes and light hair if his grandfather wasn't a free man?" demanded Landers.

"Who was your father?" asked the judge of the octoroon.

Toussaint stood in the center of the crowd with a painful compression of anger and shame in his chest and throat. He never thought about who his father had been. He took endless precautions never to let that theme linger in his mind. The gentleness, the sweetness, the refinement of his mother had built such mental bulwarks against the question that it could not be thought. Now, to have it flung in his face in this contemptuous place!

"Well, if you can't answer," snapped the spokesman. He lifted his voice: "Does anybody here know anything about Toussaint Vaiden?"

He caught sight of Miltiades and called to him:

"Colonel Vaiden, do you know anything about this boy?"

"What is it you want to know about him?" inquired Miltiades.

"He says his mother's name is Gracie Vaiden. Do you know him?"

"His mother was my father's house servant," said the Colonel, looking at Toussaint.

"Do you know who the boy's father was?"

Miltiades pondered a moment and then said:

"His mother was married to a negro named Solomon."

"Was Solomon a free man?"

"No, my father-in-law, Mr. Alex BeShears, owned Solomon and I think sold him to a nigger dealer soon after the war broke out."

"There you are," said the judge to Toussaint: "your father was not a free man, so you can't vote."

Landers interrupted:

"What color was this negro Solomon you're talking about?" he asked Miltiades.

"Why, as I remember Solomon, a light chocolate."

"Then look at this boy," protested the postmaster, shaking a finger at Toussaint. "How would it be possible for a chocolate-colored father to have such a——"

Old Judge Ashton, who was standing near by, lifted a courteous voice.

"Now, Mr. Landers, sir, the law of Alabama supposes that the child of a mother is the offspring of her husband. In a case like this the rule becomes what is known in courts as a legal fiction, sir—but it holds."

CHAPTER TWENTY-SIX

Judge ashton's jest concerning Toussaint's paternity lingered in the ears of the crowd for an amused moment; then Colonel Miltiades Vaiden forgot it because he was full of more important affairs.

The Colonel cast his own ballot, got himself out of the election crowd as inconspicuously as possible, and pursued his way along the deserted road to Gracie's cottage in East Florence.

As he walked he wondered if he would possibly have any trouble getting the money back from Gracie. The mere thought of a Vaiden negro failing to safeguard his spoil, or failing to return it when he was ready for it, filled the Colonel with a kind of anticipatory grimness.

His very freedom from criminal prosecution depended upon Gracie's faithfulness. He wondered what he would do to a Vaiden nigger woman if she should spoil the sudden and miraculous fortune which had befallen him? He did not think he would shoot her. Shooting would be too painless. He clenched his fists as he walked along, and then put the whole idea to one side as absurd. Of course Gracie would not betray him.

The peculiar half-chanting wail of negro voices caught his ears. He was passing Miss Tony's house with its foolish gate posted like a sentinel in front of the rickety door.

"O Lawd," came a black woman's voice, "don' let him!"

"Don' let him!" came a chanting response on a higher key.

"Don' let Mas' Clebelan' be 'lected an' tu'n yo' chillun back into slabes once mo'."

"O Lawd, spa' yo' people dem scorpeen whups!"

"Don' let him, Lawd, don' let him!"

There were a half-dozen voices in the tightly shut cabin chanting simultaneously:

"We knows hit's wrong to lie an' steal."

"Men runs aftah women, an' us women 'lows hit."

"Gib us one mo' chanst, Lawd, to se've you bettah. Don' let Mas' Clebelan' git 'lected!"

The logical terror of the black folk that if a Republican President set them free, a Democratic President would cast them into chains again was lost on Miltiades. To him they were a cabinful of fool niggers mouthing their nigger prayers. He hurried on toward the neat white cottage of the quadroon a mile beyond.

Gracie's cottage was deserted. The white man knocked at the door, then entered, going directly to the kitchen, where the valise was concealed.

When he entered the kitchen he saw some boards laid on the top of the kitchen stove, and the cover of the manhole in the ceiling was gone, leaving a square black aperture.

A kind of coldness went over Miltiades at these signs. It flashed on him that somehow the Handbacks had got his money. They had caught on somehow . . . the direction he had taken from town . . . they had wormed the secret out of Gracie. . . .

As the Colonel stared at the hole in the ceiling a homicidal wrath rose up against the colored woman. He tingled to do some terrible violence to her. For a Vaiden nigger . . . one his own family had raised . . . the Colonel reached in his pocket and fingered Frierson's revolver.

He turned, walked back up the hallway, and opened the woman's bedroom door. A dress thrown across the foot of the bed suggested that Gracie had left the cottage hastily. The Colonel looked at the dress intently. He decided she would come back.

He went back to the kitchen again, studied the aperture, then suddenly climbed up on the stove and felt into the dark loft. His hand touched the valise. He gripped the leather corner and almost fell off the stove. He pulled the case to the edge of the manhole. He was trembling so violently that it almost fell out of his hands. He caught it against his chest, with the boards on the stove teetering under his feet. Then he saw that the valise had been opened and one of the packages broken into.

When the Colonel saw this a queer change came into the quality of his wrath. The broken package was Gracie's own theft. It was a nigger's trick to take a little out of much, to pilfer a dollar or two, to commit beggarly thefts. The Colonel got off the stove, put the valise on the table and began examining the torn package. It had a bill or two left in it. There had been five hundred-dollar packages and thousand-dollar packages in the container. At the very least Gracie had taken something near five hundred dollars.

This increase in the quadroon's theft worked another turn in Miltiades' complicated fury.

"God damn such a wench!" he shivered, "running off with hundreds of dollars. . . ."

The noise of the opening of the front door went through his nerves like the plucking of violin strings. He closed his hand over Frierson's pistol. He did not know whether or not he would use it. He ought to beat her with a stick of her own stove wood. He took a step backward so he could look through the kitchen door into the hall.

Gracie was just entering her room when she saw Miltiades in the kitchen. She gave a little cry and stood looking at him.

The man moistened his lips.

"You have taken some of my money," he said in a monotone.

The quadroon nodded with a strange heartbroken expression in her face.

"Y-yes, sir . . . th-three hundred dollars," she said unsteadily.

"What did you take it for?" trembled the Colonel.

"For—for Miss Ponny, Colonel Milt," breathed the woman.

"Ponny! Ponny! What did Ponny want with three . . ."

"Oh, Mas' Milt!" gasped Gracie, "to buy a coffin . . . to buy a coffin for her and her little baby. . . ."

And the quadroon began weeping, with a faint gasping sound, battling against her emotions like a white woman.

CHAPTER TWENTY-SEVEN

I N THE shabbily built boom house on Cherry Street the two front windows were alight. This double lighting silently reaffirmed to Miltiades the tragedy of which Gracie, the quadroon, already had informed him.

The house where Ponny and her baby were laid out for burial was, paradoxically, more astir with life than Miltiades had ever known it. The living room on the right-hand side seemed to be full of people. The company room on the left was lighted but appeared unoccupied. But as Miltiades moved up the dark walk to his door he saw through the window, lying on the bed of the company room, a great bulk covered with a sheet.

As the Colonel entered the hallway, Rose Vaiden, his sister-in-law, opened the door of the living room. She looked at him for a moment and then said in a monotone which was full of reproach:

"You know about Ponny, Miltiades?"

"Yes."

"She's in there."

A kind of wrench of emotion went through the viscera of Miltiades. He opened the door and went into the company room. Two or three of the visitors came to the door of the living room and silently watched him enter. The Colonel closed the door behind him.

What moved Miltiades most painfully of all was the complete stillness of the great sheeted figure on the bed. Ponny always had slept restlessly, but here was not the faintest suggestion of motion. Her heavy movements had ended.

As he stood looking at her body he recalled how she had wanted to go with him to the speaking in Courthouse Square, and how he had put her off and had gone away without her. Now the dead woman reproached him for his lifelong neglect and the faint shame which he always had felt for her. It had almost emptied her life of pleasures. The Colonel thought now, with useless self-reproach, that he need not have treated Ponny like that; she had deserved better than that.

After a space he turned and went back into the hallway. Rose was still there. She asked, "Have you had your supper?" When the Colonel said no, she directed that he would find some on the table.

She stood a little out of the doorway for him to pass.

In the living room there were several persons: Mrs. Ashton, who had brought Rose to Cherry Street in her buggy; Mrs. Klem with three of her children; two more neighbor women, and young Jerry Catlin.

As Miltiades walked through the room Mrs. Ashton said in a formal voice:

"Colonel Vaiden, I want to extend my sympathy to you in your bereavement."

The Colonel thanked her and went on into the kitchen. He sat down at the table feeling the disapproval and condemnation in all of his visitors. Condemnation of his theft, and shock that Ponny should have died while he was in jail, affected the voices and manner of all the women. It was in the big eyes of the Klem children as they looked at him. It sounded in Jerry's voice when he said, "Good-evening, Uncle Milt."

The table before him was loaded with food, cold boiled ham, cold fried chicken, corn bread, light bread, cold turnip greens, jams, pickles, sweet milk and butter milk, two kinds of fruit pies with strips of brown crust crisscrossed for tops. A pot of coffee simmered on the stove.

The neighbors had brought most of this in to make a solemn feast for the watchers who sat up with Ponny through the night.

Mrs. Klem was transported to find herself on an ephemeral equality with Mrs. Ashton and Mrs. Rose. She talked excitedly, telling these great ladies what had happened while they were interested in her story.

"I jest felt something was wrong," she continued, "when I saw the sheriff and Mr. Handback coming away from Miss Ponny's. . . ."

"Yes, yes, naturally," agreed Mrs. Ashton, frowning slightly at Mrs. Klem and trying to get her to hush now that Miltiades had entered the house.

"So, thinks I," proceeded Mrs. Klem, "I'll jest step over and see what's happened to Miss Ponny, and over I goes. And there she was. . . . Law, Miss Ashton, you'll never know how she looked, there on the floor, caught in . . ." Mrs. Klem paused significantly, shaking her head. After a moment she added, "And it was all brought on by that stinking sheriff and that hawg of a Handback tumbling ever'-thing in her house upside down and digging in her yard looking for the money."

"Mrs. Klem," ejaculated Mrs. Ashton, in exquisite discomfort, "have you got a long-handled broom in your house to sweep cobwebs? . . . Would you mind going and getting it for me?"

"Why, nome . . . not at all!" cried Mrs. Klem, filled with delight to be able to do something to accommodate Mrs. Ashton. "I'll send Virgy after it this minute," and she whirled one of her little girls off after the broom.

Mrs. Rose went into the kitchen to wait on Miltiades while he ate, and also to strengthen her silent condemnation of the Colonel by being near to him.

Rose had convicted Miltiades of wife murder. If Miltiades had not stolen the cotton the sheriff would never have frightened poor Ponny into a miscarriage with his search warrants. Rose had talked this steadily all the way from her boarding house to Ponny's home. Her brother-in-law was so repulsive to her that she could hardly endure to watch him eat at the table. She knew that he had never loved Ponny. Now he had done this to her.

As Rose poured and handed Miltiades a glass of milk she

could endure it no longer. She turned abruptly, went into the living room, and said to Mrs. Ashton:

"Susie, go attend to him . . . I'm sick."

Mrs. Ashton felt equivocally about Miltiades. She felt the Colonel had gone about collecting an old debt in an unconventional manner. He had tripped and got himself in jail. That incarceration changed him for her from a gentleman into a man who had been in jail.

She went into the kitchen thinking, not without a touch of ghastly humor, that here was she, Susan Ashton, wife of Judge Ashton, serving supper to a jailbird!

Presently, to prove to Miltiades that she was not thinking about his having been in jail, she said to him:

'Augustus has telegraphed everybody: Mr. Sylvester in Arkansas, your other brother in Louisiana, Marcia up in Tennessee, and he sent word to Miss Cassandra by a nigger. . . . I imagine he'll get some replies in the morning as to who is coming. . . . It's a good thing the weather is as cold as it is."

This last phrase had reference to the keeping of Ponny's body for two or three days.

"Did anybody send word to Mr. BeShears?" asked Miltiades.

"Why, no-o . . . I don't suppose they did," ejaculated Mrs. Ashton in a concerned voice, as if the oversight were her own.

"Well, there's plenty of time for that," said Miltiades; "they live down at the Crossroads."

For a space Miltiades ate in silence. The greater portion of his thought was a cold, conscious disregard for what the women about him were thinking. He asked himself silently, what difference did it make to him what the women thought?

The thoughts of the women were so childish and unperceiving. He had had no concern with Ponny's death. It had been brought about by circumstances over which he had no control.

Then, as he sat there, a queer thought came to Miltiades. It was Ponny, whom years ago he had married for her money, who at last, with her life, had countersigned his title to the fortune he now possessed. This bizarre fact, once it had come upon him, held his mind with a sort of fascination. Ponny's death really had rescued him from jail, delivered him from a criminal prosecution, and handed him a fortune. Because what chance would Handback have in any suit after he had done Ponny to death in his mal-use of the sheriff and the search warrant?

At this turn of his thoughts Miltiades' wrath began to rise against the merchant. He wished he had been at home when Mayhew and Handback were frightening his sick and pregnant wife! It was an outrageous misuse of official power! A prospective mother: to come turning her house upside down, no doubt demanding to know where the money was and abusing her for not being able to tell! The full cruelties enacted against Ponny grew upon the Colonel. No wonder they kept him locked up in jail without bond or bondsmen! No wonder when Ponny was dying they had come flying back to the jail and had compromised on ten thousand dollars and no criminal actions on either side!

The Colonel had known of Ponny's death when he returned with the money. When he had paid Frierson he had cursed the Handbacks for damned unscrupulous murderers, and he had said to the jailer that, as far as his liberty was concerned, he need not pay a cent. But he had paid over the money because he had said he would, because the word of a Vaiden was as good as another man's bond!

Then he had sent a negro to ask a bank to take the remainder of the money in their back door, it being election day. Later he had walked openly up Market Street with the return of his old debt and had deposited it.

But the money, the compromise money which he had left with Frierson to be paid to the Handbacks, he felt had been tricked from him. It was their damned slippery double dealing again!

In the midst of the Colonel's silent wrath Mrs. Klem entered the kitchen. The woman paused beside his chair and said in a low tone:

"Colonel Milt, I don't think there's going to be a place for you to sleep here. The comp'ny room's occupied, and the setter-ups will have to be in the fam'ly room by the far. If you want us to, we'll move yore bed in the hall."

Miltiades had not thought where he would sleep. He looked blankly at Mrs. Klem, then glanced around the kitchen as if choosing a place.

"That would be too much trouble, to move the bed in the hall."

"Why, no, it wouldn't be no trouble. . . . Miss Rose said you could come down to her house," proceeded the neighbor woman, "and you're more than welcome to our house, Colonel. Jeff likes you. He says you're not stuck up . . . it's jest a few steps down there. . . ." Here Mrs. Klem's sallow face trembled, tears filled her eyes. "I—I know you're goin' to miss Miss Ponny," she gasped. "We all are, Colonel Milt. . . ."

The neighbor woman's grief suddenly invaded Miltiades. He compressed his lips, swallowed at a pain in the back of his throat. When he could speak with evenness he said:

"I believe I'll go down to your house, Mrs. Klem, I appreciate your courtesy."

He realized, by this second-hand invitation Rose had sen to him through Mrs. Klem, how his sister-in-law loathed him, how she could not bring herself even to ask him to his brother's home to sleep.

CHAPTER TWENTY-EIGHT

Aт intervals, all night long, the funeral watchers in the tenement on Cherry Street heard the boom of the cannon of the Florence Fencibles.

The women who sat up with Ponny in the fore part of the night would glance at each other and talk in low tones of the election, but they did not forget they were sitting up with the dead. Now and then one of them would say to Jerry:

"Hadn't you better look in the company room to see if everything is all right?"

The boy would move, half awake, and look into the room of the dead, and then come back and try to sleep in his chair. He was to be a watcher in the latter part of the night. When the women went home he would go on duty. From time to time he vaguely heard the booming of the cannon, and a feeling of some indefinite evil filled Jerry's brain. Now and then he really did drift into unconsciousness.

At twelve o'clock the women aroused Jerry again, and everybody went out to eat a midnight snack. The women had been looking forward to this repast for hours and ate with good appetites. But it was a solemn eating. The watchers felt the presence of the dead woman in the company room, and the food had a funereal flavor.

After their meal the women put on their shawls and went home. Mrs. Klem told Jerry she would send Mr. Klem over to sit up for the rest of the night, and for Jerry to drink two cups of coffee to keep him from going to sleep. The boy did this and presently became intensely awake. His aroused and rather awed mind began to think of his aunt Ponny. Her death struck him not with grief, because he had seen her only a few times, and then her flesh had rather shocked and

repelled him, but it filled him with a sense of solemn fore-
boding that such a thing could happen in his own family.
Death had seemed to Jerry something that came to other
folk, but his own kindred moved on in a sort of unquestion-
able immortality.

Then, as he brooded before the fire, he shifted from this
child's view of life to the mystical apprehension of existence
which he had been reading in the occult books he had found
in the college library.

He thought of his aunt Ponny's soul. He thought of the
darkness of the night extending thousands of miles into
stellar space, and he wondered if his aunt's soul would find
the light of day. Surrounded by this blackness in the shock
and horror of dissolving death, how would his aunt's soul
know where to turn?

And young Jerry thought if only he were an adept, if he
had learned to hold commerce with the bodiless dead, he
might guide his aunt Ponny through the dark immensity of
the night.

He wished earnestly that he had been more persistent and
more successful in his occult exercises. Perhaps by now he
could have developed his force sufficiently to aid his dead
aunt in this mystery of death.

The priests of many churches believed they could succor
the souls of the dead through prayer, the Catholics, the Mor-
mons, the Hindus. The possibility of such ministrations filled
Jerry with a profound desire. He began tentatively exerting
his will to make himself known to the spirit of his aunt. He
thought intently:

"Aunt Ponny, this is Jerry, your nephew . . . this is
Jerry . . . this is Jerry. . . ."

He repeated this over and over. He meant his aunt Ponny's
soul to feel his mental vibrations and be calmed and comforted by his human sympathy and nearness.

The boy's whole heart was filled with desire to comfort
his aunt Ponny. After a while this impulse widened to include
all the sorrowful of the earth, both the living and the dead.

He willed that people with griefs should come to him. He wished passionately to devote his life to the easing of the sorrows of men.

As Jerry thought these things there came a step on the walk outside the front door. A shock of embarrassment went through the boy. He got quickly up from his kneeling position and sat in his chair again. All thought of his aunt Ponny vanished from his mind in his effort to appear usual and commonplace before Mr. Klem. He hoped that Mr. Klem had not seen him through the window.

He glanced at the window to see if he had been in view from the walk, but he could tell nothing by the black face of the night pressed against the panes.

He sat waiting for several moments. Nobody came in. Jerry became curious. He looked at the windows, and a fantastic notion crossed his mind. Suppose the soul of his aunt Ponny had heard him and had made a sound in the yard! The youth arose, walked in a dream to the front door, and looked out.

At first he saw nothing at all. Then far to the south he saw a diffused light from the bonfire in Courthouse Square. He stood staring steadily, half expecting to see an aureole in the shape of a human form, as his occult books had described.

He saw nothing, but presently he felt there was someone standing in the darkness looking at him.

"Who is it out there?" he asked in a low tone.

"It—it's me," replied a voice.

"Who is me?" asked Jerry apprehensively.

"Loob Snipes."

Jerry became at ease.

"What do you want, Loob?"

"Is—is Col'l Milt heah?"

"No, he isn't here."

The negro was quiet a moment; then said:

"Could you meet me roun' at de back do', Mist' Jer'y?"

"What for, Loob?"

"Well, suh, Ah—Ah'm de niggah whut kep' Mist' Lucius f'um shootin' Col'l Milt in de sto' de oddah day. . . ."

"Yes?"

"An' . . . an' ol' Mistuh Han'back done tu'n me off'n his place fuh my pains. An' my wife Haly an' ouah fo' li'l' child'un is a-standin' out thah in de road now, hongry. We kain't git nothin' to do heah in Flaunts. . . . We'se country niggahs. . . ."

"Well, Loob, I can't do anything for you," said Jerry.

"No, suh, I knows you kain't. . . ."

"Then what do you want me to go to the back door for?"

Loob remained silent for several seconds.

"Uh—well, Ah knowed you-all have a lot fixed up to eat . . . Miss Ponny bein' dead . . . mo'n you-all could eat yo'se'ves. An'—an'—an' I wondahed if you wouldn't han' me a li'l' somep'n out de back do' fuh Haly an' de child'un, Mist' Jerry?"

The youth was annoyed that a negro should have the impudence to come around begging for his aunt's funeral snack. He thought sharply to himself:

"They'll do anything in the world to get a white person's sympathy and take advantage of it."

Aloud he was saying:

"No, Loob, it's not mine. I can't give any of it away. I am just one of the watchers here, waiting for day to come."

CHAPTER TWENTY-NINE

O<small>F ALL</small> the Vaidens to whom Augustus sent telegrams announcing Ponny's death, only Marcia Catlin, Jerry's mother, returned an answer. She would reach Florence, the reply said, on the following morning.

Jerry looked forward to his mother's coming with a certain apprehension. He felt his stay in Florence had wrought changes in him which his mother might not recognize. But when she arrived, early the second morning after his aunt Ponny's death, worn from an all-night drive through the country in a livery-stable hack, his anxiety vanished. He submitted to her kiss and did not understand the nervous pressure of her arms around him as she prayed for a second that her son would never succumb to the temptation of theft as had her brother Miltiades.

Marcia stayed with Augustus and Rose. When the neighbors heard that Mrs. Catlin was at Rose's home they came before the hour set for the funeral to see her: the Ashtons, the Crowninshields, Mrs. Bradley, other persons who scarcely knew her but had heard of her. Among them Mrs. Frierson, the jailer's wife, came to see the visitor. She introduced herself and said she had seen Marcia once before the war at the Lacefield manor, and when she heard Miss Marcia was in town she felt like she just had to see her again. She said she was Eliza Ham's niece.

Mrs. Catlin held the woman's hand and said:

"Well . . . well . . . well . . . and you are Eliza's niece. . . . Which one of Eliza's sisters was your mother?"

"Mary."

"Where is Eliza now?"

Mrs. Frierson said her aunt was living in Lenstock, Texas. When Eliza and her husband were on their way to Texas from Alabama they had stopped overnight at Bay Minette, Louisiana, and had stayed with Marcia's elder brother Lycurgus Vaiden.

Marcia said:

"Just think of that, she saw Lycurgus."

During Marcia's girlhood Eliza Ham had meant almost nothing to her. Mrs. Frierson she did not remember at all, but now she was moved to see any human being who had lived in that vanishing glory that surrounded her girlhood days.

Drusilla Crowninshield Marcia never really had liked, but now the old rivalry and the faint intellectual contempt which Marcia had felt for the daughter of the Lacefield manor had passed away. For the first time in her life Marcia was reconciled to Drusilla for breaking her betrothal to Miltiades and eloping with Major Crowninshield. Marcia now supposed that even back in those days Drusilla had divined that Miltiades was dishonest. It did not dawn upon her that if Drusilla had married her brother the theft he had committed would have been impossible. Mrs. Catlin let the whole painful episode slip into forgiveness and forgetfulness. She said in a low voice, looking at Sydna:

"Your daughter is almost as pretty as you were, Drusilla, when you were a girl."

And Drusilla turned and looked curiously at Sydna, reviewing through Marcia's eyes her own past loveliness.

A cream-colored woman came to the door of the boarding house and stood just outside the threshold, looking at Marcia. Finally, in a lull in the talk of the white women, Rose said:

"Marcia, do you know who this is?"

Mrs. Catlin looked at the quadroon's face for upward of half a minute and finally asked:

"Is that you, Gracie?"

And Gracie's dark, wrinkled eyes suddenly filled with tears, and she said in a low tone:

"Yes, Li'l' Miss, this is Gracie. How are you getting along, Li'l' Miss?"

And Marcia said:

"Very well, Gracie. . . . Well, I declare, Gracie . . . I'm glad to see you, Gracie."

"And I'm glad to see you, Li'l' Miss."

Here Mrs. Catlin's talk went back to the white women, but Gracie, standing at the door, clung uncomfortably in the ex-mistress's mind. It made her think of her dead brother Polycarp, by whom, she had always believed, Gracie had borne her child. Now the thought of Polycarp's misconduct and Miltiades' theft filled Mrs. Catlin with anxiety for her own son. She could not imagine where such a heritage had entered her family.

It was now ten o'clock, the hour set when the whole group would go to Miltiades' home on Cherry Street for Ponny's funeral services. Just before they started, Rose drew Marcia aside and whispered:

"We have a back seat for Gracie, if you want her to come along."

But Marcia, filled with the disturbance caused by Gracie's presence, shook her head slightly and turned with the others for the door.

A little later, when the group of the white Vaidens and their friends drove away in two buggies and the hack, the cream-colored woman stood at the gate and watched them out of sight.

In the house on Cherry Street Marcia met her brother Miltiades. She was so moved at the thought of his dishonesty, the color faded from her face and left visible the fine grains of chalk upon her cheeks. She could scarcely speak to him. She quavered, "Miltiades . . . I'm so sorry for you . . ." and began weeping.

She felt as if her brother had put himself into some far-off region where neither she nor any of the family could ever come near him again. That her chivalrous brother could have stolen! That Colonel Miltiades Vaiden, a gallant officer during the war, a leader of men during the tragic days of the Reconstruction, the one member of her family of whom she always had been proud, that brother, a common thief. . . .

At the contagion of Marcia's tears the other women in the house began weeping. The Christian minister with his broad face and smacking lips stood in the bare company room and spoke in Ponny's funeral. He described the rich rewards of a Christian life, extolling the patience, the charity, the faith and loving-kindness of the dead woman who lay in her coffin at the end of her empty existence.

The interment of Ponny was to take place at the family burial ground on the old Vaiden plantation. The minister and friends remained in Florence; only the family undertook the long drive of sixteen miles over a rough road.

The black hearse and the hack, in order to return to Florence that day, were forced to break into an indecent trotting and bumping over the less rough stretches of the road.

On the way to the old homestead, the cortège stopped at the Crossroads and picked up old Mr. BeShears. A half hour later, in the early afternoon, they reached their destination.

The sight of her sister Cassandra, a gray-haired old woman, coming out of the ruinous log house to meet them filled Marcia with desolation. It made the whole gay, brave past of their family unbelievable. The part which she, her very self, had lived broke away from reality and became a legend lingering over the house and the fields, as remote as the mound builders.

Buck Mosely and some negroes from the Crossroads already had dug the grave. These black men tugged and sweated and lowered the great coffin into its resting place among the slim pines growing on the hillock.

As the negroes refilled the grave and rounded the raw red mound the family stood watching in silence. Old man BeShears, balanced on his injured feet, looked at an ancient stone which bore the half obliterated epitaph:

POLYCARP VAIDEN

SON OF JAMES AND LAURA VAIDEN
BORN 1845.   DIED 1865.

A BRAVE SOLDIER, A LOVING SON, A GENTLEMAN OF HONOR.
DIED TAKING ALMS TO THE NEEDY.

It happened, through the undirected digging of the negroes, that Ponny was buried beside him.

CHAPTER THIRTY

Three days after Ponny Vaiden's burial Marcia Catlin started back to Tennessee. Her friends made a second call on the visitor to express a hope that they would see her again sometime, but Marcia did not know. It was such a long way from her home in Tennessee to Florence . . . nearly fifty miles . . . and the roads were so bad. . . .

"You'll have to come back and see Jerry graduate," they suggested.

But in her heart Marcia did not think she would. If Miltiades or Augustus or Rose should die, then she would make the long trip back again to attend their funerals, but outside of some family calamity she did not believe she would see friends and kinsfolk again.

These old friends regretted Marcia's going. In her presence they lived again in the glamour of their youth. She was like a chemical that brought out the romantic record of their past on the palimpsest of their double lives in the old South and the new.

The only person in Florence really gratified to see Marcia start back to Tennessee was her son Jerry.

His mother completely disarranged Jerry's outer and inner worlds. In the same boarding house with his mother he could not go on with his exercises in saintliness; he could not debate with Sandusky concerning men and God and things. He could not even think comfortably about Sydna Crowninshield under his mother's eyes.

However, Jerry did not realize these handicaps. He did not know that he wanted her to go. He sincerely supposed that he was delighted that his mother had come to visit him. He bought her a cheap box of candy downtown which cost

270

him his spending money for a week. He purchased tickets to a negro minstrel and then sat through it on needles and pins over obscene jokes at which he would have roared had his mother not been along. He even took a walk with her one crisp afternoon, and was keenly embarrassed because Sydna Crowninshield called good-day to him from her yard.

When Marcia finally started home, Jerry rode seven miles with her in the hack, then kissed her good-bye with tears in his eyes and walked back to Florence.

Everyone, including even Sandusky, agreed that they had never seen a mother and a son so congenial and so devoted to each other. Jerry was almost as much pleased at this report as he was that his mother finally had gone home and left him, once more, to his own devices.

He walked the seven miles back to Florence with tears in his eyes and treading on air.

The departure of Marcia acted on the Augustus Vaiden family like the dying out of an opiate, and all those small bitternesses which go to make up life in any well regulated establishment broke out afresh.

When Jerry got back from his long, filial walk, he found his uncle Augustus fretting to go to town. Rose would not let him, because she thought it was too chilly.

"I want to walk down there and lay the law down to A. Gray Lacefield," declared Augustus in a dudgeon. "I want him to know what'll happen if he publishes a word about that!"

"Why, he wouldn't think of publishing anything about it," soothed Rose.

"Of course he will!" cried Augustus, "unless somebody lays the law down to him."

"Well, you can't go down there on a cold day like this. . . ." She pondered a moment, then: "Write a note and send it by Jerry. The bitter weather would give you the la grippe."

Augustus grumbled at this deputing of his authority, but finally got up from the kitchen table to hunt a pencil and

paper. He had to search clear up in Sandusky's room before
he found any. He brought these back to the kitchen table
and wrote a fierce note:

> Mr. A. Gray Lacefield,
>   Editor *Florence Index,*
> Sir:
>   If you print any reference to my brother Miltiades
> Vaiden in your filthy scandalmongering sheet you wil
> have me personally to settle with. Yours,
>   Augustus Vaiden.

Rose took the note, read it, nodded to Jerry to follow
her, and walked out into the hall.

"Jerry," she said, tearing the note thoughtfully into little
pieces, "run downtown and ask Mr. Lacefield not to mention anything about your uncle Miltiades in his paper."
Tears formed in Rose's eyes. "It's important, Jerry. It—
it'll just ruin the family. Already your uncle Augustus has
had to give up the position he was offered at the Barham
Furniture Store. It's just ruined Augustus' business career."

She blinked the moisture out of her eyes and controlled
herself. "Tell Mr. Lacefield your mother came to Ponny's
funeral, and all her old friends enjoyed her visit greatly.
That will be something for him to print."

Jerry received this commission with a sense of importance.
He walked down to the *Index* office and told the editor what
his aunt Rose had asked.

A. Gray Lacefield was a smallish man with the whitened
face and rather overbright eyes of a printer. Now he called
his devil and went with Jerry to the forms that were already
put to bed.

"Listen to this," he said appealingly to Jerry, "wouldn't
you think this was putting it delicately enough?" and he
read from the reversed type:

" 'Last week our old friend and fellow townsman, Colonel
Miltiades Vaiden, made an overnight business visit to Mr.

Joe Frierson, our esteemed manager of Lauderdale County's detention department.' What's the matter with that?"

Jerry was sharply embarrassed to be asked to sit in judgment on the article, but he faced the situation and said honestly:

"Mr. Lacefield, everybody will know what you mean."

The editor drew a long breath. He was as unhappy over the matter as Jerry.

"Dad brim it! My duty to my subscribers . . . the whole truth, nothing but the truth, let the chips fall where they may. . . ." He bent over and read the type again. "Everybody knows it, anyway," he argued, "if I print something that is public knowledge, who does it hurt?"

"Why, Aunt Rose and Uncle Augustus and my mother," said Jerry.

Now, it happened that Jerry's mother had been A. Gray Lacefield's sweetheart during his youth. That young man had spent his attractive years trying to persuade her to marry him, but at last she had married Jerry's father. So the editor looked at the type a little longer, took his mallet, knocked the quoins loose, and neatly extracted the offending paragraph with his rule. He set it aside in a galley, then went to a case and set up in bold-faced capitals,

WATCH THIS SPACE NEXT WEEK
FOR IMPORTANT NEWS

He locked this in and started to work at his Washington hand press.

The embarrassment of quashing the newspaper article was not the only spiritual tax levied against Jerry Catlin on account of his uncle Miltiades' peculation. A reception was given to the sophomore class, and Jerry received an invitation. When he cast about for a girl in his class to go with him, he discovered that they all had escorts.

This did not greatly distress him. In fact, it was a mild

relief, because he never got on very well with girls of his own age. In addition to this he always felt a faint uneasiness at a public reception lest he say or do the wrong thing. However, the fact that he could not get any girl at all with whom to undergo the thin penetrating unpleasantness of a social function caused Jerry to mention it to Sandusky that afternoon.

The boarder immediately became virulent. He inquired acridly:

"What difference does it make whether them little stuck-up sophomore girls go with you or not?"

"Well," said Jerry, "it's improving. It learns you how to act."

"I say, the less you have to do with such people the better off you are! They're stuck-up because they were born here in Florence . . . always colluging together like they was God'lmighty's little nieces."

Jerry refrained from smiling. He knew, as did everyone else in college, that Sandusky had written a note to a sophomore girl asking her to go to a picnic with him. It was a very formal note, which he had copied straight out of the *Complete Letter Writer's Guide.* That invitation became its recipient's prize possession. She showed it to all of her girl friends and to some of the women teachers.

When Sandusky found this out he was furious. For two or three days he spent his spare time in Governor O'Shawn's law office trying to find out if he could recover the letter by means of a replevin suit. When he could find no precedent for this he contemplated a suit for slander.

Now Sandusky shook his head at Jerry:

"Stuck up and treacherous as snakes," he added.

"They've always treated me fair enough," defended Jerry mildly.

Sandusky sat straighter at his table.

"Oh, you think so, do you?"

"Why, sure," said Jerry a little surprised.

"Then I'll tell you why all them girls had beaux to go

to the reception. It's this: All the other boys' invitations had girls' names in 'em already. They didn't have to ask nobody."

"Why, mine didn't!" ejaculated Jerry.

"No . . . none of the girls wanted their names in your invite," explained the boarder maliciously.

Jerry stared at Sandusky. He thought of his uncle Miltiades.

"Oh!" he ejaculated in a changed tone. "I didn't know that."

When the boarder saw the damage he had wrought, he tried to mend it.

"Don't pay no attention to the ignorance of a lot of fatheaded Florence girls. They've got ever'thing wrong, anyway. In the first place, your uncle Milt didn't steal that cotton, he was just collecting an old debt, he's got a paper that'll show it. In the next place, if he had 'a' stole it, there's no jestice in holding it aginst you. But it's all fam'ly with these Florence folks. They don't think about nothin' but fam'ly."

"Is that really why they left any girl's card out of my envelope?" queried the youth incredulously.

"Why, sure . . . jest like I was telling you."

Jerry sat staring at a mismatched place in the dingy flowered wall paper in their room.

"I wonder how long this will last?"

"Why, I imagine four or five years after you are dead will see you through."

Jerry considered this a stroke of wit and laughed a little.

"Well, I don't know that it will make any particular difference with me," he said at length. "I don't really like to go with 'em, anyway."

"Same here," echoed Sandusky.

"Still, I do consider it improving."

"Improving for what?"

"It makes you feel at ease when you are with 'em."

"Why, hell, if you ain't never going with 'em, what difference does it make whether you'd feel at ease or not? You see that just cancels itself out."

"That's so, too," admitted Jerry gravely.

The two young men sat in silence in the bare upper room. A tiny stove, shaped like an hourglass, suddenly ceased to make a small roar, and Sandusky knew it was out. The little stove went out very easily, but it made amends by being very difficult to start. Sandusky looked around for some waste paper.

"Girls are silly as geese, anyway," continued Sandusky, rumpling up a sheet of newspaper.

"Some of 'em make better grades than I do," admitted Jerry.

"Do you know why?" demanded Sandusky sharply.

" 'Cause they're smarter, I guess," opined the hobbledehoy.

"No, it's because they have feminine minds. I read about it in psychology just the other day. A man's mind doesn't really work at anything except what it's interested in. But a woman's mind is just like a waste basket. It'll hold anything you throw in it. Why? Why, because it don't make no diff'runce to girls. They're not goin' to do anything with their minds anyway, and so they'd jest as soon have them full of one kind of junk as another. And do you know what I thought to myself when I read that?"

"Have no idyah," admitted Jerry.

"Why, this. I said to myself, 'Sandusky, here you are in college, learning in college that you cain't learn anything in college because most of what they teach here don't apply to your mind. So college cancels itself out. All right, that bein' the case, I'm going to quit all this tomfoolery and get down to law which my mind can take in. I'm going to pass the bar examinations as quick as I can and be a lawyer.' "

As Jerry was not really listening to this he did not follow it.

"So I'm quittin' today," concluded Sandusky; "this is my last day."

The brooding boy came to his surroundings.

"Last day of what?"

"College," repeated Sandusky sharply, "I'm quitting college today!"

"What are you goin' to do?"

"Why, doggone it, I told you I was going to pass my bar examination and practise law."

Jerry looked at the boarder in amazement. The fellow's quitting school gave the youth a sense of sacrilege. Jerry himself was doing nothing in college. He considered all his studies, taken separately, as unimportant, but he did believe that college in the abstract was the very foundation of any degree of enlightened existence, and the only hope of success in life. The fact that most of the successful men he knew were not college men had no bearing on this belief. Now he stared at Sandusky as if the fellow were committing economic suicide.

"You are still writing at your lessons," he pointed out weakly.

"No, I'm not," denied the boarder, "this is something about the law," and he folded what he had written and stuck it in his pocket.

"Are you going to keep on boarding here?" asked Jerry tentatively.

"I am till I pass the bar examination and get into a good practice," said Sandusky.

"Then we can look forward to the pleasure of your company for quite a while," suggested Jerry.

"I don't know whether you can or not," said Sandusky stiffly.

He took an envelope out of his drawer, addressed it, and placed whatever he had written inside of it. Then he got up and looked around for his hat, evidently about to go somewhere.

Jerry came to life at once. He jumped up and went scuttling downstairs. He found his aunt Rose and his uncle Augustus in the kitchen and excitedly told them that Sandusky was quitting college. The two asked a few swift questions and found out that Jerry did not know why the boarder was quitting. Immediately both husband and wife hurried into the hallway to head off Sandusky. They waited about a minute when he appeared on the steps. Augustus cleared his throat.

"Er—Mr. Sandusky," he said gravely, "Jerry tells me you—er—you are thinking of quitting college?"

"I'm not thinking of quitting," said Sandusky, "I've quit."

"Well, now . . . look here, Mr. Sandusky . . ."

"Mr. Sandusky," interrupted Rose swiftly, "if it's because you haven't got enough money to put yourself through college, you can stay on here and pay half board, or not pay any board at all—whichever is the most convenient."

Sandusky was amazed at such a proposal.

"Why, no-no," he said blankly, "it isn't because I haven't got the money, Miss Rose; I—I come here with two hund'erd dollars like the catalogue said . . . and I've still got it."

"Then—what's the matter?" asked Mrs. Rose, bewildered.

"Well," said Sandusky judicially, "I jest don't feel like I'm getting anything out of college."

"Not getting anything out of . . . Why, you study, don't you, Mr. Sandusky?"

"Yes, but looky here, what diff'runce will it ever make to me whether my tarsal bones are in my shins or my wrists?"

"You break one of them and you'll find out," put in Augustus, who did not know where they were himself.

"Well, I hope I don't break anything," said Sandusky, "but if I do, I'd be a whole lot more likely to get well of a sprained ankle than if I had a ruptured carpal or tarsal, or whatever it is down there. That's my way of thinking."

"We see you are a very ungrateful young man," said Mrs. Rose warmly.

Sandusky went on out the door thinking stiffly of the insult they had put upon him to think he had no money.

Augustus, Mrs. Rose, and Jerry went back into the

kitchen full of wrath at the obstinacy, induracy, and pig-headedness of Sandusky.

"It's men like that who refuse an education when they could get it that you find later in life hoeing cotton and plowing corn like a nigger in the field," said Mrs. Rose, quite piqued that Sandusky had not needed her charity.

CHAPTER THIRTY-ONE

Sandusky proceeded toward town filled with ironic contempt for the slur the Vaidens had put upon him by considering that he was poverty stricken.

On the contrary, he was rich, or at least he was potentially rich. Indeed, his decision to quit college was based on the fact that within the last few days he had made a great deal of money at his profession, and it stood to reason he would make a great deal more. Why, he would make more, he supposed, in the run of a year than the president of the college himself! The envelope in his pocket proved that.

Here Sandusky reached into his pocket, touched the talismanic envelope, and was doubly fortified.

At the cross street that turned into Pine, Sandusky paused, looked about him for a moment, then turned right and walked over to the more unfrequented thoroughfare. Presently he moved in silence townward along its mould of leaves.

As he drew near the Crowninshield home he glimpsed across the old fence a girl with bright blonde hair in a blue and yellow morning dress. She was gathering chrysanthemums which ran in all gradations from pinkish white to reddish black. Sandusky had no idea what this major chord of red did to the unfinished cadence of yellow and blue, but it had its effect on him, nevertheless. He supposed the charm of the ensemble belonged wholly to Sydna, and he felt this charm was something he could possess and touch and use, like real estate or a pie.

When he came within talking distance Sandusky began walking slowly, hoping the girl would glance around. As she did not, but continued cutting flowers, Sandusky stopped completely, cleared his throat, and said with a sense of mental strain at trying to think up something to say:

"Those are very pretty flowers you are picking, Miss Sydna."

The girl looked around with a faint start.

"Yes," she agreed, "they are very pretty," and went on with her work.

Sandusky moistened his lips.

"Are—are they your favorite flowers?" he asked emptily.

"Why-y . . . no."

"Is—is red your favorite color?"

The girl looked around at him again.

"No," she said, a little surprised and amused at his persistence, and then, not to be too curt, she added, "It's blue."

"Blue," repeated Sandusky staring at her as if this were a surprising color. "Do you . . . do you like poetry?"

"Why, no, not specially," answered the girl in growing astonishment.

The smallish man wished he had never started such a conversation, because, once under way, he could not stop it.

"Uh—er—what is your favorite dish, Miss Sydna?" he inquired next.

The girl compressed a smile from her lips.

"The one that holds the most," she said.

At this reply Sandusky became miffed. He felt himself laughed at. He thought to himself that Sydna was laughing at a very successful lawyer if she did but know it. He had half a mind to show her the envelope in his pocket. But he did not allow the girl to see that she had miffed him.

He glanced at the sky as if he were drawing some deduction as to the time of day from the position of the sun.

"Well, I guess I better be moseying along," he said.

"Good-bye," said Sydna, biting her lips.

Notwithstanding his affront, Sandusky moved away with obvious reluctance. After inching along the length of two panels of fencing he came to another halt.

"I'm stopping college," he said.

The girl looked at him in genuine surprise.

"Do you go to college?"

"Why, sure," said Sandusky, "I've been going to school nearly three——" Suddenly it dawned on Sandusky that the girl did not know who he was. This amused him. "I'm Sandusky," he said in a lighter voice; "I'm Miss Rose Vaiden's boarder."

"Why, ye-es . . . ye-es . . ." ejaculated Sydna, rather disconcerted.

"That's all right," agreed Sandusky readily; "nobody hardly ever knows me. Folks I see over and over . . . it's the dad-blamedest thing."

"I don't see how anyone could forget you," said Sydna.

"Well, they do, but I figger they're goin' to remember me from now on."

"Why?" inquired the girl, letting curiosity overcome her tact.

"Because I'm going in the legal business," nodded Sandusky. He reached in his pocket, drew out the envelope, and stood fingering it and looking at it.

"Is that why you are going to stop school?" inquired Sydna.

"That and the slights," said Sandusky.

The girl looked at him with some curiosity.

"The slights?"

"Yes, them college girls. They're so biggoty. They wouldn't any more stand here and talk to me in a nice way like you're doing than they'd fly. They'd try to throw off on me." Sandusky pulled down his mouth. "I say let 'em throw off, it's all the same to me. But now they're starting in on Jerry the same way. And I ralely think that's a shame. It'll be worse on him than it was on me, because he hasn't got the backbone I have."

Sydna laid down her flowers and approached the fence.

"What Jerry are you talking about—Jerry Catlin?"

"Yes."

"What did anybody do to him?" asked the girl intently.

"Why, they slighted him at a party they're giving. They didn't put anybody's name in his envelope. He feels it even if he pertends like he don't."

Sydna went on with a staccato catechism until she knew what had happened to Jerry.

"Why, the idea!" she ejaculated; "the idea of them treating a nice boy like Jerry thattaway. . . ."

"Oh, well," said Sandusky loftily, "I'm not supprised. You'll find Florence girls treacherous as snakes, Miss Sydna. My motto is, don't han'l' tar, or you'll get yourself black. So I let 'em alone." Sandusky glanced at the sun again.

"Well, I ralely have got to be moseying."

CHAPTER THIRTY-TWO

Sandusky's trip to town turned out not so profitable financially as he had anticipated. He was hunting for Colonel Miltiades Vaiden. When he reached the business part of town, he began inquiring for the Colonel. Everyone had seen him, but they directed Sandusky to widely separated places and had him walking from one end of the business section to the other.

Now and then some person wanted to talk to Sandusky about the glorious election of a Democratic President, but the oldish young man had neither time nor inclination for such rejoicing. He had voted the Democratic ticket in the present election because he had made up his mind to make his home in Florence, but he came of a Republican family and at heart he was a Republican himself. If his father ever found out he had voted the Democratic ticket he would not allow him to come home any more.

So Sandusky evaded comment on the election and continued searching for the Colonel.

Passers-by reported the Colonel was with Bradley, the real-estate man, and from the information Sandusky received, the two seemed to be walking in all directions at once. At last a negro in Intelligence Row pointed out Bradley and the Colonel talking in front of a ramshackle building on the opposite side of Courthouse Square.

Sandusky got out his envelope and started for them.

Both men were smoking fat black cigars. Bradley smoked his automatically with one eye closed against its string of smoke. The Colonel was very conscious of his cigar, taking it out of his lips now and then, looking at it, flipping off the ash.

The real-estate man was warning the Colonel earnestly:

"Now, Colonel, you don't want one of these damn shiny plate-glass stores . . . you're no Jew."

"But, Bradley," persisted the Colonel, "I want a location on Market Street. Nobody's going to come 'way over here to trade."

"The customers who will trade with you follow you to the jumping-off place to do it," pronounced the real-estate man positively.

This was evidently one of those conversations which would not end, so Sandusky put in tentatively:

"Colonel, could I have a word with you when you're through?"

The Colonel held up a hand of assent and continued to Bradley:

"That's exactly where you misapprehend me, I'm not looking for that sort of store or that sort of trade."

"Then what sort of a damn store are you looking for?" asked Bradley, out of patience.

"I want to put in a department store."

"A what?"

"A department store . . . you know what a department store is!"

"Why, that's city doings!"

"Why wouldn't one go in Florence?"

"I don't know, but I'll prob'ly be in position to tell you when you get through."

"You mean by that you haven't any Market Street property you could offer me?"

"This wouldn't do?" Bradley nodded at the shack behind him.

"That wouldn't do for the warehouse of what I've got in mind."

"I see . . . Could you wait till next month, Colonel, before you settle on anything?"

"Why?"

"Old man Simpson's lease on his drug store runs out next month. You offer me a little better figger, and I'll go around to old Mrs. Wood and lease it from over Simpson's head . . . he's paying sixty."

"A month!" ejaculated Miltiades.

"If you could offer her sixty-five . . ."

The Colonel hesitated. In the outlines of the business he hoped to establish, Miltiades thought in the expansive terms of his overseership before the war, but the actual details he considered in the light of the penurious years he had lived in Florence.

"I'll look around a little further before I settle on anything."

"Looky here, Colonel," cried Bradley, jerking down his cigar and opening his smoked eye, "this is no time to put off leasing or buying. The minute Cleveland gets his seat, ever'thing in the South, rents, farms, produce, ever' damn thing is going to jump sky high."

"That's a fact," agreed the Colonel, with a return of his impatience to buy.

Sandusky interposed again.

"Could I have half a second, Colonel?"

"Just a minute. . . ." Here another thought entered the Colonel's head. He said to Bradley, "Farms, too?"

"Hell, yes. They'll be a little behind other things, but the general advance will drag land up too."

"I was thinking of a farm," said the Colonel, "a small farm about the size of two nigger fam'lies. Have you got anything like that?"

"Two fam'lies . . ." Bradley considered. ". . . Two. . . . Look here, Colonel," began the real-estate man with tentative enthusiasm, "I've got a six-nigger fam'ly plantation that I can make you at such a figger you'll swear you stole it."

Miltiades asked where it was.

"Now, of course," warned Bradley, "land values are going to be a little slow in responding to the Cleveland Administration. You can't turn this over at a profit inside of six months."

"All right, what plantation is it?" pursued the Colonel, with interest.

"Well, it's the old Lacefield place," said Bradley.

An odd little feeling went through the Colonel.

"Has Handback put that up for sale?"

"He told me yesterday he wanted to sell it. He priced it at fifteen thousand for a quick sale."

Miltiades was pleased in a sardonic way at this news. While he was clerking for Handback, he wished the merchant well, but now that he had stolen from him he wished him all the evil that could befall him.

"Offer him seven thousand five hundred dollars from me," he directed.

Bradley screwed up his smoked eye a little more tightly.

"Don't believe it would be the thing to mention your name, Colonel," he said frankly, "and it wouldn't be worth while to mention that price, either."

The idea of owning the old Lacefield plantation flowed through the Colonel's nerves with a subtle satisfaction.

"What price would you mention to him?"

"Not less than twelve, five. I'd be willing to try that on him and see if it was a fit."

"I have known that place," said Miltiades musingly, "when a hundred and fifty thousand wouldn't touch it."

"M-m . . . that's not in this day and time. All right, looky here, I'll offer him the twelve, five . . . and I won't tell him who it's from. There's no use doing that. I'll say I'm buying it myself and let the deed pass through me."

"Twelve, five," repeated Miltiades. "Not that I need such a big place. I don't. I've only got a couple of nigger fam'lies to provide a place for."

The two men separated, repeating twelve, five, several times, after the fashion of men careful to have the price understood. Bradley moved off up the street in a straight line for Handback's store.

With the real-estate agent's departure, Sandusky closed in on the Colonel, envelope in hand. He was so nervous he almost dropped it. He moistened his lips.

"Colonel," he said, "here—here's a little something for you . . ." and he handed Miltiades the letter.

The Colonel took it and looked at it, rather mystified.

"What is this?" he queried.

"It—it's a bill," stammered Sandusky.

"Bill for what?"

"It says," said Sandusky.

The Colonel opened the bill and looked at it.

"It—it says, 'For legal services rendered,'" read Miltiades, puzzled. "Rendered when?"

"Why, in your trouble with Mr. Handback, sir."

The Colonel drew back a step and frowned.

"Why, I didn't have any lawsuit with Handback."

"N-no," stammered Sandusky, "but w-we avoided a lawsuit, Colonel; w-we compromised the case, you know, on your payment of ten thousand dollars."

The Colonel stood looking at the bill.

"Why, to compromise a case isn't doing anything at all. There's no work connected with compromising. A man could do that for himself. . . . Did Governor O'Shawn make out this bill?"

"I made it out as his clerk," explained Sandusky hastily.

"Do you mean to say the Governor charges me five hundred dollars for you doing one day's work? Why, damn it, he must consider your time very valuable!"

"Lawyer bills," said Sandusky uncomfortably, "are made out—er—according to the amount of money connected with the case."

"M-m . . . well, I'll take this up with the Governor personally," decided Miltiades.

"No, I'll take it back to the office," interposed Sandusky hastily. "You see, I'm responsible for the bills. I have to bring back the money or the bill."

Miltiades returned the paper to the oldish youth.

Sandusky, who was walking a little behind the Colonel, thought bitterly:

"I wish I had a license to practise law, you old skinflint, I'd collect every cent of that at the end of a lawsuit." Aloud he was saying, "Well, Colonel, could I get you to pay me my share in the matter? You know I ran around for you all day long, when—er—you couldn't run around for yourself."

"I know you talked me into paying a lot of money I really wouldn't have had to pay," said Miltiades grudgingly, "but you did skin around town for me. . . ." The Colonel ran his hand into his pocket, drew out a roll of bills, and peeled off two one-dollar bills. He added fifty cents out of his pocket change. "That's for what you did personally," he said, "although I must tell you, Sandusky, I thought you were exerting your good offices in my behalf out of friendship for my brother. Good-day to you, sir."

"Good-day," replied Sandusky, and he angled away from Miltiades with the two dollars and a half in his hand.

If Sandusky felt thwarted and bitter to collect only two dollars and a half out of a bill for five hundred dollars, Colonel Vaiden was in scarcely a less sardonic mood.

The Governor's bill had made him angry. It was exorbitant, and Miltiades thought the Governor had made his bill large because he imagined Miltiades would rather pay it than protest and drag the Handback scandal into court. That was virtual blackmail, and the Colonel was amazed at O'Shawn.

Presently he wandered from bemeaning the Governor in his thoughts and fell to thinking about his department store again. This idea was much more dramatic than realistic. He imagined a large establishment with clerks behind the counters, a procession of customers entering; cash trolleys running to a central accounting desk. What he fancied was purely an onlooker's picture of a department store, not what a proprietor would see at all. In fact, the Colonel knew nothing whatever about department stores, but, like most Americans of the pioneer stock, he assumed he could manage one if he had the chance.

In the midst of his preoccupation about such a store he saw a thin young man in modish clothes, carrying a sample case.

The Colonel angled across the street to overtake the salesman. When he was a few steps behind he called out:

"Bivins! Mr. Bivins, just a minute!"

The salesman stopped and turned about. The Colonel noticed that the fellow's eyes were ringed a little more deeply than formerly from drinking, and his nose had developed a delicate spray of veins on its end. He stood batting his eyes at the Colonel.

"What in the hell do you want?" he queried in dislike for Miltiades.

"Want to place an order with you," explained the Colonel in equal short temper.

"I'm not down here selling goods," said Bivins.

"You're not! What are you doing?" ejaculated the Colonel in astonishment.

"Collecting."

"You working for your same company?"

"Sure."

"Wouldn't you sell something if you got an order?"

"From you?" asked Bivins.

"Yes, certainly, from me."

"How you going to pay?"

"Cash."

"You mean you'll pay me the cash when you give me your order?"

"Certainly not," snapped Miltiades, "I wouldn't risk five dollars with you as far as I could throw a bull by the tail."

"But I suppose you really have got the cash this time," said Bivins, and he broke out laughing.

Miltiades was suddenly enraged.

"By God, if I had a gun I'd blow your brains out," he said in a fury, and he started back across the street.

Bivins became more sensible.

"Wait, hold on," he said in a half apologetic tone, "I'm here to sell goods, and you want to buy. I'll ship anything you want to the railroad station with a bill of lading attached. Is that all right?"

"That would protect both of us from being swindled," said Miltiades, turning back again.

"All right, what do you want?"

The Colonel thought what he wanted. The set-up that struck him as an immediate necessity was provisions for the tenants he would probably put on the old Lacefield place. He began tentatively:

"I'll need flour . . . meal . . . hoes . . . plows . . . bacon . . ."

"What grade of flour?"

"That yellow third-grade flour, 'Farm Wife's Friend.' "

"I know what you're starting," said Bivins, looking at his purchaser out of his circled eyes; "I can make out your order quicker than you can. You want the regular set-up for niggers on a plantation. Why not leave it to me and let me go? I've made out hundreds of orders just like yours."

"What you in such a rush about?" asked the Colonel irritably.

"I'm on my way to a creditors' meeting."

"Oh, you are. . . ." Miltiades fell in with Bivins and walked a little way in unfriendliness. "You've picked a hell of a time to force some merchant to the wall just when business is about to open up."

"I think so myself," agreed Bivins, "but my boss don't. He's a Cincinnati Republican. He says he's going to mark time and see which way the cat jumps."

Miltiades pondered this a moment.

"If enough firms start collecting and stop selling, the cat'll jump the wrong way," he said at last.

"Yes, but the boss can't help it," said the drummer defensively; "the banks are closing down on him, and Wall Street is closing down on the banks."

"It's a Republican trick to disorganize the country," de-clared Miltiades.

"Hell, don't I know it!" cried the drummer.

"But they can't do it," defied Miltiades; "wait till the Democrats get under way with the South behind them, every-thing will go forward."

"I sure hope that's so," said Bivins, "but I'm down here collecting."

The two men walked on, momentarily sympathetic in their common political faith. After some space Bivins began un-certainly:

"By the way, Colonel . . . I don't like to ask questions, but . . ."

Miltiades' brief good-will faded somewhat.

"Yes . . . what is it?"

"Do—do you know whether Lucius Handback is still go-ing with Miss Sydna Crowninshield?"

Miltiades was dourly amused at the question.

"I am sorry to say I haven't the slightest information on that subject."

"Well . . . all right . . . I thought maybe . . ."

The Colonel prepared to take leave of his companion.

"Well, I'm going this way. Where you headed for?"

"The Handback store," said the drummer.

Illumination broke over Miltiades. He suddenly under-stood why Bradley had offered him the old Lacefield place for fifteen thousand dollars. He now regretted his counter offer of twelve thousand five hundred. If Handback's credi-tors were pressing him, he might get it even cheaper. He ejaculated on the impulse:

"You know I've got to go there too." Then he thought how bitterly unwelcome he would be at the Handback store. He caught the drummer's arm. "Look here, Bivins, when you get there, call Bill Bradley to one side and tell him I say not one cent over nine thousand. You understand that, 'Not one cent over nine thousand.' "

Bivins glanced at him out of his reddish rimmed eyes.

"I understand that."

The two went on together a little farther. Miltiades was now loath to leave the drummer.

In the midst of the exciting possibility of getting the old Lacefield place for a picayune, the thought of his future store popped into the Colonel's head again.

"Bivins, one of these days I may give you a great big order for high-class hardware."

"That'll be fine," said the drummer.

"You won't forget to tell Bradley what I told you, will you?"

"Sure not . . . not a penny over nine thousand?"

"That's right," nodded Miltiades.

CHAPTER THIRTY-THREE

On the second day after the creditors' meeting in the store of J. Handback & Son, Colonel Miltiades Vaiden owned the old Lacefield plantation. He had bought it from Bradley for the original amount the two men had named. Bradley claimed that Slim Bivins never delivered the Colonel's final figure.

"And why should he?" inquired the real-estate man, closing completely his smoky eye, "when Bivins' house is the heaviest creditor the Handbacks have? Why should he take money out of his own pocket and put it in yours?"

What Bradley really paid for the place, Miltiades never found out. The amount recorded in the register or deeds was for one dollar paid in hand and other valuable considerations.

Miltiades was mortally sure that Bradley had lied to him and cheated him, but then anyone who had anything to do with Bradley in a business way finally swung around to that point of view.

An odd and rather absurd incident had determined the Colonel's purchase of the Lacefield place.

Three days before the meeting of the Handback creditors, Miltiades was walking home from town along Pine Street. He chose this route because he did not want to pass the wordless hostility of his brother's house, and it was a sort of pleasure to walk by the equally wordless and possibly non-existent sympathy in the Crowninshield home.

In all Florence, only in Drusilla's weathered manor did the Colonel hope for any mitigation of the moral sentence of theft which the town had passed upon him.

294

There was a curious mental tang in the way Miltiades thought of Drusilla. It had a flavor of his dead wife, Ponny, in it. When he thought of Drusilla, he felt it was without Ponny's permission. When he walked up Pine Street it was with a sense of ghostly transgression. Sight of the manor itself always reminded him that Ponny was dead. An accompanying memory of Sydna chasing the urchins who had mocked him in the street somehow took away his dead wife's disapproval.

On this particular afternoon, as he passed the manor, a notion flitted through the Colonel's head to enter and thank Sydna for what she had done for him. That, of course, was impossible.

So he was going past the house when he heard the Crowninshield gate click. Came a patter of running steps behind him and a voice calling his name.

The Colonel turned with a startled and wordless apprehension of pleasure when he saw it was a negro girl in pursuit of him. He waited for her, wondering if she could possibly have some message from Drusilla. The black girl came to a breathless stand in front of him.

"Col'l Milt," she panted, "my mammy said tell you Miss Gracie done set down on huh."

"Sat down on her?" repeated Miltiades, not understanding.

"Yes, suh, Miss Gracie set down on my mammy."

"Gracie Vaiden?" he probed.

"Yes, suh, Miss Gracie Vaiden, aw Miss Gracie Dill, aw Miss Gracie Light, aw Miss Gracie Beekman. . . . Miss Gracie got a lot o' names." The black girl was calling over the roll of men, black and white, with whom Gracie had lived long enough for her to use their names as her own.

"Do you mean Gracie is living with your mother?" hazarded the Colonel, "do you mean she is putting up on your mother?"

"Yas suh, yas suh, dat's whut I means. She's settin' down on Mammy."

The Colonel stood looking at the black girl for several moments.

"Well . . . what are you telling me about it for?"

The girl was a little taken aback.

"Mammy said she guess maybe you do somep'n 'bout hit."

"Who is your mammy?"

"Miss Tony."

"Where does she live?"

"At de house wid de gate."

This abbreviated description fitted the shack so well that the Colonel remembered it. He was sharply astonished.

"What in the world is Gracie doing living with your mother!" he ejaculated.

"She say huh kinchonce make huh."

"Kinchonce!"

"Yas suh, huh kinchonce hu't huh."

"Conscience!" cried Miltiades.

"Yas suh, huh conscience."

"Well," said the Colonel slowly, "I'll call around and see what's gone wrong with Gracie's conscience."

Miltiades was faintly amused. He wondered if Gracie had got religion and had given up her post as Handback's concubine, or had the merchant become so hard pressed for money that he had turned her out of the cottage? This last offered itself as the true cause of Gracie's homelessness and why this girl had come to him. Miltiades had brought it upon Gracie, and now he must do something about it.

The Colonel stood thinking when he could go and see the quadroon. He felt he could not go at that moment, because Ponny would be waiting supper on him. Then he remembered that Ponny was dead. He turned about and started back toward town. Pammy Lee stood in the gate of the Crowninshield residence and watched him out of sight.

At Miss Tony's shack the Colonel found a rather puzzling state of fact. He asked Gracie if Handback had turned her out. She said Mr. Handback didn't know anything about her change. Miltiades then asked why she was leaving the cottage. Her explanation was that Mr. Handback looked so terrible she couldn't bear to see him any more; she didn't want even to think of him again.

"I tells huh hit's de Lawd wuckin' to save His chile f'um dat kine o' life," intoned Miss Tony solemnly.

Both colored women were standing in the presence of the Colonel. As Miltiades did not care to sit in a negro's chair, the three stood in the shack discussing the situation.

"How came you to know anything about it?" asked Gracie, out of her depression.

"Well . . . I heard about it." He could not admit that Miss Tony had sent him word, for that would reflect on the coffee-colored woman's hospitality.

Miltiades thought of providing another cottage for Gracie, not such a house as Handback had built for her, but a good substantial negro cabin whose roof did not leak. He was grateful to the quadroon for what she had done. He really owed her his fortune.

"I have been thinking," said Gracie somberly, "of going North and educating Toussaint."

Miltiades shook his head.

"Now, Gracie, no . . . no . . . that's unpractical. . . . How do you mean, educated?"

Gracie was sorry she had mentioned the topic.

"Oh, I mean . . . know a good deal."

"Colored people, Gracie," advised Miltiades earnestly and sincerely, "are hurt more than they are helped by education. When a colored person becomes educated there is no place for him. An educated man doesn't want to do day labor in the fields. And where could Toussaint be a doctor, or a lawyer, or ever run a store bigger than a peanut stand. . . ." the Colonel continued to shake his head. "You don't want to ruin him, Gracie."

The white man's earnestness forced itself upon Gracie's mind with the merciless quality of truth. It made her dreams for Toussaint's advancement appear utterly unreal. It produced in the quadroon, in a more refined and complicated form, the ancient agony of her slave days, when she had dreaded lest Solomon, her first husband, might be sold away from her, as indeed he finally was.

The Colonel's words made her feel sick. She wanted to sit down, but kept standing in her ex-master's presence, looking into a fire of barrel staves on the hearth.

"I tells huh," said Miss Tony, "hit mus' be ag'inst de Lawd's will fuh Toussaint to go to some big school fuh Him to make huh han' ovah evahthing she got lak she is done."

Gracie looked at her chocolate-colored friend.

"That's all right, Tony," she said quickly.

"Oh, 'scuse me, Miss Gracie," ejaculated Miss Tony, clapping a hand over her thick lips.

"Hand over what . . . how?" queried Miltiades, puzzled.

"Tuh . . . tuh, Mistah Han'back," juggled out Miss Tony, who, under Gracie's prohibition, could speak only a few words at a time.

"He gave me a little money," explained Gracie drearily, "and he needed it; so I gave it back to him till he could get straightened out again."

Miltiades' heart sank at Gracie's stupidity.

"How much?" he asked in a disgusted tone.

"About four hundred dollars."

"I swear, what a fool you are, Gracie." He laughed shortly. "Well, now, that's what I say about educating a nigger. Sister Cassandra educated you . . . now look what you do!"

This almost exonerated the Colonel from helping Gracie at all. If she was big enough fool to give back an insignificant . . .

"Why, four hundred dollars won't help him at all," scouted the Colonel, "it won't be a drop in the bucket!"

"I . . . knew that . . ." said Gracie in a small voice.

"Then what the devil did you give it to him for?"

"Be-because," cried Gracie desperately, "I—I couldn't k-keep anything of h-his . . . after wh-what I'd done!" and she began weeping.

The Colonel looked at her, shaking his head hopelessly. He didn't understand her. She had gone off into some feminine flightiness which he did not understand . . . into some nigger foolishness.

"And that was the money you had saved up to send—" he tried to think of Toussaint's name, but failed—"your boy off to school?"

Gracie nodded, blinking her eyes.

"Well," comforted the Colonel, after a moment's thought, "I'm not sure if this isn't the best thing that could have happened for your boy. Put him on a farm. Let him grow up into a man who is some account. It would be a lot better than making him into a misfit in some town."

The Colonel's reasonableness and his authority, the well known fact that he did not cheat negroes but treated them squarely and honorably and wished them well, overpowered Gracie.

"Maybe it is," she agreed bleakly, "but I don't know how Toussaint will ever get along with anybody. He's a proud boy."

"Now, look here," planned the Colonel hopefully, "Loober . . . you know Loober Snipes?"

Gracie shook her head.

Miss Tony did.

"He's de niggah dat kep' Mistah Lucius Han'back f'um shootin' Col'l Milt," she explained brightly.

"That's right," said the Colonel, "and the Handbacks turned him off their place for what he did. He's been hanging around me asking me to put him on another place, and I really feel like I ought."

Miss Tony nodded deeply.

"Da's right! Da's right! I kin say one thing fuh you, Col'l Milt, you got de bigges' hea't in you I evah saw in a white pusson."

The compliment gave the Colonel a certain touch of pleasure.

"Well, here's my idyah. I'll buy a farm big enough for

two families and put Loob's family and your family onto it,
Gracie. I know I can get along with Toussaint. I never did
have any trouble with colored folks."

Gracie gave a long sigh at this final vanishing of her
dream for Toussaint.

"Yes," she said slowly, "I'm sure you'll get along with
Toussaint all right . . ." and in her thoughts she added,
"since he is your own son."

CHAPTER THIRTY-FOUR

I⊤ was dusk when Miltiades left Gracie, and it was quite dark when he reached Market Street once more. This darkness gratified the Colonel. In its obscurity he could walk the streets without that constant, unconscious screwing up of his moral resistance to meet the silent recollection of his theft in the mind of every passer-by. The darkness did not remember his transgression. Within its bosom, he and his sin might rest.

The Colonel walked slowly and delayed getting home as long as possible. The emptiness of the mean Cherry Street house oppressed him. When he was at home he was continually beset by the impression that Ponny was in another room and presently would come moving her shapeless bulk through the door.

Once or twice, when his dead wife's presence bore more sharply upon him than usual, the Colonel, sitting alone in his room, had thought, "No wonder the ignorant believe in ghosts."

So now he walked slowly, to arrive at his home as late, and to go to sleep as quickly, as he could.

A voice said out of a blur of gateposts:

"Is that you, Uncle Milt?"

The Colonel paused.

"This is Miltiades Vaiden."

A slender figure stepped out of the yard and fell in beside the Colonel. Miltiades walked on, vaguely annoyed because the presence of his nephew estopped his formless reverie.

"You know," began Jerry, after walking for a space, "people are curious creatures: they've got mighty little reason."

"Why, what's happened to you?" inquired the Colonel absently.

"Why-y . . . nothing much. . . . I was just thinking. . . . Now, look here, now . . . say something comes up and somebody doesn't want to associate with me. All right, well and good . . . but I say it's unreasonable."

"Why is it unreasonable?" queried the uncle, with a touch of curiosity.

"Why, because, if they were really my friends, then they would be in rapport with me—at least, to some extent. They would have to be, wouldn't they?—or we couldn't be friends at all."

The word "rapport," which Jerry mispronounced, was unfamiliar to Miltiades.

"Why do you say that?" inquired Miltiades with a touch of pride in his nephew.

"Because, if friendship depends on . . . well, on fitting folks's souls together, don't you think, Uncle Milt? . . . Then, no matter what the other person did, you really couldn't withdraw your friendship, because if your souls fit once, they're bound to fit always."

"Why, no-o, I'm afraid I don't quite see that," said Miltiades.

"It's very simple," said Jerry. "If friendship is a communion of souls, then if anything bad turns up in your friend, that shows there was some answering crookedness in you. And instead of condemning him, you ought to blame yourself."

Miltiades was amused at this involved reasoning, but Jerry's remarks cast also a not so humorous side glance on himself.

"How came you to think of all these things?" inquired Miltiades uncomfortably.

"Well, I have lost several so-called friends lately," admitted Jerry, "and I just got to thinking about them."

"What did you do to lose them, Jerry?" inquired the uncle with concern.

"Why . . . nothing."

"But that's very strange for you to do nothing and lose your friends and then think up all this rigmarole to condemn them. I think you'll have to admit that's a little queer."

"It's not what I did, it's what I am," said Jerry gloomily.

"What you are?"

"Yes."

"You mean . . . your family?"

"Yes."

Miltiades dropped his catechism.

"Pay no attention to them," he advised. "Remember you're a Vaiden. You are equal to the best and better than the most."

"Yes, I think of that, too," said Jerry.

The boy slackened his gait and let his uncle get ahead.

"Well, good-night, Uncle Milt," he said, stopping entirely.

Miltiades came back and shook hands with his nephew.

"Good-night, Jerry."

When the two separated, Jerry rubbed the hand his uncle had touched up and down on the leg of his trousers. He did not like to touch his uncle Miltiades.

CHAPTER THIRTY-FIVE

Young Jerry Catlin had talked and walked with his uncle
Miltiades Vaiden as a last resort. He had been standing at
the boarding-house gate with a wrought-up feeling that he
must talk to someone or lose himself in the endless circlings
of his own thoughts.

But there was one droll difference in young Jerry Catlin's thoughts when he was alone and when he was in company with his uncle Miltiades. Alone, Jerry thought piti-
fully and helpfully of the pupils in college and the people
in town who had more or less ostracized him, owing to his
relationship to his uncle. He thought of them as people
whom he wished he could help to a better understanding of
life; he would inform them, lift them up. But in company
with his uncle Miltiades he had broken out into a diatribe
against them; they were fools and idiots. His uncle left him
vibrating with wrath and intolerance for such a folk.

When Miltiades had gone, this militancy quieted in the
youth once more. His heart beat. He felt as if he had been
through some strong exertion.

"I must control myself," he thought, and after a few
moments he added, "this is an opportunity for me to practise composure and humility of soul."

No sooner had he thought this than an extraordinary notion dawned on Jerry. He walked back down the street,
astonished at himself, thinking it over, wondering if it were
possible. What he suspected was this: it might be that his
uncle Miltiades had taken the cotton, that his friends had
withdrawn from him as a preordained test. Perhaps the
mystic brotherhood had brought these tribulations upon him
to observe how he endured them and to see if he were worthy

of acceptance in their order! The thought of walking the
earth in constancy and humility filled young Jerry with its
ancient poetry.

A great sweetness filled the boy at the thought. His
ostracism suddenly became wings to his heart. He wished,
after he had met the test, after he was transfigured, that he
might lay his hands on the people who had misprized him,
and heal them.

When he reached his aunt Rose's boarding house Jerry
was too excited to go inside. He did not want to be around
Sandusky, who had grown brusquer and more impatient
than ever. He did not want the carping law student to be-
devil him out of his mood of messiahship.

In his exaltation Jerry walked on past his boarding house,
down the street, beneath the high jeweling of the night. He
felt himself native to the very sheen and quiver of the stars.
In their luminous mystery he sensed his own eternal past.

Presently he found himself on Pine Street, in the profound gloom of the trees. As he walked, he could see the
stars moving above their foliage in the tiniest needle pricks
of light. Jerry went on down the street, touching the fence
posts to keep his direction.

His emotion presently lost some of its mystical quality
and became an unordered trembling and suspense. He
stopped in front of a box-scented gate and stood with little
shivers of sweetness passing through him. He wondered if
Sydna were busy. It seemed to Jerry the old manor was the
goal whither all his restlessness and exaltation had tended.

He wished Sydna would come out so that he could ask her
frankly if she would mind seeing him and talking to him
again. He would tell her that he was very lonesome, but if
she did not want to see him, he would bless her and think
tenderly of her always.

Then a notion came to Jerry to will that Sydna should
come out to the gate. It would test that phase of his occult
training.

He tried this for a few moments. He stood looking fixedly

in the direction of the front door, willing that Sydna should appear in it. He tried simply to will her to appear in the doorway, as he thought that would require less effort than to make her come clear to the gate. If he got her to the door he could call her the rest of the way.

He had hardly begun his concentration when he heard a sound toward the house. Jerry was surprised at himself. His heart began beating. He peered toward the manor. He could see nothing, but he heard steps on the graveled path.

Before he could see anything at all a voice quite near him gasped in a startled undertone:

"Who is that?"

Jerry realized that Sydna did not know she was being willed to come.

"It's me . . . Jerry," he said, trembling.

A figure appeared close to him at the gate. It was the negro girl on her way home after her work. She peered at Jerry curiously.

"Is—is you waitin' fuh somebody, Mist' Jer'y?" she asked.

"Listen, Pammy Lee," said Jerry in a hurried whisper, "run back in the house and tell Miss Sydna I'm out here."

"Yes, suh, Mist' Jer'y, I jess whispah to huh, unbeknownst to anybody else, 'Mist' Jer'y's at de gate.' "

Pammy Lee turned and vanished in a murmur of gravel on her exciting errand.

The tall youth stood outside the gate, staring through the darkness toward the house. The odor of the box came to him like some remembered sweetness. Romantic impressions which he had received as a child from his mother's tales roused to life in Jerry. He felt as if he were all the lovers who ever had waited for their ladies. All their impatiences, doubts, and tremors suffused him. He thought in a kind of tentative desolation, "What if she won't come after all!" He felt he could not possibly go back to his humility and saintliness for comfort. He did not know what he would do.

The moments lengthened into minutes, and the minutes

stretched into an endlessness that lost the character of time. A throbbing was in his temples, and a weight at the base of his throat. Presently he knew that Sydna was not coming. Then every moment he thought that the next moment he would go away. After a while he had no hope left that Sydna would come, but continued standing at the gate with his power of withdrawing paralyzed. Then he heard a different quality of steps approaching along the graveled path.

The youth leaned toward the rustling and whispered: "Sydna! Sydna!"

A darkness that was her form and a paleness that was her face appeared before the boy.

"Jerry," she asked in reproach, "why didn't you come in?"

"Why-y . . . Sydna . . . I didn't know whether you would want me or not."

"The idea! The idea of such a thing!" cried Sydna.

Jerry reached to unlatch the gate and found Sydna's hand at the same task. The two hands suddenly gave up the latch and squeezed each other. The feel of Sydna's fingers pressing his own overwhelmed Jerry with sweetness. He fumbled the latch open with his other hand. He stepped inside, still clinging to her fingers. He moistened his lips and whispered, "Where will we go?"

The girl hesitated.

"We . . . might go to the hammock," she said unevenly.

"Well . . ."

Sydna went in front, leading him by the hand through the unseen curves of the box. At the end of their walk both groped with their free hands for the hammock. Jerry touched it and said in a broken voice:

"Here it is."

He drew her to it. They held it and tried to sit in it.

The yielding netting tipped them backwards and pressed their bodies together.

Jerry lay utterly still, filled with a mixture of rapture

and sharp apprehension lest Sydna pick herself up again. She at least did not do so at once.

"I heard about you," she said protectively.

"Heard . . . what?" said Jerry, hardly observing what either Sydna or himself was saying.

"The way those little flippety second-year girls have treated you."

"Oh, that . . ." said Jerry, ". . . that. . . ." With the melting sweetness of Sydna's hip and shoulder against his own, the second-year girls were as remote from the hobble-dehoy as the Great Wall of China.

"What have you been doing with yourself all these days?" she asked gently.

"Nothing at all."

"Seeing nobody?"

"Nobody but Aunt Rose and Sandusky and Uncle Augustus."

At this Sydna ejaculated, "Sandusky!" with a notion of telling Jerry of the law student's conversation with her, but she broke off her sentence and sighed.

All this talk had not the faintest connection with the ecstatic torment rising in Jerry's motionless body. A trembling seized him of which he was ashamed and which he tried to control.

"Did you finally go to that reception?" asked Sydna.

"What reception?"

"Why, the one the girls wouldn't go with you."

"Oh . . . yes . . . no . . . no, I didn't go."

"Don't you know whether you went or not?"

"No, I didn't go."

The girl hesitated a moment.

"How came you not to come here, Jerry?"

"I didn't know whether . . ."

"Have you wanted to come?"

"Oh, yes, Sydna . . . of course." He turned toward her, filled with a sort of prickling sensation, and half threw his arm about her waist.

Sydna caught his hand and pressed it against her breast. "You should have come!" she stressed impulsively. "I wanted you to come! When I heard about what they were doing to you, it almost made me sick!"

The feel of her supple bosom moulded around the back of his hand struck a kind of voluptuous terror through the youth. With a sort of anguish he desired to cup his palm over the mound and explore its amazing pliancy. But a feeling of profanation kept him motionless. He focused all his sense of touch into the back of his hand. The softness of her breast made him want to melt into her and lose his existence in her own. Any closer intimacy with her body seemed immeasurably remote and impossible to Jerry. She was utter sweetness as they reclined.

He lay with his arm bent awkwardly across her waist and torso. All he desired was merely to turn his hand. His body was charged with a growing desire which, somehow, was as far away from him as the reception he had missed, as the sophomore girls who would not go with him. At the tension of his body he felt a kind of shame.

Sydna lay for a long time in the passive sweetness of a woman. She would have liked Jerry definitely to put his arms around her and fondle her, but she found this timidity like a delicate rapture after her anxiety about the boy. She felt in all the nerves of her body a safety with Jerry, and a delight in him. All his ascetic exercises were like gold which he had saved and which he was now spending, silently and unawares, upon her.

Never in her life had she known a man who resembled Jerry; never had she known a man who had thought of some other thing than money or position or ribaldry or women.

Their talk was hushed to silence in the greatness of their sensations. They made no further attempt to conceal their dual rapture in talk.

After a long while Sydna sighed and said she would have to go in.

"I guess Mother wonders where I am," and she thought

yearningly how innocent Jerry was and how sweet it was for him to be that way.

"I hate to go home," said the boy.

"Sleep here in the hammock," she invited with a little laugh.

"When you go away it'll be too cold."

She said nothing, but smoothed his hand and then slipped her fingers between his hand and her bosom, as if she were consoling him momentarily for his loss. She thought to herself pensively and wistfully, "I am four or five years older than he is . . . three or four. . . ." She had an impulse to pick him up and hold him always in her bosom, never to let anyone wound him; aloud she repeated regretfully, "Well . . . I *must* go in."

Here she loosed herself definitely, got up from the hammock, clung to Jerry's hand as far as she could reach, said, "Good-bye," and went into the house.

When she was gone, Jerry became conscious of the strong passion of his body It was as if some opiate had expired in him and left him flooded with the pain of desire for some woman. He got up from the hammock and adjusted his twisted clothes. He hated to go home. He hated to go to bed and be tortured all night long by unsleeping desire.

As he groped his way among the hedges toward the gate a voice in the bushes gasped out:

"Oh, Mist' Jer'y, is dat you?"

Jerry was shocked.

"Yes, it's me."

"Did—did she gwi' off'n leave you lak dat?" moaned the voice in bitter disappointment.

Jerry went groping toward the hidden one, and his hands touched and moved over the excited, the curious, and the erotic form of Pammy Lee.

CHAPTER THIRTY-SIX

Wʜᴇɴ Pammy Lee reached her mother's cabin in East
Florence, the girl acted so oddly and broke out giggling at
times so foolishly that Miss Tony inquired into the matter,
and presently knew the particulars of her adventure.

The coffee-colored woman was wrathful. She clumped
Pammy Lee's corkscrew wool.

"Be 'shamed of yo'se'f!" she admonished. "Whut if
Brothah Lump Mowbray knowed you was a-carryin' on like
dat! He'd say, 'Shame on you, Pammy Lee!' wouldn't he,
Miss Gracie?"

"Yes, he would," agreed Gracie, who knew that Lump disapproved of any woman having any relations with any man
except himself.

"An' whut would de Lawd say?" went on Miss Tony, appealing to a still higher authority. "He'd say, 'Be 'shamed
of yo'se'f, you stinkin' little niggah gal, breakin' my commandments!' " The mother reached out to give Pammy Lee
another thump, but the girl ducked out of the way, and
Miss Tony's mind slid off to the practical consequences of
her daughter's indiscretion.

"Now, ap' as not, you'll be havin' a baby, an' wha in de
worl' is I gwi' put hit, I don' know."

"Hit kin sleep wid me, Mammy," piped a very small voice
from the common bed of the children.

"Shet yo' mouth, Hezekiah. Dat baby wouldn' sleep wid
a great big ol' stinkin' niggah boy lak you is. Dat baby
would be a pa'tick'lah baby. Hit would be a fine baby. . . .
Shame on you, Pammy Lee. . . ." She paused in the midst
of her mechanical shaming, "Well, you ain't gwi' back to
Miss Drusilla's no mo' aftah this, Pammy Lee."

"Why?" asked the daughter in surprise.

" 'Cause you's a woman now. You's wuth mo'n any fifty cents a week. I'm gwi' sta't out in de mawnin', lookin' fuh a place wid mo' pay fuh you. I'se gwi' send Jinny Lou up to Miss Dru's in yo' place." She turned to a smaller girl and directed, "Jinny Lou, you go to Miss Drusilla's in de mawnin' an' let huh lea'n you to cook. An' you lissen to what she tells you, you aimpty-haided li'l' niggah!"

Miss Tony's monologue might very well have run on with its homilies and reproofs until morning, but it was broken into by Hezekiah exclaiming:

"Dah goes Mist' Han'back, Miss Gracie!"

The tiny boy was peering out of the single pane of glass set in the side of the cabin.

Miss Tony flew into her little son.

"Hezekiah Hampton!" she cried. "What has Miss Gracie got to do wid Mistah Han'back fo' you to be tellin' huh who's a-goin' by? Now, you jess lay back down in yo' bed an' shet yo' eyes an' hush . . . tellin' Miss Gracie, dah go Mistuh Han'back . . . dat's a nice thing fuh a li'l' boy to say!"

The man in the alley whom Hezekiah had recognized continued on his way to Gracie's cottage. He walked slowly, not thinking of the quadroon at all, after the manner of a man going to the home of a long-kept mistress.

The merchant was turning over and over in his head a multiplicity of plans to obtain money. On one plantation he had some corn; on another, hay; here were a few hogs, and there a bin of oats—pitiful odds and ends left over from a vast and ravaged granary. He was trying to meet certain immediate obligations without selling other plantations.

Now, in the midst of his planning, he thought of Colonel Miltiades Vaiden. He stopped his mental arrangements with a sort of spasm and wished the Colonel in the bottom of hell. He wished his son Lucius had shot the Colonel! He wished . . . here he blew out a long breath, and his thoughts went back to his bills.

He had to pay them or go under. His whole life's work
was about to vanish. He had spent all his life, ever since he
was seventeen, working every single day in a dark, smelly
store. His holidays had been Sundays, Christmas, a week
that he had been sick, and the day he had got married.

When he was a boy he had started clerking for a man
named Alley in Haleyville, Alabama. Then through a drummer he had got a job in Florence with a merchant named
Stout. He had bought a fourth interest in Stout's business;
then, during a business depression, he purchased the other
three fourths. By the time the Civil War broke out he was
doing the largest business in Florence. He financed nearly
all the big plantations in the county through his cotton
broker in New Orleans. He carried a large stock of merchandise. The Civil War completely destroyed his credit and his
trade. It forced him into involuntary bankruptcy, and he
came out with nothing whatever, not even the technique of
how to get wealthy again. As a matter of fact, the war
ushered in a new mode of accumulating money. This was the
method of working the negroes under mortgages instead of
under simple chattel slavery. Handback and thousands of
merchants like him perfected this method. It did away completely with the great landowners, or, rather, it shifted the
proprietorship in the land from the manor to the store. Now,
when Handback had built up this great organization, Miltiades Vaiden, with a little wildcat claim against him for
five bales of cotton, had come and stolen all he possessed—
every liquid dollar he had in the world.

He spat out his acrid thoughts of the thievish Colonel.
He had come to the cottage he had built for the quadroon.

The mere dark shape of the cottage soothed away to some
extent the rancor that filled the merchant's heart. It
promised him a respite. He meant to drink some rye whisky,
talk to Gracie a while, and finally go to bed and drop into
the profound sleep of alcohol and a woman and escape his
worries for a space.

The cottage was dark. The merchant did not ring but

groped under the doormat and found a key. He let himself in.

From the hallway he called in an undertone:

"Gracie . . . this is me."

He thought she must be sleeping soundly, because she usually answered at once:

"Come in, Mr. Handback."

That was one of the pleasant things about Gracie. She was always quiet and respectful and ministered to him with the agreeable solicitude of a highly trained servant. He always felt that this was his cottage where he could come and drink and sleep, and that the quadroon took care of it for him. It was his house. It was his chapel, and Gracie was his acolyte.

The merchant opened the bedroom door and listened for, but could not hear, the sound of the quadroon's breathing.

"Gracie!" he said in a low tone. "Gracie . . ."

Then he observed the room was unaired, and he wondered about that.

He drew a match and struck it almost silently on his trousers. He held the little flame above his head and saw the bed was empty.

This surprised and disappointed him. Usually Gracie was in the cottage. She was, he supposed, gone over to one of the neighbors. He went to a lamp on the dresser, conserving his match, and lighted it.

In the full light the bed was neatly made, but somehow it had the look of not having been used for two or three days. What details gave it that appearance, the merchant did not know.

"I wonder where she's gone to?" he thought with some concern. He took the lamp and made the round of the house, the kitchen, a dining room, two extra bedrooms, all a little musty from disuse.

The merchant returned, very puzzled, to the bedroom. On the center table he saw a pink envelope with his name on it. He picked it up, a little annoyed at this certainty that

Gracie was gone at least for the night. The note would tell him where. He wished resentfully that she had chosen some other time. He felt that she had treated him badly. She knew of this crisis in his affairs; she knew that he was in trouble. She had returned to him the four hundred dollars he had given her. Now, for her to be away from home on the night he chose to visit her, that showed an indifference toward him. She really was, he supposed, quite indifferent to him . . . as he was to her. She was just a colored woman whom he hired.

He opened the envelope and read the enclosure,

> Mr. J. HANDBACK, City.
> Mr. Handback, you need your house. I am going away for good. I can't keep house for you any more. I haven't done you right, and I keep thinking about it all the time. Don't try to find me, because if you knew what I did you wouldn't want to employ me any more anyway.
> Very respectfully,
> GRACIE DILL.

For several seconds Handback stood with the note in his hand, simply looking at it. Its statement that Gracie had gone away and would not come back did not seem real. He read the letter over again with a feeling that he must have overlooked something—some sentence telling where he could go find her.

Then his mind gathered the lines, "Don't try to find me. If you knew what I did, you wouldn't want to employ me any more."

The merchant sat down by the table. His hands began trembling so he could hardly hold the note before his eyes:

> If you knew what I did, you wouldn't want to employ me any more anyway.
> Very respectfully,
> GRACIE DILL.

Whatever it was that Gracie had done was a minor matter. Behind that, to the merchant, lay the blank emptiness that she was gone . . . that she was coming back no more.

The man sat looking at the note with a faint sensation of weight and chilliness in his cheeks. He looked around the room and tried to think what he would do now, but the effect was like trying to get some heavy, lifeless thing in the top of his head to move.

"I don't see how she could go away," he murmured aloud, "when she knew I was so worried . . . when she knew I was in such trouble."

He tried to think again what he could do. He did not see how he could get through this tangle into which his affairs had fallen if he had no mental release, for a few hours, from his debts. He had never dreamed that Gracie was so necessary to him until she was gone.

He read the note again, holding it at a distance from his eyes, like an old man. He speculated this time on what she had done that would cause him not to want her any more . . . given herself to some other man, he supposed . . . possibly a negro.

This last thought revolted Handback. It was a stimulant after the numbing blow of her desertion. He thought, bewildered and resentful:

"I don't understand her. . . . If she did it, why in God's name did she have to tell me?"

He tore the note up with its formal opening of "Mr. Handback" and its formal closing of "Very respectfully." It was thus negroes always addressed the whites in their infrequent letters. They would not presume upon the familiarity of "Dear Sir."

During their years of joint occupancy of the cottage neither Gracie nor the merchant had ever uttered the word "love."

J. Handback locked up the cottage he had built six years before and walked back through the darkness to his store.

G<small>RACIE</small>'s actual removal to the Lacefield place did not occur until two weeks and three days later. She stayed on with Miss Tony, who was now quite content and even pleased with her guest, since she knew that Gracie finally would go away. A little visit two or three weeks' long was nothing to Miss Tony; only the vista of a perpetuity dismayed her.

Once during this period Gracie went back to the white cottage for something she had left behind, but she could not get in. The key which she had kept under the mat was gone.

During this interval Miltiades was fixing up the Lacefield place for Gracie. He purchased a horse and rode leisurely about the countryside, picking up a few mules and some farm implements where he could find them. Mules were obtainable only by trading around like this. There was no regular mule market nearer than Columbia, Tennessee. The farm implements the Colonel also bought second hand, matching his trained sense of value against that of the tenant farmers. Some of these tenants made very poor trades.

Take Gibeon Dalrymple, for example. Gibeon sold the Colonel three mattocks, a shovel, and a "possum" dog for four dollars. Gibeon then agreed to keep the dog for the Colonel until the latter called for him.

Later in the week, Miltiades traded the dog and eleven dollars to Alex Cady for a farm wagon.

When the Colonel finally drove the quadroon and her son to the plantation he outlined what he wanted Toussaint to do. During the winter months Toussaint would paint up the houses, renew the fences, grub out the sassafras sprouts that had sprung up in the fields.

"I want to get everything into the shape it once was," explained the Colonel to the octoroon youth.

Toussaint nodded at each of these injunctions, saying: "Yes, sir. . . . Yes, sir. . . . Yes, sir. . . ."

It was an odd, inexpressive sort of agreement. There was something blanketed about the youth, something which the Colonel, in all his experience with negroes, had not met before.

But the boy would come out all right. He was of the old Vaiden stock of negroes.

The Colonel would rehabilitate the old Lacefield place, built up its productiveness, restore its style. The idea came to him that he might have a country estate with stables and kennels to which he could repair from time to time from the grind of business in his store.

As the Colonel drove past BeShears' Crossroads, a group of white men and negroes were loitering on the platform. One of the white men called out:

"Hey-oh, Colonel, is that the town nigger you're goin' to make a farmer out of?"

And the whole group broke out guffawing at the idea.

"I think he'll work all right," returned the Colonel genially.

"Yes, an' that nigger woman there with you, she looks like she would work all right, too," called out some lickerish wag.

The Colonel made no reply to this, and the group laughed again as if his silence admitted improper relations with the woman he was installing on his farm.

Alex Cady walked out toward the buggy.

"What house you goin' to put 'em in, Colonel?" he inquired, with the assurance of a tenant on the same place.

"Haven't decided, Alex," responded the Colonel, with the evasiveness of a business man.

Miltiades sensed that Alex was fishing for his choice of houses. The crowd laughed at Alex's discomfiture.

"You might 'a' knowed you wouldn't git nothin' out of

the Colonel, Alex," they twitted. "Nobody knows what the Colonel's goin' to do tull he does it. . . . If you don't believe that, go ast ol' man Han'back!"

Some of the white men on the platform laughed violently at this. The negroes maintained a shocked silence at such a jest against the owner. The allusion abruptly destroyed for Miltiades his elation at taking possession of the old Lacefield place.

Gracie looked back at the men on the platform and said with controlled contempt:

"There certainly has been a come-down in country folks."

"A come-down," repeated Miltiades in a flatted tone: "they're gone . . . they've been gone for years."

The thought filled the Colonel with a passing melancholy. Gracie's remark made him realize the change. As he had ridden about the countryside, he had hardly observed its imperceptible, steady decline. It was like the face of an old acquaintance whose scars and wrinkles accumulate so gradually that only by an effort of memory one reconstructs the vanished countenance.

To Gracie the weathered Crossroads store, the old spring behind it with its pool surrounded by dead stumps; the thin acres of the Reserve with an occasional negro shack here and there; all held the shock of a first discovered change. She had not been back to the Crossroads since the year old man Jimmie Vaiden, her white father, had died.

Now her surroundings filled Gracie with the most painful memories. Down this rutted Reserve road, her little Missy, the gray-eyed Marcia, had ridden to be imprisoned in the Yankee camp. At the Crossroads store, old man Be-Shears had sold Solomon, her first husband, to a negro dealer.

The last time Gracie had seen the Lacefield plantation its meadows were full of Yankee tents. In one of these tents she had sojourned as the mistress of a Federal officer named Beekman. Her father, old man Jimmie, had tried to reclaim her as his property from Beekman, but the Yankee soldiers had laughed at him; and she saw her father, who was also her owner, ride away cursing her and on the verge of apoplexy.

But above all the scene around her reminded Gracie of Beekman. She and Beekman had walked along these lanes. An old sedge field which she was passing had been a meadow then, and here was pitched the tent of her uncandled honeymoon. The impression of the Yankee officer became so strong that she almost expected to see him at some turn of the road. The cream-colored girl had loved Beekman.

The old Lacefield manor itself was deplorable. The silver poplar grove that had stood on its lawn had long since been used for firewood. All that was left of a flower pit that had lain back of the mansion was a depression three or four feet deep and choked with weeds. The great gate was gone, and Miltiades could have driven his buggy anywhere across the scattered stones of the wall. He drew up in front of the chipped columns of the portico.

"Gracie," said the Colonel, "you can stay here, or I'll put you in one of the cabins on the place. You have your choice."

"I wonder if the roof leaks?" speculated Gracie, looking at the heavy, lifeless pile.

"I imagine it does," said Miltiades.

"Maybe some of the rooms are dry," said Gracie hopefully.

"I want to put a new roof on the whole house," said Miltiades, looking at the sloughing columns and the little wrought-iron balcony at the level of the second story. The banisters sagged at one side and were evidently held by a single rail.

"If you're going to do that," decided Gracie, "we'll take this place."

"And I'm glad you will," said Miltiades. "I'm glad there is some connection between you and what the manor used to be."

"This is a strange thing that I am going to live in the Lacefield manor," said Gracie.

And for a moment she and the Colonel stood as man and woman who felt each other's involved and tragic rôle in a catastrophe which was so great that it stretched beyond both their comprehensions.

The Colonel gave more instructions to Toussaint about the rehabilitation of the place, and then started to his buggy to drive away. Gracie told Toussaint to hurry and unhitch the Colonel's buggy for him.

The son moved deliberately. He undid the bridle from the ancient hitching post, hooked it over the catch at the top of the collar, and stood holding the bits, looking at the white man with appraising gray eyes. There was a quality in him which Miltiades could not quite fathom. The Colonel referred this to the man who he thought was the boy's father. "If he takes after Beekman," thought the owner of the plantation, "he will at least be energetic." And a droll notion struck him that the solitary benefit of the Yankee invasion during the war was that it had improved the energy of some of the negroes in the second generation in the South.

CHAPTER THIRTY-EIGHT

AT A cold turn in the weather Toussaint Vaiden drove to the hills beyond BeShears' store for a load of wood.

This was free wood to be had for the taking. Nobody inquired its ownership. An industrious negro could even have cut some of this wood and sold it in Florence, but the tenants very seldom supplied themselves, much less anyone else.

Toussaint, both going and coming, drove past the cabins of the other tenants in a morose daydream which was his habitual mood.

When he reached home again his mother said that she had heard a knocking down at the stables while he was gone, and she didn't know what it was. He asked her what did it sound like, and she repeated, with a woman's vagueness, that it was just a knocking. She evidently had been nervous about going down herself to see what it was.

The son said he would look around as soon as he unloaded his wood. In the barn lot the white negro forgot this commission. As he unhitched his animals his mind returned to the continual theme of his reveries: how he and his mother would move to a place where they were not known, and Toussaint would slip off his negrohood and would become a white man.

He would be white. He would be free of being a servant, of being bossed and swindled and stoned. He would be the equal of any man.

The octoroon led his mules to their stalls with an inner warmth at what he had borne. That would all be changed. He would use the money he made here on the plantation to send himself and his mother North.

Without a break in his thoughts he set about following Colonel Vaiden's directions. He went to a shed, got out a small keg of oxide of lead, and began mixing it in a gallon of linseed oil. He picked up a stick and stirred and poured and stirred and poured. After a while he took the new cheap brush which the Colonel had furnished and began spreading the paint on the wagon.

The brilliant red stood out against the uniform gray of the stables and colored the painter's mood. He thought in this new place where they were going he and his mother might pass for Spaniards. They could say his father was an American who had married his mother in Cuba.

In the midst of this reverie a dry nasal voice behind him said:

"Hey-oh, paintin' her up, air ye?"

Toussaint glanced around with a startled feeling that the speaker had read his forbidden thoughts. A few steps away the smallish figure of the white tenant stood leaning on an ax. The white negro instantly became uncommunicative.

"Yes . . . I'm painting it."

Cady looked on for several moments in silence, then asked in a curious voice:

"What you paintin' it fer?"

"The Colonel told me to."

"Why, hell, what of that? He ain't got no way of makin' you. It ain't in yore contrack. . . ." After a moment another thought entered the white tenant's head: "He ain't payin' you extry fer it, is he?"

"No."

"I didn't imagine he was."

As Toussaint made no reply to this, the white man finally added:

"Especially as that's my waggin."

Toussaint was a little disconcerted at this; he turned around and asked:

"How came it yours?"

"Why, by God, because I paid for it," exclaimed the white man instantly belligerent.

"I mean, how did the Colonel come by it?"

"Oh, he jest borryed it from me to do a little haulin' on the place."

Toussaint hardly knew whether to go on painting or not. His strokes slowed down under his indecision, but he said nothing.

"I may be taking it back one of these days," said Cady, "when I get ready fer it."

Again Toussaint remained silent. Something about his silence irritated Cady.

"I see you are one of them there shut-mouth niggers," observed the white man disagreeably, "like that there Lucy Lacefield that lives in the house next to mine."

"I don't see what there is to say if you're going to take the wagon."

Cady considered this judicially.

"Well, I God, now, they ain't—if that's what ye're thinkin' I guess it's all right."

The belligerent little white man hesitated, walked back down the line of doors in the stable, entered one, and presently came out with an armful of fresh red cedar wood. For Cady to get freshly cut cedar out of the tumble-down stalls struck Toussaint as an odd thing. He quit his painting, walked to the door of the stall, and looked in. All of the stalls were made with cedar posts. In this particular one, the posts were cut down and split up. Red and white chips lay over the earthen floor.

The octoroon looked at the white man's sabotage.

"Did you do that?" he asked in blank amazement.

"Ye—naw," hesitated Cady. "I jest saw these sticks layin' in here, and I thought I'd take a few home fer my ol' woman to cook with."

"Why, the devil," exclaimed Toussaint, "that's right fresh cut, and my mother said she heard you down here chopping this morning!"

"Yore maw heard me chopping!" demanded Cady warmly.

"She told me so the minute I got home," said Toussaint.

"Well, if yore maw told you that," nodded Cady deliberately, "she told you a damn lie . . . the yellow ol' devil!"

A kind of tingle whipped through the octoroon from his chest to his finger tips. He flung his brush, and it hit the white man on the side of his head, giving the impression of a sudden horrible wound.

Cady swore, lifted his ax, and rushed at the white negro. Toussaint dodged aside, and the bit cut into the ground amid sparks of fire. The boy's heart was drumming wildly. He caught up a stone and almost let drive at the red-splashed little man who was rushing at him again.

"Stop! Stop there, Cady!" he yelled with the stone drawn back.

The white man came, in spewing oaths and obscenity.

"You damn yellow bastard! Drive yore waggin by my house an' never turn yore damn head!" The ax crashed down again. The throat of the handle banged down on a tire and stung the white man's hands. Toussaint dodged again, trembling over throwing the stone. Visions of white revenge danced before his eyes if he touched a white man, and as he thought, he threw.

Came a crack. The ax fell one way and Cady fell another. Horror swept over Toussaint. There was a spot of deeper red on the white man's temple, and this gave the impression that the whole side of his head was torn away.

Cady sat up, looked about him, and began violently abusing the octoroon. The negro's heart pounded. He was more frightened of the white man on the ground than when he was up charging with his ax. This might mean any sort of punishment for him, a jail term, a sentence to the coal mines, a visitation of white men. . . .

He was babbling:

"Mr. Cady, I had to do it! You'd 'a' killed me, Mr. Cady! Are you much hurt, Mr. Cady?"

"You God-damn nigger! Throwin' a rock!"

He tried to get up, but fell down again.

Toussaint ran to him.

"Mr. Cady, don't hit me, an' I'll help you up!"

The white man held out his hand and was helped up. He cursed steadily. When he was on his feet he told Toussaint to hand him his ax. The octoroon did this, holding it by its blade and reaching the handle to the white man at arm's length. Cady tried to jab it at the negro. Then, with a great effort, he stooped, picked up the pieces of cedar, and moved uncertainly out of the gate and down the road. As he went he called back:

"I'll git ye fer this, nigger! Hittin' a white man with a rock! Yore day's a-comin', nigger!"

And he staggered down the road and out of sight.

Toussaint stood in the stable yard, sick with fright. He was not afraid of Cady or anything Cady could do. He was afraid of white men. If he were brought before a court, any sort of punishment might be put upon him.

The white negro picked up his paintbrush from the ground. He looked at it and was distraught because he had thrown it.

He did not want to go back to the manor as excited as he was; his mother would be frightened. He pondered what he should tell her.

"My God," he thought desperately, "I wish I had turned white long ago! If only I had been white!" He clenched his fists at the scurrilous names Cady had heaped upon his mother. If he had been white he would have killed Cady. He would have beaten his head to a jelly with stones!

A girl with a troop of black children behind her came hurrying up the road toward the manor. The girl herself was of a tan color. Who she was and why she hurried up the road with the children following her, Toussaint had not the slightest idea. He stood watching them go by.

A moment later a chorus of soft-toned negro voices piped out:

"There he is, Miss Lucy! There's Mistuh Toussaint, stan'in' in de lot."

The girl Lucy came up to the gate.

"Toussaint, what did you do to Mr. Cady?" she asked in a shocked voice.

"Why—he called my mother names. . . . I hit him with a rock!"

"Will he die?" gasped the tan-colored girl.

"Oh, no . . . that was paint," recollected Toussaint.

At this the children began laughing and ejaculating:

"Lawzy me! He sho' was painted up! You sho' painted dat white man's haid, Mistuh Toussaint!"

"Hush," said the girl to the children, and then to the youth:

"It scared us all so. We came over to find out. We didn't know what had happened!"

She was evidently very frightened.

"Well, as I say, we did have a fight," admitted Toussaint, "I threw my paintbrush first. I guess I oughtn't. Then he struck at me two or three times with his ax. Finally I hit him in the head with a rock and knocked him down."

The girl stood with her hand on the fence, thinking intently.

"Children, you may go home," she directed; "there won't be any more school today."

The children with the humorous mouths and long, sleepy eyelashes of negro children started back down the road, walking in crooked lines for amusement. Some of the children touched the others and then walked a little faster in order not to be touched in return . . . slow little games. They were all cold, underfed, and underclad.

The girl teacher remained at the gate.

"I certainly am glad it's no worse than paint," she breathed. "Is your mother at home?"

"Yes, but I was hoping she wouldn't hear about this."

"She really ought to know," said Lucy. "It might be a good idea for you to go and tell Colonel Vaiden, too, so if Mr. Cady gets out a warrant the Colonel will bail you out."

The tan-colored girl spoke with the certainty of a thought-out plan.

"Well, all right, I'll do that," agreed Toussaint, feeling much relieved himself at some definite thing for him to do.

The girl Lucy spoke a careful English which Toussaint had never heard from any other colored person than his mother. He went out into the road and joined her.

"Do you teach those children every day?" he asked curiously.

"When they are not picking cotton or hoeing."

"Where do you teach 'em?"

"We've been using an empty cotton pen. The boys are going to ask the Colonel for some bricks from the manor to build a fireplace in it."

"In the cotton pen?"

"Yes, we put up poles and thatched it with hay. I told the children that that was the way the negro people built their homes in Africa. I thought it would leak, but it doesn't."

There was a touch of pride in Lucy's voice that she and her pupils had overcome the difficulty of the roofless cotton pen.

"Well, I know I can pick you up enough loose bricks around the manor to build you a fireplace," promised Toussaint.

"When you finish painting your wagon, let's do it," suggested the tan-colored girl.

Lucy herself was going to the manor. She had been intending to call, she said, ever since Miss Gracie had come to the plantation.

As she walked on up the road, Toussaint called after her that he didn't know whether to finish painting the wagon or not, as Alex Cady said it was his.

"Oh, don't pay any attention to that white man," cried Lucy; "he traded that wagon to Colonel Vaiden for a coon dog. I heard all about it." And she went on up to the manor laughing.

Toussaint finished the wagon in a brilliant burst of vermilion. The passing of Lucy Lacefield had made his difficulty with Cady less menacing. There was something he could do about it.

After he had finished the wagon he made shift to put a light bed on it, hitched up the mules, and drove it to the sunken pit at the back of the manor. This had once been a flower house and was lined with brick. Toussaint cut away the weeds, then took a shovel and began digging out the bricks.

As he worked his mother and Lucy came out and watched him.

The two women had not stood on the edge of the old pit for many minutes before the tan girl began cleaning off the bricks and putting them in the wagon bed.

There was something attractive about Lucy as she stooped and scraped and piled the bricks in the wagon. When Toussaint had first seen her in the lane he had thought of her as a mulatto. Now, as she stood on the edge of the pit, her complexion lost its suggestiveness of a negro in Toussaint's eyes, and Lucy became a woman just like his mother, to whom the accident of color did not apply.

As Lucy worked she was telling Gracie about her mother, Presh Lacefield, who had been seamstress for the Lacefields in the days of the old manor's glory before the war.

Her mother had gone to Huntsville and set up as a dressmaker right after the war. Finally she had married Luke Anders, who was a farmer, and they had moved back to the Reserve. Lucy said her mother sometimes wished she had stayed in Huntsville, everything was so changed in the Reserve.

The colored tenants of the ruinous old manor stood talking of the old days and digging bricks out of a former flower

house to make a fireplace for a negro school in a deserted
cotton pen.

That afternoon Toussaint hauled the bricks to the field,
improvised a bright red mortar out of clay, and began setting up the fireplace at the end of the pen.

The roof was not a very good piece of thatching, but it
was so steep that it did not leak. The seats were a bench,
two or three stools, and a split-bottom chair which Lucy had
brought down for herself. The blackboard was an old piece
of oilcloth, and marks were made on it with pencils of blue
clay which the children whittled out of the bottom of rivulets.
On a large pumpkin beside the teacher's chair was scratched
a map of the world with the stem for the North Pole.

Everything Lucy Lacefield did, she did rapidly. She made
up more clay plaster for Toussaint than he needed. She kept
bricks to his hand and recleaned them before she laid them
down. In the midst of this work she had leisure. Woman-
like she talked to Toussaint about himself, his life in Florence, what he was going to do here on the plantation.

"I tell Luke he ought to fertilize his cotton," said the
girl; "this land's worn out."

"You mean manure it?" queried Toussaint. "You couldn't
get enough."

"No, I mean commercial fertilizers."

Toussaint did not know what she was talking about.

"Where do you get that sort of fertilizer?"

"I don't know exactly, but there is such a thing. I've read
about it in the farm papers."

"I wonder if it would make the land grow much more?"

"It says it doubles and trebles the yield," said Lucy.

The girl's tone immediately made Toussaint want to get
some of this miraculous stuff.

"If I had some of that, Mammy and I could get away
within a year," hazarded Toussaint.

"Get away," echoed Lucy. "Where are you and your
mother going?"

"North, I suppose," returned the boy, "but I had thought of going West, too."

"White people go West," said Lucy looking at the youth, "but colored folks hardly ever do."

"Ye-es, I know that," admitted Toussaint, thinking of his real purpose in fleeing the South.

At his vague answer the girl looked at him curiously.

"If you made a success here, it looks as if you'd stay."

"Well," said Toussaint, drawing a long breath, "colored people don't get their rights here. My trouble with Cady, for instance: if he takes me with a warrant, I won't get a fair show."

"If you make a good tenant and grow lots of cotton, you'd have a better show than just an ordinary negro," stated Lucy crisply.

"I suppose that's so," admitted Toussaint.

"And if you really made a success you'd help all the colored folks around here," persisted the tan-colored girl rapidly. "It would show people that negroes could be industrious and prosperous. It's a responsibility to be a colored person now. A white man like Cady can do anything, and nobody will think any worse of white people for it, but if a negro does anything, everybody says, 'Oh, well, all negroes are like that.'"

"I wish I hadn't thrown that paintbrush at Alex Cady!" cried Toussaint. "I ought to have just let him talk."

The girl came over and touched his hand.

"They tell me what is without help should be without regard," she quoted philosophically.

While the maxim was sober enough, her faint touch on his hand was pleasant to Toussaint. Just then a nasal feminine voice called:

"Lucy! Lucy! Air you in that cotton pen, Lucy?"

This caused the tan-colored girl to step away from Toussaint and move to the door, where she could see who was calling her.

"Yes, I'm here, Miss Mamie!" she called back.

Toussaint now had the fireplace up as high as his chest and was trying to contrive how to swing in the hips of the little chimney.

A white girl, a trifle younger than Lucy, came walking across the rain-flattened cotton rows.

"Oh, you-all are makin' a farplace," she said, looking curiously at the rising structure.

"Yes, the children can't study in the cold."

"Well, I declare," repeated the white girl in astonishment.

Lucy had an impulse to say, "Miss Cady, this is Toussaint Vaiden," but to have introduced a negro to a white girl would have been an offense.

Mamie Cady stood near Lucy with an occasional curious glance at the white negro who was laying the bricks. Finally she said:

"Lucy, would you mind looking in this?" and she handed an envelope to the colored girl.

The envelope was addressed in a copperplate handwriting with many flourishes. The whole address was inscribed on a scroll. Above this flew a pen-drawn bird bearing the scroll in its beak. On the outstretched wings of the bird was written:

"Fly away little bird and carry this letter to . . ."

On the scroll itself was the address:

> MISS SLATIE CADY,
> BeShears Crossroads,
> Lauderdale County,
> Alabama.

Lucy drew out a letter in the same florid handwriting and looked at it.

"What does it say?" asked Mamie.

Lucy nodded faintly at Toussaint to ask if Mamie wanted the letter read before him.

"Oh, yes, go ahead," said Mamie.

"DEAR MISS SLATIE," read the tan girl, "I seat myself to write you a few lines to let you know Pap's hawgs took the colry just as he was fixin' to kill 'em, so he didn't, and Pap says that is the first time he ever knowed the colry to lengthen a hawg's life. Ha! Ha! Ha!——

"Some robbers was through this part of the country the other week and blode up Railroad Jones' office in Lanesburg. I regret to inform you that cousin Hepzy Catlin is dead. They buried her in Mount Moriar burial groun's. We heard about Colonel Milt Vaiden stealin' out old man Handback.

"Hopin you all is enjoying the same blessins, I am

"Your cousin,
"PHILO SMOTHERMAN."

The name Catlin caught Toussaint's attention.

"Are the Catlins kin to you, Miss Mamie?" he asked.

"My mammy was a Smotherman, and her great-aunt was Miss Hepzy Smotherman who married old man Philo Catlin. That's why Uncle Henst, Mam's brother, named his boy Philo, after Philo Catlin. . . . So Aunt Hepzy's dead."

"That's what the letter said," nodded Lucy.

"When Mammy got that letter," said Mamie, "she was mortal shore that somebody was dead. She handed it to me and said, 'Mamie, go take this to Lucy and see who's dead.'" The white girl stood looking at her letter for a minute or so and then said:

"I don't reckon you could learn me to write, Lucy?"

"Why, I am sure I could," said Lucy, entering the pen and picking up a stick of blue clay.

The tan girl evidently was about to begin.

"What do you charge?" asked Mamie.

"Why, I charge ten cents a month."

"Ten cents a month," repeated Mamie. "I could make that with eggs. . . ."

This bargaining was interrupted by Alex Cady's voice shouting:

"Mamie! Mamie! Come away from them stuck-up yaller niggers, or I'll skin you alive. First thing they know, I'll pitch a pine knot into that nigger mess they're buildin', and the whole shebang will go up in smoke."

Mamie's face whitened. She turned about and started walking rapidly across the worn cotton rows toward her father's cabin.

CHAPTER THIRTY-NINE

At noon the next day after his bricklaying with Lucy Lacefield, Toussaint Vaiden saddled one of the mules and rode to Florence.

The octoroon was in a hurry for two reasons. That morning Alex Cady had come to the manor and demanded his wagon. Toussaint and Gracie and Lump Mowbray held a council. Lump had said that they had better not raise any more ruckus with that white man, but for Toussaint to go tell Colonel Vaiden about what had happened and see who the wagon belonged to. Another reason that spurred Toussaint was an apprehension that a constable might ride up and take him with a warrant for what he already had done to Cady.

As he urged his mule to a running walk he turned over in his mind his fight with Cady, thinking how he could put himself in the best light before the Colonel. Another reason for his rush, he wanted to get back and see how the fireplace worked that morning.

On the previous day, when he had come home to the manor and had dinner with his mother, he had sat restlessly at the old table in the kitchen and finally had said he believed he would step out that night and try to get acquainted with their neighbors.

Gracie had forecast suspiciously:

"Now, Toussaint, you're going to Luke Anders' house to see Lucy Lacefield again."

Toussaint had become very uncomfortable.

"I thought I'd go by all the cabins," he protested, "except that white man's, and see everybody."

This second time Toussaint had seen Lucy the fact that

she was a tan girl and not so white as he vanished completely from his mind.

Lucy's mother, Presh Lacefield, had told Toussaint at once that Lucy had had a year in a colored school in Nashville, that she was a Christian girl and was trying to see how much good she could do. "Her only fault is, she's too good," declared Presh, "they put a lot of foolishness in her head up there in Nashville, which I don't suppose I would take out if I could, but it won't do her or anybody else any good."

Toussaint saw that Presh was extremely proud of her daughter, and this was her way of boasting about her, to decry her. It was the old Lacefield way of boasting. Presh had been a house servant in the manor before the war and the modes of speech among the old white aristocrats were Presh's modes.

Presh reminded Toussaint somewhat of his mother, but Gracie held a pensive sweetness to her son that was almost mysterious. He never knew of what she was thinking, whereas, after his first five minutes with Presh, he never knew anything except what Presh was thinking. Toussaint had come away from the Anders' cabin at midnight with an uncomfortable certainty that his mother would disapprove of his long stay.

When the white negro reached Florence he hitched his mule on one of the back streets and approached Colonel Vaiden's store as inconspicuously as possible. He was still afraid of being arrested for his assault on a white man.

The Colonel's store was the same ramshackle affair on the wrong side of Courthouse Square which Bradley had shown to Miltiades in the first instance. No amount of subsequent looking had found another building for Miltiades. It was the worst store in Florence actually to be in use. Its theoretical rental had been seventeen dollars a month, but the Colonel had got it for eight silver dollars piled in a stack before Bradley's eyes.

"This is a hell of a department store I'm leasing you,"

said the real-estate dealer, and he felt that the Colonel had got several of his best cigars under false pretenses.

Toussaint entered a building that was absolutely unlighted from one end to the other except by a front and a back door. A large brass lamp hung from the middle of the ceiling, but lamps were designed for the night and not the day, so it was unlighted.

Toussaint stood in the doorway, blinking his eyes and seeing nothing. From the interior Miltiades asked without enthusiasm:

"Do you want anything, Toussaint?"

"I'd like to speak with you a minute, Colonel," said Toussaint in a lowered tone.

Miltiades instantly perceived that his tenant was in trouble.

"What have you done now?" he asked in a voice that suggested that Toussaint was always running to him with some difficulty.

"Is anybody here?"

"No."

"Well . . . I . . . I had a little trouble."

"Yes, I know that."

"You heard about it?" ejaculated Toussaint, in alarm.

"No."

"Well . . . Mr. Alex Cady come and took his wagon back."

"You mean the one I let you have?" snapped the Colonel.

"Yes, sir."

"Why, the little runt!" ejaculated the Colonel, annoyed. "I gave him eleven dollars for that wagon. You tell him that. Tell him I told you to tell him, and for him to give that wagon back to you."

Toussaint was disconcerted at this message.

"I'd rather not tell him myself, if you don't mind," said Toussaint appealingly.

"Have you already had a fight with him about it?" asked the Colonel sharply.

The white negro stood silent.

"What did you do it for?" demanded the Colonel. "You knew I'd get the wagon back for you, or you should have known it. What did you want to start a fight for?"

"It wasn't for the wagon . . ." stammered Toussaint.

"What was it for?"

"He called my mother a bad name."

"Oh . . . and he took the wagon after that?"

"Yes, sir."

"What did you do to make him call your mother a bad name?"

"Well, he was cutting up some posts in one of the stalls for stove wood, and I told him to stop."

"I see," nodded Miltiades.

The Colonel wondered if this were the truth. He always doubted a negro. But it was a reasonable explanation. He knew the tenants burned the fences and the weather boarding of their houses rather than get out and cut their own firewood in cold weather. He had expected this. He had figured it in the price he had paid for the old Lacefield place.

"Were you wanting to use the posts for firewood yourself?" he asked Toussaint almost whimsically.

The octoroon grew warm.

"I had just come back with a load of wood from the hills," he replied, "when Mother told me she heard a hammering down at the stable. I went down to see, and when Cady denied cutting the posts I told him Mother had heard him hammering, and that's why he called her a name."

"M-m . . . is that all your trouble?"

"Then I threw a paintbrush at him and smeared his face, and I thought he might get out a warrant for me."

"I see," nodded Miltiades. "If he does, let me know."

"All right, sir," said the white negro gratefully.

"And, Toussaint," added the Colonel reflectively, "you . . . you oughtn't to raise trouble with a white man just offhand like that."

"I know I oughtn't," said the youth in a monotone.

The Colonel didn't exactly like the way he said this, so he dropped the subject.

"Is there anything you are going to have to have on the farm?" he asked in a negative voice.

The white man's invitation not to purchase anything recalled to the youth what Lucy Lacefield had said.

"Colonel," he began tentatively, without much hope, "I—I've been thinking about something for the planta-tion. . . ."

"All right . . . what is it?" inquired the Colonel in a discouraging tone.

"Well . . . it's ferterlizer," said Toussaint.

"Fertilizer!"

Toussaint nodded vaguely.

"You mean you want me to get you some manure from somewhere?"

Toussaint really did not know what he meant himself.

"No-o . . . it's not manure. You call it commercial ferterlizer. I think it comes in bags."

Miltiades was astonished.

"Where did you get such a notion in your head, nigger?"

"I—I just heard about it," stammered Toussaint. "They say it makes more cotton."

"Well, I be damned!" ejaculated the merchant. He himself had heard of commercial fertilizers, but he had never seen any. Now, for one of his negroes to pop up and ask for commercial fertilizer!

"How much do you think you would need?" he inquired.

"They say . . . about twenty-two pounds an acre."

"Well . . . we'll see about that . . . if I can get it and it doesn't cost too much. But, look here, if I do get some I'll put it down against your account!"

"Oh, yes, that's all right," cried Toussaint, delighted at this half promise.

When Toussaint was gone, Miltiades stood in his deserted store, thinking over such an extraordinary request from a negro. It was as if a baby should display an interest in higher mathematics. Then he thought of Beekman again, whom he supposed to be Toussaint's father. That explained the white negro's initiative, and also his tendency to get himself into trouble with anybody who crossed him.

CHAPTER FORTY

It was five o'clock, and Colonel Miltiades Vaiden locked his store and started for his home. Other businesses in town kept open longer, but his trade came from the country, and by five o'clock all of his customers were out of town.

As Miltiades crossed Courthouse Square he was disappointed in his heart about his store. He had meant to found a large, handsome store, but he had reproduced, almost automatically, Handback's store, BeShears' store, and a thousand other stores throughout the South.

The real object of the darkness and uninvitingness of all these stores was to discourage trade. The less merchandise the negro tenants bought, the greater profit the merchant-landlords would have at the end of the year. Therefore the storekeeper arranged his goods not to sell. He specialized in unattractiveness.

But all this was precisely the opposite of what the Colonel had in mind when he embarked upon his enterprise.

At first Miltiades thought his establishment in Courthouse Square was a temporary affair, and that later he would found a dignified mercantile establishment. But the store that he had started expanded swiftly. He accepted more and more first mortgages. He had even foreclosed one of these mortgages and now had another plantation on his hands. Then a debtor had given Miltiades what purported to be a first mortgage on his place, but which later had turned out to be a second mortgage. The Colonel had been forced to buy in the first to make his second good. This deal had set him back about thirty-five hundred dollars.

He could, of course, have sent the man who made such false representations to the coal mines, but then he would have had a plantation on his hands that was completely idle. The Colonel had given the fellow a wigging and let him go. But the point was, he saw his dream of a fine business vanishing because all his money was being tied up in this gloomy little hole on the Square.

So the Colonel walked home through the cold dusk with a number of disagreeable things in his head. And then the people he passed on the streets gave him a bare, "Good-evening, Colonel Vaiden," or did not speak at all.

Not that he gave a damn for that. He had enough to think of, God knew, without worrying about whether the people in Florence liked him or not.

They never had liked him, but since the Handback episode their attitude toward him had changed from silent indifference to silent distrust and condemnation. It was queer how different could be the emotional content of two silences . . . in folk walking past without a word.

A few days before this an odd break had occurred in Miltiades' isolation. On the corner of Pine and Laurel streets some workmen were laying the foundation of a brick church. They were excavating a large basement with a place for a furnace. The hole in the ground with its stone foundations for the walls and partitions caught the Colonel's fancy and suddenly put him in mind of the fact that, as yet, he had started no mansion of his own. The Colonel wanted some such magnificent home. He wanted it to escape the turmoil of his tenants, the ugliness of his store, and the silence of his acquaintances.

Of course, he couldn't get it now, because he had too little money. But when his circumstances eased up he was going to build himself a home that was a home.

As Miltiades stood looking at the foundation, a man in a long black coat came up Laurel Street, and he too stopped and began looking at the foundation.

The Colonel knew the man. He was a Reverend B. Alvin Puckett, minister of the congregation who were building the new church. Miltiades could see the Reverend Puckett

glance at him from time to time. Presently the minister took
open notice of Miltiades and came around to him with rather
a breeze.

"This is Colonel Vaiden," he said, offering his hand. "I
am Puckett, the preacher in charge of this congregation. I
have been intending to call on you, Colonel, but you know
how it is, a minister never has a minute of his own."

Miltiades returned the preacher's hand rather blankly.

"I suppose you are kept busy," he agreed, wondering
what a minister did with the week-days.

"So I'm very glad to meet you now and here," pæaned
the divine.

The thought crossed Miltiades' mind to say drily, "You
form a minority of one," but instead of that he said he was
pleased to meet him, too.

"I'm glad to see you take an interest in our prospective
building," went on Puckett with enthusiasm. "Now, this is
going to be the vestry, there the robing room for the choir.
The organ is going to be situated yonder, at the end of the
nave. Its pipes will be gilded and form an arch with a gold
cross in the center. . . . What do you think of lighting the
building with acetylene?"

Miltiades answered vaguely that acetylene jets gave a
nice light.

"Could you make some suggestion about the lighting?"
inquired the Reverend Puckett earnestly.

"Well . . ." said Miltiades, thinking of possible ways to
light a church, "you might have 'em hanging from the ceiling."

"A good idea," nodded Puckett, "the ceiling is going to
be arched; middle Gothic. The acetylene plant will cost about
two hundred and fifty dollars. Dr. Simpson the druggist
suggested fifty dollars. Judge Ashton suggested seventy-
five. I thought it would be nice for just three men to arrange
the lighting of the church. You know how nice such reports
look when you hand them in at conference, just three names
making up the amount. Gives such a generous character to

the congregation. So much more so than a number of names with small contributions."

"Yes, that's true," agreed the Colonel.

While the fellow talked, Miltiades had been mentally adding what already had been suggested and subtracting the sum from what might be called the superior limit of suggestibility, and he arrived at the amount of one hundred and twenty-five dollars as a field for further suggestions as to how the acetylene lights should be arranged in the new church.

The dry humor of the situation appealed to the Colonel. He reflected again that he was thirty-five hundred dollars short. But the great advantage of having a full-bodied shortage is that small extravagances have no influence on it.

"I believe I'll suggest fifty dollars," said Miltiades. "I hate to put you to the trouble of finding another man, but I just happen to have fifty dollars in my pocket"; and to the Reverend Puckett's amazement the Colonel drew out a long purse and handed him four tens and two fives.

After that Miltiades did not get away for a good hour. The Reverend Puckett discoursed on the generosity of the Florence people, on the need of an up-to-date church, one that the Methodist congregation would have no need to be ashamed to meet their God in. In brief, he kept Miltiades so long that the Colonel regretted having given him anything at all. He ruined his begging with his gratitude.

The Reverend Puckett himself was thinking piously:

"Who knows but what this may be the thief on the Cross, turning his eyes toward his Saviour?"

To Miltiades his contribution of fifty dollars had no meaning at all beyond his brush of dry humor in giving it and his boredom with Puckett after he had given it.

But when the report of his donation got abroad at the next meeting of the Methodist deacons, gossip was much more ingenious than that. The malevolent said it was conscience money. The ambitious said Colonel Vaiden was trying to buy his way into respectable society again. The vain said he was trying to make a splurge on what he had stolen. One or two of the kind-hearted believed the Colonel was trying to put himself right with God.

Miss Sydna Crowninshield thought that, notwithstanding all the scurrilous and untrue things said about Colonel Vaiden, he was still the magnanimous Christian gentleman. Tears came to her eyes when she heard of it. It was so like the chivalrous knight who had comforted her dying father on the battlefield even after her father had cost the Colonel his love.

The point that really stuck in Miltiades' mind after his contribution was the manor which the bare foundations of the church had suggested.

So now, today, as he walked up Pine Street, he was thinking that for all the edification he was getting out of his money he might as well be J. Handback and have done with it.

He had no store; he had no manor; he had no liberal and cultivating amusements, nor was he a patron of the arts. He pursued none of the *post bellum* graces of life, and for all he was getting out of his money, he might just as well be Handback, or his father-in-law Alex BeShears, or any other of the ten thousand money grubbers in the South. He was disturbed and disappointed in himself. After he had transferred the ownership of the cotton from Handback to himself it was a sort of moral duty for him to use it at least with more enlightenment than Handback had been doing.

At the moment the Colonel was passing Bill Bradley's residence on Pine Street. An impulse moved him to step in and ask Bradley what a two-and-a-half-story brick house of fifteen or twenty rooms would cost. Not that he meant to buy or build such a structure: he wanted to know what it would cost.

Bradley, the purveyor of magnificent homes, lived in a single-story wooden house that needed paint. It would continue to need paint. Mrs. Bradley refused to let Bill paint the house or clip the lawn or do anything at all to the outside of the place, because, she said, if he did so, he would sell it.

Mrs. Bradley had lived in dozens of houses in Florence which she had fixed up and which Bill had sold. She told her friends that Bill would sell her last shimmy at high noon in Courthouse Square and deliver the goods on the spot, if anybody made him an offer. She said she liked her Pine Street home, and she was determined to keep it if she had to let it rot down on her head.

Mr. Bill Bradley answered the Colonel's bell. He appeared in the hallway with one eye slightly closed out of habit, although at the moment he was not smoking.

Bill was surprised to see the Colonel. He knew that he was the only man in town who had been friendly toward Miltiades, but he did not consider that his friendliness had gone far enough to warrant the Colonel in calling on him at his home. If it had gone that far, it had slipped out from under his control.

So now, with a trace of surprise in his manner, he asked the Colonel into the living room, as there was no fire in his parlor.

Miltiades, who read Bradley's unwillingness, said no, he wouldn't go in at all, he had just stopped by to get an estimate on a house.

The real-estate man grabbed his friend's arm.

"Nonsense! Nonsense!" he cried. "Come on in to the fire. Me and Lily was just wondering why you didn't come around sometimes. Lily, here's Colonel Vaiden come to see us. See if you can't trot out some of that blackberry wine your mother sent us. Colonel, my mother-in-law makes the best blackberry wine you ever put in your face. Now, what kind of an estimate are you looking for, Colonel?"

"Now, look here," explained Miltiades, trying to put everything straight, "I want you to know here and now that I am not going to buy anything. I just want an estimate."

"Colonel," cried the real-estate dealer, "I'm the very man

you're looking for. I haven't got a thing in the world I want to sell you."

Mrs. Bradley began laughing.

"Colonel Vaiden," she said, "when Bill doesn't want to sell you anything, you might as well get out your check book and start paying him for it."

With the uncommercial aspect of this investigation thoroughly before them, Mr. Bradley ran through an expert catechism as to the sort of house Miltiades did not want.

"Is it that department store idea again?" he inquired.

"No, a dwelling house. I simply want an estimate."

The real-estate dealer turned to his wife.

"Listen to that, Lily, this old fox is thinking about marrying again."

"No, not at all," said Miltiades, with a widower's soberness.

"You'd say that anyway," coquetted Lily, lifting a brow at the Colonel.

"All right," re-began Bradley in a business tone. "Do you know any house in this town of the sort you want?"

"I was thinking of building to suit myself."

The real-estate dealer drew a long face.

"Don't try that. You'll suit nobody else in the world and finally not even yourself."

"You'd better let *her* see your plans," advised Mrs. Bradley archly; "and remember, she'll want plenty of closets."

"Go ahead and tell me what you want," advised Bradley.

The Colonel pondered. He could explain neither to the Bradleys nor to himself that he wanted a spiritual retreat from the commercial mechanism into which he was falling. He not only could not explain this, but the Bradleys were so conjugal that it was impossible, in their presence, to think of a manor being put to any other use than for an uxurious married couple to live in.

So the Colonel began on what already had crystallized in his mind: an old brick manor with green jalousies, a colonnaded piazza, an observatory on top; and he went on describing the sort of manor one saw anywhere in the South.

Bill looked at his wife.

"Very unusual, Lily, ain't it?"

"Very," nodded Lily earnestly; "only he hasn't mentioned closets."

Bradley got to his feet.

"Look here, Colonel, let's take a walk and be to ourselves. If we don't, Lily will turn your house into one huge collection of closets."

Miltiades arose with a touch of regret at leaving this hearth with a pleasant woman beside it. It was like going out of a warm room into the cold again. He followed Bradley to the door. Outside, the night had grown quite dark. The moment they were out of the presence of Lily their talk lost its undercurrent of deference and humor and became more flat-footed.

"A house like you've been talking about will cost you around fifty thousand dollars, new," said Bradley.

"That's what I wanted to know."

"But, look here, damn it, I can sell you the same damn house, already put up, for a third of that price."

"Sixteen and two thirds," calculated the Colonel.

"I'll say fifteen in round figgers."

"But it won't be what I want," declared the Colonel.

"How in the hell do you know it won't be what you want?"

They had reached Bradley's gate. The real-estate dealer remembered something else he had to tell his client, so he walked on with him.

"The rest of them deeds, Handback swears he give 'em to me."

"Well, it doesn't make much difference anyway."

"No, but when I sell you a place I want you to be able to show a clear title to it in your safe."

"Don't worry about it."

"I'm not worrying, but I like to do business in a business way."

The two men were talking about the old deeds to the Lacefield place. The whole collection was transferred to each new purchaser of the plantation. They were a formidable pile that derived title from the original Indian grants.

While the two men discussed the old deeds which should have been delivered to Miltiades, Bradley paused, opened a gate, and headed the Colonel into it.

The real-estate man changed to an optimistic strain.

"Talking about that house, saying you just want an estimate . . . inside of twelve months you'll be ready to buy."

"What makes you think so?"

"Because by that time the Administration will be on its feet, ever'thing will be moving. . . . Did I tell you about a order for a site for a fertilizer factory?"

This made the Colonel think of Toussaint.

"Yes, you told me about that. . . . Where are we going?"

Miltiades discovered that he was walking up a circular graveled path between borders of box. Bradley stopped with a full-armed gesture toward the dark mass of a manor.

"What's the matter with that?" he demanded with the mechanical but glowing commendation of a salesman.

"Matter with what?"

"Why, the Crowninshield place?"

Miltiades saw where he was and became rather embarrassed.

"I don't know what's the matter with it."

"Does it suit your needs?"

"Aw, pshaw!" ejaculated the Colonel in an annoyed tone, "it isn't for sale."

"Make me an offer for half what it's worth, and it's yours," said Bradley in earnest tones. "I know who owns this house. I don't mean who holds the deeds, I mean who actually owns the house."

The Colonel became incensed at being dragged onto Drusilla's lawn and offered such a nefarious bargain.

"I wouldn't buy it the way you're talking about for fifteen cents!"

"Well . . . it would cost you more than that, even my way," said Bradley, evidently laughing.

"Bradley, I don't appreciate this," said the Colonel severely.

"M-m . . . it's business."

"You know the owner of this place doesn't want to sell!"

"Of course not . . . they never do. . . . But the man with the mortgage always wants to sell, and usually does, sooner or later. Now this man is especially keen to get his money now. I know."

"What's his rush?"

"Why, with this financial depression coming on us, gold dollars are going to be worth their weight in gold, I can tell you."

"I thought you expected flush times. You got a commission to buy a site for a fertilizer plant."

"Hell fire, that order was canceled two weeks ago—by telegraph. No, sir, this property is going to be foreclosed, Colonel, and if you don't buy it some damned skinflint will, and Miss Drusilla will be turned out of her home."

At this moment the door of the manor opened, and a youth and a girl appeared against the light in the hallway. They lingered for a moment, after the fashion of the young, when the girl probably saw the coal of Bradley's cigar, for she said in a startled undertone:

"Jerry, there's somebody out in the yard!"

"Out where?"

"It's just us, Miss Sydna," interposed Bradley in the casual tone of a neighbor. "I was just showing a prospect your house to see if it was anything like what he wanted."

"Mr. Bradley, you're not going to sell him our place!" called Sydna in apprehension.

Bradley broke into a laugh.

"How could I sell your mammy's own property if she didn't want me to?"

The couple on the porch hesitated a moment.

"Who is your prospect?" asked Sydna.

"Colonel Milt Vaiden."

Sydna gave a little gasp. She felt as if a violin string had been twanged in her chest.

"Come on up. You-all can't tell anything about our house in the dark."

"M-m . . . we might make a guess what it weighed, maybe," replied Bradley.

The two men walked up the ample wooden steps.

"Come in," invited Sydna. "Jerry, you bring me that book the next time you come."

"No, no," objected the Colonel, "we haven't time to come in, Miss Sydna, I was just passing by. . . ."

"All right," said Jerry's voice, "I won't forget it." He passed the men on the piazza and said, "Good-night, Uncle Milt. Good-night, Mr. Bradley."

"Good-night, Jerry," returned the uncle.

"Jerry, I hear they're about to kick you out of school again," called the real-estate man cheerfully. "What's the matter this time?"

"Not having any brains," returned Jerry just as cheerfully.

"That's the only reason they'd ever kick you out, Jerry —because they haven't got any brains. Now, Colonel, you're in better hands than mine to see this house. I'll walk to the gate with Jerry."

"I meant I didn't have any brains," said Jerry, waiting for the real-estate man.

"Oh, you . . . well, I never would have suspected that, Jerry."

Sydna was peering at the Colonel in the light from the doorway.

"Really, won't you come in, Colonel Vaiden?" she invited, in some excitement.

Miltiades was disconcerted that Bradley had got him into such a situation. He thought sharply to himself, if he ever did buy anything at all, it wouldn't be from Bradley.

"I wish I could, Miss Sydna, but I haven't time. I was not making a call."

"I know you are not," caught up the girl; "you never do, but I see you go past every day."

"I really don't call much anywhere, Miss Sydna," defended Miltiades inexpertly.

"I know it, but you can't do that way, Colonel," protested Sydna. "You and Mother are such old friends, it looks as if . . ."

"Well, yes . . . I suppose I ought . . . Drusilla and I——" He broke off, oppressed by the enigmatic complication of their two lives, their changing relations to each other, until now he stood on her lawn in the darkness, with a real-estate dealer, planning to foreclose the mortgage against her home. . . .

"There really isn't much to say, Sydna," he concluded grayly.

"Why, I think there is everything to say," pressed the girl, with the anxious excitement of a person who faces suddenly a long desired and solitary opportunity. "We were talking about you the other day . . . giving the lighting system to the Methodist church. I hope you'll remember the Episcopalians too, some time."

She had not at all meant to switch off onto this topic. It had come by accident.

"You belong to your mother's church?"

"Oh, all the Lacefields are Episcopalians."

"Well," said Miltiades more lightly, "if the Episcopals start a new church, they can rely on me to give them light," and the Colonel moved to go.

"But, look here, won't you really come in and see Mother? You can't come up on her porch like this and then go away!"

She was in earnest; in fact, she sounded on the verge of tears. She forced Miltiades into seriousness again.

"I don't think your mother would like to see me, Sydna," said the Colonel.

"I'll run ask her."

"Sydna!" cried the Colonel, shocked at the idea.

"Well, then, how am I ever going to get to see you myself?" asked the girl.

"Do you want to see me?" inquired the Colonel incredulously.

"Why, of course."

"What for?"

"Why, to thank you."

"Me?"

"Yes, you know that night at the political speaking," she lowered her voice, "when you corrected Mr. Handback . . ."

The Colonel had a bad moment when he thought she alluded to J. Handback, but it dawned on him that she was calling Lucius Mr. Handback.

"You forgot what you said to him!" cried Sydna reproachfully.

"I'm afraid I have."

"You said, even if he wasn't a gentleman, he should act like one, or something like that. . . . It squelched him."

The Colonel was slightly amused.

"If you liked it, I am very happy to have done you that service."

"As if that were all the services you've done me," said Sydna, shaking her head.

"I hope I can do more," said the Colonel, extending his hand.

"But, look, you really are coming back to see Mother?"

"If she should give me some assurance that she would like for me to come," suggested Miltiades.

"I'll see that she does that," exclaimed Sydna.

At that moment an interior door opened, and a voice called:

"Sydna darling, it's getting late. Who are you talking to, honey?"

"I'm talking to Colonel Vaiden, Mother," called back Sydna triumphantly and expectantly.

Came a pause; then Drusilla's voice said:

"Oh!"

And the interior door was shut.

CHAPTER FORTY-ONE

For several days, on the strength of Sydna's suggestion that her mother would see him, Colonel Miltiades Vaiden pondered writing a note, asking permission to call at the Crowninshield home. But the impulse somehow held within itself a queer unrealizable feeling, and so it was delayed and delayed.

Then the pre-Christmas rush set in and eddied even into the store on the wrong side of Courthouse Square, and Miltiades had no time for social amenities. Two weeks later Christmas day came and put an abrupt end to all trading whatsoever.

The only customers left in town during the holiday were the small boys who had exhausted their supply of firecrackers and roman candles. As Miltiades did not handle fireworks, he sat on a stool at the bookkeeper's desk quite alone. He turned through the accounts of the tenants to get a notion of whom to curtail. But instead of putting his mind on his business he thought that it was Christmas, that Drusilla Crowninshield had her home decorated, that Rose probably had fixed up her boarding house. . . . He wondered what his sister Cassandra was doing . . . very likely teaching Buck Mosely's brood of pickaninnies that Santa Claus was a myth. The fancy of his old maid sister doing this gave Miltiades a sort of sad amusement.

Presently other members of his family floated into his thoughts: his brother Sylvester in Arkansas and Lycurgus in Louisiana. Ponny always wrote a semi-annual letter to the wives of these two brothers, and now it occurred to him that unless he took up the correspondence himself he would likely hear from them no more.

The Colonel reached for his pen and paper, but when he got them together he had nothing to say. Where Ponny would have thought of pages full of news, the Colonel could think of nothing at all. Then, as he sat there, dipping his pen from time to time, a suspicion came to his mind that probably his brothers' families would not care to hear from him. If the report of the Handback affair had reached their ears, very likely they would not appreciate a letter from . . . He did not finish his thought but simply let it drop

Then he began writing:

DEAR MRS. CROWNINSHIELD:

The writer would greatly appreciate the honor of calling on you and your family at any time today that is convenient for you.

With my greatest respect and best wishes of the season,

MILTIADES VAIDEN.

Christmas Day.

The Colonel looked at his handiwork, which he certainly had not set out to write. He put it in an envelope and walked to the door with an idea of finding a negro to take it.

The Square outside was empty of black folk. From here and there came the report of giant crackers. A church bell was ringing.

The Colonel stood in his door with note in hand when he saw young Dalrymple Love strolling toward his store. The clerk wore his Sunday suit, a new derby hat, and polished shoes.

Wearing his best clothes and moving aimlessly along the street, the clerk produced, somehow, an acute impression of loneliness. When he came up to Miltiades he touched his hat.

"Good-morning, Colonel. I hope you had a good trade this Christmas."

"Fair enough, and I hope you did, too."

"It might have been better," said Love; he paused a

moment and then added, "I'm leaving Mr. Handback on the first."

Miltiades was quite surprised.

"Got a better place?"

"Haven't got no place at all." He hesitated a little uncomfortably. "The fact is I thought I'd walk down this way and see if you didn't need a clerk. You know what I can do. You've seen me clerk."

"How came that?" asked the Colonel.

"Well, Mr. Handback is gettin' rid of a lot more of his places . . . our trade's fell off something fierce. You see the nigger trade goes with whoever buys the places, so nachelly he don't need as many clerks as he used to need."

"M-m . . . I see," nodded Miltiades.

As he said it a gust of acquisitiveness went through the Colonel. If Handback were selling more of his farms they must be going cheap indeed, and Miltiades began silently counting up his resources to see if he could purchase another.

"What are you doing for Christmas?" he asked of Love, passing over the boy's inquiry about a job.

"Why, nothing much. The saloons are shut up, and me and Stebbins can't get in to play pool nowhere."

"Why don't you go to see your girls?"

Love turned his forward foot on its heel and said:

"Huh, I ain't got no girl."

"What are you doing now?" inquired the Colonel.

"Why-y . . . Lucius give me a note and a dime and told me to go out and find a nigger to deliver it. . . . I'm a dad gum mind to tear it up."

"Why?"

"I'm not Lucius' erran' boy."

"Well, I wouldn't tear it up."

"I don't see no nigger. I think they are all over at a big to-do in East Florence."

"Who's the note to?"

"Oh, that Crowninshiel' girl," said Love in distaste; "stuck-up city girl."

Across the Colonel's mind floated a contempt for Lucius, dangling after Sydna. Aloud he said:

"By the way, Love, if you decide to go over there and take the note yourself, I have one to—er—to Mrs. Crowninshield."

"I'll take yours," announced Love at once, with some reference possibly to the fact that he had applied to the Colonel for a job.

"That's nice of you. You can bring back my answer here, if you don't mind."

"Oh, no, I don't mind."

Mr. Dalrymple Love took the Colonel's note and started across Courthouse Square toward the entrance of Pine Street. He was still rather hopelessly on the lookout for a negro. He did not want to enter the Crowninshield home as an errand boy. Then he tried to think of something to do after he had delivered the notes and come back with the answers. He looked at the corner saloon on the north side of the Square, where he and Stebbins might have played pool all day long had not the place, unhappily, been closed on this, their single holiday.

Across the town other church bells were ringing out the glad occasion of Christmas. A notion came to Love that next Christmas he and Stebbins would rent a saloon and shut themselves up inside and play pool all day long. As he walked along, his imagination added other enjoyable details. He and Stebbins would take a couple of cans of cove oysters and plenty of pepper sauce and crackers, and they would have a regular Christmas dinner. They would eat and play pool at the same time. He could fancy himself chewing a bite of canned oysters and crackers, chalking his cue, and deliberating over how to shoot a combination. The church bells rang out charity, peace, and good-will to all men. Love walked along planning a gay, delightful Christmas twelve months distant from this lonely day.

Angling across the Square, Love saw a party of three going to the courthouse: Judge Ashton, a negro girl, and what at first appeared to be a white boy, but a second glance showed it was the white negro who had lived in East Florence.

The white negro promised relief from the ignominy of delivering the note at the Crowninshield home, and Dalrymple went striding across the Square, calling:

"Oh, nigger! Say there, nigger! I want you to deliver a note!"

The blond negro looked at Dalrymple through the cold sunshine.

"I can't, Mr. Love," he excused himself, "I'm going with Judge Ashton."

"Where to?"

"The courthouse."

"Why, hell, you're already there. Come along and take this note, there's a dime in it."

"You'll have to excuse me this time," demurred Toussaint.

"I'll be damn' if I do!" cried Love. "You're the only nigger left. All the rest are over at East Florence at some sort of nigger to-do."

"But we are going there too, just as soon as we get through with Judge Ashton, Mr. Love."

"I be damn' if you do. Now, you can run up to the Crowninshield place with a couple of notes; then you can go."

Judge Ashton intervened to say he would have to see the two negroes in the courthouse first, and then they could do what they pleased.

So Dalrymple went in with them and stood on the cold porch until the Judge and the negroes had finished their business inside.

When the white negro and the tan girl came out again Love said:

"Now, here are the notes and a dime. Run on up to———"

The white negro interrupted in a kind of taut monotone:

"I'm sorry, but we've just got to get to East Florence."

Dalrymple Love, in a hillman's fury, cursed them for

being a couple of damned unaccommodating yellow pole-
cats. After this outburst he said more soberly and reproachfully:

"This is a nice howdy-do for Christmas, when everybody's
supposed to be nice and friendly . . . refusing to take a
Christmas note."

And the tan girl said in a low tone:

"You haven't helped our Christmas much, either, Mr.
Love."

The white negro shushed her and said:

"Come along. . . . Don't say anything to him."

Mr. Dalrymple Love delivered his two notes at the
Crowninshield home on Pine Street and returned one answer
to Colonel Vaiden and the other to Lucius Handback at the
Handback store. With the latter answer he offered Lucius
his dime with the observation that he wasn't able to find no
nigger except a damn yellow stuck-up devil that ought
to be shot.

Lucius said keep the dime for a Christmas present, and
the country boy said, "Hell, I don't want any Christmas
present for taking a note," and flung the dime on the floor.

Lucius read his note and became angry in his turn. He
glanced at the silver piece on the floor and snapped out:

"All right, sweep it out in the morning," and he went to a
show case and replaced a tie which he had taken out.

The country boy's wrath at the negro served him in lieu
of any other Christmas entertainment. He found some
pleasure in thinking how he would like to kick that nigger
from one side of Courthouse Square to the other. The white
nigger was uppety, he supposed, to show off before the
nigger wench . . . and he'd like to kick her from one side
of Courthouse Square to the other, also.

However, here he was, deprived of those pleasures, back
in the store with nothing to do, nowhere to go, and his job
coming to an end on New Year's Day. . . .

The litany of Mr. Love's woes was interrupted by a very

extraordinary spectacle. Down the steps from the upper story came a short compact figure in a new stiff hunting coat. He wore ordinary trousers, but his legs were cased up to the knees in cheap canvas leggins. He carried a long breechloading shotgun in his hand, and his coat bore the imprint of a box of shells.

Dalrymple stared at the figure in the utmost amazement.

"Mr. Handback!" he ejaculated at length, "what in the world are you going to do?"

"What does it look like I'm going to do?" asked Handback.

"Why—why, it looks like you're goin' a-huntin'!"

"That's right, I am. I'm taking a day off"; and he laughed at the stupefaction written in his clerk's face.

From the other end of the store Lucius called:

"Dad, are you rigging up for a costume ball?"

"I'm going hunting," repeated the merchant; "I'm going rabbit-hunting."

"Well, I be danged!" cried Dalrymple in amazement. "Imagine, the boss going rabbit-hunting. . . . Look here, I believe I'll go with you!"

"Come on, if you've got any way to go."

"What way do I need?"

"You'll need a horse. I'm going to ride out in the country a piece. I wouldn't have gone if Lucius hadn't got turned down by his girl. He won't need the mare now, and I just thought I'd go."

"If I'd dreamed you'd gone hunting I wouldn't have written the note in the first place, Dad."

"Well, that's pretty nice of you, Lucius, you're a pretty nice sort of son, isn't he, Love?"

"M-huh," said Love, then added with a bit more heart, "Yes, there are lots worse fellows than Lucius."

"A whole lot worse," said the father.

The huntsman went back to the bookkeeper's enclosure and began fiddling with his books, putting things away in his safe. He called to Lucius:

"Tell your maw I won't be home to dinner."

"All right."

He continued with his papers for several minutes and presently called again:

"By the way, here are them deeds Bill Bradley ought to have. He swore up and down I never give 'em to him, and sure enough he was right. Now, don't forgit that, Lucius, you and Love."

"I won't," promised Love, and the papers passed out of his mind even as he promised to remember them.

The merchant squatted on his heels looking into his safe for a minute or two longer. Then he closed it and walked forward behind the dry-goods counter to his cash drawer and took out a little pocket change, Love thought. Then he went on to the door with his gun.

"Not going with me, Love?" he inquired.

"No, sir, I haven't got no horse."

"Well . . . Merry Christmas to both of you boys."

"Same to you, Mr. Handback."

"Merry Christmas to you, Dad."

CHAPTER FORTY-TWO

T HE Handback mare was hitched to a post in an alley by the side of the store. In the cold sunshine her hair looked a little unkempt. She shied around at the odd sight of her owner in hunting clothes, but presently stood and allowed the inexpert horseman to bestride her saddle.

J. Handback got himself set, feet in stirrups, gun balanced inside the pommel of his saddle, and moved his mount carefully into the street. He looked back, saw Love and his son standing in the door of the store laughing at him. He waved awkwardly and rode on.

J. Handback was in better spirits than he had been for many, many days. He was ruined. All that he owned he would be forced to sell in these depressed times, and still it would not pay what he owed. Now that he saw this and agreed with it; now that he had quit struggling mentally for some combination that would pull him through the crisis, he felt better. He had the limp, restful feeling of a man when a long and violent fever suddenly leaves him.

The motion of the mare beneath him was vaguely pleasant. He thought, if he saw a rabbit on his way to the place where he was going, he might find a kind of Christmas pleasure in killing it.

His thoughts hung around his catastrophe, no longer as frenzied rescuers working in a wreck, but as spectators viewing a ruin, reconstructing its fall, pondering what might have been done, but with no thought of doing anything.

That which had taken the last breath of hope from the merchant was a very odd thing which had no financial connection at all with his affairs.

Several days before Christmas he had attended a meeting

of the board of deacons of the Methodist church, of which he was a member. He had heard his minister, the Reverend B. Alvin Puckett, make the announcement that Colonel Miltiades Vaiden had contributed fifty dollars toward the lighting fund of their new church. The minister went on to say that he and all of his deacons hoped that this gift to the church betokened a man who was right with his Maker. Then the Reverend Puckett had placed all the contributions he had received on a table in the assembly room, and had lowered his head, and in a few well chosen words had asked God's blessing on the gifts and the givers.

When that happened Handback somehow became certain that he would never pull through his difficulties. He knew that Colonel Miltiades Vaiden was going up, and he had an irrational conviction that he was going down. He and the Colonel seemed to be counterpoises balanced fatally against each other.

But now, as the merchant rode along, a little coal of happiness kindled and burned in his heart amid the gray ash of his ruin. He was on the road to the home of his runaway mistress. When he had started from town he was not quite sure that he was going to Gracie, but as he rode forward in his hunting coat and leggins, his destination grew upon him. An increasing haste filled his mind. He visualized the different points on the road before he reached them. He could see BeShears' store, the Reserve road, the old Lacefield manor, long before he reached them, but he could not see Gracie. He peered about the old place for her in his thoughts; physically he was urging his mare to a faster gait.

In the course of time the merchant really came in sight of the weathered brick house with its peeling colonnade. Around its ancient observatory the wrought-iron grilles were twisted and broken away in places. It was like an advertisement of the indignities suffered by the ancient manor of the Lacefields.

There was no Gracie at the gate, and the merchant was

touched by a fear that she had gone away to some Christmas gathering. This did not seem probable, however, as Gracie seldom associated with negroes. The merchant was remembering this last fact hopefully when his attention was caught by a very small, queer structure in a field. It looked like a large child's playhouse with a tall thatched roof and a miniature chimney.

He wondered what the thing could be, then went on to the manor, stepping his horse over the scattered stone fence and riding around behind the old pile where the mare would be out of sight from the road. He lowered his gun, got down carefully, and looped his bridle over the end of a pole in the woodpile. As he turned toward the house he heard a gasp, and a woman's voice breathed:

"For God's sakes—Mr. Handback!"

Gracie stood, a picturesque figure, in the doorway of the kitchen. She had resurrected from somewhere a black lace dress and a red lace shawl, and there were brilliants in her hair. Her dramatic eyes stared at the man from a colorless face.

Handback was not quite sure whom he was seeing.

"That—that's you, isn't it, Gracie?"

"Y-yes, sir, Mr. Handback."

"Is there anybody in . . . are you expecting anybody, Gracie?" he asked, with disappointment and a twinge of jealousy in his voice.

"No, sir, Mr. Handback."

The merchant stood looking at her for a minute or two, and then with a kind of start picked up his catechism again.

"Then what are you so dressed up for?"

"It's . . . Christmas." Gracie glanced down at herself.

"I didn't know you had any such clothes as that," said the merchant a little curiously.

"Governor Beekman gave them to me a long time ago," said the quadroon.

"Oh . . . he did . . . well, Beekman was a Yankee thief during the war. He used to go around stealing spoons."

"Yes, sir," said Gracie in a far-away voice.

As the merchant continued staring at her, an odd, irrational gust of shivering invaded him. It was faintly annoying. His hand shook, a muscle in his cheek would jerk, his lips tremble. Then he became quiet again.

"Are you glad to see me?" he asked.

"Uh . . . ye-es. . . . You scared me at first, riding up with a gun."

"I did?"

"Yes, I thought . . ." She hesitated, with the beginning of a smile on her colorless face.

"What did you think?" he pressed curiously.

"Why-y, that you and ol' Pap had caught me and were going to take me back to the Big House."

"Oh . . . I see."

With her explanation a queer change came over Gracie for the merchant. It was the first time in all their relations that Gracie became not a negro but a woman. Somehow the imaginative quiver that had thrust her in her Christmas finery back for a moment into slavery, that had stung her nerves and flesh for a single moment with the horror of flight and armed capture; that instant, somehow, transformed Gracie from a quarter negress into a comely and sensitive woman whose whole life had been tragic and heartbreaking.

"Won't you come in?" said Gracie. "It's dinner time."

The two had drunk together in the cottage in East Florence and had eaten candy and fruit together. They had, of course, slept together any number of times, but they had never sat and eaten together at the same table.

Now this social distinction passed through Handback's mind as he followed his hostess through the great kitchen of the old manor into the vast dining room.

Under a tall window, some of whose panes were broken and mended with greased paper, stood a little table with a snowy cotton cover. On it were laid out a roasted chicken, hominy, beans, cranberries, stewed tomatoes: an excellent meal arranged for one.

"I wish I had known somebody was coming," regretted Gracie; "I could have had a lot more things."

"That looks fine." The white man hesitated on the edge of saying, "Get another plate for yourself, Gracie."

The Spanish costume with which the quadroon had adorned herself urged mutely that Gracie be treated with the courtesy due any woman. The white merchant drew a long breath; then sat down at the table alone.

"The old place is pretty badly gone," he said, looking about; "it really isn't worth much more than the nine thousand dollars."

Gracie glanced about the dining room.

"Wait a minute for your coffee."

The white man withheld the carving knife from the chicken. Gracie went into the kitchen and returned with the coffee. As she did this, the very femininity of her movements filled the merchant with a kind of sweetness and restfulness. It gave him a feeling as if he had been without food or water for a long time and now suddenly, at the mere sight of her coming toward him, he was replete. His fingers and palms had a tingling feeling of wanting to touch her hands and arms. He recalled to himself that she was really a negress. She was an illusion. Behind her creamy contours and the drama of her eyes stood a negress.

Gracie attended the merchant as he ate his Christmas dinner alone. The solitariness of it was the single flaw in his pleasure. It was a small flaw. Gracie always had been first his maid and then his mistress. He ate with his food sweetened by the pleasure of seeing her again. He had been away from her a long, long time. His ruin was now like a dark cloud rolled away to the horizon of his mind, and the sun was shining again.

"What is that funny little house yonder?" he asked, pointing through one of the glass panes.

"A schoolhouse," said the quadroon.

"For who?"

"Why . . . the children."

"Nigger children?"

"Yes, sir."

"Does Vaiden allow that?"

"Why-y, I . . . suppose so," said Gracie uncertainly.

"I'll bet he doesn't know it."

"I don't know whether he does or not."

Handback had a sharp thought that he ought to tell the Colonel about this. He ought not to let their trouble stand in the way of information like this.

"I'm against that. It'll make trouble finally," he said aloud.

Gracie looked through the window at the little schoolhouse.

"I hope not," she said.

The dinner was ending. The merchant had carefully left half of everything for Gracie. The thought came to him to ask her, after she had eaten her dinner, to give him her body.

He knew that she would give herself, but today, somehow, that knowledge carried with it not a prospective pleasure, but a penetrating pathos. He did not want Gracie's body given so. Indeed, he did not want the gift of her flesh at all. He was tired and ruined and beaten. He wanted the real Gracie; the gentleness of her sympathy; the kindness of her heart.

"Gracie," he said, out of these vague desires, "it seems a long time since I saw you last."

"Yes, it does, Mr. Handback," agreed the quadroon; "here on this old place every day is like a week."

Handback glanced around him at some of the old stucco ornaments still clinging to the ceiling.

"I imagine it would be like that. . . . How soon will anybody be coming back here, Gracie?"

"I don't know. I sort of expected Toussaint for dinner."

"Well . . ." He moved slightly in his chair, under compulsion to go. "At least, I'll take a smoke," he decided aloud.

He drew out a cigar, and Gracie held to him a lighted match. He mentally limited his visit to the length of his smoke. The fact that his cigar would, as far as he knew, finally conclude his relations with Gracie touched the merchant with melancholy.

He began talking half to Gracie and half to himself about the catastrophe that had befallen him.

He said that it was queer that it should have happened to him. He had always tried to do right and to treat everybody right, and then, just when the depression of the new Administration was coming on, to have all of his operating capital taken away at a stroke. . . . "But, then, I don't suppose the kind of life a man leads has anything to do with what happens to him," said the merchant in a monotone to his ex-mistress.

"I wouldn't say that, Mr. Handback," chided Gracie.

"Well, if there is a God, for Him to reward justice and right living and generosity . . ."

"The reward for those things comes after we are dead," said Gracie reverently.

"Yes, yes, that's true," agreed the deacon of the Methodist church.

For Gracie to repeat this ancient and accepted doctrine bestowed a new verity upon it. God comforted His dead. God made atonement for the wounds they had borne in life.

The quadroon's dark dress and red lace shawl and crimson brilliants in her polished hair bestowed an odd piquancy upon her simple and crystalline faith. It was as if the innocence of a child somehow had survived in Gracie. It would, the white man divined, live on and on. When the charms of her person were quite gone, the gentleness of the quadroon, the anodyne of her sympathy, would linger with her until she laid down her life in God.

No other person in the world had ever given the merchant this impression. Gracie never had before. While he had had money he could not see the woman with whom he had consorted for six years. In the midst of his bankruptcy he saw her at last.

With a tang of dismay Handback noticed that his cigar was almost gone. He pushed his chair a little way from the table and looked at the cream-colored woman with a questioning frown.

"You don't like it here?"

"Why-y . . . I don't know, Mr. Handback. It's lonesome . . . but I'd be lonesome anywhere."

"Would you go away if you could?"

"I can't."

"Would you go away with me somewhere?"

"With you!"

The man nodded, a brief quick nod, looking steadily into her eyes.

"Where?" breathed the woman.

"Well . . . I don't know . . . down toward Louisiana or Mexico . . . where French or Spanish women are common."

A kind of melting went through Gracie's bosom.

"To . . . for us . . . to live together?" she whispered.

It did not cross her mind to marry a Southern white man, but to live openly with a white man once more; to have him not hide her; not to slip to her house in the dark and let himself in with a secret key: that much honesty of existence pierced Gracie's heart.

"I can pull enough money out of my business tomorrow to get us away somewhere in the Southwest. . . . I always treated you good, Gracie."

"Oh, Mr. Handback, you've always been just as good to me . . ." Her eyes suddenly filled with tears.

"Then you can go?" he asked eagerly. "You can be my housekeeper. People live most anyway in New Orleans. Gracie . . . Gracie . . . say you'll do it. I'm sick of the way I'm living now."

The quadroon was trembling at the sudden and amazing prospect of a life openly lived with Handback. It was the most nearly honorable overture she had ever known. The thought of New Orleans went through her heart like a gay song. Her eyes, glancing through one of the unbroken panes, fell on the queer little house with its high thatched roof and miniature chimney. The flutter of her anticipation suddenly dropped. She stood looking at the queer little building.

"What's the matter?" asked the man at the change in her face.

"I . . . can't go."

Handback frowned, got up, took a step toward her, and caught her arm.

"Look here, why can't you go?" he demanded.

His ungentle touch hurt her arm with a kind of sweetness. She thought, "Why shouldn't I go?" Aloud she said unsteadily:

"On account of Toussaint."

"What! Toussaint!" cried the merchant. "Why, he's a grown man! Do you expect to keep him tied to your apron strings!" He gave her arm another shake.

"But, listen," begged Gracie, holding her mind by a great effort to her objection, "Toussaint is a-l-m-o-s-t white. If I go off and leave him he's sure to marry some dark girl. Then he'll be lost again. He'll be a nigger . . . his children'll be niggers. . . ."

"What do you expect his children to be?"

"Oh, I don't know . . . I don't want them to go through . . ."

"Gracie . . . who do you expect him to marry?"

The quadroon's face went as colorless as when Handback first had ridden up with a gun.

"I—I don't know," she breathed.

The man looked at her hard.

"You do know. You—you're planning for him to marry a——" He broke off with scorn in his eyes and on his lips.

"I—I never said anything at all," defended Gracie, trembling violently. "You—you just think bad things of me!"

The merchant stood filled with repulsion at the bare notion of a negro woman wanting her son to marry a white girl. The thought of a reversal of the usual sexual relation between the races horrified him. And Gracie, such a clean, such a nice negro woman . . . to plan it.

"Gracie, you . . . didn't really . . . mean that?" he asked with a sickened feeling.

"I meant . . . some—some girl as—as white as he is," stammered the quadroon.

"Oh, that!" agreed Handback. "Yes, that. . . ." A sudden notion struck him. "Why not take him to Louisiana? He might marry a French girl. They say such mix-ups don't amount to much down there."

At this sudden agreement to all of her plans Gracie caught her breath with a great dawning happiness. The whole of her uttermost dreams abruptly had come into sight.

"Could he go with us?"

"He could go with us," conceded the merchant, "but of course, after he got there . . . You must realize, Gracie, he's a man. He's old enough to look after himself."

"Yes, yes, that's true. . . ."

The woman stood in the old dining room thinking for several moments.

"Mr. Handback," she said, turning to him slowly, "you don't know why I left your house in Florence, do you?"

"Because you thought I needed the rent?"

"No—that wasn't it."

The merchant then recalled Gracie's note and the suspicions he had felt as he stood in her empty cottage.

"Well," he said, after a moment, "it doesn't make any difference why you left me, Gracie."

"Oh, yes, it does," persisted the cream-colored woman quickly. "I couldn't possibly go to New Orleans with you . . ."

"Then what?" asked the merchant reluctantly.

"Because . . . Colonel Miltiades Vaiden . . . is my half brother."

The man looked at her curiously.

"You were taking up the family quarrel?"

"Oh, no. . . . When—when you were hunting every-where for your—your money, Mr. Handback, I—" her voice sank to a bare whisper—"I had it. . . ."

"You . . . had it?"

"I was keeping it for him."

The merchant stared at her, at first, almost with simple astonishment, then his comprehension went dropping down through the gulfs of his business cataclysm, his agony and despair and final ruin. For Gracie to have helped her white half brother to steal him out!

The woman groped behind her for a chair and sat down, for the first time in the white man's presence.

Handback said:

"I——"

He stopped and started again with a dry mouth:

"Didn't I always——"

Gracie understood everything that he could not say. She nodded faintly and whispered from chalky lips:

"Yes . . . you always did. . . ."

Handback saw the carving knife on the table. Then he thought of his shotgun. He started into the kitchen to go out the back door. He turned once to ask a question. He could not frame it because he could imagine no answer at all. Why she should have betrayed him, why turn all he had over to her white half brother, who, he knew, had never been anything to her. Of the lingering dominance between ex-master and ex-slave he understood nothing . . . nor did Gracie. It was all as insane as the cursings of the mad.

The merchant walked through the kitchen into the back yard. His shotgun leaned against the woodpile. He knew if he went back and killed her nothing would be done to him. His trial would be postponed court after court and finally dropped. He picked up his gun with a shaking hand to go back and kill her. His very unsteadiness halted him for a moment. Suppose he shook so that he crippled her and would have to stand firing shot after shot into her breast. He could not mutilate the creamy, graceful thief.

He loosed his mare's rein and then held to the saddle as if he were about to fall. He led the animal to the doorstep and got shakily on her back. He drew up his gun, turned the mare through the weed-grown lawn, and went out into the public road again.

He rode at a walk for nearly a quarter of a mile.

A negro boy on a mule passed him at a long trot and called out hopefully:

"Chrismus' gif', Mistuh Han'back."

A little farther on at a gap in the fence the merchant rode into an old field. He got down and hitched his mare to the fence and cocked his gun. He looked about, then walked up the fence row for twenty or thirty yards. He laid the stock of the gun across the top rail with the muzzle toward him. He thought of some money which he had put in his cash drawer and which would have been enough to take him and Gracie to some other country . . . a little money which she had not got.

Around him stretched the plantations which once were his. He had done no wrong thing. He had given no cause of offense to any man. The work of his life had been taken away from him by a woman he had kept . . . more gently than his wife . . . for years.

Not once did it pass through Handback's mind that he loved Gracie Vaiden; not once, even up to the moment of his death, did he realize that he was doing this thing not for the loss of his wealth, but for the final loss of his love.

The negro boy on the mule trotted merrily on to the manor. He was the bearer of happy news. When he came in sight of the white-faced woman in the door he yodeled gleefully across the unkempt lawn:

"Toussaint sho' wucked a Chrismus' trick on evahbody today, Miss Gracie. Him an' Lucy Lacefiel' got married at Mount Olive chu'ch in Eas' Flaunts 'bout two houahs ago."

Nᴇᴡs of the nigger wedding already had circulated about Florence, to the amused interest of the white folks. The white folks, of course, approved of negroes marrying one another, but really, in their hearts, they did not see why the darkies took the trouble to do it. This particular nigger wedding had another fillip of interest besides the general unnecessariness of black folk bothering to get married anyway. Judge Ashton phrased it to his wife when he got home from issuing the marriage license:

"Susie, there's a nigger downtown, just as white as I am, marrying a brown girl."

"I don't see how he could do it!" ejaculated Susie.

"Well, I don't know . . . it may be a provision, Susie," speculated the Judge, who was of a religious turn of mind.

"How's that?" inquired Mrs. Susie automatically, without any intention of listening to a philosophical discourse from her husband.

"These white negroes, if they didn't instinctively mate with the darker members of their own race, they might keep getting lighter and lighter and finally threaten the integrity of our own people, Susie. I believe Providence regulates their selections."

"Oh, fiddle!" scoffed Mrs. Susie.

"Well, anyway, one menace has been removed," said the Judge comfortably. "I had thought about that boy. I was very glad to fill out his marriage license to a brown girl."

When the news came to Handback's store, Dalrymple Love then realized he had been trying to tear a prospective groom from a prospective bride to dispatch the two notes to the Crowninshield home, and it amused him very much.

It was the only jest the clerk had known during that long, lonely Christmas Day, and he thought about it now and then and laughed. Finally the clerk brought the day to a premature close by climbing to the second story and going to bed at seven o'clock. If he only had waited up half an hour longer he would have had excitement enough to fit out a week of Christmases . . . but such was the Dalrymplian luck.

Information of Toussaint's wedding was not so much brought as it was insinuated into the Crowninshield home by Jinny Lou.

Jinny Lou was a saddle-colored little girl with black glistening curls instead of the screwed-up pigtails of Pammy Lee. Owing to her general gracefulness, Jinny Lou stood in a fair way to be promoted in the culinary world of Florence, Alabama, much more promptly than had been her darker and less attractive sister, Pammy Lee. But of her superior fortune Jinny Lou at present knew nothing.

The leggy light-brown child came into the Crowninshield home giggling behind her hand. When Mrs. Drusilla, who was entertaining Colonel Vaiden, asked what was the matter, Jinny Lou whispered amid her embarrassed giggling that Miss Lucy Lacefield had got married to Mistuh Toussaint Vaiden . . . she had seen 'em.

There was something queer about weddings that Jinny Lou did not quite understand, something mysterious about them. She did not know why the bride and groom went off together to live instead of returning to their own homes, as would appear the rational thing to do.

Mrs. Drusilla Crowninshield did not touch this point of the child's quandary, but she set her right on another topic. She corrected the little girl very kindly for saying *Mister* Toussaint and *Miss* Lucy Vaiden, as those titles were reserved for the whites.

Since these instructions conflicted with those given her by her mother, Jinny Lou always fell into confusion and never ventured a remark above a whisper, in the hope of conveying her news but concealing her words.

"That white negro boy we used to see around here," ejaculated Sydna.

"Drusilla, do you remember that Yankee Beekman?" asked the Colonel in a tone that was meant to impart to the mother information not intended for the daughter.

"You mean Toussaint is General Beekman's child?" ejaculated Sydna, whose brain worked a bit more quickly than those of either of her elders.

"Why . . . yes . . . naturally," admitted the Colonel, a little embarrassed. "Toussaint's mother lived with Beekman while he was Governor of Alabama."

Sydna shook her head.

"I can't possibly understand the taste of Yankees."

"Why, darling, of course you can't," agreed Drusilla; "they're tradespeople."

"Mother . . . Colonel Milt runs a store!"

"My dear, Miltiades has to run a store to keep his business going. It's not because he wants to run a store. . . . By the way, have you ever been in his store, Sydna?"

"No, I haven't."

"Well, it's a sight, and I consider that a great honor to the keeper, because it shows that he doesn't care a thing in the world about the store as a store."

"I see that," nodded Sydna, acquiescing in the compliment.

"The thing that caught my attention about the wedding was *who* were marrying." Mrs. Drusilla stressed the "who" faintly, to carry concealed information to the Colonel.

"Oh, you mean a Lacefield and a Vaiden," observed Sydna.

"Well, yes," admitted the mother, "the two families have always been on such friendly footing, and yet somehow nothing ever did come of it; now these negroes of those names marrying . . . it seems odd."

"It seems odd because it seems natural," suggested Sydna.

"Well, honey, I don't see exactly how 'odd' and 'natural.' . . ."

"Well, Mother, that's about the only reason for it to

'seem' at all. You know Uncle A. Gray was really after Miss Marcia Vaiden all his life, and——"

"Listen, Sydna . . . be respectful."

"Why, I am respectful. I'm more than respectful. I think he's the finest man I ever heard of. I think he's the noblest, purest——"

"Darling, you aren't suppose to be so vehement in a person's presence."

"Well, all right. . . . I've wanted to tell him that all my life, and now I've done it." She drew a long breath and looked into the fire with a faint smile on her lips.

"Well, Miss Sydna," protested the Colonel, as if he had just wakened, "I can't possibly imagine you are talking about any person in this room. Such an opinion is so utterly beyond the deserts of any man I know."

"Listen, darling, we don't want all of us to get embarrassed on Christmas night. Suppose you play us a carol."

There was an old square piano in the corner of the living room. Sydna looked at it and said she didn't believe she knew anything to play.

Drusilla shook her head.

"I declare, such a change has come over girls. When I was young all girls knew enough music to play, but we couldn't teach. Nowadays all girls know enough music to teach, but none of them can play."

"Maybe music has become a silent miracle," suggested the Colonel, "that is passed from the initiated to the neophyte, like the apostolic blessing by the laying on of hands."

"The blessing is passed on at twenty-five cents a lesson," laughed Sydna; "that's why so many of us work at it."

It was all very light and Christmasy talk. Sydna's brief outbreak was the only expression of genuine feeling during the evening. The girl now sat entranced, listening to the Colonel. The voice she heard was the same voice that had promised her father on the battlefield to care for his baby daughter. And through all her twenty-two years the Colonel had been her silent, almost unseen protector. He had done that because he loved her mother. The Colonel's own marriage to Miss Ponny BeShears had been really a pitiful accident in the Colonel's unbroken fealty to her mother. Now it moved the very depths of Sydna's heart to think that after all that had happened, Colonel Vaiden and her mother might live their lives in happiness together.

A step on the piazza caused the whole party momentarily to become quiet. Sydna got up and looked through the window and then said in a flat tone:

"Oh, it's Jerry."

"Ask him to come in where his uncle Miltiades is," suggested Mrs. Drusilla.

Sydna stretched her hand toward the fire, then went through the hall onto the portico.

Young Jerry came up, looking at her with a rapt questioning expression.

"I ran over for a minute," he explained. "All my folks have gone to meeting."

"Won't you come in to the fire?" invited Sydna, loath to waste any time on the juvenilities of Jerry.

"I'm not cold," announced the youth triumphantly. "I've been up in my room for nearly two hours, and I'm not cold at all."

"Without any fire?"

"Not a coal," boasted the mystic.

The girl looked at him in reproof.

"What in the world do you act like that for? You look frozen. You'll give yourself pneumonia."

"No, I won't. I believe I've got myself so I don't feel either cold or heat. You know . . . just concentrate . . . draw your feelings away from your body like the fakirs do."

Jerry's vagaries suddenly bored Sydna. He was so harebrained.

"That's silly . . . freezing yourself, trying to . . . well, I don't know what you're trying to do. . . . Come on, let's go to the fire."

Jerry's Christmas ebullition vanished. He had dashed

over to tell Sydna of the successful combat of his soul against refrigeration.

An hour or two before, the youth had gone up into his room, and the fire was out in his little stove. And it just occurred to him that the adepts did not pamper themselves with heating apparatus. No, they concentrated and left their bodies like insensitive shards while their souls joined the harmonious brotherhood of other yogis in some mystical realm. Jerry had tried the experiment. He had taken off his coat, sat down on the bed, and withdrawn.

He had got cold, of course, but he succeeded in making his chill feel afar off. He had shivered violently, but the shivers too seemed remote. At last his fingers and toes ached so he had to give it up, but he considered his experiment, taken as a whole, a success. Then he had run over to Sydna as the solitary human being to whom he could mention such a thing. And now here she stood on the portico, calling him silly and foolish, talking exactly as his aunt Rose would have talked.

As Jerry stood there with his Christmas elation gone, it occurred to him that Sydna had found out what had happened between him and Pammy Lee. He was sure she knew, because she appeared disgusted with him.

"If you think I'm silly," he said, "then folks going to college are silly. They're trying to do things with their minds, and so am I."

"They're trying to do things that can be done."

"I just told you I came out all right."

"But they learn practical things at college—something that will be of some use to them afterwards."

"Why, they don't. Look at Sandusky. He quit because he said college was a waste of his time."

"Sitting in the cold isn't good for anything in the world."

"It's about like geometry. Geometry strengthens the reason, and cold strengthens the will."

"Well, please let's go inside to the fire. My will's strong enough."

"Who's in there?" asked Jerry, who had wanted to be alone with Sydna.

"Nobody but Mamma and your uncle Miltiades."

"My uncle . . . well, for goodness' sake! No, I'll run on back."

Sydna studied her caller for a moment.

"Look here . . . you don't hold anything against your uncle Miltiades, do you?"

"Me? Naw. I say if your soul is attached to another soul, and that other soul steals or murders or does something of the sort, then what he does can't make any difference to you at all, because the possibility of that sin was already in his soul when it attracted yours. So maybe that's why he attracted you. Or maybe there is something in you that corresponds to that, or maybe you are that same sort of person yourself but don't know it because you never had a chance to find out. At any rate, it shows you something about yourself and not about the man who did the act."

The first part of this rigmarole Sydna followed very well; the latter part escaped her but left her with a feeling that it was not very complimentary to somebody—possibly herself.

"Well," she said, "I know I'm not going to stand out on this portico and be called a thief and a murderer. If you won't come in, good-bye and a Merry Christmas."

Jerry was quite taken aback.

"Why, I didn't mean you. . . ."

But Sydna was already walking into the hall. She held the door open for him. After a moment she said, "Well, if you won't come in . . ."

Mrs. Drusilla's voice called from the living room.

"Come in and join us, Jerry. Your uncle Milt is in here."

"No, thanks, Miss Drusilla. I just ran over to say Merry Christmas and Happy New Year."

"Same to you, Jerry," called Mrs. Crowninshield, and she added in an ordinary tone to Miltiades:

"Jerry's a nice boy."

The nice boy moved down the box-lined walk pondering somberly the cause of the change that had come over Sydna. It must be, he supposed, Pammy Lee. Sydna had found it out and had withdrawn her friendship from him on account of his animalishness. He let himself out the gate and moved along with a feeling of argumentative shame. He had made a misstep, but he had renewed and redoubled his austerities. He would not allow a nigger girl to halt him on the road to perfection. Pammy Lee might be an accident, but she would never become a habit. His weakness with her had thrown him back physically and spiritually. The physical matter he had wasted on her might have been transformed into some worthy spiritual accomplishment.

His error in ever accepting Pammy Lee must be repaired. It had, he supposed, postponed his meeting with some spiritual instructor, some mystical member of the world brotherhood of adepts. He didn't blame them. No doubt they had to be very strict about entrusting the subtle powers of a mystic to a man who would debase his body with a little kinky-headed nigger.

But he would climb back up to where he had been, and he would work on further than that in saintliness.

And Sydna holding Pammy Lee against him. Well, she could if she wanted to. It made no difference to him. He had put all women whatsoever completely out of his mind.

CHAPTER FORTY-FOUR

WHEN Sydna Crowninshield returned to the living room, her mother arose and said she had to go to the kitchen and help Jinny Lou.

The daughter protested that she could help Jinny Lou, but Mrs. Drusilla said no, that Jinny Lou's helper had to have long experience in the handling of food and men, and that Sydna did not qualify for such a post.

The girl was really chagrined to see her mother go to the kitchen. She went to her mother's chair and sank into it. The seat and back were still gently warm from Drusilla's occupancy, and this warmth was like a caress after her chill five minutes on the piazza. The hickory logs in the fireplace were an emblazoned mass with little purplish and bluish flames flickering here and there. She kept glancing at the Colonel across the hearth, sometimes with direct scrutiny, sometimes out of the corners of her eyes. . . . He was a powerfully built man, with his shoulders heavier than his girth, even in the middle of middle age. Sydna thought he looked like a general. It was comfortable to sit in the room with Colonel Vaiden after listening to the moonstruck vagaries of Jerry.

"What were you and Mother talking about?" she asked, smiling faintly at him.

"Of your grandfather's place. It's melancholy to see it now. 'The harp that once through Tara's halls, the soul of music shed' . . . You know the poem."

"I've read it, but I don't know how it goes."

"Drusilla used to say it to me sometimes when we lived there. Neither of us dreamed then that the very house we were living in might very well be the original of the poem."

383

"All of it is like a story or a poem to me," said Sydna.

"Do you remember living in any of those times?"

"Well . . . I know I have . . . Mother has told me. . . ."

"Do you remember sitting on my knee once, up in your mother's room?"

"Was that you?" asked Sydna, looking curiously at him.

"I hope you are remembering me," said Miltiades, smiling a little.

The thought came to the Colonel, if he married Drusilla now, Sydna would be his daughter. She would come and go under his eyes. She had the sweetest smile he had ever seen except that of Marcia, when Marcia was Sydna's age.

And then, comparing Marcia and Sydna, the Colonel thought what a strange thing was Time, creating beauty and love and passion to exist a moment in its curling wave before it broke upon the lifeless strand of eternity. He had seen Marcia at Ponny's funeral: his sister's girlhood grace was quite gone. And even Drusilla was sedate and wise. She looked upon life with the epicene eyes of a woman past forty.

"I told you the other night," reminded Sydna, "if we ever had a chance, I wanted you to tell me about my father."

The Colonel translated himself to the past.

"Well, your father had reddish hair, Sydna."

"Yes, Mother has a lock of his hair."

"Oh . . . has she?"

"Well . . . yes, she has," hesitated Sydna, instantly sorry she had mentioned this.

"I was sitting here wondering," said the Colonel, "with your father's hair as dark as it was, how yours is so fair. From here your hair looks like pale silk with gossamers of flame sliding through it as the logs blaze up. It turns your eyes into dark mysteries."

"I never thought you were so imaginative," said the girl.

"I am not required to imagine anything when I look at you, Sydna."

The girl drew in a caressing breath and thought how sweet it would be to have Colonel Vaiden for her stepfather.

"Go on," she said, "tell me more about my father."

"To tell you of him, Sydna, would be to sum up the whole tragedy and romance of the South. But when I look at you like this I am convinced that you feel far more of that tragedy and romance than any of us oldsters can ever know or tell."

"Why do you feel like that?" asked Sydna, gazing at him pensively.

"Probably because only children conceived and reared in the midst of a great social upheaval ever truly record it. I was twenty-eight when the war came up. It could do nothing to me except kill me, but you were dreaming under your mother's heart when Yankee troops ransacked your grandfather's home. . . ."

"I couldn't remember that," said Sydna in a low tone.

"No, but you are made up of that romance and tragedy. Its shocks and emotions are yours. I have thought that every era of history is written not on books by withered scribes but upon the hearts and souls of the children of that generation. All historians can do is to make a few passing footnotes to explain why your eyes are pensive and your lips wistful."

Sydna thought how beautifully the Colonel talked of her father. It seemed impossible to her that all of Florence could think so illy of him.

She wondered if the Colonel were sensitive about being misunderstood. Of course he was sensitive. A man who could feel so keenly the poetry and beauty of life and who remained faithful to his love for her mother, could not help being affected by the harsh and mistaken judgment of the public.

A desire to comfort the Colonel, to assure him that she was his faithful friend and believer, filled the girl's heart. At the same time young Jerry passed across Sydna's mind with a mental tag of how callow and silly he was.

"You must have been surprised," the Colonel was saying, "to see us standing there in your yard?"

"I'm never surprised at Mr. Bradley," replied the girl, carrying on the conversation mechanically while she sat thinking about the Colonel in an entirely different vein. "I wouldn't be surprised to find Mr. Bradley anywhere, pricing anything to anybody."

Miltiades was amused at these universal inclusions.

"He's a salesman. I was trying to tell him the sort of house I wanted, and he brought me in here and showed me yours."

"Was it like it?" inquired Sydna with more interest.

"Not exactly. . . . I want the sort of house that you are a girl, Sydna, if you understand what I mean."

"Why, Colonel!" ejaculated the daughter with a return of her sweet feeling, "what a lovely thing to say!"

"Oh, no, it's just an easy way of saying what I mean."

"Well, I still think it's awfully nice. . . ." Sydna hesitated and then asked in a different tone, "Have you mentioned your home to Mother, Colonel Milt?"

"No-o . . ." dragged out Miltiades, understanding what the girl meant.

Sydna was faintly embarrassed at the intimacy of her own question. She said half apologetically:

"I feel like we've been friends, Colonel Milt . . . always. I really do remember seeing you on the plantation. You and Mother were sitting on a settee. Mother called me to you. You took me up on your knee and kissed me."

The Colonel sat for several moments in silence. Preceding that scene with the child he recalled Drusilla's sudden and amazing bestowal of herself upon him, and after their gust, little Sydna had come in, and he had kissed her.

And now here sat he and Sydna before this Christmas fire. His gustiness for Drusilla was quite gone. Indeed, his gustiness for all women had changed into a kind of poetry. They could be exquisitely sweet and comforting to him across the expanse of a whole hearth, as was Sydna.

The Colonel's thoughts wandered on and on and presently came out an odd door.

"I imagine," he said, "the first man who ever built a church completely bewildered all the women of his tribe."

"Why so?" inquired the girl curiously.

"Because it was the first house ever built not to be used as a home. The women must have been astonished and antagonized."

The girl studied the Colonel intently for several moments.

"How came you to say that?"

The Colonel tried to think his thoughts backwards but could not.

"I haven't the slightest idea."

"I believe you were thinking about that house you want to build. You don't want it to be just a home—you want it to be something more than that."

"Well, that's true, but I couldn't have been thinking about that just then."

"That's all right. . . . Tell me, why do you want more than a home?"

The Colonel sat some moments looking into the coals.

"I want a justification."

"A what?"

"If I have money I think I ought to do some beautiful thing with it. It's a kind of obligation to live a fine life, Sydna. The old South before the war realized this. They tried to create around them a magnificence that had nothing to do with making more money. That's why Handback always gave me a sort of repulsion. Besides starting out with my money, he did nothing beyond make more money. He was like an unfriendly boy in a ball game who grabs the ball and then refuses to play but just sits and holds it. . . ."

In the midst of this illustration came the sharp clacking of a woman's heels on the piazza. The hall door was flung open. The steps hurried to the sitting room. A hurried tap, and the door opened while Sydna called, "Come in."

Mrs. Ashton thrust in her head.

"Sydna, where's your mother?"

"In the kitchen. . . . Why . . . what's happened?"

"Mr. Handback's killed himself! He went down to your mother's old home place and blew his head off with a shotgun. I hope Miltiades Vaiden is satisfied now!"

And Mrs. Ashton clicked hurriedly down the hall toward the kitchen.

CHAPTER FORTY-FIVE

Aʟᴛʜᴏᴜɢʜ Mrs. Susie Ashton, and indeed all Florence, believed that J. Handback had committed suicide on account of business reverses, the *Florence Index* took a more charitable view of his death. The paper attributed it to the fact that he carried a new style hammerless shotgun which would fire prematurely upon a mere jar, and the merchant had jarred his gun as he climbed the fence into the field.

The article went on to relate how Handback's last act had been to arrange some deeds relating to the old Lacefield place ready for delivery to its present owner, Colonel Miltiades Vaiden, but since his death, the son of the deceased, Mr. Lucius Handback, had been unable to locate the papers.

The article concluded with praise of the dead man as a tender father, a kind and loving husband, and a consistent member of the First Methodist Church in Florence for a period of more than twenty years. The *Index* extended its profoundest sympathy to the bereaved family and bade them remember that their loss was heaven's gain, and that while their loved one's death had brought them heartaches and tears, it had brought to those relatives and friends who had preceded J. Handback to the abode of the blessed a joyful reunion that would never end.

This appraisal of J. Handback's character, everyone, under the shock of his death, felt should have been true, even if it were not; and the announcement of his arrival in heaven everyone felt, in God's mercy, was true, even if, in strict justice, it should not have been.

In the upper story of Mrs. Rose Vaiden's boarding house this article started what promised to be a sharp theological debate on the pardoning power of God, but Mr. Sandusky, who was one of the principals in the argument, suddenly abandoned his wrangling, got his coat and hat, and said he was going out.

Young Jerry Catlin felt the natural annoyance of any disputant whose opponent suddenly vanishes and leaves him charging the air. He watched Sandusky go out the gate from their upper window and wondered what he had in his head: nothing good, he ventured.

Jerry's argument had been that God could not pardon J. Handback and accept him in heaven, because only the righteous could enter the abode of the blessed. So in the pardoning God would have to change J. Handback into one of the righteous. But such an arbitrary change would be the equivalent of annihilating the original Handback and creating another soul, *de novo*, in his stead. But God could not do this because a soul was immortal. Therefore Jerry thought J. Handback would have to sweat it out the best he could. At this point Sandusky had walked off, leaving these arguments unanswered.

But Mrs. Rose's boarder was not flying from a beaten field, as most certainly seemed. He walked briskly and purposefully to town, with his long greenish great-coat flapping in the air, and he carried the newspaper in his hand. When he reached the business section, he turned off Market Street toward the Handback store. When he came in sight of the place he saw a group of negroes standing desolately about the entrance. The law student walked in among them and, seeing their dejection, asked what was wrong.

"Do's locked," answered one of the blacks; "we kain't git in to buy nothin'."

"What's wrong with the store?" inquired Sandusky, looking at the closed door.

"Man inside say de sto's made a designment an' ain't gwi' open up no mo'."

"Why don't you go somewhere else and trade?"

"Cause Mistuh Han'back's runnin' us. Ain't nobody else

gwi' sta't runnin' us wid Mistah Han'back's fingah already on ouah crops."

"Look here," said Sandusky, "I'm a lawyer. You niggers have a claim for support against this stock of goods. Why not put it in my hands and let me see if I can get something out of it for you?"

The black men began mumbling either acquiescence or refusal at this, and moved away from the law student, rolling their eyes at this new trap that was spread before them.

Sandusky let the negroes go and turned to the closed shutters of the store. A knot of black crêpe around the knob published the death of the owner. The law student peered through the keyhole and saw Lucius Handback, Stebbins, and Sheriff Mayhew working on the inside. He rapped on the shutter and peered again.

"Hey, Stebbins," he called through the shutter, "this is Sandusky. Come let me in."

The clerk came to the door, opened it, and looked questioningly at Sandusky.

"We can't sell anything," he said. "The Sheriff shut us up."

"I wanted to see Mr. Handback a moment," said Sandusky.

"Why . . . he's dead!" ejaculated Stebbins in a low tone.

"I mean Mr. Lucius Handback."

"Oh, well . . . there he is." Stebbins nodded at his employer.

The three men were invoicing the stock preparatory to delivering it over to the creditors. There was no fire in the stove, and it was very cold. Sandusky went back to where Lucius Handback was at work counting the bolts in a revolving bolt case. The young man paused in his work as Sandusky stopped near him.

"Want to see me?" he inquired in a lowered voice.

"I wanted to express my sympathy for your family," said Sandusky in the same tone.

"I thank you," said Lucius, not recognizing his caller.

Sandusky moved his paper.

"I—I notice in the *Index*," he began carefully, "your father—er—misplaced some papers in regard to the Lace-field plantation."

Lucius nodded slightly, looking closely at the oldish youth to see how that concerned him.

"I'm a lawyer—er—a student of law," explained the hill youth at once. "I read law in Governor O'Shawn's office. The Governor requires me to look up all the legal points that come out in the newspaper . . . for practice, you know. The Governor criticizes my reports."

This rôle of a student asking for simple aid in understanding the law was entirely unobjectionable.

"Is there a legal point about the papers that went with the Lacefield place?" asked Lucius.

"I don't know. I read the notice in the paper and thought I would come around and see. What were the circumstances, if you don't mind telling me?"

"Why, no, not at all. They were some old deeds that had passed the property along from one hand to another."

"M-m . . . I see," nodded Sandusky.

"And that's all there is to it."

The law student stood thinking over this situation.

"Well, I thank you, Mr. Handback. . . ." He seemed about to go, then turned for a last question. "They are all recorded at the courthouse, of course?"

"I suppose so," said Lucius with the lack of interest a man usually feels in academic questions.

"They may not be all recorded," observed Sandusky after another pause. "When the Yankees were running things right after the war a lot of the Southern people refused to record their transfers in the county courthouse with a Yankee register."

"Oh, they did!" ejaculated Lucius. "I didn't know that."

"Yes, they were mad at the Yankees . . . wouldn't have

anything to do with 'em," explained Sandusky, purely historically.

"Well . . . what effect does it have if a deed is lost and not recorded?" inquired Lucius curiously.

"The title would probably lie in the last owner of record," said Sandusky.

"And that would cut out everybody whose deeds were lost and not recorded?"

"It would cut out everybody from the time the first unrecorded deed was lost. You see the title passes through every deed in the whole string, and from the point where any one of them is lost and has not been recorded, then all the rest are no good."

"Oh, yes . . . I see," nodded Handback, enlightened. "That doesn't seem right, does it?"

"Nothing seems right in law. You have to get used to it."

"I suppose that's so," agreed the son of the store.

"I was especially interested in this, because I did a little business with your father before he died. I—I arranged the settlement between him and Colonel Vaiden, if you remember."

"Oh, you are Mr. Sandusky," ejaculated Lucius.

Mrs. Rose's boarder nodded, quite pleased at being remembered.

"I recognize you now. You did save my father ten thousand dollars out of . . . very unfavorable circumstances."

"And do you know what I got for it?" smiled Sandusky bitterly. "I went to Colonel Vaiden and told him I was not a licensed lawyer, that I was just a student, but that I had done exactly the sort of work any lawyer would have done, and I would appreciate whatever he thought my services was worth, and do you know what he gave me?"

"No," said Lucius, "I have no idyah."

"Two dollars and a half," said Sandusky.

Lucius dropped his hands from the bolt case.

"You don't mean he gave you two dollars and a . . ."

Sandusky nodded again and smiled.

"That was another reason why I was interested to see just what deeds were lost. If there's a link out in the recorder's office, it wouldn't make me feel so very bad to point out to Colonel Vaiden that the deed he's holding to the property isn't worth the paper it's written on."

Lucius gave the slight smile which a man in grief gives to a pleasing idea.

"I don't see how that would benefit us much, Mr. Sandusky," observed the merchant's son. "The deed Father had wouldn't be any good either."

"Well, at least there would be no harm done if I ran over to the courthouse and see if there is a skip, and if there is, find out just who filed the last deed of record and in whose hands the title lies."

"All right," said Lucius; "when you find out I'd like to know."

Sandusky buttoned another hole in his shabby great-coat and walked out among the negroes, who still stood planless before the closed doors of the store that once had supported them.

CHAPTER FORTY-SIX

His clerk, Dalrymple Love, first broke the rumor to Colonel Miltiades Vaiden that Lucius Handback and Sandusky proposed to bring an action in chancery against the Colonel's title to the old Lacefield place.

Miltiades was surprised and amused.

"How did you get such an absurd story?" he questioned.

"Stebbins told me about it. He heard Lucius and Sandusky talking about it in the store."

"Well, that's perfectly impossible," assured the Colonel. "You see, I hold my deed from the Handback estate. It's a regular guaranty deed and binds their heirs and assigns forever. All right, if Lucius breaks down my title in chancery, he would have to make it good himself, because he is Handback's heir."

Love opened his eyes and began to smile.

"Then you can't lose!"

"If I lose, I win; if Lucius Handback wins, he loses." Miltiades laughed.

The clerk was sweeping out the store. He had a large mass of oily dirt and refuse rolling before his broom, leaving behind it a kind of eggshell finish of fine dust particles which the broom would not pick up from the oiled boards. That eggshell finish was considered clean, and to this state Dalrymple meant to bring the whole store.

The Colonel walked to the door and looked out. There was no trade. The winter was getting well on into spring, but instead of a prosperous jam of wagons and buggies in the streets there was only a scattering of pedestrians; townsfolk without conveyances. And these urbanites bought nothing beyond the clothes they wore and the food they ate.

As the Colonel looked out on this signal of hard times he thought of J. Handback's suicide. It had caused his own life in Florence to become a little more isolated than it had been formerly. In the irrational way such things work, public opinion had balanced the merchant's suicide against Ponny's death, and this left Miltiades with the theft of the Handback cotton unatoned for. It would be held against him with renewed bitterness until Handback's tragedy also drifted out of the common mind.

But although the suicide worked against the Colonel socially, it looked as if it might aid him financially. All the Handback plantations were put up for sale, and Miltiades had bargained for three more with long extensions of credit. It was the Colonel's idea to buy. He wanted to buy to the limit of his cash and credit during the present depression and enjoy the benefits of recovering prices within the next few years. While he executed this financial maneuver he damned Wall Street and the Yankee nation for their plot in creating a panic just to discredit the Democratic Administration.

In the middle of these thoughts, the Colonel glanced into his store and called out:

"Love, I'm off a few minutes; if any of my niggers come in and try to run up a great big bill, hold 'em down to what they have to have."

"All right, Colonel."

"If that nigger Toussaint comes after his fertilizer, give him all he can haul off . . . it's all his."

"All right, Colonel."

"If . . ." Miltiades tried to think of something else for Love to attend to, but was unable to do so. He left his "if" hanging in the air and started out across Courthouse Square toward Pine Street.

As the Colonel moved along, other questions began to disturb him. He wondered if it would be a proper act for him to visit the Crowninshield home under the renewed opprobrium of J. Handback's death. He would not want to bring

Sydna's and Drusilla's name under the shadow of that tragedy.

He recalled how Mrs. Susie Ashton had shouted into the Crowninshield living room the news that J. Handback had shot himself. Sydna had leaped up, run across the room to him, put her arms about his neck, and gasped out:

"Oh, Colonel Milt! Don't mind her! Susie Ashton's a gossip! She's a mean woman! Oh, what makes people treat you so awful!" and she began weeping over him, holding his arm and shoulder to her breast.

Of course such a demonstration of partisanship made the Colonel all the more careful not to compromise the girl in public estimation. She was too loyal, too generous, too exquisite a creature for him to dream of bringing a whisper against her, "And of course," added Miltiades at the end of his soliloquy, "the same is true of Drusilla, also."

Under these circumstances, therefore, Miltiades did not feel that it would be prudent for him to call at the Pine Street residence. He would write a note to that effect. He and Drusilla were intimate enough now for him to be perfectly frank with her. He would explain in a note why he felt it best to discontinue his calls, at least for a period. If she disagreed with him, she could say so. In fact, he rather hoped she would disagree with him. If she did, he meant to ask her to marry him.

A kind of faint questioning tremor went through the Colonel at this belated and imaginary satisfaction of his life-long romance. If she wrote him a note asking him to come and visit her anyway, then at last he would marry Drusilla.

Colonel Vaiden continued up Pine Street, thinking of the Crowninshields, but turned into Bill Bradley's house two lawns below it.

Mrs. Lily appeared at the door and told him that Bill was asleep.

"Why don't you wake him up and put him to work?" inquired the Colonel.

"Really Bill stays abed because he is so industrious and

energetic," explained Mrs. Bradley seriously, then she went
on to say if Bill woke up and had no prospects to sell he
had gemeeny fits all day, so he stayed in bed and slept all he
could so as not to wear himself out.

"Is he going to hibernate all through the Democratic
Administration?" inquired Miltiades.

For some reason this question reminded Mrs. Lily of some
plans and estimates Bill had drawn up for Miltiades and she
hurried inside the house to get them. Presently she returned
with a large envelope.

"This gives you down payments and deferred payments
and everything," she explained.

"No, I don't want it," said Miltiades. "I just came by to
tell your husband I am not going to build, after all."

"Oh, so you won't build," repeated Mrs. Lily in the casual
tones of a wife to whom her husband's business is something
remote and of slight personal consequence.

"Yes, I've decided not to."

"Well, all right. . . ." Mrs. Lily held the envelope for a
·moment and then said, "I suppose I might as well burn this
and get it out of the way. If I don't burn 'em when I get the
chance, Bill will get our whole house stacked full of plans."

The idea shocked Miltiades.

"No, no, don't do that. After all, I might as well take 'em,
they were meant for me."

The Colonel had a notion of rescuing the plans and later
returning them to Bill.

The housewife handed over the bundle, and Miltiades
moved back toward the gate, opening the envelope just to
see what terms he could have had. It was a linen envelope,
and Miltiades was shocked again to think that Mrs. Lily
would have burned it.

The paper told him he could get his house for a down payment of seven thousand dollars and an annual payment of
three thousand, five hundred and sixty-one dollars for a
term of sixteen years. A letter accompanying the plans explained that these terms were offered on account of the sharp

decline in the building trade, and that such long-term payments would not be extended again.

Both letter and terms impressed Miltiades sharply. If he were going to build a home, certainly now was the time to do it.

The notion came to the Colonel that before declining such an offer he ought at least to consult with parties who were likely to be interested. As this mission seemed outside the boundary of purely social calls, but lay more in the sphere of business which would not brook delay, the Colonel, after some further dialectic, went up to the Crowninshield door and rattled the disabled bell.

Sydna was in the living room, reading. Drusilla was in the kitchen, going into the higher mysteries of corn lightbread with Jinny Lou. The little negro girl eventually noticed the scratching of the doorbell and came out and showed the Colonel into the sitting room.

Sydna arose quickly and gave both her hands to the caller.

"You've been away a long time, Colonel Milt," she said reproachfully.

The Colonel immediately became concerned,

"Well . . . considering everything, Sydna, I thought that was the best thing to do."

"I think the best thing to do is to follow your heart, Colonel Milt."

"A person's heart, unfortunately, says different things. It says hurry to your friends; it says stay away from them for their sakes; it says guard your friends' reputation even if you lose your own."

Sydna looked pale and tired. She gave the caller a faint smile and led him to a chair.

"When it said, 'Hurry to your friends,' that was your heart; the rest of it was your reason, and you shouldn't have paid a bit of attention. . . . What have you got in your hands?"

"You mean besides these two lilies of the valley?"

Sydna withdrew her own hands with a touch of color in her face.

"Now, what is it?"

"It's the plans and prices of that house we've all been talking about."

"Oh, you want to show them to Mother!" exclaimed the girl.

"Well, I thought I would, if she had time."

"She'll take time. I'll do whatever she's doing in the kitchen and send her in."

"If you will, Sydna," agreed the Colonel, watching her.

"And—and, Colonel—I do hope she . . . likes everything."

The Colonel looked at the daughter.

"I hardly know what I'll do, Sydna, if she doesn't."

The daughter was moved. She came forward and squeezed the Colonel's hands.

"And listen . . . please . . . may I come back afterwards . . . and see if she did?"

"Yes, Sydna, I wish you would."

The girl, still pressing his fingers, leaned forward and kissed him.

"That's for luck," she said.

As she disappeared through the doorway Miltiades had a queer impression that the Drusilla whom he had known on the plantation in the Reserve was tripping away from him once more.

Sydna really was not at all like Drusilla. She was taller, slenderer, with blonde hair and more melting brown eyes. In temperament she was quite different from her mother, yet to Miltiades, some transposition of personality seemed to have taken place, and in Sydna, during little glimpses like these, the real Drusilla laughed and moved and breathed again.

This odd impression, which lingered for perhaps half a minute after Sydna had gone, was presently dissipated by Drusilla entering the door.

The Colonel's enthusiasm for his manor mounted again as he took his hostess's fingers.

"I've just got the figures on that house, Drusilla." He opened his linen envelope again. "I can get it built on payments of three thousand a year. It's on account of bad times. The contractor says I'll never get such an offer again."

"Well," said Drusilla, smiling, "I never had an offer yet but what it was the only one like it, and if I didn't accept it instantly I would never get it again."

"You sound as if you had been in the market."

"I've had to sell some things . . . and buy some things."

"It's a shame for a woman to have to be subjected to commercial life," said the Colonel.

"What have you decided about the plans? Are you going to accept them?" inquired the woman pleasantly.

"I thought I would consult with you before I decided on anything."

"That's very nice." She regarded him a moment. "I have wondered why you want to build a house at all, Milt."

The Colonel drew a long breath. "Well, Sydna . . . I mean Drusilla . . . I've always wanted a home like your father's old place, ever since . . . well, ever since I was big enough to want anything at all."

Drusilla drew her brows down in a surprised, tender expression.

"You mean . . . since you were a child?"

"From the time my father let me ride behind him on Old Joe down into the Reserve. We were going to a speaking . . . to hear Yancey. He made a speech from your father's piazza. Of course he was eloquent and poetic and passionate, but it seemed to me that the old manor was a sort of . . . well, I can hardly explain it . . . a sort of embodiment of his oration. The manor was his eloquence and dignity in brick and stone. I never wanted anything so much as to live in a manor like that, to live a life that was high and noble and passionate, like the speech . . . and like the manor."

Drusilla looked at her old lover with a film of tenderness in her eyes.

"I declare," she said softly, "how you Vaidens hang onto everything. You never quit. Miss Cassandra read books and taught negroes. Marcia daydreamed. Augustus avoided doing anything at all. . . . Every one of you is still going right on without a pause or a change of pace. I have never known anything but death to stop any of you . . . if death does stop you?"

The Colonel gave his companion a curious look.

"Do you mean that for a compliment, Drusilla?"

"Not especially. Your family trait makes you all seem very stupid at times. You go butting your heads against stone walls. The Vaiden motto seems to be *'Caveat muros.'* "

Drusilla began laughing as she appraised this particular example of Vaiden obstinacy before her.

"No," said Miltiades, laughing with her, "that isn't a compliment."

"The whole truth seldom is," said Drusilla; "a compliment, if it is really meant, is nothing more than the bright side of a dark truth."

"You make my family out very silly."

"You really aren't that. Your family follows some interior purpose. My family lived their lives with an eye out to make the best of things as they were. I suppose that is why all of us Lacefields had a tendency to lean on you Vaidens. We felt in you a kind of interior solidity. And the Lacefield tendency to gather in whatever blessings there were made us want to collect Vaidens along with the rest."

"Well, Drusilla," said the Colonel, in a monotone, "you could have had this Vaiden years and years and years ago, if you would have taken him."

"Of course, I knew that, Milt, but I was always something of an opportunist, even when I was young. I always thought, 'Well, I believe I'll wait a little while longer . . . and see what happens. Maybe something better will come along.' "

"And did," interpolated the Colonel with a wry smile.

"I don't think so now," said the woman.

"Why, Drusilla," ejaculated the man, surprised into frankness, "you know Emory Crowninshield wouldn't have done what I did!"

"No, he wouldn't," agreed the woman at once; "he wouldn't have set aside public opinion like that, because he was a politician. And he wouldn't have set aside his conscience like that, which is the other side of public opinion. In other words, he couldn't have wanted anything badly enough and persistently enough to go through what you've gone through to get it."

Miltiades sat for several moments in a judicial silence.

"That's bad," he finally said at length; "if I'm that sort of man, I'm bad."

"If that's bad," declared the woman, "then the spirit back of every great fortune, every great invention, every great religion is bad. Jesus Christ himself was ruthless moving toward His own goals."

The Colonel sat pondering this violent partisanship. Finally he said:

"I am going to start building that house, Drusilla. I want to see what you think of it"; and he unfolded his envelope.

He spread his blueprints and estimates out on a table, and the two looked at them together.

"The real house," suggested Drusilla, "when it's up, and a lawn and trees around it, will look much softer and more livable than this."

"Yes, of course, an architect's drawing always looks hard." He paused a moment, and then saw an opening toward his original point: "What a home finally looks like will depend a good deal on who lives in it, Drusilla."

"Yes, of course, that's true."

"If it's a manor at all, it will have to have a woman in it."

Drusilla looked at him thoughtfully.

"And you are going to ask me to be the woman?" she suggested slowly.

The Colonel was not expecting such a remark, but he said simply:

"I have wanted you for a long, long time, Drusilla. When I ask you to be the mistress of my home I must tell you I have done many things I could wish I had never done. If you are willing to take the sort of man I am, Drusilla, it would be far beyond my deserts if you would marry me."

The only sign Mrs. Crowninshield gave of any feeling was a little lift of her dark blouse. She leaned across and touched the blueprints on the table.

"How many rooms will you have in your home, Miltiades?" she asked gently.

"Fourteen, I think, Drusilla. . . . Why?"

"What do you want with a woman of my age in a house of fourteen rooms, Miltiades?" she asked with a faint propitiatory smile.

"Why, Drusilla, because I love you," exclaimed the Colonel, quite taken aback; "because I have loved you ever since—ever since your father gave me my first job as a man. Now, look here," he pleaded in a lighter tone, "you might as well marry me. You said yourself we Vaidens kept after what we wanted till we got it."

"Well, you are going to get it, Milt," ejaculated Drusilla.

"Do you mean you are going to marry me?"

"No."

"Then I'm getting what?"

"Why, the manor. You're going to build a finer one than Father ever possessed."

"But I want you!" cried the Colonel. "I've thought of you every day through all these years. I have walked past your home here at night, and stopped and thought of you being just across here behind these brick walls, until I was ashamed of myself for thinking such thoughts when I was married to Ponny."

"I know all that, Milt," said the woman softly; "in fact, I've seen you once or twice. I have always been a kind of symbol to you of the manor and the station you wanted. Once you thought you saw a way to get it through Ponny. Your marriage to Ponny taught me a great deal, Milt. Up to that time I thought you wanted me because I was I. . . . People said you married Ponny because I had jilted you. But I knew better. I saw that you never had wanted me, you had always wanted the manor."

She sat looking at him without reproach or resentment, simply telling at last what the years had taught her.

Miltiades had never dreamed of such a view of himself and his life. He knew he had married Ponny for the money her father was reputed to possess. But always he had supposed his passion for Drusilla sprang out of the charms of the woman herself.

"Why do I want you now?" he asked at last. "I can get the manor without you."

"Why, you think probably that I am part of the interior decoration of a manor. . . . You've seen me in one."

"But, listen, Drusilla," begged Miltiades, getting up and going toward her: "Be the interior decoration of one!"

"No."

He stopped, looking at her intently.

"It really isn't . . . Handback, is it?"

"Miltiades!" She arose with a little stamp of her foot. "Of course it isn't Handback! Didn't my father build that first manor . . . out of slaves?"

And she turned and walked out of the room.

CHAPTER FORTY-SEVEN

COLONEL MILTIADES VAIDEN sat for some time in the living room of the woman whom he supposed he had loved all his life long, but whom, according to her analysis, he had never loved at all.

He could not believe it. As he lingered before going away finally from the house he tried to remember just how he had felt toward Drusilla in the days of her flowering. He recalled only a pervasive unrest, pricked with lovers' quarrels and the one moment of their lives which men call love but to which women deny the name.

The Colonel folded his plans and returned them to the linen envelope. He would not now build the manor. This whole desire had centered upon his marriage with Drusilla. Before her refusal of him he had not known this. Then he began reasoning if this were true he really must love her and that she was wrong in her charge against him.

A faint noise caused the merchant to glance up. In the doorway stood Sydna, looking at him with the intentness of one who divines bad news.

"Colonel Milt," she whispered in a shocked undertone, ". . . wouldn't she?"

Not until he heard the tragedy in Sydna's voice did Miltiades perceive the full measure of his loss.

He shook his head slowly.

"No, Sydna."

The girl came toward him with distress and sympathy in her brown eyes. She glanced at the door.

"What reason could she have had?"

A growing feeling of having been done a deep injustice welled up in Miltiades.

"Why . . . she said I didn't love her . . . !"

The daughter stared incredulously.

"Mamma said . . . you didn't . . . love . . . her?"

"That's what she said," repeated the Colonel bleakly.

"What a terrible thing to say! What could she have been thinking about?"

Sydna was close to his chair. Miltiades fumbled about in his head, trying to recall Drusilla's arguments that proved he did not love her, when he suddenly saw that Sydna was weeping. She maintained a surface composure of her face, but tears trickled down her cheeks. Something squeezed painfully in the Colonel's chest. He got up and put an arm about her shoulders.

"Sydna, don't cry for me, honey. After all, I have never got anything I ever wanted in this life. Folks don't, I think. Happiness of any kind is like a will o' the wisp, our very motion toward it causes it to float away."

Sydna began sobbing outright.

"But you've been so brave, so constant, so loyal, so utterly unselfish. Life . . . life can't do you like that. . . ." Her voice broke. "It . . . just . . . mustn't. . . ."

The Colonel tried to comfort her, stroking her hair, her shoulders.

"But, darling, it happens frequently in anything you do; and in love affairs it happens all the time."

The girl wept unrestrainedly upon his shoulder. The Colonel stood murmuring, "Now . . . now . . . honey . . ." caressing her blonde hair, which was so fine it stuck like silk to his fingers. Presently he lowered himself into his chair again and let her sit, weeping, in his lap.

"Colonel Milt . . . in the hardest hearted novels I . . . ever read . . . if the hero doesn't . . . marry his sweetheart when . . . when she's young . . . he . . . he does when she's old. . . ."

Miltiades took the girl's two hands and patted them.

"Novels are written the way people wish life could be lived, Sydna, not as things really happen."

The girl sat thinking a moment.

"Colonel Milt, what other reason did Mother give for not taking you?"

"Why, darling, if she thinks I don't love her, that's enough, isn't it?"

"Ye-es . . . but she always gives several reasons for everything she does."

"Well, aren't they her real reasons?"

"Oh . . . sometimes they are. . . . What else did she say?"

The Colonel was surprised to find Sydna skeptical about Drusilla, to whom he always had attributed the utmost frankness. Now he pondered what other reason the mother had given him.

"Well . . . she picked up the blueprints and asked me what I would want with a woman of her age in a house with as many rooms as that. . . ." Miltiades cleared his throat. "Now, you may not understand her allusion. . . ."

"She means she won't have any more children," interpreted Sydna absently.

"She possibly had that in mind," agreed the Colonel, relieved that Sydna could put it so unobjectionably.

"I wonder really why she didn't take you," speculated Sydna, looking at Miltiades with a puzzled frown.

"You think she has still another reason for not marrying me?" ejaculated the Colonel.

"Why, of course, and that will be the true one, and she'll never tell you in the world unless you just make her."

"Well, by George," said the Colonel, "if I knew the true reason I might be able to argue her out of it."

"Whether you do or don't," said Sydna, beginning to breathe unevenly again, "I think you deserve to know the real reason after a whole lifetime of devotion to her."

The Colonel also felt this to be a fair reward. He hesitated a moment at putting Sydna off his lap to go to Drusilla, because he saw no reasonable hope of ever getting her to sit there again, but of course he had to sacrifice this minor pleasure in his effort to reach the one great happiness of his life.

"Where is she?" he asked.

Sydna got up, as he had anticipated.

"In the kitchen," she said encouragingly, "and make her tell you, and then you can argue her down. That's why she always tries to put you off with something else, because she's easily argued down if you can ever find out what it really is."

"All right, you just wait here a few minutes, and I'll go back and have it out with Drusilla."

"Do! Do!" encouraged the daughter; "and, for heaven's sake, make her take you this time!" She squeezed his fingers and let him go.

If the Colonel had been leading Sydna herself to the marriage altar, the daughter could not have been more vividly excited over the suitor's second solicitation of her mother. Her heart filled her chest with its clamor. Her pulse beat in her neck. How wise and sad and noble the Colonel was! How like a hero out of a book, if only she could contrive to make it end like a book. . . . She thought of living permanently with the Colonel as the daughter of his manor. She picked up the prints which he had left on the table to see what the manor would be like, but she was so excited she could not fasten her attention upon them.

Miltiades moved toward the Crowninshield kitchen, determined to have the real reason of his rejected offer of marriage out of Drusilla. As he walked, the place on his knees where Sydna had been sitting felt chilly and deserted. It was the uncomfortable sensation that any area on a man feels when some woman has been lounging there for a few minutes and gets up and goes away.

The Colonel tapped at the kitchen door with a certain trepidation. It was very unconventional to pursue the mistress of a manor into the remoter parts of her house after she has refused a suitor's hand. Nevertheless, he tapped discreetly and stood choosing some words with which to start talking. The door opened at once, and Miltiades saw the little tan-colored girl with the glossy curls.

The Colonel looked around the kitchen.

"Jinny Lou . . . where's your mistress?"

"She . . . gon' to de garden," whispered Jinny Lou, overpowered by the entrance of the Colonel in the kitchen.

"Gone to the . . ." The Colonel halted, embarrassed at the tan child's possible implication.

"Oh . . . oh, no, suh, 'tain't that," hurried Jinny Lou, equally upset. "She—she tuk huh gloves an'—an' hoe."

"M-m," grunted the Colonel, not amplifying the point on which he and Jinny Lou had come to an understanding. "Which way is it to the garden?"

Jinny Lou silently reached up, unlatched the back door, and let the Colonel out into the Crowninshield back yard. Two strings of planks led away from the back door. Jinny Lou pointed the one to the right.

"That 'un goes to de garden," she whispered, "an' that 'un goes to de well."

After these road directions, the little negro stood in the kitchen door and allowed the Colonel to choose his destination. The Colonel started for the garden, walking along the loose planks with a slight uneasiness lest one should fly up and hit him.

Drusilla was digging in the garden with a hoe. The most conspicuous things about her were her white cotton gloves and the dark modeling of her hair in the sunshine. When she looked up and saw who was coming she grounded her hoe in the dirt.

"Why, Miltiades!" she ejaculated.

The Colonel hastily assembled the sentence he had planned to say.

"Drusilla, I know it is unconventional to follow you out here, but we are such old friends. . . ."

"I didn't know lovers were ever friends," interrupted the woman.

"Well, that may or may not be. . . . Sydna sent me out here."

"Sydna!"

"Yes," nodded the Colonel seriously. "Sydna is all cut up over this, Drusilla . . . the way everything has turned out. She's been crying about it."

The mother stirred her blade in the plowed earth.

"Sydna weeps pretty easily," she observed.

The remark incensed the Colonel.

"If she's sensitive, that's all the more reason your daughter should be considered, Drusilla."

The woman stood surveying Miltiades with a faint smile on her lips.

"You seem more wrought up about Sydna's weeping than you were about my refusal to marry you."

The Colonel was slightly disconcerted at this, but he faced the matter.

"Yes, I am. Our marriage certainly wouldn't do either one of us any harm, and if it would make Sydna happy, I think we ought to do it. At least, I'm more than willing. Sydna has been loyal to me in a way that no other human being in the world ever has, not even members of my own family. God knows why she has done it. I don't deserve it. But if I can act in the future in such a way that I would have deserved it, I'm going to do it."

Drusilla nodded slowly.

"She has been more than loyal to you, Miltiades."

"Yes, she has been much more faithful to me than I have been to myself."

"What do you mean?"

"I mean she believes I have not done what I know I have done."

Drusilla stood looking at him and shook her head faintly.

"Aren't you sorry, Milt?" she asked.

The Colonel nodded in the direction of the old Lacefield place.

"I'm sorry for that—that last. I wish it hadn't happened.

It was really his own fault . . . to give up and quit like that."

Drusilla continued shaking her head hopelessly.

"You really are an outrageous man. You always have been. You appear to people who don't know you as a most conventional man, but you really stick at nothing and regret little."

"Drusilla, we've both known that for a long time. Will you or will you not marry me?"

"Would you marry a woman who didn't love you, Miltiades, even for the sake of Sydna?"

"So you really don't love me at all?" queried the Colonel incredulously.

"Do you imagine a woman who loved a man could analyze him like that, aloud, before his face?"

The Colonel was a little taken aback.

"I suppose not." He stood looking at the woman he had loved for twenty empty years, and then said curiously, "I would really have to get acquainted with you over again, Drusilla. You are not the same person I used to know. You have grown very wise."

"I've been lonely. I've had to think. Sometimes it seems impossible to me that my life—*my* life really has been lonely."

"We have both been," said Miltiades. He stood for a moment and then said simply, "Sydna told me to ask you the real reason why you wouldn't marry me."

"The real reason?" repeated Drusilla.

The Colonel smiled faintly.

"She said you always gave a number of reasons for what you did, but if a person wanted to find out the real reason he would have to pin you down and make you tell."

The mother smiled back at him but grew serious.

"I . . . I'm afraid I can't tell you my real reason, Milt," she said in an odd voice.

"Then you do have one!"

"Oh, yes . . . of course."

Colonel Vaiden felt a tang of reproach.

"Were you really going to let me go away without knowing . . . when this concerns me so vitally?"

"You went off and left me without knowing, Milt . . . when it concerned me vitally."

"Why, Drusilla," said the Colonel in a shocked voice, "I didn't dream . . . you remember you . . . you went away once with Colonel Crowninshield. . . ."

"I was a romantic girl then, Miltiades, but you deserted a woman who loved you."

Colonel Vaiden stood looking at her with nothing at all to say.

"After you married Ponny you became a sort of ghost to me," went on Drusilla. "I would see you passing along the street, the ghost of somebody I had loved."

Miltiades listened, moistening his lips with his tongue.

"Sydna watched you too," continued the woman. "When she was a little thing she would call to me 'Mamma, there goes Colonel Milt.'"

"Yes?" said the man in a low tone.

"She has looked for you and talked about you all her life. Here, of late, since this trouble came up, she cannot bear to hear anyone speak ill of you . . . no matter what happened."

Miltiades nodded. He could well believe that.

"That morning when she ran out in the street and chased away those boys, she went back to her room and cried all the rest of the day."

"I declare," breathed the Colonel with a fixed frown, "I didn't know . . . I didn't dream . . . that's pitiful. . . ."

"Here, lately, she can't endure any of her usual callers. Young Jerry, Lucius Handback, Alfred Thorndyke . . . she says they are so silly and kiddish. . . ."

"Yes?" nodded the Colonel, looking intently at her.

"And these last few days, when you have persistently stayed away from us, she has been sick. . . . You see . . . Sydna has loved you a long time, Miltiades."

"Me! *Me!*" whispered the Colonel. "Sydna love *me!* . . . How is that possible? . . ."

The mother made a helpless gesture.

"I have wondered a thousand times, Miltiades. . . . God knows why."

CHAPTER FORTY-EIGHT

COLONEL MILTIADES VAIDEN moved in a kind of daze from the garden to the living room of the Crowninshield home. That Sydna loved him, that she might, according to the belief of her mother, even marry him, seemed an impossible, almost a sacrilegious idea. The girl seemed so perfect, so innocent, that the thought of marriage with her filled the middle-aged man with a kind of exquisite dismay.

As he passed through the kitchen he asked of Jinny Lou in a trepidant tone:

"Is Miss Sydna still in the living room?"

The little negro walled up her black eyes.

"Yaas, suh, you fin' huh dah. . . . Miss Sydna nevah stir huhse'f to do nothin'."

The Colonel moved on through the house, filled with the oddest perturbation. He thought Drusilla must be wrong. The fact that the mother herself had just refused his hand vanished from his thoughts in the face of this amazing intimation about Sydna.

"If it is true," he thought, "I must explain to her the kind of thing she is getting into . . . the inequality of our ages . . . the different . . . overtones . . . of what we feel for each other. . . ."

The shadow of possible tragedy wavered before the Colonel's mind. He walked on filled with concern about Sydna's future happiness.

The girl herself heard the Colonel's step and met him halfway down the hall. At the sight of his face she said in a pinched voice:

"She . . . didn't change?"

The Colonel moistened his lips.

"Well, yes . . . she changed."

"Oh, she's accepted you!"

"No, not exactly."

"Then . . . how has she changed?" asked Sydna, quite at sea.

"Sydna," answered the Colonel, "I—— Come, let's go back into the sitting room. I will have to explain that to you."

Sydna moved wonderingly at the Colonel's side. When they entered the sitting room again, both felt an impulse to resume their original position in one chair, but the Colonel drew two chairs tête-à-tête.

The girl looked questioningly at Miltiades as she lowered herself into one.

"All right. . . . Tell me."

Ordinarily the Colonel would have put his palm over the girl's hand, but now he did not.

"Sydna," he said seriously, "I am a middle-aged man. I feel about as I always have felt, but in reason I know I must be going down the other side of the hill."

The girl looked at him, quite at a loss.

"Mother is nearly as old as you are, Colonel Milt."

"M-m . . . she's a good bit younger."

"But, look here," cried Sydna, narrowing her brown eyes "do you mean to tell me she has refused you on account o, your age?"

"Now, now, don't get miffed at your mother," soothed th' Colonel in embarrassment. "No, it wasn't that."

"Then what reason did she give you this time?" pressed Sydna with the greatest concern in her face.

"We-ell . . ." The Colonel did, after all, touch her hand. He felt almost sick. She was just a girl. Only a few years ago she was a little child who had come to him gravely at her mother's behest and given him the wet, formless kiss of childhood. Now she sat beside him, a lovely girl, deeply concerned about his own and her mother's happiness. He had to approach her question.

"If I should tell you, Sydna, I am afraid it would shock you . . . painfully, perhaps."

"Well . . . tell me."

"Sydna, the mere idea of what she said was an utter bewilderment to me. . . . I never dreamed . . . Sitting here, looking at you soberly like this, I know Drusilla must be mistaken. . . ."

"Looking at me . . . *me?*"

"Yes, I know she must be. I know what she said was utterly impossible."

"Colonel, are—are you going to tell me or are you not?" she begged in uneven breaths.

"Yes, yes, yes, dearest. . . ." He hardly knew how to go on. He drew a breath. "I hope you'll forgive me. . . . I hope you'll forgive us both, Sydna. Your mother said that she thought that you . . . you were fond of me. . . ."

The girl opened her eyes and leaned forward a trifle.

"Why, I am."

"I mean . . . that you cared for me. . . ."

"Of course I do," agreed the girl.

"Sydna, I mean," despaired the Colonel in a morass of embarrassment, "she meant that . . . that . . . that you loved me and . . . and might honor me by . . . becoming my wife. . . ."

The girl became perfectly motionless. The color dropped from her face and left her dark eyes in a pale oval setting. The Colonel held up a hand toward her.

"I beg of you to remember this presumption is not my own. To me such an idea would never have occurred, as I see it never has to you. It was Drusilla's fancy . . . her imagination. . . ." He broke off, patting her fingers slightly with the ghost of a smile, and withdrew his hand.

Sydna continued staring at the Colonel with wide eyes.

"Do you mean I . . . I have come between you and Mother?" she whispered.

"Why, I had never thought of it in that way. . . . No, no, I don't think so . . . not at all."

"But doesn't Mamma still love you?" she asked in a pinched tone.

Miltiades suddenly perceived that the girl was suffering. A feeling of helplessness came over him.

"Why, no . . . she doesn't . . . she said she didn't," he returned uncertainly.

"And you . . . don't you love Mother?"

The Colonel simply sat and looked at the girl, unwilling to put into bald words a denial of what he himself, for so many years, had held to his heart as a great possible happiness.

The daughter shook her head slowly, almost incredulously. "And both of you found you . . . didn't love each other . . . after all this time!"

And then, to the Colonel's dismay, he saw that she was weeping.

"Sweetheart . . . honey," he comforted earnestly, "you needn't feel so bad about it, precious. After all, if she doesn't want me, and . . ." he was on the verge of saying, "and I don't want her," but his courtesy forbade, so he finished a little incoherently, "then why should it hurt you so, Sydna?"

The girl composed herself, blinking her wet eyes.

"It . . . it's not so much for . . . for you two . . . if . . . if you really don't . . ."

"Then why . . . what is it, darling?" asked Miltiades in the utmost concern.

"Why . . . it's just life," said the girl in an aspirate. "I have never found any . . . any great love in my life, but . . . but I always thought . . ." She put her hand to her mouth and pressed her lips.

The Colonel looked at her aghast as her idea dawned upon him.

"You mean . . . us . . . me?"

She nodded dolefully.

"If—if you aren't faithful, Colonel Milt, then—then there isn't any faithful love in all the world. . . ." And she began weeping silently, with the tears dropping from her lashes at this final destruction of a lifelong ideal.

The Colonel came to a disturbed pause at this new direction developed in Sydna's grief. He felt a sharp impulse to justify Drusilla and himself, and in the same breath shrank from shaking the girl's inherent trust in the immortality of the passion of youth.

He pondered how to begin, and finally asked gravely:

"Sydna, do you believe my nephew Jerry Catlin is at present precisely as he will be twenty years from now?"

The girl steadied herself somewhat to think where this question led.

"Why, no, Colonel Milt, of course he is not exactly . . . Do you mean people change, the very center and heart of them must change?"

"Everything else about a person changes, Sydna: one's appearance, the way one thinks, the very inmost personality that makes one an individual—all shift and change with the passing of time."

"Then what becomes of love?" asked the girl, in a low voice.

The Colonel thought for a moment.

"When you say love, Sydna, you don't mean the kindliness and gentle amiability that Judge Ashton has for his wife, or Rose has for Augustus, or Bill Bradley feels for Lily?"

"No," admitted the girl slowly, beginning to see the position into which the Colonel had drawn her, "I wasn't talking about that."

"You are talking about something in your own heart which you are sure will exist forever?" questioned Miltiades tenderly.

The daughter nodded faintly.

"I know I have something to give somebody . . . which will never change."

The Colonel sat looking at the girl, thinking how to

agree to the reality of the emotion which Sydna felt in her heart.

"Honey," he said at last, "I know the tenderness and sweetness of what you feel. It is a kind of heaven waiting for someone to come and dwell in it."

"But, Colonel Milt . . . you don't think it will last?"

"Yes, I do, darling."

The girl gave a pitiful smile.

"But the only one I ever thought would last . . . didn't."

"It endures, Sydna, the passionate love of youth endures always, but it is transformed to the keeping of others. Your feeling that it is deathless is utterly true, but Love walks the earth stepping from generation to generation. It lights up all hearts with its undying flame as it moves on its mission of ecstasy. The very intensity of every moment provides for the immortality of the goddess. You must remember, Sydna, that Venus was born of the foam of the breaking waves of the sea; but her reign is eternal."

The girl sat filled with sadness at this pensive elegy to Love. It made her feel helpless to think that the time would come when she, too, would sit beside the ashes on a deserted altar. She drew a long breath.

"I don't see what's left," she said at last; "I don't see what there is to live for."

"Why, for the loves of our children," assured the Colonel. "They come as close to our heart as our own. I sometimes think, Sydna, only as the goddess leaves us and moves on to the next generation, only then, from a distance and with no thought of self, do we behold her amazing beauty and grace."

The middle-aged man drew a long breath, sat for a moment longer. The actual reason why he had come to Sydna a second time recurred to him, and now its impossibility gave him a touch of ironic amusement at himself. He and Drusilla, in a manner, he supposed, had been two doting simpletons. After all, what did either of them know about Sydna? A touch of admiration passed through the Colonel at the

delicate way the girl had turned aside his marriage offer. It
somehow had got lost in their talk, and he himself did not
know exactly when. "That," thought the Colonel, "is because her forbears have been, for generation after generation, gentlefolk."

He picked up his blueprints mechanically and began replacing them in the envelope. He would return the specifi-
cations to Bradley.

At this earnest of his going away a trembling set up in
Sydna. While they were talking of the evanescent eternity of
love, the girl had had an impression that such an eternity
enwrapped her. Now, abruptly, this was gone, and she felt
more lonely and unhappy than ever. She followed the man's
movements with her eyes.

"Colonel," she said in a low voice, "you have never had
any children. Now you will go through life . . . quite
empty . . . of anything?"

"I think that was my own fault, Sydna. Your mother says
I never did really love her. . . . I don't know. . . . I always thought I did." The Colonel slipped the envelope into
his pocket and was about to rise.

The girl leaned forward impulsively.

"Colonel . . . don't go," she said.

Miltiades thought of the exquisiteness of her courtesy
that bade him stay after what had happened.

"I should have been back to the store long ago, Sydna,"
he smiled.

"Colonel Milt," repeated the girl, stretching a hand
toward him, "please don't go. . . ."

"But, honey, I must. . . . I really should never have
come."

The girl began trembling again, "Oh, Colonel Milt, I
don't want you to go away. Everybody sounds so . . . so
foolish and . . . and so far away, except you. Nobody tries
to understand me, except you . . . and now . . . you're
going away . . . for good, maybe. . . ." She lifted her

hands toward him. "Don't go away and leave me, Colonel
Milt. . . ."

The man looked at her in amazement. He took her small,
workless, almost useless hands in his own.

"Why, Sydna, honey, you don't mean . . ."

She nodded faintly, her dark eyes fixed on his.

"Yes . . . I do . . . I—I think I have meant it all my
life."

As he leaned toward her, his hands slid up her slim girlish arms and around her shoulders. She was unbelievably
soft; her shoulders bent to his pressure with the flexibility
of youth. Her age, her innocence, came over the Colonel with
its penetrating sweetness, and following this, like its
shadow, drifted the possibility of tragedy. This last, he felt,
as an honorable man, he must tell her; the disparity of their
ages, the probable disparity of their tastes and needs.

He began in a serious tone:

"Sydna, dear, do you believe it is possible for you really
to marry me, when . . ."

The girl gave his neck a convulsive pressure.

"Dearest Colonel Milt, months ago it quit being possible
for me to marry anybody else. . . ."

The Colonel sat holding the girl in his lap, patting her
shoulder, kissing her ear. A strange feeling came over him
that the years had melted and he was free in Time. He might
have been with Drusilla in his arms; or a girl he had known
during the war in Virginia, or with Ponny at the beginning
of their courtship: all these memories revisited his heart, like
the ancient Magi, bearing gifts of myrrh for Sydna.

To the girl herself, she rested in the embrace of that romantic figure, who on the battlefield of Shiloh had promised
her dying father to care for his little daughter Sydna.

CHAPTER FORTY-NINE

D RUSILLA thought it best to make the wedding a very quiet affair: just the two immediate families, a few intimate friends, with the Reverend Mathers, the Episcopal minister, officiating.

Sydna told her mother that she was willing to stand on the highest mountain before all the world and marry Miltiades. She said she only wished her own character measured up to his.

Drusilla reminded her daughter that it was not what people were, but what other people thought they were, that counted, and that she still considered it best to make it a very quiet affair.

As to the actual quietness of the affair, only the form of the announcement was subdued. The news traveled over the town instantly by back-yard telegraph.

Within six hours it was known from old Florence to East Florence that Sydna Crowninshield was going to marry her mother's old beau for his money.

A great many experienced persons applauded Miltiades' wisdom in picking a young nurse for his old age.

Old Mrs. Waner on Tombigbee Street prophesied spitefully,

"This 'un'll run off the night before the weddin' jest like her mammy did before her."

Old Mrs. Waner disliked the whole kit and bi'ler of the Vaidens with an old woman's thoroughgoing detestation, because her brother, old Parson Bennie Mulry, a Methodist circuit rider, now dead, had praised the Vaidens too enthusiastically when he was at home.

Nobody in Florence could understand how Sydna could

take a man old enough to be her father, and who came with-in an ell of being it, too.

These old women gossips quite forgot how charming cer-tain middle-aged men had appeared when they were girls; those recollections having been effaced by more recent mem-ories of how middle-aged men had appeared when they them-selves were middle-aged.

In this round of gossip Jerry Catlin was not forgotten. Sydna Crowninshield was marrying that old thief Milt Vaiden, with Jerry Catlin, his nephew, head over heels in love with her.

That was exactly like the Vaidens . . . and the Crown-inshields!

This matter of young Jerry was not without some pith. For months now Mrs. Rose Vaiden had been concerned about Jerry in regard to Sydna Crowninshield.

Spring had come, not only to Miltiades and Sydna, it had spread across Pine and Market streets and included the Rose Vaiden boarding house. It affected Jerry's studies adversely. In truth, it had become a fairly well established fact that young Jerry Catlin was going to fail in his term examinations that spring. None of the college faculty held out any hope for Jerry's scholastic efforts. Mrs. Rose Vai-den reproached herself bitterly for this outcome. She at-tributed it to the influence of Sydna, and it was she who had first sent Jerry to the Crowninshield residence with a pie. But for this, Rose felt, young Jerry might never have be-come acquainted with Sydna Crowninshield, and he might have done handsomely in college, because, being of Vaiden descent, he had brains.

Augustus and Rose were talking of this very matter in the kitchen. There were tears in Augustus' eyes, but this was caused by some shallots and had no reference to his nephew. As far as Jerry was concerned, Augustus' eyes were hard and blue.

"We might just as well send him back to Marcia now," Augustus was saying, "as to wait and let him disgrace the

Vaiden name by failing. Didn't even have the brains to keep up with that fathead Jefferson Ashton. . . . Jefferson's getting through all right!"

"He's got the brains," said Mrs. Rose, "Jerry's been . . . troubled."

"What's he got to be troubled about, I'd like to know!"

"Well . . . I don't know," said Mrs. Rose, in a tone that meant she did not think it wise to tell what she knew.

"Nothing . . . nothing at all. I gave him a fair chance, and he didn't take it. He's his mammy made over. Sister Marcia was one of the laziest-headed girls I ever saw in my life. She was mentally almost as lazy as she was physically, and that's the superlative. There wasn't anything that lived that was any lazier physically than Marcia Vaiden."

Augustus' wrath at his nephew was increased at these remembered shortcomings of his nephew's mother. He lost all patience with Jerry.

"I'm going upstairs and tell that boy to pack up and be ready to take the first boat down the river. I won't keep any such numbskull in my home! Hasn't got ambition enough to pass the examinations of a little two by four college like this!"

"Finish your shallots," said Mrs. Rose, seeing Augustus putting down his pan.

"No, I'll finish Jerry first."

"But, Augustus," cried Rose in genuine alarm, "he hasn't actually failed yet: people just think he's going to fail."

"The teachers in the Florence college are no fools," growled Augustus: "when they are unanimous that a boy's a numbskull, he's a numbskull"; and Augustus tramped off through the dining room toward the front hall.

In the upper story of this same boarding house another acrimonious conversation was in progress. It had been getting sharper for some time.

"If she is not marrying him for his money," inquired Sandusky tartly, "what is she marrying him for?"

"Because . . . because she . . . honors him," replied

Jerry warmly. "There's something in marriage besides either money or sex, Sandusky. And even if you don't know what it is, it's still there!"

Sandusky began laughing in an annoying manner.

"What is that other thing?"

"Why, it's a—a spiritual correspondence . . . or a relation of honor and—and adoration."

"You say Sydna Crowninshield *honors* Colonel Vaiden?"

"That's what I imagine."

"And he adores her?"

A thin pain, like the thrust of a hatpin, went through Jerry's chest.

"Yes—I imagine he does," said the nephew.

Sandusky laughed with thin down-curved lips in his sharp face.

"What you say doesn't make any sense at all. She couldn't really honor a cotton thief and a skinflint, and he couldn't adore a stuck-up town gal that would sell herself to a old man with a bunch of stolen money!"

At this point the long truce between young Jerry Catlin and the boarder came to an end. Jerry got up, almost leisurely, from the bed, stepped across, and swung at Sandusky's head.

The smaller man dodged, jumped up, scattering his law books, and grabbed Jerry.

Immediately began one of those inexpert short-winded struggles between two men who are not in form and know little about fighting. Jerry choked Sandusky's throat and pounded at the boarder's detestable skinny face. His blows seemed to land wrong. They hit but did no visible damage. Sandusky was thumping the hobbledehoy in the stomach. Pain rang through Jerry's diaphragm like a bell. His breath was shut off. He continued choking and pounding as best he could under the sharp disadvantage of not being able to breathe. He pulled his stomach back out of Sandusky's reach when the boarder began to pound him in the face.

Jerry was so nearly blinded and so frantic to make some

impression on his antagonist that he hauled off and kicked the little man in the shins.

Sandusky let out a yelp, then screamed:

"Kicking, air ye! You coward! I'll learn you to kick!"

And with that a terrible blow struck Jerry in the groin. Agony flooded the adolescent's abdomen and legs. He staggered and fell curled up on the bed. Sandusky stopped, shocked at his roommate's face.

Just then the door opened. A voice boomed out:

"What in the thunderation are you boys doing . . . fighting?"

"We . . . were . . . playing . . ." gasped Sandusky, who could talk.

"What in the world were you fighting about?" cried Mrs. Rose, right behind her husband. "Look at Jerry there on the bed. He's bad hurt!"

Jerry shook his head in a world quivering with pain, to show that he wasn't hurt. He was terribly frightened at what his uncle would do.

"P-playin'," he gasped, trying to back up Sandusky.

"Of all outrageous conduct!" roared Augustus. "Fighting like niggers! What in the thunder were you fighting about? Jerry—you started this!"

Jerry shook his head.

"Well, I came up here anyway to ship you home. You've disgraced the name of . . . What in the nation did you start a fight with Sandusky for, anyway?"

Jerry became able to speak through cottony lips.

"He—he—insulted—Uncle Milt."

Augustus frowned at Jerry, then glanced at Sandusky.

"What did he say?"

"Called him—cotton thief. . . ."

The room abruptly became still.

"Sandusky . . . did you say that?"

"Why! Why, me and Jerry got to squabbling," explained the boarder nervously. "If I said it I didn't mean it. I don't know what-all I said."

"Sandusky," said Augustus, his own face growing sallow with wrath, "Rose and I accepted you in our home more in coöperation with the college than to make any money out of your board. You have quit college. I will have to ask you to give up your room to some more ambitious and dependable young man. I can't extend the hospitality of my home to a clod of a person who is willing to drift with the current and make no effort to do something and be somebody in the world. I'll get another boarder in your place who is willing to work and study and try to achieve something. In the meantime I will have to ask you to vacate your room."

"Now, look here, Gussie," put in Mrs. Rose, "Mr. Sandusky didn't start that fight for nothing."

"I said Miss Crowninshield was stuck up," repeated Sandusky, "and Jerry hit me."

"You said Uncle Milt was a thief," repeated Jerry hotly, unable to hear Sydna's name mentioned.

Mrs. Rose divined Jerry's feelings, and it struck her that the best thing that could happen to Jerry was for him to go home before Sydna and Miltiades were married. So now she said:

"Augustus, you came up to send Jerry home. If you did that, Mr. Sandusky wouldn't have anybody to quarrel with."

"Send Jerry off for defending the good name of my brother!" cried Augustus.

"No, for failing in his exams!"

"He hasn't failed yet. He's a Vaiden. Give him a night or two, and he can study up and pass the confounded examinations. They don't amount to much, anyway. They're mainly trick questions. All the pupils say that."

"Do you still want me to leave this house, Mr. Vaiden?" inquired Sandusky stolidly.

Augustus said he did, but said it with much less fury than before.

The reader of law set about packing his things. He had accumulated too many books to go in his paper valise, so he said he would have to go to town for a box.

Mrs. Rose went down the stairs with him. She was sorry to see Sandusky go. It meant ten dollars a month less for their groceries.

When these two were out of hearing, Augustus asked Jerry:

"Didn't Sandusky kick you foul a while ago?"

Jerry nodded.

"The dirty pup—you should have kicked him foul first." And he began telling Jerry of a fight he once had had with one of Forrest's troopers.

CHAPTER FIFTY

THE moral result of his fight with Sandusky dismayed young Jerry Catlin long after the pain of the kick had passed away. Why had he ever started the fight? Why had he not used the wisdom of the adepts and retired from the argument instead of hitting Sandusky? His occult books had warned him if he hoped to gain the great power of the initiated he must banish anger and revenge from his soul.

Up until this fight Jerry had been trying to look upon the boarder as an unenlightened spirit. He had resolved at times to bring light and soothing to Sandusky's soul. But these periods of good resolutions had been at intervals when he was not in Sandusky's presence. When he and the boarder were together they never agreed on anything, and here at last he had started a fight with the fellow and had caused the law student to be dismissed from the boarding house.

As young Jerry pondered ruefully over this he realized that before he could proceed further along the path of illumination he would have to straighten up his misstep as best he could.

So he got himself off his bed with an undecided feeling in his midparts, as if they might begin to ache again. He moved around the room gingerly and satisfied himself that he could walk all right, then started downstairs to see his uncle about Sandusky.

In the kitchen Jerry found his uncle working at the shallots again. Augustus and Rose were talking, and the nephew awaited with some misgiving for an opportunity to suggest that Sandusky be forgiven and readmitted to the boarding house.

As he considered how he would put this request, his uncle looked up from his shallot cleaning.

"Jerry," he said in a severe tone, "Sandusky will be back for his things in about an hour."

"Yes, sir," nodded Jerry, and he drew in his breath to begin to say, "and, Uncle Augustus, I hope you won't turn Sandusky out after all . . ." when Augustus proceeded in a deliberate, purposeful tone:

"And when he does come back, I'm going to make you lick him."

"What?" ejaculated the nephew.

"You'll fight him again," snapped Augustus, "fair this time. I'll stand by with a pole. We'll teach the dirty rat how to fight foul!"

"But, looky here," began Jerry in a panic, "I came down here to—to ask you to forgive Sandusky and take him back, Uncle Augustus!"

"Take him back!" ejaculated the uncle.

"Yes, sir."

"You—you're not afraid of him, are you?"

"N-no, sir, but I—I thought we might forgive him."

"Forgive him? Forgive that skunk?" Augustus put down his shallots. "Do you suppose a Vaiden would ever forgive an insult or a foul blow? No, by George, not till it's settled! You've got to take the skin off of Sandusky's head, or I'll take it off your back, sir. You've got to lick Sandusky."

"But, look here, Uncle Augustus!" cried Jerry in confusion, "I'm not afraid of Sandusky, honestly. Personally, I'd as soon fight him as not. And if he licked me, well and good, and if I licked him well and good. . . ."

"Why, thunder and Tom Walker!" roared Augustus, "that's no spirit to go into a fight! You've got to go in to lick or die. You mustn't even think of losing!"

Jerry nodded agreement to this desirable mental state before fisticuffs.

"But, look here, Uncle Augustus, it—doing that will throw me completely out."

let a little dried-up runt like Sandusky kick you around like a puppy, I think you'd better pack up and go home."

The threshold of the kitchen seemed to sink under Jerry. He held to the door jamb.

"Well . . . all right, sir," he said in a strained voice.

"Gussie!" cried Mrs. Rose, "you are not going to do any such thing!"

"I certainly am! Go to your room and pack your things, Jerry!"

"All right, sir"; and Jerry returned to his room from his mission of forgiveness.

The moment he was gone Mrs. Rose turned on her husband.

"Augustus, you're nothing but a blind, bust-headed Vaiden!"

"Why, what's the matter?"

"The idyah, a book on character kicking up all this shindy!"

"Well, isn't it?"

"Of course not. It's puppy love. He's head over heels in love with a girl old enough to be his mother."

"What girl?"

"Why, Sydna Crowninshield, of course."

"Why, the idyah! That's worse than ever . . . an engaged girl!"

"Did Jerry know she was going to get engaged when he started going over there?"

Augustus reflected on this.

"Well, if Sydna is keeping him from studying, what's the use in his staying here?"

"Well, I, for one, am certainly not going to send Marcia's boy home for falling in love with a sweet girl like Sydna."

"Well, what does he mean by falling in love at his age?" inquired Augustus.

"You were married when you were two years younger than Jerry," pointed out Mrs. Rose.

Augustus blinked.

"Boys matured earlier then than they do now."

"I'm going up to Jerry's room and tell him you've changed your mind," said Mrs. Rose, "and that he can stay and finish out his year at college."

"Tell him he can stay if he will buckle down and work and have ambition and determination, like a Vaiden," agreed Augustus.

"All right. I'll do those shallots. You go in the living room and lie down and take a nap. All this has upset you. You must rest your nerves."

CHAPTER FIFTY-ONE

Young Jerry Catlin, in the upper story of the boarding house, was unaware of the reprieve his aunt was bringing him. He sat on his bed filled with a widening realization of the ill fortune which had descended upon him. Everything that went to make up his life was about to be taken from him. If he were forced to return to his home in Tennessee there would be no possibility for him to pursue the path of illumination. The endless bickerings of his smaller brothers and sisters would preclude that. Florence had given young Jerry a respite from the *sturm und drang* of his own family, but his uncle's decision had forced him back into it, and now he would have to give up all hope of a spiritual flowering.

But this loss of the actual physical silence in which the hobbledehoy hoped to cultivate some mystical psychical power was the mere beginning of his misfortune. His real loss was that he should see Sydna Crowninshield no more. Sydna was the only person Jerry had ever known with whom he could talk of the confused and tumbling vagaries of his soul. Sydna was the only human reality in his nebulous groping after some great mystical goal. He planned every detail of a vague messianic life with some reference to Sydna. He thought if he should ever gain the power to dematerialize himself he would send his soul across from the Vaiden boarding house into Sydna's bedroom and appear before her bed in a white mist. The thought of himself being a white mist bending above Sydna sleeping in her bed filled Jerry with ecstasy and tenderness.

But if Sydna were married, the boy could foresee a kind

of homelessness for his disembodied spirit. It would have nowhere to go.

The very idea that Sydna would marry some other man seemed much more fantastic to Jerry than that his soul should be able to loose itself from his body. He really could not conceive Sydna married. It would be as if she were destroyed, as if she, and not he, were about to de dematerialized and some other sort of woman substituted in her place.

Young Jerry sat staring at the tiny stove, long since fireless now that spring had come. He revolved the horror of Sydna's approaching marriage. He wondered if she knew that a person's spiritual and astral progress depended upon the subjugation and eradication of all sexual desire?

He and she, to gain enlightenment, would have to free themselves from all desire of the flesh. . . . A sudden chill came over Jerry. He sat shivering, and then he tried to exert his will and prevent himself from being cold, but he almost instantly forgot this detail in his absorption in Sydna.

If Sydna married, he would be utterly alone unless one of the brotherhood of adepts came to him and initiated him in the higher mysteries of life. . . . If he had to go back to Tennessee, in the noise and hubbub of his own family, he would never in the world prepare his soul for initiation.

He got up from his bed. Instead of packing his clothes and getting ready for the steamboat, he took his hat, went downstairs, out the gate, and started down Market for Pine Street.

When Jerry Catlin reached Pine, spring had hung the trees with gauzes of greenish yellows and reds against the virginal blue of the sky. All this color filled Jerry with an advance nostalgia for Florence when his uncle should have sent him home.

On one of the lawns two little girls already had begun their spring-long task of knotting violet chains.

Farther on Jerry entered the Crowninshield gate and circled up to the piazza. Jinny Lou opened the door to him and went flying off to tell Miss Sydna who had come.

From where he stood, Jerry presently heard Sydna and Mrs. Drusilla talking. The mother said:

"Tell him to come in here, Jinny Lou."

The daughter said:

"Tell him I'll be out, Jinny Lou, when I try on this dress. Mother, I need a breath of air."

Presently Jinny Lou reappeared with this last message.

Jerry waited upward of half an hour on the portico. He looked unseeingly at the lawn, which was spaced by the gray wooden columns of the piazza. A small sulphur butterfly flew onto the long porch and lighted on a spot of sunshine on the floor. The butterfly lifted its wings slowly up and down in the weak light. Jerry thought it must be cold.

Sydna greeted her caller with her habitual invitation to come into the living room; then she asked him what was the matter, for, of late, Jerry had come to her only in periods of distress.

"I'm going home," said Jerry, staring at her.

"Right away?"

"Next trip of the *Rapidan*."

"Not before school quits?"

"That doesn't make any difference, the teachers are going to fail me anyway."

Sydna drew a breath.

"Why, Jerry!" she reproached, with a feeling that she herself was about to fail. It was an induced emotion. Sydna herself had never known it. She had gone through college with a glib certainty. Not once in all her course had she ever failed to make an honor mark, and not once had she ever been distracted by an idea outside of her books. She had the feminine ability to keep her school work completely disengaged from her everyday thinking.

"What have you failed in?"

"Nothing yet, but I guess I'll fail in everything when the time comes."

"You're not even going to stay and try the exams?"

"Uncle Augustus said there wasn't any use in my staying any longer."

Sydna studied her caller. If school books did not suggest ideas to Sydna, everything else did.

"Let's go out in the yard and talk about this," she suggested.

They picked their way to the hammock and tested it gingerly before sitting in it. With Southern negligence Sydna had left it out in the yard all winter, and it was probably too far gone to hold them up. But after a few muffled snaps it settled back to work again, and Sydna even swung herself a little with the toe of her slipper.

"What did you do to your uncle Augustus?" she inquired.

Jerry drew a long breath.

"We-ell . . . I had a fight with Sandusky."

"Jerry Catlin!"

The youth nodded with a heavier heart.

"What in the world did you fight Mr. Sandusky about?"

"Oh . . . we got to arguing, and one word led to another. . . . We never did get along very well."

"And Mr. Augustus is going to send you home for that?"

"No, he shipped Sandusky for that. Then, after it was all over, I got to thinking about Sandusky, and—and you know what I believe about that sort of thing—I thought I ought to forgive him, not because I care a tinker's dam about him, but because it was for my own good."

"Surely—I know about that."

"All right, that's why I was forgiving him, you might say, purely as a matter of business."

Sydna ran her tongue across her lips and nodded seriously.

"Well, I went down to Uncle Augustus and told him I forgave Sandusky and wanted him to take him back . . . and he sent me home."

"What!"

Jerry nodded.

"He wanted me to have another fight with Sandusky and

lick him. He sent me home because I wanted to forgive him."

"Oh, did Mr. Sandusky—er——" Sydna broke off her involuntary question. She had supposed, of course, that Jerry had whipped Sandusky in the first instance.

Jerry turned a dull red, but he could not explain that Sandusky had defeated him on a foul kick, so he was forced to pass over that detail of his disgrace in silence.

After a moment Sydna began again:

"Couldn't you have explained to your uncle Augustus why you wanted to forgive him?"

"I tried. I told him I was following a book of instructions on character building, but that made him madder than ever. He said if my character permitted a little runt to kick me around like that, he didn't want to have anything more to do with me. . . . Well, I can see how he felt that way."

"So can I," nodded Sydna.

The two sat in the hammock, Sydna moving it faintly with the tip of her toe. They sat on one edge and used the other side as a back against which to lean. Jerry's back sagged down with his head tilted forward at a sharp angle by the taut selvage, but he was content. He knew that Sydna knew everything about him and was concerned about his difficulties. He lay at rest because he was perfectly understood.

"I won't be able to do anything at home," he mumbled.

Sydna knew he meant his yoga exercises.

"We really must keep you here somehow, Jerry," she said with concern.

"I wonder if I'll ever get to be that sort of a person, even if I did stay here?"

"Why-y . . . ye-es. . . . Look here, Jerry, what good would it do you if you did get to be that sort of a person?"

"Why, Sydna!" ejaculated the boy; "for a soul to gain command over itself . . . for it to know itself! . . ."

"Yes. How would that help you get along in life, Jerry . . . help you do something . . . make something of yourself?"

Jerry looked at his solitary sympathizer in a dawning amazement.

"You don't believe it would be good for anything?"

"Well . . . honey . . . nothing very practical," she suggested gently.

"Sydna," he said, shocked, "it's like Franklin said when he discovered electricity, there's nothing very practical about a baby."

Sydna withdrew from the stand she had taken. She touched her companion's arm to reëstablish herself with him.

"Listen, Jerry, I've been sitting here thinking. If your uncle Augustus does send you away, why—why couldn't you stay with—with Colonel Milt? He's your uncle, too, and—and I'll be just as much your aunt as Miss Rose. . . ."

At this suggestion of her marriage a swift, an overwhelming despair rushed over Jerry. He turned out of the hammock and knelt before Sydna with his arms clasped about her knees and his face in her lap.

"Sydna! Sydna! Sydna!" he sobbed. "I kain't stand it! I kain't bear it! If you marry, I—I'll kill myself!"

CHAPTER FIFTY-TWO

W HEN young Jerry Catlin knelt sobbing and clutching at her knees, a kind of quivering tenderness had flooded Sydna Crowninshield. She felt an impulse to hug the boy to her breast, to caress him, to cover his wet face with kisses. Instead of that, she put her hands against Jerry's shoulders and pushed against her own trembling sympathy, and along with it, against Jerry himself. She had begged him to stop, hush, don't. Eventually they had talked together in a sort of unstable rationality and had decided, between the two of them, that the best thing for Jerry to do was to see Sydna no more until after the wedding. This wedding, they seemed to believe, would end their mutual strain and unhappiness. So Jerry had disappeared up Pine Street under the lacy trees.

Sydna's perturbation did not vanish with the going of the youth. She charged herself with Jerry's failure in school. He had spent his time with her. She even accused herself as the cause of his occult vagaries. His infatuation for her had moved him to try to do impossible things. It was a thousand pities she had ever permitted their intimacy.

During the following days she was always thinking about Jerry, fancying him alone in his attic trying to transform himself into some magical something or other. Or waiting for some master adept to appear out of nowhere and initiate him into heaven knew what. He was so serious about the thing, that was what disturbed Sydna. He was wrapped up in it, and it was her fault.

The only relief Sydna found from these self-reproaches was when Miltiades came to the Crowninshield home. The presence of the older man, the solid yet poetic character of his talk, made Jerry's adolescent fumings appear boyish and more or less trivial. It was as if Miltiades lifted Sydna to his own middle-aged point of view, and from this elevation she looked down on Jerry's devotion both to herself and to his chimera with the tenderness and perception of a woman of experience.

A mechanical aid to this serenity were two saddle horses. One day Colonel Vaiden arrived at the Crowninshield gate leading one of these horses and riding the other. When Sydna came out and saw the two animals she had exclaimed:

"Colonel Milt, have you hired a horse for me?"

And he had said casually, no, he hadn't hired it for her.

"Well, I'm to ride it, am I not?" she asked, a little at sea.

"That's entirely with you," said the Colonel with a faint smile. "The mare belongs to you."

"Oh, Colonel Milt!" cried Sydna, staring at the mare. It did not occur to her to run to him and kiss him for this spectacular gift.

Drusilla chided the Colonel for spending so much money on his fiancée. He ought not to do it, as hard as times were getting. But the Colonel explained that now was the time to buy anything; he was getting the mare very cheap, and later he could use her on their plantation.

Sydna looked at Miltiades' heavy-set figure with a thrill of proprietorship in such a handsome, generous husband. She must needs run off at once and put on her riding habit to try the animal, and this left Miltiades and Drusilla at the gate to look at the new mare.

"She looks a little bit like Madelon," said Drusilla, with an eye for fine points in horseflesh.

"She's the same strain as Madelon, but I bought her from Columbia, Tennessee."

"Father bought Madelon from Lexington, Kentucky," recalled the woman.

"Well, they are both blue-grass countries."

There was a pause, and then Mrs. Crowninshield said gravely:

"Miltiades, don't you really think you are buying too many things all of a sudden?"

"If I'm going to buy, now's the time."

"Yes, I know, but another big house here in Florence . . . and me to live alone in this one . . . I think that's foolish."

Her question suggested a fear of loneliness in Drusilla's heart, and a little shock went through Miltiades that this middle-aged woman was really the Drusilla he had wooed in the old Lacefield manor before the war. Now, for that Drusilla to dread a coming loneliness . . . it was very strange.

"Are you suggesting that we stay here?" he asked, putting his thoughts aside.

"Why, certainly, that's the thing for you both to do."

"Well, Drusilla, that's very generous——"

"Why, it's nothing of the sort. If you were poor, it would be generous of me to offer you a home, but when you are wealthy, it's generous of you to accept. You see, that's one of the peculiarities of the rich: you are laid under deep obligations to them, no matter whether they give you something or take what you've got."

The two middle-aged persons laughed a little at this observation.

"If I accept your home, I wonder if I might put you under further obligations to me by changing it a little?" suggested Miltiades tentatively.

"Why, what do you want to do to it?" inquired the woman, with a suggestion of defense in her voice.

"Well . . . its columns."

"Columns . . ." The woman turned to look at them. "What's wrong with its columns?"

"Nothing, but they are wooden, and they're square. All my life, Drusilla, I've wanted to live in a manor with round granite columns."

Drusilla looked at her house, imagining it with round stone columns.

"It won't be that sort of a house any more."

"No-o . . . I suppose it won't."

"How in the world came you to want to live with a row of round granite columns?"

The Colonel tried to grope back to the beginning of his desire for such a piazza, but it was lost in the past.

"Well," decided Drusilla, "I believe I would rather you would bring your six round granite columns and stick 'em up before my house than for you to build a whole new mansion as a background for them."

At this point Sydna reappeared.

"I'm going to have to have a new riding habit, Mother," she said, holding up her arms and turning around.

"Why, honey, what's wrong with that one? It looks exactly like it always has for the last ten years."

"I know it, and this habit has been all right for borrowed horses, but it won't do for one of my own."

"You shall have the new habit tomorrow," promised Miltiades, holding his hand to receive Sydna's boot.

"Now, Milt," protested Drusilla, "you can buy Sydna a horse and put columns around my house, but you can't buy her a riding habit yet. She will have to get along with what she's got."

"Now, isn't that absurd!" said Sydna from the saddle.

"Perfectly absurd," agreed the Colonel, "and by the way, Drusilla, we may not be back for lunch, we're going to ride out to your father's old place in the Reserve."

"You'll be sore when you get back, Sydna. And about that habit, Milt, a line has to be drawn somewhere."

The Colonel lifted his hat in final adieu to the woman at the gate and rode on with the daughter.

There were little flashes of a continual irony permeating Miltiades' relations with Drusilla and Sydna, and now, in this riding away, he felt it, but presently it vanished before the youth and slenderness and flexibility of Sydna sitting the mount he had given her.

The ride aroused in him a dream-like feeling. At any moment he felt he might wake up and find himself in his

Cherry Street house with Ponny. At the thought of Ponny's
bulk Sydna's lissomeness filled the Colonel with sweetness.
The notion of marriage with the girl came to the Colonel
as a sort of sacrilegious thing. In the light of Ponny's
death it seemed terrible to subject Sydna to the hazards
of maternity. There was something so sweet and girlish
about her that Miltiades was touched even at the thought
that she should be lent to the violences of love. He would
have kept her thus, cantering along in her trimness and
elegance, always.

Presently the Colonel began telling of his plans to rehabilitate the old Lacefield manor and to install Gracie and
Toussaint as housekeepers.

Sydna fell in with this at once and began planning the
details with quite a housewifely air. She said it would be
foolish to attempt to replace the burned portions of the
grand staircase with real mahogany. They could do it with
ordinary wood and paint, and that would look more like a
summer place, anyway; they were always painty.

Miltiades talked against this. He did not want a painty
place. He hoped to reproduce the solid amplitude of life
that had flourished before the Yankee invasion swept it
away. Sydna began to count the cost of such repairs, and
mathematics is always on the side of the patch worker. She
seemed very sensible as well as graceful and charming.

After a long ride the two came in sight of a shack by
the roadside brightly spotted with circus posters. On the
platform before it lounged a gang of negroes. As the
riders passed this place Miltiades drew down his horse to
see if he knew any of the loiterers.

"Hello, Loober," he called out to one of the blacks, "can't
you find anything to do in your cotton during such fine
spring weather as this?"

The other negroes began laughing at Loober, who was
disconcerted.

"Well . . . uh . . . Col'l Milt . . . tell you de troof
. . . I wuzn't speckin' to see you come ridin' pas' heah

today." And Loober flung up his bugle-like lips and began laughing at his own admission.

"Well, suppose you move yourself back to the cotton field and get to work," suggested the Colonel.

"Yes, suh, but my ol' 'oman an' chil'un is hittin' de weeds rat now, Col'l Milt."

"Get along, get along," hurried the Colonel, in good temper but with decision.

"Yes, suh, yes, suh, I'se gittin' uhlong. F'um de way you gwi' wuck me, Col'l, I mout jess as well been bawn a gal."

And Loob shuffled off down the southward fork of the road that led into the Reserve. The other negroes on the porch laughed loudly and hooted at Loob, asking him why he didn't come back.

At this noise, a dark, poorly dressed white man limped out of the door of the shack. He stood looking at the crowd.

"You niggers make less noise," he said harshly. "I kain't hardly hear what Miss Ham's a-sayin' in here."

The group on the platform quieted at once. The crippled man then observed the riders.

"Oh, is that you, Miltiades?" he said. "Well, I see you're settin' up to another gal sence Ponny's dead."

"Miss Crowninshield came down with me for a ride," answered the Colonel in a dignified tone.

"I hear you two are gwine ter git married," said the merchant.

Miltiades admitted the report was true.

"An' you old enough to be her daddy," added Mr. BeShears disapprovingly.

A very fat old woman came to the door with a round home-made splint basket on her elbow.

"Hello, Colonel Milt," she called in a cracked cheerful old voice. "Now look at that . . . ain't she the picture of her mammy made over again?"

"How's Mr. Ham, Aunt Polly?" inquired the Colonel.

"Oh, complainin', as usual. He's drinkin' sass'fras tea now to thin his blood for summer."

"Hope it thins out all right," said Miltiades, laughing.

"I tell Erasmus healthy is as healthy thinks," nodded the old woman. "You don't take nothin' for your blood in the spring, do you, Colonel Milt?"

"No, nothing at all."

"Well, Milt, that shore is a purty gal. I s'pose you figgered if you couldn't git the ol' hen her chicken'd do?" and old Mrs. Ham began cackling as if she were a hen herself.

Such chaffing made Miltiades uncomfortable before Sydna. He was afraid the old woman would embarrass the girl.

The Colonel introduced the two as a possible safety valve for old Aunt Polly's high spirits. Sydna said that she almost knew Mrs. Ham, her mother had spoken of her so often. At the girl's well bred voice and courtesy Aunt Polly became a little more considerate.

"By the way," she ejaculated, "I guess our quit-claim deed fixed you up all right, didn't it, Milt?"

"Fixed me up how?"

"Why, our deed to the Lacefield place that got lost before it ever got recorded in the courthouse."

"Did you make out a quit-claim deed?"

"We shore did, me an' Erasmus."

"Who did you make it to?" inquired the Colonel, with interest.

"Why—to Lucius Han'back. He said make it out to him so he could make you a clear title."

The Colonel pondered a moment.

"If you wanted me to have a clear title, why didn't you make it out to me?"

"Well, that lawyer of his'n said you got your lan' through the Handbacks, and our quit-claim would have to come through the Handbacks, too."

"What did Lucius pay you for it?"

"Why, nothin'. If we sold a track of lan' to a neighbor oncet, you know we ain't goin' to turn around and make him pay us fer it twicet. Now, of course, if it had of been a

Yankee we sold it to, and he'd 'a' lost his deed, why he wouldn't 'a' got it back a-tall, not fer love ner money."

And the old woman took her snuffbox out of her apron pocket, rolled her hickory bark brush in it, and scrubbed it positively against her teeth.

CHAPTER FIFTY-THREE

THE middle-aged man and the girl rode from BeShears' store to the ancient Lacefield manor. Irregular stretches of decaying rail fences bordered their way. Sassafras bushes, sumac, and elder stalks unfolded their greens to the flattery of the sun. Plums were in bloom, a white perfumed lace wound about crinkled black bushes. The whole thin, neglected plantation was touched here and there with accidental beauty.

Miltiades had ridden away from the store, thinking with some concern of the quit-claim deed Aunt Polly Ham had mentioned; but presently his thoughts drifted to the people who lived in the Reserve, a people as worn out and impoverished as the thin acres of the old barony itself.

Sydna, who had been riding along in silence, asked curiously:

"Was that BeShears Crossroads?"

"Sydna, don't you know where we are?"

"I thought it was, but I remembered it as a great big place, with huge show cases full of candy, and dolls hanging from the ceiling."

"Haven't you been back here since you were a child?"

"I don't believe I have. There was no reason why I should come back with Grandpa while he was alive. I thought it was a tremendous journey from Florence."

"Then you are really passing over the threshold of your new home," exclaimed the Colonel. "I think I ought to kiss you."

The girl looked at him.

"Do you want to kiss me, Colonel Milt?" she asked with a faint and dubious smile.

450

He maneuvered his horse closer to her.

"Why, Sydna, of course I do." He touched the small hand on her bridle and put his arm about her waist.

The girl flushed a trifle but said with composure:

"When I'm with you, Colonel Milt, I never think of kissing. It seems trivial, somehow. I just want to be near you, where I can look at you and hear your voice. . . ."

"You love me, don't you, Sydna?" asked the man, with concern.

"Why, Colonel Milt, I'm sure I love you. I feel as if you were about to crown me queen in some sad, romantic country . . . and I do hope I'll make you a good queen. . . ."

"Sydna," said Miltiades, with a sudden humility, "I am not worthy of a look, much less a kiss. . . ."

"Oh, Colonel Milt," she protested with a rush of compassion.

She leaned toward him from her horse. A thought went through Sydna of the war and the field of Shiloh. She saw again in her fancy the cyclorama of the battle which her mother had shown her when she was a small child. . . . Now she lifted her mouth as if to receive the eucharist.

From the roadside behind a rail fence and a curtain of briars came a sudden coughing. The lovers turned in their saddles. Then they saw it was Loober Snipes, whom the Colonel had sent home from the store.

Loober was far more disconcerted than the two he had disturbed. He stood bobbing uneasily with his felt hat in his hand.

" 'Scuse me, Col'l Milt! 'Scuse me, Miss Sydna! 'Scuse me! 'Scuse me!"

"We'll excuse you," said Miltiades. "What made you bob up like that?"

Loober became still more confused and apprehensive.

"Wuw-wuw-well, Col'l Milt, Ah—Ah bob up lak dat, tut-to tell you-all, Ah-Ah wouldn' have no ca'in's-on like dat, not . . . not rat heah . . . nohow."

"Just how does one of my niggers decide where I am to

salute my future wife?" inquired the Colonel with dangerous courtesy.

Loober perceived he had crossed a deadline. He could hardly stammer:

"Please, please 'scuse me, Mas' Milt, b-but Ah don' want h-him to git he eye on you-all."

"His eye?"

The Colonel glanced around to see who else was spectator.

"Y-yaas, suh . . . he eye . . . you-all sta'tin' out lak you-all is. 'My Lawd,' sez I to muhse'f, 'I gwi' stop de Col'l an' Miss Sydna if'n he skins me alive fuh muh trouble.' "

"Loober," asked the Colonel, frowning, "who in the devil are you talking about?"

"Why, Col'l . . . rat in dat fiel' . . . jess inside dat fence is wha' he stood. He may be stan'in' tha yit. . . ." Loober stared into the empty field. "I don' know. When we foun' he, we tuk whut fell down, it an' he gun, an' haul 'em off. But whut di'n' fall down but still kep' a-stan'in' tha, I guess is stan'in' tha yit."

Loober shook his head portentously and began walking away from the sinister spot.

"Ah sho' God woul'na stop heah, Col'l, you an' Miss Sydna, Ah sho' God woul'na."

With the passing of Loober, Sydna and Miltiades rode on silently without the kiss. The girl continually looked at the briars and weeds and cockleburs on her side of the road to keep Miltiades from seeing that she was crying.

She was weeping partly from shock that her betrothed should have paused on the very spot where J. Handback had killed himself; but mainly she wept out of pity for Miltiades, to have the suicide flung at him like that, the first time he had ever asked her for a kiss.

And the Colonel was so blameless through it all. Luck, fate, chance, were persistently against him and through no fault of his own.

He had been robbed. When he found opportunity to

retake his money, all Florence had ostracized him. He had occupied the first place during the Reconstruction, but later everyone had dropped and forgotten him. And then even Sydna's own father and mother had betrayed him. . . .

But this invincible man went on. No matter what happened, he went forward without complaint or reproach. An almost religious emotion welled up in Sydna. She prayed that she might have the greatness of soul to be a worthy wife to so noble a man.

In the midst of her meditation the Colonel pointed out over a field and said in a surprised tone:

"Sydna—look at that!"

The girl left off her hero worship, but saw nothing.

"What is it, Colonel Milt?" she asked with the tenderness of her thoughts in her voice.

"Why, the cotton," said the Colonel in increasing surprise; "that's the way cotton grew before the war!"

Sydna looked again and observed a glimmer of green over the level brown field. It was the first leaflets of some crop breaking through the soil.

"I'm afraid I'm stupid . . . but what is there to be surprised at?"

"Why, the stand, the color. They are excellent. If that cotton keeps on the way it has started, it will mean a bale or a bale and a fifth an acre."

"Is that lots?"

"For the last ten years this land has been running from three quarters to half a bale."

"Maybe I've brought you good luck?" smiled Sydna.

"Of course you have . . . spiritual luck. Then I hired some of the old Vaiden negroes on this place—that's going to be commercial luck."

"Oh, I hope it will be."

"It will. I already feel as if they were part of the place since I own it. Look yonder how Toussaint has been painting things."

"Toussaint . . ." repeated Sydna curiously, "where do they get such names?"

"Make 'em up, I suppose. That's the nigger in 'em, to make absurd names." He turned to a more serious theme. "I'm going to employ Gracie and her boy as regular tenants. They are the very ones to keep everything in shape for us to come out in the summer. They'll take a pride in it. They're Vaiden niggers."

From where they were Sydna could see the manor, a gaunt, solitary pile between the blue sky and the brown fields.

The girl looked at it for several seconds.

"Is that the manor?" she asked in a shocked voice.

"That's it."

"Doesn't it look deserted?"

"It needs trees. When the Yankees fired the place they killed most of the silver poplars . . . the niggers chopped down the rest—for firewood, because they were close by."

"Isn't that a shame!"

"Our troubles are over on that score now. We've got Vaiden niggers with us. I'll put the manor in condition, and they'll keep it that way."

Sydna sat shaking her head.

"I don't see how we can ever get things like they were."

"Why, trees will grow again, paint will brighten the houses; it seems that fertilizer will enrich the fields. . . ."

"But the people; who will ever come out on week-ends to dance and fox-hunt? And will there ever be an orator again to make a speech on our lawn?"

Miltiades, who had seen the old life, thought it might be renewed, but Sydna, to whom it was a kind of fairy tale, was hopeless of recapturing the mood of a vanished society in a single old manor house, crumbling and about to fall.

As the girl looked she caught sight of figures on the opposite side of the field. She drew Miltiades' attention to the inconspicuous workers.

"Hoeing, I imagine," said Miltiades. "While the other

niggers are loafing at the store, these Vaiden niggers are at work."

"I don't think they are hoeing . . . one of them is pushing something."

"What is there for them to push?" queried the Colonel, puzzled.

"Looks like a wheelbarrow."

The Colonel could not make out the wheelbarrow.

"I can't imagine what they're doing with a wheelbarrow."

By common consent they moved their horses down the road to the end of the rows on which the negroes worked. The field hands at their task came slowly toward the horses. Presently the Colonel recognized the nearest woman. He was a little surprised, and called across the field that Gracie should not be working like that. She had been one of the house niggers on the old place when she belonged to his father, and it was no time for her to start making a field hand now.

The quadroon straightened and began fanning herself with an old straw hat which she wore to save her complexion.

"Toussaint was in a press," she called back in her soft voice. "I thought I would help him out."

"If you help a farmer when he's in a press," warned Miltiades good-naturedly, "you'll help him every day in the year."

Gracie was walking toward them to talk, after the fashion of a hostess receiving guests.

"I'd really rather work here with Toussaint and Lucy, than—than to stay by myself in the manor," hesitated the quadroon. "How are you, Miss Sydna?"

"Very well, Gracie, and how are you? You don't look very well."

"I'm not, Miss Sydna," she said, lowering her voice, "Toussaint marrying like he did."

"People marry, Gracie," smiled the girl.

"So I've heard," agreed Gracie, lifting her eyebrows and

returning the white girl's smile with delicate feminine humor. But she immediately became serious and drew a long breath at the dream in her heart for Toussaint, which had died. "Not that I'm saying a word against Lucy. She's a mighty good girl. I'll call her over to talk to you."

Gracie leaned against the fence, and both the white persons began talking to her at once. The quadroon answered both with the verbal facility of her race, and between sentences called Lucy to come there.

After the Southern fashion, when white employers find negroes at work they stop them and talk to them; when they find them idle they put them to work.

Miltiades began explaining what he wanted done about the manor. He wanted it restored and kept in ship-shape all the time. It would be something permanent for Gracie and Toussaint and Toussaint's wife Lucy.

In her heart Gracie did not want this. The last shocking tragedy had made the plantation hideous for her. However, she took an approving stand on the Colonel's idea. She said Lucy and Toussaint were bent on staying here, and she knew the Colonel's plans would suit them exactly. She called again to Lucy that the Colonel wanted to see her.

"Who's that nigger on the other side of the field?" inquired Miltiades.

"Oh, that's Lump Mowbray. When he saw you-all he said he believed he would work on the far side of the field. I told him not to bother, you wouldn't run him off."

"Why, no, and what good would it do if I did? He'd be back on the place the minute I turned my back."

"He helps Toussaint in a pinch," defended Gracie casually.

"The Colonel and I didn't understand what you folks were doing with a wheelbarrow," questioned Sydna.

"Oh, sprinkling fertilizer," said Gracie.

"Is that it?" said Miltiades. "I believe that's going to turn out fine. It's got a good stand."

"That was Lucy's idyah," said Gracie.

"What did she know about it?"

"She read it in a magazine. She subscribed for a farm magazine."

"Imagine such a thing!" ejaculated Miltiades, looking now at Lucy, who was approaching the group.

Toussaint's wife was of a darker color than either Gracie or her son. As she came closer, Sydna suspected from the heaviness of her breasts that Lucy already was with child.

The young tan-colored woman came to the fence armed oddly, with a long-handled iron spoon with which she had been dropping the powder on the side of the cotton rows. Gracie said by way of introduction:

"Miss Sydna and Colonel Milt, this is Lucy."

Lucy said she was glad to meet them in a very simple tone without anything servile in it.

"I understand you are the cause of this flourishing cotton," complimented Miltiades, in a pleased voice.

Lucy repeated what Gracie already had told about reading of fertilizer in a magazine.

"Well, by George," said Miltiades, "a lot of folks are against educating negroes. I wish they could see this."

Lucy hesitated a moment and then said:

"Some people don't want to treat the colored people right and that's why they don't want them educated."

"Not every time," denied Miltiades. "I must admit, I've had the same notion myself. I was afraid if you educated a negro he wouldn't work, and I'll bet you the most of 'em wouldn't, either. There's a lot of difference between the ordinary black riff-raff and the Vaiden negroes."

"It's nice for us to feel that we are going to be treated well," said Lucy, alluding to the Colonel's reputation for honesty among the black people.

The tan girl's English subtly amused the Colonel. It seemed affected because it was grammatical. He came back to the point in which he was interested.

"I'm glad you and Toussaint are bright, educated negroes. I was just telling Gracie that I intend to restore the manor, and I want you and Toussaint to keep it in order for me and Sydna while we are in Florence."

Lucy looked at the white man quickly.

"You mean you and Miss Sydna will live in the manor?"

"That's my plan. I will build houses for you and Gracie and Toussaint."

Lucy became thoughtful.

"We hadn't thought of doing domestic work, we intended just to run the farm."

"Couldn't you do both?"

"I wouldn't want to take the time to run two houses," demurred Lucy, "and one of them such a big one."

"But, Lucy," protested Gracie, "I thought you and Toussaint were keen to get here in the manor and keep house."

"But don't you see, Mother Vaiden," said Lucy earnestly, "Toussaint and I don't want to go into domestic service. . . . We just prefer not to . . . that's all."

This was perhaps one of the most remarkable sentences Miltiades had ever heard from a negro. It suggested there was a plane of life outside of personal service to white persons which negroes might occupy. It suggested Toussaint and Lucy settling down to a social independence quite like that of any well-to-do white family. The tan girl's social attitude was like her speech, irreproachable and unnatural, highly affected and utterly absurd. She annoyed the Colonel with her uppishness.

Toussaint himself was coming down the cotton rows, pushing a wheelbarrow. Miltiades called out a compliment to the cotton as he had done to the other negroes. The octoroon put down the handles of his barrow and agreed that it was pretty good cotton.

"Best I've seen on the place for twenty years," praised the Colonel.

"This is the first crop I ever saw here," said the white negro, looking around the field.

"I imagine Lump Mowbray must have given you advice," speculated Miltiades.

The blond negro gave a brief laugh.

"He objected to everything Lucy and me did. He can prove by the Bible that it's a sin to use fertilizer."

The whole group began laughing at Lump.

"What are you pushing fertilizer around in a wheel-barrow for, Toussaint?" inquired the Colonel. "Why don't you use your wagon?"

The octoroon looked at his barrow and then at the Colonel. Lucy the tan girl answered for him:

"Why, he never could get the wagon away from Cady," she said.

"Cady!"

"Yes, sir."

"Toussaint, didn't I tell you to go get it?" asked the Colonel in a harder voice.

"I asked him for it, but he broke out to cussin' and said it was his, and I didn't want to have another row with him," explained the octoroon impassively.

Until that moment Sydna almost had the impression that she was talking to a white group. Now she suddenly felt their position and its disadvantage.

The Colonel was irritated.

"Now, look here, Toussaint, when I tell you to do a thing, you do it."

"But, Colonel, what if I get into trouble?" protested the white negro.

"Why, thunder! I'll get you out!" cried Miltiades. "Do you think I'd see one of my niggers imposed on by riff-raff like the Cadys?"

"Well, that's why I didn't do anything," explained Toussaint lamely; "I didn't want to make him any worse than he is."

"Now, look here," ordered Miltiades crisply, "Alex Cady and his ilk don't tell me when I can use my own wagon. Come ahead. You catch out your mules, and we'll go over to Cady's and get that wagon."

Immediately all the women, both colored and white, began to object.

"Honey, I wouldn't go over there myself!" pressed Sydna apprehensively.

"I don't want Toussaint to have anything to do with him," cried Gracie, "he's a mean man!"

"I think we'd better send an officer," said Lucy.

"The devil and Tom Walker!" cried Miltiades. "He's got my wagon! Toussaint, if you're not afraid to go with me, get your mules and come along!"

"I'm not afraid of anything," said the white negro somberly. "I'll bring my mules, but I won't squabble with him."

"I'll do the squabbling for both of us," promised the Colonel.

And the group moved out of the field toward the manor.

CHAPTER FIFTY-FOUR

THE only person who had the information to understand the full drama of the situation was Gracie: Colonel Miltiades Vaiden and his white negro son riding away with a horse and two mules to maintain the octoroon's property rights in a wagon. Gracie knew of the relationship, but fear at what would happen prevented the quadroon from appreciating the brackish irony.

The cream-colored woman stood in the weed-choked gate of the manor, beside Sydna, the Colonel's betrothed, and watched her son and the father of her son disappear together down the road.

Miltiades himself rode along the gully-washed lane with anger and a dignified contempt for the poor white trash he was about to visit.

Toussaint rode behind him on the harnessed mules. The young husband of Lucy meant to take no part whatever in the row between two white men. To do so would have been a kind of insanity. If he had hurt Cady he would have been jailed; if Cady had killed him nothing would have been done about it.

To the Colonel, Toussaint's backwardness was a cowardice which he attributed to all members of the negro race. They were all cowards; even to the negroes of the old Vaiden plantation—a set of rabbits.

"How long has he had that wagon?" asked Miltiades, without looking around.

"Ever since I came to you about it before Christmas . . . he claims it's his'n."

"Well, I be damned!" ejaculated the Colonel, since Sydna no longer was in hearing.

461

Cady's shack was only half a mile up the road toward BeShears' store. They came in sight of it presently, set back in a little field with a lane leading to it. In the field sprouted a hit-and-miss stand of cotton with a growth of weed already threatening to crowd it out. At the far end of the field Miltiades saw the Cady women at work.

As the Colonel turned up the lane a small figure came walking diagonally across the field to meet him. As horsemen and walker drew near each other, Miltiades made out the sharp features of Cady. A little later the white tenant called out in apparent good spirits:

"Hey-oh, Colonel, glad to see ye. Light an' rest yore saddle."

"I'm glad to see you," returned the Colonel. "A good deal of your cotton failed to come up, didn't it, Cady?"

"I didn't figger it would do much," said Cady, "I didn't git furnished no fertilize' like some of the tenants did."

"You didn't ask for it," said Miltiades.

"Well, I figger to take whut you furnish me and not go baggin' fer no fool fixin's," said Cady drily.

This brought the diplomatic overtures of the interview to a close.

"Cady," said the Colonel in a commonplace tone, "I would like for Toussaint here to use that wagon I bought from you."

The hillman put his hands on the fence.

"I had a idee you didn't bring them two mules over to haul me no load of fertilize'," he said drily.

"No, we just came over for the wagon."

"Well, Colonel," dragged out the hillman with a metallic sound entering his nasal voice, "you never did ralely pay me fer that waggin, did ye?"

"Why, I paid you eleven dollars and a possum dog," snapped the Colonel sharply.

"Did je deliver me the dawg?"

"No, but Gibeon Dalrymple did."

"Did Gibeon ever give you my receipt fer the dawg?"

"Look here," said the Colonel, "I didn't come over here to argue a lawsuit. I came to get my wagon. Of course I have a receipt for the dog. Not from Gibeon but from you. I put the dog in the receipt you signed for the eleven dollars."

A sharp change came in Cady's satisfaction.

"But you didn't deliver me no dawg when you handed me the money!"

"No, but I delivered you an order on Gibeon for the dog." Cady swung his head from side to side.

"Now, by God, you kain't steal me out like you done ol' man Han'back!" cried the hillman. "I God, Milt Vaiden, you're up agin one of the blue hen's chickens this time!"

Mention of Handback sent a warmth of anger over the Colonel. He looked around. The wagon in question stood in front of Cady's shack with one of its wheels and a part of its frame still a dirty red.

"I've no time to wait on a damned fool," snapped the Colonel. "Toussaint, hitch your mules to that wagon."

"Toussaint!" whipped out Cady, "you damned yeller son of a bitch, lay a hand on that waggin and I'll blow you into Kingdom Come!" With that he turned and went running toward his cabin. As he ran he glanced back over his shoulder to see if Miltiades was drawing a pistol.

Full wrath filled the Colonel.

"You shoot anybody!" he derided. "You haven't got the guts to shoot a fattening hog! Toussaint, get off that mule!"

The octoroon swung down and stood beside his harnessed animals.

"Now, stand out of the way, I'll hitch 'em up myself!"

"He's li'ble to shoot you," warned Toussaint in a low tone.

"A blow-hard hasn't got the guts to shoot anything!" rapped out the Colonel.

He took the lines from Toussaint and started jingling toward the wagon.

Cady disappeared in the hut. From the field came the high calling of women's voices:

"Pappy! Alex! Pappy, what air you-all doin' down thar?"

The Colonel swung one of the mules on one side of the tongue and began deliberately hooking the traces to the singletrees.

In the midst of his work the cabin door opened and Cady stood in it with a preternaturally long-barreled shotgun.

"Colonel," he said in a shaky voice, "unhook them mules, or I'll put a load of buckshot through 'em!"

"Through the mules!"

"That's my word, Colonel. Them mules kain't haul my waggin away frum my own gate an' me with a gun to stop 'em! I'm in my rights, Colonel," he added through his nose. "I got possession o' that there waggin!"

The Colonel stopped his hitching and looked at Cady. The little man had his long gun at attention, ready to aim and fire. And he would do it. He would never have had the courage to fire at the Colonel himself, but he would shoot a mule.

Miltiades was infuriated. To have such a spindling rat of a man hold his wagon illegally.

"God damn you, Cady! I'll send the sheriff after this wagon tomorrow, and I'll put you off my land! You know damn well I bought and paid for this wagon! I have your receipt."

"Now, Colonel," whanged the hillman insolently, "jest cool off, now. You're not dealin' with ol' man Han'back. If one or t'other of us is got to kill hisse'f on account o' yore thievishness, hit a-goin' to be you, Colonel, 'tain't goin' to be me!"

CHAPTER FIFTY-FIVE

THE Colonel was thoroughly angry and disgusted at the outcome of his visit to Alex Cady. The ex-leader of the Ku Klux had the passion of all commanders of men never to allow himself to be made ridiculous, and his scene with his dried-up little tenant had ended ridiculously. The Colonel had been forced to unhitch his mules and lead them away.

When he and Toussaint were in the Reserve road again they mounted their animals and rode back to the manor. The Colonel assured Toussaint that Sheriff Mayhew would deliver the wagon to him on the following day, and then he added in disgust:

"That's what I should have done at the start."

The white negro said nothing but rode the jingling mules just behind the Colonel.

At the manor the two colored women and the white girl were waiting anxiously the return of the men. Lucy, the tan girl, was stationed far down the road. When she saw them coming she waved a white cloth as a signal to the other women that the men were safe.

When Miltiades and Toussaint came up with her she said in the greatest perturbation:

"Oh, we thought one of you was shot! We heard a gun fire!"

"No," said Miltiades glumly; "it was somebody hunting, I suppose."

Toussaint dismounted and walked beside Lucy.

"Are you still shaky, Lucy?" he asked anxiously.

"No-o . . . no, I'm all right now."

Toussaint put a hand on her arm. He evidently would

have put his arm around her and comforted her fright if it
had not been for the Colonel.

Miltiades found Sydna in the greatest disturbance. She
began crying as the Colonel rode up.

"We thought one of you was killed," she wept. "We heard
a gun in that direction, and we knew you didn't have one."

All of the women had been sickened with fright. Sydna
was so shaken the Colonel was afraid she could not ride
her horse. He wanted to go over to the Hams' and borrow
their old buggy, but Sydna would not let him out of her
sight again. The Colonel kept repeating soothingly:

"There wasn't any danger at all. . . . The little rat
threatened to shoot my mules. Toussaint, I'll have Sheriff
Mayhew deliver that wagon in the morning."

"Colonel Milt," ventured Gracie, "I don't believe it's a
good idyah to bother that white man any more. He doesn't
care what he does."

"But, Gracie, he can't keep a wagon after I pay for it!"

"He sure will be mad. . . . He'll be madder than he
ever was at us, because he knows you're fixing to give the
wagon to us."

"What will he be angry at you-all for? I can roll that
wagon into a creek and let it rot if I want to."

The whole group went on back into the manor.

"He'll be mad at us," repeated Gracie with certainty.

The tan-colored girl made coffee and gave it to Sydna,
after which the white girl felt calm enough to start back to
Florence. The Colonel assisted her to mount on the moulder-
ing block in the weed-grown yard. It reminded him of the
innumerable times he had handed Drusilla up at that same
block. In those days such an ignominious thing as a difficulty with a worker on the plantation would have been
impossible. Around the horse block, the Colonel's fancy
reconstructed the old smooth lawn and the glinting leaves
of the silver poplars, the pleasant, obsequious, and obedient
slaves. . . . Miltiades compared that liberal life with the

desolation about him, and the belligerent and dishonest white family now on his estate.

"Sydna," he said, deeply moved, patting her hand, "you are the only bit of the old South left. You are an angel, remaining on earth to remind us there once was an Eden."

Sydna pressed his fingers convulsively, and then, on an impulse, leaned down and kissed him.

As the two rode away Miltiades' conversation veered to casual topics to wean Sydna's thoughts from her fright.

"Lucy is a very odd girl, isn't she?"

"Doesn't she talk good English?"

"Oh, well, that's affected."

"But, Colonel," said Sydna thoughtfully, "if any girl tries to improve her speech, she is bound to be affected for a while."

"What I don't understand is Lucy not wanting to enter domestic service. What else is there for a nigger woman to do?"

"They are very queer darkies," agreed Sydna, "except Gracie."

"Toussaint and Lucy are young. They are these new uncomfortable colored people who are springing up in the place of the good old-fashioned nigger."

Back at the manor the same theme was handled in a different set of words. Gracie was saying:

"Lucy, I couldn't imagine what you meant, telling Colonel Milt you didn't want to run the manor for him and Miss Sydna."

"I explained it to him."

"Yes, but if you're going to stay here, why not get a good position?"

"Well, first," said Lucy, "I want me and Toussaint to lead our own sort of lives. I don't want to be too close to white folks."

"Too close to white folks . . . why, everything we get is from white folks."

"We don't get our hair, or our color, or our voices."

"M-m . . . we get 'em changed a good deal," observed Gracie obscurely. "But why do you want to stay here at all if you don't want to be caretaker of the manor?"

"Because I would like for the colored people in the Reserve to see that a dark woman can live and talk and act with correctness and fineness without being associated with the whites all the time."

"Lucy," said the quadroon uneasily, "I don't like the way you look at things. You take a kind of stand against white people. Toussaint thinks everything you do is just right. I hope you'll never get him into any trouble."

"The reason I ever loved him is because he didn't bow his head to anybody."

"The reason you loved him," said Gracie with an undertone of bitterness, "is because he is a white man, and you know it."

The mother turned away, filled with anger and frustration at her daughter-in-law. It filled Gracie with despair to know that Toussaint kissed and fondled Lucy . . . her white son, who might have married a white girl. . . .

The bitterness of her disappointment overwhelmed Gracie. If she had known, if only she had known of Toussaint's marriage on Christmas Day, she would have gone away with Mr. Handback.

The dead man, now that he was lost, had gained complete possession of the quadroon's imagination. He had offered to live with her openly as man and wife. That was as honorable an offer as Gracie had ever had. The merchant had walked out of the dining room maddened when he learned that she had betrayed him. But, even then, if she had said she would go with him, she believed he would have taken her back.

And when she confessed that she had used him treacherously, he had not killed her . . . he had killed himself.

The cream-colored woman turned away from the kitchen and the antagonizing ambition of her daughter-in-law. She entered the great desolate dining room of the manor.

At a table by the window, with its glass and greased paper

panes, sat a figure wearing a new cheap hunting coat. It was a heavy figure with its back turned toward Gracie.

The quadroon looked at it in silence for upward of half a minute. She was not frightened. She had seen it several times before. But her heart began beating. She said aloud, in a low tone:

"I'm sorry for what I did, Mr. Handback. . . . I loved you, Mr. Handback."

In a few seconds more the figure melted away.

It was the first time the word "love" had ever been used between them. Gracie could say that to the dead.

CHAPTER FIFTY-SIX

Night spread her concealing robes over the wounds of the ancient manor.

To Gracie, standing at the gate, the last illumination in the west seemed to be a doorway leading into vast chambers of light wherein Mr. Handback and all the innumerable dead awaited the rolling up of the scroll of Time. That was their home. Sometimes they came back to earth to warn or comfort the living, but their domain was the towers of sunrise and the pavilions of the evening.

She pondered why he had kept his face turned from her. And she remembered a passage in the Bible, quoted by Lump, how God himself, when He was displeased with a people, turned His face from them.

Well, she had done enough against Mr. Handback . . . she had done more than enough against him. She began weeping silently, her face impassive, her tears gathering tiny specks of the final light.

A querulous voice said reproachfully:

"You stan' heah thinkin' 'bout some man, Gracie. You gittin' too ol' fuh dat, Gracie. De Lawd done tuk His blessin's away f'um you. An' desiah shall fail, an' de days shall be a bu'den . . . 'at's whut He say, Gracie . . . desiah shall fail."

The old negro touched Gracie's arm with the uncertainty of a man endlessly repulsed.

"Oh, Lump," said the woman, in patient distaste, and moved a little away from him.

The gray negro remained where he was with an old man's compensating ability to enjoy a woman's beauty without touching her. To the old preacher with his advancing age,

Gracie's curves and voluptuousness had changed subtly from firebrands to an entranced shining. He would sit and watch her with motionless eyes, or simply stand near her like this in the darkness, and something about her, her aura, the emanation of her soul, filled him with a profound content.

But Lump was so constructed that if anything made him happy, he did what he could to make it unhappy. Tonight he had a little better whip than usual to increase his enjoyment of Gracie's distress.

"Whut dat Alex Cady go'n' do to us tomah when She'f Mayhew come an' go go'n' be a Gawd's plenty."

"He can't do anything to Toussaint," defended Gracie. "Toussaint didn't do anything to him. The Colonel made him ride the mules down there."

"Huh, if a white man di'n' fly into uh niggah tull he done somep'n to him, all us niggahs be settin' in easy chai's."

Gracie drew a long breath.

"I shouldn't be a-tall supprise' if'n dat Alex Cady di'n' come roun' dis ve'y night an' try some sawt o' flapdoodles wid us."

"What do you suppose he'll try?" asked the quadroon in alarm.

"Oh, I dunno . . . somep'n . . . somep'n. . . ."

The woman peered down the dark road in the direction of Cady's shack.

"Lucy say suppah is ready," added Lump.

"I certainly am not hungry," said Gracie, turning mechanically into the manor with the old negro following her.

The colored Vaidens ate in the old Lacefield kitchen. There was a table in the large dining room, but it had never been used since Gracie, out of whim, had laid her Christmas dinner upon it and Mr. Handback had come and eaten it.

Two oil lamps illuminated the kitchen, a glass goblet-shaped lamp and a bracket lamp against the wall. The two seemed to make a very clear bright light, although they left the greater part of the kitchen in semi-darkness.

Lucy and Toussaint were already seated, and this sight always gave Gracie a little pang of frustration at the marriage her son had contracted. He had fallen back that much toward the negroes. She herself almost had climbed away from the race that barely creamed her skin and tinted her finger nails and curled her hair. Toussaint was white. At the table Lucy was saying:

"You didn't say anything to him, did you?"

"No, I just stood there when the Colonel left me."

"What he's really angry about is not the wagon at all," said Lucy, "it's the manor."

"When you and Mother Vaiden first moved in here, Mrs. Cady used to come around to Luke Anders and tell my mother it was a shame for a colored family to live in the manor. That's why Mr. Cady chopped the posts out of your stall."

"De Lawd sen' de plague on de 'Gyptians cause dey di'n' do right," reminded Lump solemnly.

"What can we do about it?" asked Lucy of Toussaint.

"De Lawd spa'ed de chillun of Isr'el when dey painted dey do's wid blood."

"What do you mean by that, Lump?" demanded Gracie sharply.

"Why, I don' mean anything by dat 'cep'n' I'se tellin' you whut's in de Bible."

"You don't mean we ought to do something to Alex Cady?" questioned the quadroon in another tone. "But Toussaint would have more sense than to do anything like that."

"All I say is de 'Gyptians stain' dey do's wid blood."

"Toussaint certainly has a right to defend himself if Alex Cady starts to do anything to him," said Lucy.

The old negro preacher paused in his eating to listen to this and then changed sides completely.

"Got a right . . . whut you mean by got a right?"

"Why, a legal right to protect himself . . . that's something everybody has."

"Yeh . . . legal right . . . niggahs ain't had no legal right in dis county sence dat ol' Yankee Judge Britton got run out o' de Flaunts co'thouse."

"If enough of us tried to take up for ourselves in a legal way, the white people would finally notice us."

"Yeh . . ." drawled Lump; "an' when de white folks fin'ly notice us, de black folks come lay us away."

The tan girl breathed more quickly, lifting her swelling breasts in the lamplight. Gracie thought silently:

"Toussaint could have been out of all this, now he's back where he'll never get out at all."

They finished supper. Lucy took a bucket and started for the well. Gracie deserted her dish washing and followed her. She overtook the young wife at the well curb. The older woman stood for a moment listening to the creaking pulley and trying to restrain her impulse to scold. At last she succeeded in remonstrating in a reasonable voice.

"Lucy, you oughtn't to be putting notions like that in Toussaint's head. He's been proud all his life. I've had trouble keeping him civil and well spoken to white folks. You oughtn't to hold up for lawsuits and things. He's got to get along with white folks somehow or other."

"We would do very well with white folks if it weren't for these miserable crackers!" declared the tan girl passionately.

"Yes, but they're here, and they're going to stay here," pointed out Gracie.

"You don't have to tell me that," said Lucy in a tired voice. "Do you know why Alex Cady had a fight with Mr. Luke Anders?"

"No-o," dragged out the quadroon, who now knew why.

"Because I wouldn't have anything to do with him. He kept after me and after me. Finally he cursed me for being a whoring negro school teacher and quit." The girl's voice shook at the remembered insult.

"You've never told Toussaint?" questioned the quadroon in anxiety.

"No, I never did."

"Well, for God's sake, don't, Lucy. If Cady ever crossed Toussaint again there'd be trouble."

"In such a case, don't you know the law would defend Toussaint?" pressed the daughter-in-law earnestly.

"Lucy, I don't know anything about the law, and I don't ever want to. White people made the law to use for white people."

"Miss Gracie," said Lucy solemnly, "if our race ever gets a better position, we educated negroes have got to lift it up and make it respected. The president of our school said that on graduation day. He said black people and white people stood equal before the law."

"Was he a negro?" asked Gracie.

"No—he was a white man."

"Was he a Southern white man?"

"No-o-o . . . Dr. Bennett came from the North."

The way Lucy called Dr. Bennett's name reminded Gracie of Governor Beekman, who had kept her in Montgomery. A touch of jealousy for Toussaint moved the quadroon as she wondered how deeply and in what manner Lucy had cared for her Northern teacher. Gracie wondered if Toussaint was to Lucy what Mr. Handback, for six years, had been to her. The mother magnified the possibilities and tortured herself through the mere mention by Lucy of her teacher's name.

A faint light northward across the fields interrupted Gracie's absurd and harassed imaginings. The girl paused in filling the buckets,

"That's a fire," she announced.

"Wonder where it is?"

"It's in the direction of Mother's place," said Lucy apprehensively.

The women stood watching the diffused light when tongues of flame flickered into view much closer than they had expected them to be. Lucy gave a breath of relief.

"It's in the field," she said. "Somebody must be burning the old corn stalks or something like that . . . I smell it."

The girl stooped to pour the water with an easy mind. As she did so, the flames suddenly increased. They stood up in the night and illuminated the under side of a heavy pall of smoke that mounted upward. The water girl gave a sudden scream.

"Mother Vaiden!" she cried. "It's the schoolhouse. . . . Run tell Toussaint!"

She left buckets, water, and everything on the curb and went running and stumbling through the darkness to the kitchen door, screaming:

"Toussaint! Toussaint! The schoolhouse is burning down! Oh, Toussaint, you and Uncle Lump, the schoolhouse is on fire!"

Out of the kitchen door came the young man and the old one, shouting:

"What is it? What's the matter?"

By this time the manor and its grounds were bathed in a dull light from the pyre. Toussaint ran into the kitchen, snatched up an armful of buckets, and rushed out again. He gave buckets to everyone. All the colored Vaidens set out down the road to save the negro schoolhouse.

As they hurried along with buckets jingling, the flames mounted higher. Lucy cried out:

"Oh, Toussaint, my books are in there! Run and try to get my books. Maybe the roof's burning and you can get in and out."

Toussaint drew away at a faster speed when the runners heard women's voices calling from the field:

"Toussaint! Lucy! Gracie! Is that you-all? Wait! Stop! For God's sake, you-all stop!"

Lump Mowbray and the two colored women halted at this desperate summons. Then in the light they saw two women running toward them through the field.

"Pappy's down there with his shotgun," they screamed, waving their arms. "He says he's a-goin' to shoot any nig-

ger that comes to that far! Fer God's sake, don't go nigh
hit!"

Slatie Cady and her daughter Mamie reached the fence
and stood exhausted, holding to the rails.

Immediately the negroes in the road began screaming:
"Toussaint! Toussaint! Come back! Stop! Oh, Lump,
run tell Toussaint he'll get shot!"

But Lump was already spent. He shouted, "Toussaint!
Toussaint!" and went hobbling after the young man.

Lucy started to run, but Gracie caught her.

"Don't! You'll kill yourself!"

And she began running desperately herself with the slowness of a middle-aged woman.

"Toussaint! Toussaint!" and all her breath was gone.

She came down to a walk with legs so weak and trembling
she could hardly move at all. She could see the fire plainly.
The thatched roof was a bright flaming cap upheld by four
burning posts. The whole field was lighted with a clear
yellow-red light. Gracie peered for Toussaint but saw nobody.

Suddenly she knew that he already had been shot. He was
lying somewhere in the firelit field.

She tried to run again, but stumbled. Just then a figure
quite near her at the fence hurried to her out of the shadow
of some blackberry bushes.

"Why, Mother!" it cried. "What have you run like that
for? There's no use getting any closer. Everything's burned
up."

CHAPTER FIFTY-SEVEN

A GOOD deal of mystery eventually collected around the burning of the negro schoolhouse. On the actual night of the fire it was not at all mysterious, because the mystery had not collected as yet.

Slatie and Mamie Cady told a very connected if almost hysterical tale of how the fire originated. Alex, they said, had got so mad because Colonel Vaiden meant to take his wagon back that he grabbed up his gun and swore he'd go out and kill ever' damn Vaiden nigger he could see through the windows.

Neither of the Cady women had the slightest doubt that he would do this, and Mamie, the daughter, grabbed his gun and tried to keep it.

This added to Alex's wrath. He swore that Mamie had been slipping out to that nigger schoolhouse trying to learn a lot of rot from Lucy, and he'd put a stop to that. By God, he'd burn down the schoolhouse and shoot ever' damn nigger, big or little, that come to look at the fire. He then wrenched the gun loose from Mamie and dashed out into the night.

Thereupon the Cady women had set out running across the fields to warn the Vaiden negroes to stay away.

That was the explanation the Cady women gave when they stood in the Reserve road with the negroes and watched the last of the flames.

Indeed, the two white women were so frightened they were afraid to go home and asked Gracie to let them stay that night in the manor. They reasoned that Sheriff Mayhew would come in the morning to get the wagon. They would go to their home with the sheriff. Then Alex would get so mad at Mayhew that he would forget them and everything would be all right. Alex, they said, was a good-natured man at heart, until somebody rubbed him the wrong way.

The Vaiden negroes did take the white women to the manor, and put them up in what they called "Miss Drusilla's room." It was a large front room on the left-hand side of the manor, and it belonged to Miss Drusilla Crowninshield, the negroes said, when she had lived at home. The implication being here, that since Drusilla had moved into Florence twenty years before, she had never been at home.

Anyway, the Cadys had stayed in Miss Drusilla's room. Next morning, when Sheriff Mayhew came, Toussaint harnessed up the mules, allowed the two Cady women to ride them, then Toussaint and the sheriff and the Cady women had set out to reclaim the Colonel's wagon.

Sheriff Mayhew, who had been apprised by the whole household of Cady's threats of murder and actual arson, went over with pistol in hand and deputized Toussaint to carry his gun.

"Toussaint, if I yell," Mayhew had directed, "you shoot the damned dried-up little devil, and don't stop to ast me why, nigger. . . . You shoot!"

Toussaint said he wasn't afraid of anybody, and the quartet had started for the Cady cabin.

When they reached the house, the sheriff with his pistol, Toussaint with his gun, ready to shoot without inquiry into the necessity or feasibility of shooting, Cady met them as smiling as a basket of chips.

He asked them wouldn't they light and come in and set awhile . . . specially his women folks.

Sheriff Mayhew had answered briefly that they had come for Colonel Milt Vaiden's wagon.

"It's right out there in the barn lot," said Alex. "Jess walk out an' he'p yorese'ves, gentlemen . . . an' ladies. I thought hit was my waggin, but if the Colonel says it's his'n, it mus' be his'n. Bekase when he thought ol' man Han'-

back's cotton was his'n, why, I God, it ralely did turn out to be his'n."

Here Alex burst into loud laughter as he entered the barn lot with the officer and Toussaint. He made a generous gesture.

"Jess he'p yorese'ves, gentlemen," he invited cordially. "Don't stan' back on my account."

The wagon lay on the ground, chopped all to pieces. Not a wheel was whole. Even the hubs were split and their thimbles broken.

Sheriff Mayhew said:

"Alex Cady, you're the god damnedest white man I ever heard of in all my life."

"I wonder if I can git these ladies to visit my cabin," said Alex, "after they've been enjoyin' the high society of educated niggers in a mansion?"

The two Cady women crossed the lane and went into the cabin. Toussaint and the sheriff rode back to the Reserve road again. When they reached the end of the lane, they heard Mamie Cady shrieking and Slatie her mother screaming:

"Stop! Stop, Alex, stop! You'll kill her!"

And Alex yelling out:

"God damn it, that's what I aim to do!"

Now, the above is almost a verbatim transcript of the evidence given by the sheriff and the Vaiden negroes in the case of the State of Alabama versus Alex Cady in the spring term of the Circuit Court in Lauderdale County, Alabama.

What made the origin of the fire so mysterious was the testimony of the Cady women. Mother and daughter bore witness that they had no recollection whatever of Alex Cady making threats against the Vaiden niggers. Mrs. Cady said she saw the fire in the field was nothing but an old cotton pen burning down. She and Mamie had started to the fire to watch it. On the way they had thought of a joke to play on the niggers and skeer 'em. So they ran over and told them Alex was sitting by the fire with his gun waiting to shoot any nigger that came in sight. To carry out the joke they pretended to be afraid to go home and stayed all night in the manor.

When they went to bed in the upper room the ladies swore they nearly laughed themselves to death, thinking what a good joke they had on the niggers.

The state attorney asked what the women meant the next day by Mamie shrieking and Slatie screaming, "Stop, Alex, you'll kill her!"

"That was a cat," said Slatie. "Alex was kicking the old cat off the churn, and I was warning him not to be too rough with her."

Judge Watson, who was sitting on the case, called to the jury's attention that this might or might not be admissible evidence in a charge of arson or attempted murder, but it had no bearing on the case before the court, which charged Alex Cady with wilfully and maliciously destroying a wagon which belonged to Colonel Miltiades Vaiden.

In regard to this latter charge, the Judge made a ruling and so instructed the jury that if they believed Alex Cady chopped the wagon to pieces they were not to believe that Alex Cady thought he owned the wagon, because no man would chop up his personal property, and that if Alex Cady did chop up the wagon, then they were to return a verdict of "Guilty as charged."

The twelve men were out only three or four minutes, then brought back a verdict of "Guilty as charged." Judge Watson sentenced Alex to six months in the Lauderdale County jail.

The mystery of the burning of the negro schoolhouse and the attempt at murder never came up before the grand jury.

CHAPTER FIFTY-EIGHT

The jailing of Alex Cady came as a grateful, although temporary, relief to all of the hillman's friends and relatives. To the colored tenants on the old Lacefield place it was a boon, it was like getting a tack out of their collective shoe. But the greatest beneficiaries, of course, were the Cady women. When they awakened each morning and realized that Alex was spending a semester in the Lauderdale County jail, it was balsamic; it spread a charm over the day.

All they had to do was to milk the cow, make breakfast, go out and hoe cotton all day, then back to the cabin to eat and sweep and wash dishes; it was like a vacation.

Mamie saved eggs and bought herself a book and went to the manor twice a week for lessons. The fact that she was learning to read from negroes gave her an odd feeling. She was not quite sure that she would be reading in exactly the same way white people read, but it would beat not reading at all.

At the end of every month she promptly paid her tuition fee of a dime.

The Cady women were good for their debts. At BeShears Crossroads they could run up an account as high as four or five dollars. They paid their account in eggs.

Satisfaction at Alex Cady's imprisonment did not stop at the Crossroads neighborhood. It extended to Florence. A few merchants who had been so unadvised as to allow Alex to get a dollar or two in their debt now smiled to hear that Mr. Cady had been sent to jail for chopping up his own wagon.

The hillman's confinement was a source of deep satisfac-

tion to Colonel Vaiden. Alex was a cause of constant trouble with the negroes. The fact that he was taken away from
his own crop made little difference. Cady's principle office
on the plantation was to interfere with his women folks who
really worked his land.

When Miltiades was talking to Drusilla about it he
laughed and said it was well worth a wagon to pen up Alex
for six months and give the niggers and the Cady women a
chance.

During these days his approaching wedding held the
Colonel in a state of dreamlike cheerfulness. Sydna was per-
fect. Sydna was all the things that Ponny had never been.
And he was getting his manor at last.

Miltiades' passion to build finally had settled on the remodeling of the Crowninshield home. A contractor already
had torn away the old piazza and was now replacing it with
a tiled floor above which presently would arise six great
granite columns.

The family had planned for the wedding to take place
when the piazza and the observatory were finished. Then the
old place would be a worthy foil, thought the Colonel, for
the flower-like charm of Sydna.

While the contractor worked, the lawn was littered with
sand and lime and tiles and cylindrical monoliths crated
against chipping and shipped to Florence from a Georgia
quarry. Miltiades was perpetually at the Crowninshield
home, overseeing the work.

He discussed all the points with Drusilla, where the building materials should be placed, the design of the tiles, the
size of the observatory, and the pattern of the wrought-iron
balustrade that was to go around it.

The Colonel and Mrs. Crowninshield disagreed on the
columns. Miltiades stood out for Corinthian capitals, while
Drusilla wanted Ionic. Sydna said she thought, since Miltiades was paying for the columns and giving them to her
mother, he ought to be allowed to give her what he liked.

Drusilla observed drily that that was what gifts usually were—something the giver liked.

Miltiades did not entirely understand his prospective mother-in-law. She seemed pleased with her daughter's approaching nuptials and used toward Miltiades a humorous and slightly ironic wisdom. The Colonel fell in the way of asking her advice about all sorts of things.

One day Miltiades received a letter from his brother Sylvester in Arkansas. The letter said that Sylvester's wife was suffering from goiter and he had sent her from one doctor to another with no relief. He would like to borrow five hundred dollars from Miltiades. He did not know when he could pay it back.

The Colonel showed the letter to Mrs. Crowninshield.

"You'll have to send him the money," said Drusilla.

"Yes, I know that. . . . Do you remember Sylvester?"

Mrs. Crowninshield said she had a vague recollection of him, but she had not. Before the war the Vaidens had been poor whites to the Lacefields, and they had not come under Drusilla's eyes until Miltiades Vaiden became her father's overseer. But before that time Sylvester had migrated to Arkansas. To the second set of children of the old Vaiden family, Sylvester had been only a name.

"I suppose his wife must be an old woman," speculated Drusilla, looking at the letter.

"I suppose she is," agreed the Colonel.

He knew what Drusilla was thinking. She was comparing Sylvester's old and goiterous wife with the young girl Miltiades was about to marry. After a few moments, Drusilla added:

"And the letter shows, too, that Sylvester has forgiven you."

It required a moment for the Colonel to understand what she meant, that Sylvester had forgiven his brother for stealing money and was willing to use some of it.

Drusilla continued in faint ironic explication:

"Of course, it was a blow to your family for a while, but

to be successful carries in it the seeds of forgiveness and admiration."

"Look here, Drusilla," said Miltiades uncertainly, "do you approve of me or not?"

"Of course I do, Miltiades. I was the first one to accept you. Then came the ministers of the various churches, then the poorer members of your own family. In the not distant future everybody in Florence with any claim to station and respectability will accept you warmly and sincerely, but I was first, Miltiades, because you loved me once."

An interruption of Colonel Vaiden's idyllic mood was created by the service upon him of Lucius Handback's bill of complaint in chancery.

It was a long document, and it stated in one unending sentence that Lucius Handback had come into possession of the title of one Erasmus Ham and Polly Ham, his wife, which title was of record in Volume 86 Page 714 of the Deed Book in the Lauderdale County Courthouse of the State of Alabama.

Such was the meaning of the complaint, but it required three foolscap sheets of paper with a multitude of "whereases" and "aforesaids" to make the bill sufficiently obscure for legal consideration.

Although Miltiades had had many warnings that such a bill would be filed against him, he was both surprised and incensed at its actual service.

He inveighed to Drusilla against the dishonesty of Lucius Handback trying to reclaim a farm after he had paid Lucius' father for it in a fair, square trade. "Now he's trying to get it back for nothing," declared the Colonel contemptuously: "it's the Handback blood in him cropping out."

The bill, however, had to be answered, even if it was nefarious. So in the course of a day or two the Colonel went down to Intelligence Row to the office of Governor Terry O'Shawn.

The Governor came back to Florence now and then from

his administration in Montgomery, and today Miltiades found him in his office. He sat at a desk covered with a mass of papers, leather-bound law books, notarial seals, and newspapers.

The window near which the Governor sat looked out on the gnarled and distorted mulberries which spaced Intelligence Row.

When Miltiades entered, Governor O'Shawn creaked around in his swivel chair, then got up and shook his caller's hand.

"Fine spring morning, Colonel," he said in a complimentary tone. "I like to watch the yellow buds of that mulberry unfold. Did you read about the robbery in Dothan in today's paper?"

"Is that the same set of thieves that have been going from town to town?" speculated Miltiades.

The Governor said they probably were; then, abruptly, after the fashion of such conversations, he switched to the object of the Colonel's visit.

"Why, it's that damned Lucius Handback," complained Miltiades. "He's trying to get back that place I bought and paid his daddy for."

"You don't mean it!" ejaculated the Governor. "Who's his lawyer?"

"It's Sandusky, the boy that's reading law here in your office."

"He's not any more," said O'Shawn. "He passed the bar examination at the spring term of court, and it is very unlikely that he will ever look at another law book again, if he turns out to be the average jack-leg lawyer."

"This suit he is bringing," said Miltiades warmly, "is the most inequitable suit I ever heard of being brought before a court of chancery."

"Well, if one side wasn't inequitable," observed the chief executive blandly, "the chancellor wouldn't be able to hand down a decision."

"Well, perhaps not. . . . By the way, speaking of Sandusky, did you ever send me a bill for five hundred dollars through Sandusky?"

"What for?"

"For the settlement of my difficulty with—er—John Handback?"

"First time I ever heard of the settlement."

"You didn't telegraph instructions from Montgomery and tell Sandusky what to do?"

"First time I ever heard of that either."

"Well, I be damned. . . . I'll just be damned! He handed me a bill for five hundred dollars and said it came from you."

"Now, I've heard of that sort of thing before out of Sandusky . . . several times," said the Governor drily.

The Colonel was outraged afresh.

"I suppose he used you because he had no license to practise law himself?"

"Certainly he couldn't legally present a bill of his own."

"I gave him two dollars and a half," said Miltiades.

Both men broke out laughing, the Governor roundly and lubricatedly, Miltiades drily and almost in silence.

"That's one reason I suspect," added the Colonel after the laughter, "why Sandusky is so eager in his suit against me now."

"Probably not," said O'Shawn. "Sandusky has bobbed up with a number of little suits since his admission to the bar. He searches the old magistrates' dockets for judgments that have not been collected, and he collects for half."

"Does he get many?"

"He's busy all the time."

"He ought to be disbarred for barratry!" declared the Colonel.

"Oh, well, Alabama has to have enough attorneys to conduct the business of her courts," observed Governor O'Shawn.

Miltiades dropped the topic of Sandusky and came to the matter in hand.

"Look here, Governor, what worries me, I've got all my money tied up in farms. If I should lose the Lacefield place it will upset my plans a great deal."

"Well, now, about your place," said the Governor coming down to business at last, "you got your deed from old man Handback?"

"That's right, one that his heirs and assigns guarantee forever. Now, I say, if his heir should take my place back I would recover it because the heir himself guarantees my title."

"According to that," smiled the Governor, "the title would travel round and round between you and Lucius Handback, and perpetual motion would be discovered at last."

The two men laughed at this.

"Now listen," concluded the Governor. "Usually I can't accept suits, you know that, but chancery is a very convenient court to defend in. We can easily put it off until my term of office has expired, and even then our suit in chancery will be young, a mere spring chicken of a suit."

Both men laughed again. There was something comforting about the Governor.

"And even if we never get the title cleared up, at least you will have the plantation you paid for. And in the meantime, in order to meet necessary legal expenses, file answers, and so forth and so on, probably it would be a good idea for you to deposit a small retainer."

"About how much?" asked Miltiades.

"Oh, about five hundred dollars," said the Governor, who enjoyed a dry, dignified practical joke.

CHAPTER FIFTY-NINE

O<small>N THIS</small> same point of the action in chancery, old man Erasmus Ham came around to Miltiades some days later and expressed his regrets that he had given a quit-claim deed to the Lacefield estate to Lucius Handback.

"Of all damned undermining tricks I ever heard of," berated old Mr. Ham, "pertendin' to me like he was goin' to clear up yore title, and then, be dad brimmed if he ain't tryin' to take away what title you've got!"

"It was Sandusky's idyah," said Miltiades.

"I know it! I know it! I heard that, too, the damned little legal crook. Using the law for a sandbag to hold up honest men with!"

The two men fulminated for several minutes against such practices, and then Miltiades asked his old friend how he came to be in town that morning.

"Oh, I had a little lawsuit with your daddy-in-law, Milt," said old man Erasmus cheerfully, "set at twelve o'clock today."

"Over an account, I suppose?" suggested Miltiades.

"Of course. I don't think Alex BeShears credited Polly with all the eggs and butter she brought in. It's a frien'ly suit. We ain't mad, and your daddy-in-law ain't mad. We jest want a magistrate to decide it."

"Who's your lawyer?" inquired the Colonel.

Mr. Ham hesitated.

"Well," he said after a moment, "I—I ast—er—Sandusky to look after it for me. . . . You see, I figgered if the lyin' little devil could win a bad suit he ort to do wonders with a good 'un like mine."

The casual irony and the naturalness of old man Ham's

use of Sandusky persisted in the Colonel's thoughts for some time after his old friend had gone away. He himself, Miltiades fancied, would not have stooped to such a thing.

The Colonel was on his way to the Crowninshield residence to practise his wedding ceremony with Sydna. The idea of practising such a ceremony at all struck Miltiades as a very Episcopal thing to do. He could imagine what his father, a Hardshell Baptist, would have said about a man practising his wedding ceremony.

When the Colonel reached the home on Pine Street, he found already assembled the Reverend Mathers, the Episcopal minister, and a number of children from the neighborhood who were to act as flower girls. As Miltiades came up the walk all the group were affected by him: the little girls left off chasing each other on the piazza; the Reverend Mathers came a few steps down the walk to meet the Colonel. He cleared his throat, making the effort of a preacher to meet a business man on common ground. He commented on the new columns that were being set in place on the portico and hoped the workmen would get through in time for the wedding, which was only three days off. The Colonel could never get accustomed to the Reverend Mathers wearing his collar backwards. It seemed to act as a brake on casual conversation and set their intercourse on a plane of slightly unpleasant formality.

Sydna came down from an upstairs room in a simple house dress for the rehearsal. The costume gave the girl almost a childish appearance, and another delicate pang of apprehension and doubt came over Miltiades as he went through the mimic ceremony with her.

It was a strange doubt. The Colonel felt himself entering some sphere in which he was an alien. The girl's delicacy and freshness, instead of appealing to him esthetically and emotionally, filled him with a kind of vague self-reproach, as a flower might have done when he broke it from its stem. He stooped and kissed her fingers with this feeling on him and said that she looked utterly lovely.

"Not in this dress," said Sydna, glancing at her short skirt.

Two of the little flower girls, holding empty baskets on their arms, took their places in the end of the parlor, where a bower of roses was to be placed. At the square piano a neighbor girl struck a chord and began playing Bartholdi's wedding march. Other little flower girls entered the parlor bearing empty baskets; then Miltiades and Sydna approached the minister, who stood in the place where the bower was to be built.

The emptiness, the undress of everything, gave the Colonel a faint feeling of symbolism, as if the little girls with their empty baskets might, in a way, be Sydna . . . Sydna going through life with an empty basket which was designed to hold flowers.

In the parlor doorway Drusilla stood watching the rehearsal with an expressionless face. She was behind Miltiades, who had his back to the door, but he could feel her as plainly as if she touched him. He sensed the half-mannish, half-womanish equivocation of her personality, and the odd thought came to him that if he had married Drusilla years ago she would have been quite different now. With this came the associated idea, if he did marry Sydna, would not she swing away into a not quite usual personality? Was such an aberrance good or bad? . . . He went through the ceremony, repeating the words the minister had taught him, placing the ring on Sydna's slender, almost translucent finger.

When the rehearsal was finished Miltiades excused himself on the plea that he must return to the store. The store, really, was not in his thoughts. The impression of the rehearsal disturbed him, and he wanted to be alone and think as carefully as he could about Sydna. Would Sydna's life unfold beautifully after their marriage?

As Miltiades passed among the unfinished columns of the piazza, for once in his life he wavered in the self-sufficiency of his own judgment. He felt he would like to talk over his subtle disturbance about his fiancée with some discerning person. A notion came to Miltiades to ask the Reverend Mathers to walk part of the way with him and place his problem before the minister. He paused, turned back to the parlor door until he could see the minister inside talking to Sydna and Drusilla. The sight of his formal garb caused the Colonel's impulse to die away. The middle-aged man walked on across the piazza, through the box-grown yard, and let himself out into the street. Here, he moved on down the thoroughfare slowly with no conscious objective.

Sydna persisted in his thoughts, her marriage with him, her future happiness, the effect he would have upon her flower-like existence. He felt a wish for some wise divining person who could say to him, "A woman's life is thus and so. If you have this girl's happiness most at heart, do thus . . ." except, of course, that no such person lived.

When Miltiades became aware of his surroundings again he found himself passing the post office. Out of habit he stepped into the lobby and went to his box. A circular of some sort was in it. He tapped on the little glass window, the yellow envelope vanished from sight, and a moment later Landers poked it under the general delivery grille.

The Colonel stood opening the unsealed envelope slowly. The postmaster continued where he was with his hand on the delivery window, watching the merchant's face.

The circular was about plows, and Miltiades dropped it to the floor.

"Mr. Landers," he said tentatively to the man inside the grille, "I'm troubled . . . about a curious thing. . . ."

"It isn't your mail?" questioned the postmaster.

"Oh, no, it isn't that at all."

The postmaster waited a moment for something more, and finally said:

"Then perhaps you will tell me what it is?"

"My marriage . . . I'm about to be married. . . ."

The Colonel looked at Landers with a quirk of a smile so that the fellow could pass it off lightly if he were so minded.

But the postmaster accepted distress about marriage with gravity.

"How are you troubled about that, Colonel Vaiden?" he asked.

Miltiades was relieved to be talking of the matter to someone.

"Well, the girl is very young, Landers," he said slowly; "she is little more than a child. If she isn't happy with me . . ."

The postmaster nodded slightly.

"You are distressed about her?"

"Yes, certainly. . . . What a young girl could do adversely to me would hardly be worth worrying over."

The postmaster let this observation pass. He stood considering the merchant.

"You don't strike me as an impulsive man, Colonel, I wonder why you didn't think of this before you asked her to marry you?"

"Well, I did," began Miltiades conventionally, and then it struck him that Landers was not the sort of man for one to give petty evasions, so he added as frankly as he could, "I think I may say marriage was in the girl's thoughts as well as mine."

The postmaster looked at him oddly.

"This young girl?"

"Yes."

Landers stood inside the grating, pulling at his long chin and gazing at nothing with odd inward-looking eyes.

"Were you ever friends with this girl's mother?" he inquired at length.

"Yes . . . a long time ago," nodded the Colonel.

The postmaster looked at the Colonel as if an idea were dawning on him.

"Was this friendship before the date of this girl's birth, sometime close before it?"

Curiosity as to where this was leading constrained the Colonel to answer questioningly:

"We were engaged to be married."

The postmaster revolved this for some moments, and finally asked in an odd tone:

"Were you two . . . ever married?"

From any other man in Florence the Colonel would have been indignant at such a question, but from this fantastic fellow it was relatively simple. Then, too, the fact was provocative that Landers had reached the question through a mere statement that Sydna herself had thought of the marriage.

"Yes," he answered briefly, "once." And he wondered what Landers would say next.

The mystic considered this information.

"This girl, Colonel," he proceeded carefully, "for yourself . . . do you greatly desire her?"

"Landers," returned the merchant earnestly, "that is a question I ask myself. To me she is hardly of this earth. I no more think of her the way you mean than I would think of an angel. That is why I am uneasy about her happiness. . . . Of course, there are all kinds of women, God knows, even if there is only one kind of man."

The postmaster was nodding faintly and slowly at this sentiment.

"Had it ever occurred to you, Colonel," he asked at last, "that you might be this girl's father?"

Miltiades straightened. "Oh, you mean my relations with her mother? No, that is impossible, she was born years before this other thing occurred."

"No," said the mystic, "I don't suggest that you are her physical father. You would have known that yourself. I mean her spiritual father."

"Spiritual . . . I'm afraid I don't understand."

"I mean her mother, before the daughter's conception, had your image so impressed upon her soul that she bore her daughter to you instead of to the actual physical father of her child."

The Colonel stood shocked intellectually at such a suggestion.

"Why, Landers, that's absolute moonshine. I, Sydna's father . . . because her mother was in love with me before Sydna was conceived by another man . . . that's nonsense."

"I wouldn't be sure of that," answered the postmaster. "A great many races believe in telegony. The Jews made laws on the subject."

Miltiades continued smiling a little and shaking his head.

"Very well, then, how do you explain yourself?" inquired Landers. "You never felt this way toward a woman before. It is so extraordinary that we are standing here talking about it. Did you ever see a human being before to whom you would sacrifice yourself?"

But the Colonel continued the negative shaking of his head.

"A man loves every woman differently, but how or why, he can't tell."

"What is love, to begin with?"

The Colonel had a ready-made answer for this.

"It's the attraction between the sexes," he defined at once.

"But what's the base of that attraction?"

"Why, the giving of sex, I suppose."

"But sex reactions are very much alike, whether the woman is beautiful or plain, chaste or lewd, but a man, instead of wanting any woman, desires just one. Even if her face is plain, it means more to him than does any other face in the world. He waits for her, he denies himself for her. Even when the woman is an ideal, even when a man is not sure such a woman exists, still he waits and denies himself for her."

"Well . . . assuming some man might do that," assented the Colonel skeptically, "what do you make of that?"

"It suggests to me," said the postmaster, "that love is directed by spirits who are not yet born. They use matter to frame a universe for themselves; just as the first effort of life in the scum of a pond is to frame a universe for itself."

"And you think that is love?"

"I think the force that matter feels when it is being drawn to serve life is love."

The Colonel stood looking curiously at the man in the grating.

"You stay too much by yourself, Landers. You don't talk to other men enough."

"There was another man, who lived centuries ago," said the postmaster, "who also stayed much by himself."

CHAPTER SIXTY

Although Landers' notion was absurd that some sort of telegony existed between Miltiades and Sydna Crowninshield, still, it visited the Colonel's mind up until the day of his marriage.

When that day actually arrived, Miltiades dressed for the ceremony at the store. Love, his clerk, helped him. To Love, as there would have been to any other man, there was something subtly droll in decking Miltiades out in his wedding garments. The clerk went about his chores as valet with a fixed grin on his face, except when he knew the Colonel was looking at him.

In contrast to this were the women and girls dressing Sydna. All were excited, and they talked in flatted tones on account of pins held in the corners of their mouths. They fluttered around Sydna, making imperceptible adjustments in her billowing train. Now and then they gave the bride little hugs and pats. All were in love with her in a kind of induced voluptuousness, even those who ordinarily did not care much for Sydna.

Only the betrained girl herself remained impassive. She stood before a long mirror in a sort of dream and watched the arrangement of her wedding gown. In a little while, in an hour or two, she would be the wife of Colonel Milt. Her feeling of disembodied romance revisited the girl. She thought of the Colonel promising her dying father to protect his baby daughter, and now here she was, Sydna Crowninshield, on the very verge of becoming her protector's wife. Aloud she asked what time it was. A girl ran and looked at a clock.

"Ten minutes after seven."

Two girls had found an almanac that told fortunes and were trying to read the future of the bride. One of them said:

"There's a full moon tonight, Sydna."

The other horoscopist cried out:

"What a pity they didn't have those columns done. Here it says to move into an unfinished house brings a change of luck."

"Yes, but the house isn't finished, it's the remodeling that is unfinished."

Mention of the full moon brought across Sydna's thoughts a wraith of Jerry. She could see the hobbledehoy once more kneeling and sobbing at her knees.

The girl continued dressing, thinking of Jerry, of his mystical obsession which, even at that moment, annoyed her and at the same time touched her almost to tears. He was such a foolish, foolish boy.

She became aware that one of the volunteer maids was sticking pins in her flounce and saying that the dress would have to come off. Hands began lifting the dress over Sydna's head, and she raised her arms to let them slip it off. She asked how long the tacking would take. A girl said about ten minutes. Sydna got into a house dress and said she would run downstairs for a few minutes. Two or three voices objected; another said:

"Let her run out and get a breath of air before the ceremony."

The two fortune tellers began looking in the almanac to see what sort of luck that would bring.

The lower floor and parlor already were filling with guests. To avoid these Sydna went down a back stair and into a corridor that gave on a side porch. Outside, a full moon lay huge and smouldering behind the western trees. Sydna stepped off the porch, looking at it, and moved out of habit toward the decaying hammock and the garden set. As she advanced through the avenues of musky box she saw something near the hammock that made her catch her breath. She went closer, looking with astonishment at the tall figure standing in the dim light.

"Why, Jerry," she whispered, "what are you doing out here?"

The youth was staring upward toward her window. At the sound of her voice he gave a little start.

"I was wishing you would come down."

"Well, I needed a breath of air."

"I was really trying to make you come down," he said.

A kind of dismay came upon Sydna.

"Why, Jerry . . . what for?"

"I wanted to see you one more time. . . . I'll not see you again."

She caught his arm with a sharp fear seizing her.

"Jerry . . . you're not going to do anything to yourself?"

The adolescent made a slight impatient gesture.

"No, I mean after tonight . . . you won't be you . . . there'll not be any Sydna to see. . . ." He paused, looking at the girl in the filtered radiance. "Sometimes I think there never has been one."

"Jerry . . . what do you mean?" asked the girl in a lowered voice.

"I mean you pretended to think I could do something with my exercises, but you really never did."

"Jerry, I do believe in you . . . but what is there to believe?"

A faint irony colored the hobbledehoy's voice.

"You can at least believe I made you come down here."

"Oh, Jerry! Jerry! Poor Jerry!"

A little quiver ran through her chest to comfort him. She could sense the protracted pain and discouragement her accidental skepticism of a few days before had caused him. He was such an objectless boy. What he studied and experimented with led nowhere at all. He was like a baby groping in the dark. She wanted to embrace him, to hold him close against her and comfort him. This desire came upon her with an intensity that set her nerves shaking and her pulse beating in her throat.

Voices from the old manor became audible, calling Sydna's name.

They were girls' voices in different musical keys.

"Sydna!"

"Oh, Sy-y-ydna!"

"Where are you, Sydna?"

The conversation in the boxes came to a sudden pause.

"Well . . . good-bye, Sydna."

The girl suddenly put her arms around his neck and kissed him over and over in an aura of perfume and soft flesh.

"Good-bye, good-bye, Jerry," she whispered, "good-bye."

She loosed him and ran back to the manor.

Late that night the last of the revelers in the manor had gone away. Drusilla had wished her new son-in-law and his bride a long and happy life. She had wished it tenderly and had gone her way to her own solitary apartment on the first floor, next to the sewing room.

Miltiades and Sydna went up the stairs together. Each was exquisitely conscious and shy of the other. To Miltiades the girl he was escorting lived in some pure remote zone of a child's dream. The gentle blossoming of her bosom and the curve of her waist were to the Colonel the unfolding buds of spring, and not the fruit of summer. He went with her into her boudoir, where the neighbor girls had laid out a lace gown on the foot of the bed. The Colonel observed the gown; he complimented Sydna upon being a princess in her wedding dress and presently asked if she would excuse him and let him smoke a cigar on the little balcony in the front piazza.

The girl flushed slightly and said he might. The Colonel went through the upper hall and stepped out on the little inset balcony. He was up within ten or twelve feet of the ceiling of the piazza. Three of the granite columns were not yet finished and stood dressed in dark scaffolding. The moonlight rounded the other three with its soft radiance.

The Colonel smoked his cigar in slow, meditative puffs. Sydna, disrobing in their boudoir, was quite near and intimate to him at one moment, and then seemed to recede at a great distance the next. It seemed quite unbelievable. His long-gone courtship and relations with Drusilla were a hundred times more credible than this. That had been a flesh-and-blood affair. This was a dream, a sacrament, a kneeling before an altar.

The Colonel smoked slowly with long intervals between his puffs. The moonlight shifted imperceptibly on the new columns.

The most poignantly awake person in the whole of Florence was a youth in the second story of Mrs. Rose Vaiden's boarding house on Market Street.

To Jerry, sitting on his bed, the fence and the street in the moonlight outside appeared pale and lifeless. It seemed not a thoroughfare where people walked and drove, but an avenue through some colorless cemetery. By extension, all of Florence seemed dead except one single chamber, and this was filled with a horrifying activity. That was Sydna's boudoir in the Crowninshield manor. Of life there, Jerry was aware with an intensity that boarded on physical nausea. That his uncle Miltiades should kiss Sydna, that his hands should touch her, overwhelmed the watcher with a horror of desecration. He turned and lay on his face to shut out of his eyes the persistent profanation. For Sydna in a gown of lace, Sydna, the exquisite, the fair, the slender, the sculptured . . . with his heavy, sallow old uncle . . . Oh, that he could stand with a sword by her bedchamber door and keep her untouched forever.

CHAPTER SIXTY-ONE

THE marriage of Sydna to Colonel Miltiades Vaiden emptied Jerry Catlin's world of force and purpose. Even his mysticism, which he had supposed to be universal, without relation to time or space, faded into emptiness with the going of Sydna.

For a while, for several days, in fact, he simply lay on the bed in the upstairs room of his aunt's boarding house, watching the first flies of summer wing their endless rounds against the ceiling. He no longer wanted to see Sydna, or talk to her, or sit in her company, or touch her; no more than he would have liked to sit and talk to the dead.

He did not attend these last days of college because life in the school seemed as senseless as the weaving of the flies above his bed.

Against such lethargy, Jerry's uncle Augustus mounted a high horse and would have bundled his nephew off home, but for once in her life Mrs. Rose grew angry at her husband. She told him sharply to leave Jerry alone, that she took on herself anything that Jerry did. At mealtime she made delicacies and carried them up to Jerry, to Augustus' enormous disgust.

Mrs. Rose and Mrs. Drusilla were the only persons in Florence who apprehended that young Jerry was as truly wounded as if he had been shot through the lungs. That his trauma happened to lie in his emotions was a detail.

When these two met, Mrs. Drusilla would ask her neighbor:

"How's young Jerry?"

And Mrs. Rose would return:

"He's still just lying around."

And Mrs. Drusilla would shake her head meditatively and say:

"I declare . . . Marcia's boy. . . ."

She meant this was simply a recurrence of the fatal hopeless interplay of Vaiden and Lacefield blood.

On an afterthought Mrs. Rose would ask:

"How is Sydna?"

"Why, she seems perfectly happy."

To Mrs. Rose this was incredible. She had never liked Miltiades, and she loved Jerry.

One day Mrs. Rose went to her nephew and suggested that he make a try at the final examinations.

"Just study along when it suits you," she advised, "and remember it doesn't make a particle of difference whether you pass or not."

"What's the use in doing that?" asked Jerry, as if he were talking about something in which he had no concern.

"Just to see what classes you pass in . . . so you won't have to take them over next year."

"I've missed a lot of recitations."

"Some of your classmates might help you make them up."

"I don't think any of the boys would."

"One of the girls, maybe?"

Jerry laughed a little at this.

"Why, Sarah Crowe even refused to go to a reception with me."

"Yes, I had heard about that. That was some time ago. I don't think she would mind helping you now."

Jerry doubted this. Eventually he did start back to school to please his aunt, but the assistance of Sarah Crowe was too improbable even to be remembered.

However, a few days later, this same girl, Sarah Crowe, stopped Jerry in the lower hall and asked in a friendly way how he was getting on with his math.

Jerry looked at the girl in surprise and said he did not know even where the class was working.

Sarah produced a book and showed him a page with the corner bent down.

"Right here," she pointed out, "but to do these at all, you have to know what's back here." She turned back to some more pages, whose corners had been turned down but which were now straightened up again.

The youth looked at these elucidatory pages quite innocently.

"Why don't you get somebody to go over this back work with you?" inquired Sarah.

"I don't know anybody to get, and you know the prof wouldn't do it with me that far behind."

Sarah pondered.

"What are your study periods?" she inquired. "I wouldn't mind coaching you a little."

"Why, Sarah, I wouldn't want to put you to all that trouble."

"Won't be any trouble at all. Besides, I'm going to have to pass the final same as you. It'll be a good review for me."

It turned out that the matter of study periods could be adjusted, and Jerry started reviewing algebra with Sarah.

Young Catlin did not know why Sarah Crowe so unexpectedly had offered her services in helping him with his work and he did not speculate much about it. She was a large, full-bodied girl with brown hair and blue eyes, and she was not the type about whom men speculated much anyway. Jerry forgot his first engagement to read with Sarah under a great elm on the right-hand side of the college campus as one entered the gate. Later, he did find her there, and the reviewing began.

Miss Crowe, who was quick in mathematics, soon divined Jerry's tempo and gave him all the time he required for his uninterested absorption of algebra.

Jerry liked the spattered sunshine and the buttressed roots of the tree. Sarah was not feminine enough to suggest women to the youth. She did not disturb him either by attraction or repulsion.

One day she said to him:

"You were not at home yesterday after school."

"Wasn't I?"

"No. I stopped by your aunt's, and you were not at home."

"I must have been out somewhere."

"That's logical. I wish you were that clever in quadratics," laughed the girl.

"I suppose I am pretty bad," admitted Jerry listlessly.

"Well . . ." the girl paused a moment, "I suppose you have a right to be."

At this unusual sentiment Jerry looked at the girl.

"What do you mean?"

"Your aunt and I talked a long time . . . about you, mainly."

"Me?"

Sarah nodded.

"She told me a lot."

"A lot of what?" asked Jerry, frowning.

Sarah hesitated, "Well—" she lowered her voice—"she said when Miss Sydna Crowninshield got married . . . it nearly killed you. . ."

A sense of shock, a feeling of enormous outrage spread through Jerry. He was unaware that Sarah had dramatized him, that she reveled sympathetically in his past sufferings as she would with the hero on a stage. Jerry got slowly to his feet with a colorless face. Sarah suddenly saw that he was going away. She was stricken. She caught his hand to hold him.

"Wait, wait, hold on, Jerry," she begged in a whisper, glancing around to see who saw them, "I'll take it back, Jerry."

The idiocy of taking such a revelation back disgusted the youth.

"I—can't imagine what Aunt Rose meant. . . . Sydna Crowninshield didn't have a thing to do with anything."

"Sit down again, Jerry." Sarah patted the ground earnestly.

"It was something else."

Sarah looked at him with intent eyes.

"Your experiments?" she asked quickly.

"My experiments?"

"Yes," breathed Sarah, "trying to learn how to float up in the air."

Jerry felt as if the campus were swaying beneath him.

"Did . . . Aunt Rose . . . tell you that?"

"No, no. . . . I told her," chattered Sarah.

"You told her! . . . How in the thunderation did you know it?"

"Why—why—I read it in the book in the library," said Sarah, equally disturbed. "We girls watched you. We saw you were always reading the same book, so we went to see what it was. We had a right to . . . it was a library book."

Jerry had a feeling as if he had been coming to school for weeks without any clothes on. He was brick red.

"I'm going to be a choir singer myself," hurried on the girl; "that is, if I have a voice. Oh, I do want to sing so. I hope I can go off and study. Sometimes I pray God to let me go off somewhere and study." Jerry did not realize Sarah was trying to tell him her innermost desires so they would be on a confidential equality. She sounded foolish to him.

He really was going away.

"You'll come back and study some more, won't you?" asked the girl bleakly. "I'm sorry I mentioned anything, I really am. And Miss Rose didn't tell me that yesterday, Jerry. She told it to me when she first asked me to help you. I promised her faithfully I'd never breathe a word of it to you. . . . I wish I hadn't now."

CHAPTER SIXTY-TWO

Young Jerry Catlin had determined fully to see Sarah Crowe no more. But the next day, at the same hour, it struck Jerry that Sarah Crowe already knew of his dabblings in occultism, and apparently she was very interested in and sympathetic toward them; besides that, he really ought to review his algebra. . . . When the hour came he found himself back under the academic elm.

The girl received him seriously and devoted herself to the problems in the book like a benevolent abacus. But after a while she came back gingerly to the boy's fantastic experiments.

Sarah was particularly interested in temptations. She had read the book, and she really remembered its details better than Jerry. She wanted to know if Jerry had found the path of illumination beset with subtle and ghostly temptation; had spirits sown his path with sorrows and trials to see if he were steadfast and incorruptible.

Jerry stated briefly that he supposed not, nothing of the sort had happened to him.

Sarah seemed vaguely disappointed. She came out of her musings on the subject and asked Jerry what he had to do that afternoon.

Jerry said uninformingly that he was going to be busy that afternoon, and Sarah dropped the subject.

As a matter of fact, Jerry did have something to do that day after school. He was going over to take Mrs. Sydna Vaiden for a drive.

That morning Jinny Lou had entered Mrs. Rose Vaiden's kitchen by the back door and had stated baldly that Colonel

Milt say fo' Mistah Jer' to come over that evenin' an' drive Miss Sydna some.

No doubt the Colonel had phrased his request much more diplomatically than that, but Jinny Lou had shed the niceties of her message in transit.

Mrs. Rose was angered. She ejaculated:

"The idyah of such a thing! Well, I for one won't give Jerry any such message . . . after what he's been through . . ." She continued grumbling negatives.

Jinny Lou, who stood silently in the kitchen, finally asked in a low tone:

"Am he comin'?"

The child's innocence of grammar for once annoyed Mrs. Rose.

"Oh, yes, I suppose he am," she said. "When does Sydna want him to come?"

"When she take huh drive."

"That's about three o'clock. Go back and tell her I'll send him over when he comes home from school . . . though I oughtn't to send him a step. . . ." She continued her objections in her thoughts as Jinny Lou went back home.

At the breakfast table she had delivered the message in a reserved voice, and she hoped that Jerry would quash the plan, but it had come from his uncle Miltiades, and there was nothing else to do but go.

At fifteen minutes before three that afternoon Jerry Catlin considered whether or not to dress himself up to go over to the Crowninshield manor, which was now his uncle's home. He had not been to the place since Sydna's marriage. Now the thought of going there was more embarrassing than if it had been the home of a complete stranger.

He did not dress, which is to say that he did not change from his everyday suit to his Sunday suit, but went over to Pine Street as he was.

When he reached the place, the manor was so changed that Jerry would hardly have recognized it. The dilapidated wooden fence was gone, and in its place stood an iron fence anchored with great square brick pillars. Vertical iron bars tipped with spearheads were arranged in wave-like curves between the pillars. The maze of box hedges in the yard were clipped, the trees had been trimmed so that Jerry had a view of the manor behind the foliage. In the piazza gray granite columns reached up to Ionic capitals. On the roof of the manor the iron balustrade of the observatory was a repetition in miniature of the wave-like yard fence. This repetition of design quite took Jerry's breath.

Indeed, the ensemble was so handsome and dignified that it kept Jerry standing at a small postern gate which was a few panels removed from a large double carriage gate that opened on an unfinished driveway.

A negro man, clipping the box hedges, told Jerry that Miss Sydna was waiting for him. The negro's tone bespoke the importance of poor white folks not keeping rich white folks waiting.

Jerry resented the black man's unconscious innuendo. This resentment was directed not so much at the caretaker as at Sydna and his uncle and more vaguely at the manor itself. He was sorry he had come. He hated to be toadying to a rich uncle, and the thought passed through his mind that his uncle had got his money by stealing it.

When Jerry stepped on the columned piazza he saw through a window Jinny Lou dusting and heard her high voice call, "Miss Sydna, Mistuh Jerry's come!" and then he heard Drusilla's voice reprove, "Jinny Lou, go to her and tell her, don't yell like that!" And Sydna's voice from upstairs say, "I know it now, Mother," and Mrs. Drusilla's reply, "Of course you do, but have her come to you and tell you."

Then, through the window, Jerry saw Jinny Lou give up her dusting and start upstairs to tell Mrs. Sydna that Jerry had come.

Jinny Lou was no longer the cook; she was a maid in embryo. The present cook was a black woman of amplitude

who made biscuits as light as she was heavy. Nowadays
Drusilla never entered the kitchen, and Sydna hardly knew
where it was.

The stairway of the manor had been re-done, and Sydna
came down trailing her hand on its curved, polished rail.

"It was awfully good of you to come for me, Jerry," she
said with a faint smile.

"I was glad to come," said Jerry automatically, and as
he looked at Sydna he was shaken with nervousness.

"You haven't been over for a long time."

"Well, you k-know," stammered Jerry, embarrassed into
complete frankness, "y-you know I said I wasn't c-coming
back."

The young wife changed from her easy manner.

"Yes, I know you did." Then continued in somewhat
hurried tones, "We go this way to the porte cochère."

The two walked in silence through the hall and out of a
side exit. Here a porte cochère with square brick pillars at
the corners had been added to the manor, with pleasant
effect. Under its canopy two black horses stood harnessed
to a carriage. When they stamped the brick pavement, quick
multiple echoes clapped from the dome.

Jerry handed Sydna in the carriage and stepped in himself. The black man on the lawn walked with dignity to the
carriage gate and opened it for Jerry to drive out.

The two drove for some minutes, listening to the rhythm
of the trotting blacks. The novelty and luxury of driving
gave the youth a kind of surface impression of pleasure, but
he was mainly aware of some sort of change in Sydna. It was
as if another woman whom he did not know had entered into
her.

Presently she began speaking, taking up the topic she had
mentioned in the hall.

"You ought not to feel that way, Jerry," she said gently;
"nobody has many friends who understand them."

A great sadness came over the youth.

"I ought to know that, Sydna."

"And if a person really needs you some time, Jerry, I think you ought to come to her, no matter what you said."

"Well . . . I did."

"And after all . . . I'm your aunt now, just the same as Miss Rose."

Jerry gave a little laugh.

"That hasn't got anything to do with anything."

"No-o . . . I don't suppose it has."

Here she began talking to him about himself, asking what he had been doing these last weeks. He told her that she already knew, meaning that he was still engaged in his esoteric practices.

A tender regret came into Sydna's heart for Jerry. Ever since Miltiades had remodeled her home it seemed more pitiful than ever for Jerry to throw away his time on such foolishness. Her home, somehow, stressed the necessity of centering one's energy on good valuable material things. She gave a sigh at his obduracy and yielded herself to the upholstery and the soft motion of the carriage.

"How are you getting along at school, are you going to pull through?"

"I don't know."

"You ought to get someone to help you," suggested Sydna in a tentative tone.

"I am," said Jerry.

"Oh, you are? Who?"

"Sarah Crowe is helping me with algebra."

"Well, Jerry," ejaculated Sydna, "I had heard that, but I didn't believe it."

"Why not?" asked Jerry at sea.

"Sarah is such a big, frowsy girl. . . . I don't believe she will have a good influence on you. . . . I'm afraid she will influence you away from your occult studies."

"She's never said a word against them. In fact, she seems very much interested in them."

Sydna looked around at her companion in astonishment.

"Jerry, you haven't told her about that, I hope!"

"She already knew about it," defended Jerry, flushing; "she watched what book I read and went and got it."

"How unladylike!" condemned Sydna.

"Oh, it was a library book. She had a right to read it."

"But do you think that was just exactly . . . courteous?"

"I didn't at first . . . but I guess it's all right."

"Jerry, I wish you'd get some really nice girl to coach you in algebra . . . snooping around, reading your book . . . it just outdoes me to think of it."

Sydna really believed that she felt this. She thought she hated Sarah Crowe to exert her coarsening influence on Jerry's dreaminess and spirituality. She added aloud, in what she thought was complete truthfulness, "I wouldn't mention this at all, Jerry, if I wasn't your aunt."

"I didn't suppose you cared one way or the other what became of me," said Jerry bitterly.

"Why, Jerry Catlin!" cried Sydna, looking at him with the initial sting of tears in her eyes. "How unkind of you to say such a thing. Why, I care more for you now than I ever did before, of course."

Jerry drove on, silently thinking:

"Well, I don't for you. . . . I don't even know you. I can't imagine who you are."

Part of this he was saying because he resented her fine house.

Presently Sydna said that she was to call at the courthouse for Colonel Milt at four o'clock, and would Jerry drive down there.

"What's he doing at the courthouse?" inquired the nephew.

"Oh, it's that Lucius Handback matter. The chancellor is going to hand down his decision at four."

This was of little interest to either the wife or her escort. Jerry immediately returned to his impression of Sydna in her new rôle and what she had said about Sarah Crowe. She

had given the boy a faint distaste for the wholesome, clear-
eyed Sarah.

Absorbed in this new and delicate discomfort, he trotted
the horses to the courthouse, left Sydna in the carriage with
the reins while he went in after his uncle Miltiades.

Two or three minutes later, when Jerry entered the small
chancery courtroom in the second story of the county building, he saw his uncle standing with a paper in front of the
chancellor's desk. The chancellor himself was placing a number of legal documents in an envelope.

The dramatic figure of the group was Governor O'Shawn.
He stood just in front of Miltiades and was saying in his
orotund voice:

"Your Honor, am I to understand that your respondent's
plea of adverse possession of the Lacefield estate for a period
of twenty years is set aside?"

"It has not been adverse for twenty years," corrected the
gray-haired judge, in a mild, expository voice; "it has been
twenty-five years since Erasmus Ham recorded his deed, but
he owned the place for only six years; then he sold it. In
the meantime it appears to have been owned and sold by
a number of different men. That evidence is reviewed in the
decree."

"Your respondent excepts from such a ruling," boomed
the Governor.

"His attorney has thirty days in which to file his exceptions," stated the chancellor, who continued packing his
envelope with the effect of a teacher dismissing a rather dull
school.

"This whole suit has been proved to be the sheerest case
of fraud," went on the Governor; "it is founded on a quit-
claim deed cozened out of a simple old man. It is one of the
most damnable legal outrages ever perpetrated in the courts
of Alabama!"

"That is exactly the opinion I set forth in my decree,"
stated the Judge crisply; "and when you carry up your

case, I trust the superior court reverses my decision as a matter of sentiment, if not a matter of law."

Young Jerry Catlin tiptoed across the floor to his uncle. Then he saw that Miltiades' face was colorless and sallow. It began to dawn on the nephew that something devastating had happened in this quiet dusty courtroom. When he reached the Colonel's side he whispered in an apprehensive voice:

"Uncle Milt . . . what's the matter?"

The merchant looked around, then apparently became aware of his nephew. He batted his eyes quickly a time or two, then asked:

"Jerry . . . where did you come from?"

At his air the nephew's heart sank.

"From the carriage. . . . Miss Sydna's waiting. . . ."

Miltiades lifted an unsteady hand.

"Go tell her I've . . . I've lost the Lacefield place. . . . Tell her . . . no . . . no . . . I'd better do it myself. . . ."

"Why, Uncle Milt!" breathed the youth, horrified. "Who . . . what happened to it?"

The merchant waggled a thumb across the courtroom at a small, triumphantly smiling, wizened-looking man.

"It's that damned lying crook of a lawyer."

Jerry recognized his former roommate with amazement.

"You don't mean . . . Sandusky?"

The Colonel nodded briefly, then looked earnestly at his nephew.

"Which of us had better go down and break it to her, Jerry—you or I? . . . She thinks a lot of you. . . ."

CHAPTER SIXTY-THREE

Nemesis had overtaken Colonel Miltiades Vaiden, and Florence was variously glad.

There were multiplied reasons for their pleasure. Not only was Miltiades a dour, thievish man, but Lucius Handback was a tippler, a gamester, a pursuer of women, and of such frailties are often compounded very lovable and popular men. Moreover, Miltiades had used his wealth to build a beautiful home, and nobody enjoyed seeing Cherry Street riff-raff bloom out in a mansion on Pine. Behind all this lay the basic distaste of any self-respecting, order-loving, God-fearing community to see a poor man suddenly turned prosperous . . . it always seems such a waste of money.

Even the preachers whom the Colonel had subsidized felt a quiet satisfaction in the thought that, no matter how far the ministerial judgment might be betrayed by wolves in sheep's clothing, God was not mocked.

Colonel Vaiden himself did not inquire into the heavenly machinery that had led to his downfall. He asked Governor O'Shawn to make the best terms he could with Lucius Handback.

Sandusky, Lucius' lawyer, would agree to no terms at all except delivery of the plantation. Sandusky said he was sure Miltiades was headed for bankruptcy, and he did not want the Lacefield estate mixed up with the common funds of a bankrupt.

The two lawyers talked this over in the Governor's office, since Sandusky had no office. O'Shawn then dispatched a negro to the Colonel's store saying that he could come to no arrangement with Handback's attorney.

When the negro entered the store, Bill Bradley, the real-estate man, had come around to see about collecting the installments on the smaller plantations the Colonel had purchased.

Miltiades took the note from the negro and continued remonstrating with Bradley.

"Look here, Bill, my note on the Sweeny place wasn't due till last month, and I thought, times being hard, you wouldn't push me."

Bradley took his cigar from under his closed eye and opened it a trifle.

"I meant if everything got along all right, Colonel."

"You mean you would not force me to pay right on the dot as long as I could do it, but if I couldn't do it, then I had to?"

Bradley made a wry smile.

"Well, I can't help knowing how you stand, Colonel, seeing as I put through most of your deals. I've got to protect my clients. That's my business."

"Yes, but my deed to the Lacefield place came through you, Bill. You gave me the usual warranty clause. If I lose that land I have recourse against you."

Bradley nodded.

"That's just another reason why I'm going to have to shut down on you, Colonel. I know you haven't got any responsible guarantors back of your title to the Lacefield place." The real-estate man laughed at this situation.

Miltiades moistened his lips.

"Look here, Bill, I've got a little money coming in next month that will more than meet your installment."

"Where from?"

"Hell, if I tell you I've got some coming, it's coming, isn't it?"

"It won't hurt you to tell me where from," persisted Bradley. "I'm not going to try to garnishee you."

The Colonel hesitated with an uncomfortable and oppressed feeling.

"Well, I've shipped a bunch of hawgs to Chicago. I'm waiting for the returns."

"Oh, I see. Did you ship 'em at the market, or did you ship 'em at a figger?"

"I put a figger on 'em," said Miltiades.

Bradley nodded.

"I don't know whether that's a good idyah or not. The hawg market is shot to pieces these days. If you put a figger on 'em they are liable to stay there in the pens and eat their heads off."

"If they don't move in a week or so I thought I would wire 'em to sell."

"Well, it's a bad time to sell hawgs or anything else," complained Bradley. "This damned Democratic administration we was all whoopin' our heads off about . . ."

"We really haven't got a Southern man in the White House," pointed out Miltiades.

"You know why that is, don't you?" inquired Bradley. "It's because you have to pick the Democratic candidate from a doubtful state."

"You mean the South is not doubtful?"

"Of course not. Everybody knows that no matter what damn platform they write out, or what damn Yankee they nominate to run on it, if they call it Democratic, why, the South has got to vote for it solid."

"Yeh, that's right," nodded the Colonel, "of course we have to vote the Democratic ticket, to keep the nigger down."

"There you are," complained Bradley bitterly; "of course we can't have but one party in the South on account of the nigger. But as long as we've got just one, none of the other states are going to pay any attention to our opinions. We kain't write out our own platforms; we kain't run a Southern man on our platforms; we kain't do a single damn thing politically because, by God, we ain't doubtful. I say the best thing for the South to do is to get doubtful and get doubtful quick."

"You mean have two parties and let the niggers vote?" inquired Miltiades sharply.

The real-estate agent came to a pause.

"No . . . no," he said slowly, "I wouldn't advocate that. I guess it's better judgment in the South to give up her voice in our national affairs than to let the damn niggers have the ballot."

Bradley was in the pleased mood of a man whose views have been listened to. He bade Miltiades good-day and went his way. If the Democratic party had brought on the panic, it had simultaneously put off the collection of the installment Miltiades owed on the Sweeny place.

A little later in the day a drummer came into the store, not to sell but to collect an outstanding account. The Colonel told this man about the hogs he had shipped to Chicago, but the drummer wanted some sort of payment at once. The Colonel stood at his desk, thinking over the amount of small change he actually had in his store.

"How much will you take to get out of my store and stay out?" inquired Miltiades caustically.

"What cash you've got on hand," said the drummer, unperturbed.

Miltiades paid him fourteen dollars and took his receipt. Then he told Love to stay in the store. He said he was going out for a while.

"If anybody calls when you are out, what will I tell them?" inquired the clerk.

"Tell 'em I'm out on one of my farms seeing about shipping more hawgs to Chicago," directed the merchant sardonically.

He deserted his store and walked diagonally across the Square toward Pine Street. He was profoundly depressed and wounded in his self-esteem. What disturbed the Colonel were his hogs in Chicago. He had no hogs in Chicago. The invention popped into his head to stave Bradley off for another month. The collector had believed it, because Miltiades always had been rigidly truthful with him. Now, for the sake

of a few days of grace, Miltiades had let go his truthfulness
and perhaps his reputation for truthfulness. He had sold
out for a month's reprieve, and Heaven knew what he was
going to do in that month. The Colonel was annoyed at the
small reward he was getting for his lie to Bradley. He had
lied cheaply, like a nigger about to be whipped.

Colonel Vaiden stopped by the post office on his way to
Pine Street. His box was full of letters. When Crowe, the
clerk, pushed the bundle through to him, he asked the Colonel if he knew whether Jerry Catlin had given up his course
at the college and gone back home.

"I don't think he has. Why?" asked Miltiades.

"My sister was inquiring about him," said Crowe.

"Well, I'm sure he has not," repeated the Colonel, riffling
through his letters.

They were all accounts payable sent in by wholesale
houses. Notice of Miltiades' financial difficulty had reached
some Wholesale Creditors' Association; hence this united de-
mand for the payment of all outstanding obligations. The
man who had notified the association so promptly was Sandusky, its agent in Florence.

The post-office clerk stood watching Miltiades' face as
he opened bill after bill.

"By the way," said Crowe, "Mr. Landers told me to tell
you, if I saw you, that he had a message for you."

The Colonel slipped an envelope into his pocket.

"I imagine I know what it is about," he said.

"Well, all right," nodded Crowe without interest.

The Colonel had no stomach for any message Landers had
to deliver. It was probably a questionnaire from R. J. Dunn,
inquiring into the Colonel's financial standing. The big
credit houses very often sent the postmaster these interroga-
tories together with a twenty-five-cent book of stamps to
pay him for his trouble in having the questions filled out.

Miltiades walked out of the post office a trifle more quickly
than usual because he did not want to see Landers.

He proceeded eastward to the corner, then turned up Pine

Street toward his home. The downtown end of Pine Street was very shabby, disfigured by a livery stable and some hitching posts. On a goods box, in the hot summer sunshine, sat a negro, drumming his hands on the boards and crooning a tune.

Five or six blocks up the street the Colonel came within sight of his own home. The handsome fence and the stately manor behind the parked trees set up a kind of helpless ache in Miltiades. Just to have achieved such a home and such a wife, just to have touched for a moment the goal of his life, and then suddenly to lose it. He thought again, with a self-contemptuous thankfulness, that the home belonged to Drusilla Crowninshield and could not be sold for his debts. But he doubted if he would live more comfortably as a hanger-on in Drusilla's home than he had done in his own mean tenement on Cherry Street.

The conversation of feminine voices floated to him across the street. Both were a little excited and were very formal with each other. One of them asked:

"Well . . . where is he?"

The other answered:

"I don't know, he hasn't been here today."

The first said:

"Well, it's important. I think he will pass if he works hard."

"Well, after all," said the second voice, "it wouldn't make any difference to you personally if he doesn't pass."

"I am sure it would make a difference to any friend of Jerry's," returned the first girl.

Both speakers stood at the small gate of the manor. For a moment Miltiades had a fantastic notion that he was looking at Drusilla and Ponny BeShears when they were girls. Then he saw it was Sydna and a girl whom he did not know.

He stood looking and listening to their slightly excited voices. He glanced back down the street and saw the lanky form of Landers following him. The postmaster was walking rapidly, and when he saw Miltiades he waved a hand.

The Colonel was forced to wait for him, and he stood berating Landers for working so conscientiously for a twenty-five-cent book of stamps.

The postmaster came up solemnly as usual.

"Crowe said you'd been in the office," he explained a little breathlessly, "and Mr. Maggus said you had turned up this direction."

For a moment Miltiades was at loss to know who was Mr. Maggus; then he realized it was the bullet-headed negro thumping the goods box. It disgusted the Colonel to hear Landers call a negro "Mister."

"What do you want?" he asked, with his repulsion in his voice.

"I have a message for you," said the postmaster.

"What is it?"

"It's from a man, a young man, not quite as tall as I am but much heavier set . . . a very jolly young man."

"You don't know him?"

"No, he just asked me to take this message to you, and I said I would."

The Colonel looked at the postmaster a little curiously. He was exactly the sort of man to accept a commission and never ask for whom he was doing it. There were some good points about Landers if he wasn't such a damned nigger-lover.

"Well . . . what was the message?" asked the Colonel at last. "Was it about some bill?"

"I don't think so," said Landers, a little puzzled in his turn.

"Well, what did he say?"

"He said you would find what you needed in the cash drawer."

The Colonel frowned in surprise.

"What I *needed* . . . in the *cash drawer?*"

"That's what he said," nodded Landers.

Miltiades laughed the brief laugh of amazement.

"What I need usually stays in cash drawers, but I be damned if it's in mine."

Landers appeared a little taken aback.

"Well . . . that's all I know," said the postmaster uneasily. "I didn't ask him anything else. I thought you would know what he meant."

"You didn't think to ask the man's name so I could get in touch with him again?" asked the Colonel, with a hint of reproach.

"No, I didn't," said Landers regretfully. "I was sure you'd recognize him . . . a youngish man with a wide forehead . . . gray eyes and very level eyebrows, like your own. And somehow, when he appeared before me, I got the impression that he had come to his death by violence . . . probably shot and killed."

CHAPTER SIXTY-FOUR

THE postmaster's explanation left Colonel Vaiden in a state of shocked incredulity. The Colonel, of course, went and looked in his cash drawer. He found four dollars and eighty cents, the amount which Love had sold since the drummer had ascertained the color of his money. The cash drawer did hold what Miltiades needed, but not in sufficient quantity. The thought came to Miltiades' mind that possibly an astral wag had visited the postmaster; some ghost with an annoying sense of humor.

The merchant had gone to his store very early next morning because he meant to ride out to the country and stay all day, in order, mainly, to avoid being dunned.

Now, as he stood in the faint morning light behind the counter, he was startled by the apparition of a figure in the rear of the store with a glimmering pistol leveled on him. When he straightened from over the cash drawer, the figure said apologetically:

"Oh, is that you, Colonel? By geemeny, you gave me a skeer. I thought you was one of the burglars come to Florence at last. I heard somebody come in; then I saw a man at the cash drawer."

"If a burglar broke open this drawer," said Miltiades, "we'd have to pay him a little something out of our pockets for his trouble."

Love remained silent for a moment and then said uncomfortably:

"You're mighty early, countin' your cash."

Miltiades saw that his clerk interpreted this as distrust and began a partial explanation:

"Somebody told me I would find what I needed in the cash drawer," said the Colonel, in a voice that was half amused at himself. "I'll be in the country all day today, and I thought I'd look before I started."

The clerk stood listening to this odd explanation.

"Why, of course, that's what you need . . . cash," said Love.

"Yes, I'd figured that out for myself."

Love stood in front of the counter.

"Do you mind tellin' me who told you to look?" inquired the clerk.

"No-o," agreed the Colonel dubiously, "it was Landers."

"Landers! You mean . . ."

"The postmaster . . . Landers."

"How in the nation did you come to be talking to Landers a-tall?"

"Well . . . Landers is a funny bird . . . he—he's a very odd character."

"I can't imagine any white man talking to a nigger-lover like Landers," said Love with rustic frankness. "So he told you to look in your cash drawer."

"No-o," expanded the Colonel, really wanting to go into the matter with Love, but doubting the wisdom of doing so, "no, it wasn't Landers. Some other person sent me the message through Landers."

"To look in your cash drawer?"

"Yes."

"Well, who was it?"

"Landers didn't know."

"Didn't know who sent the message by him?"

"No. . . . As a matter of fact . . . Landers said the man who gave him the message . . . was dead."

There was a silence of about half a minute when the Colonel ejaculated in exoneration of himself:

"That's what Landers said."

"Is the man crazy?"

"Why, sure," agreed the Colonel, relieved, "stays by him-

self all the time . . . hardly ever speaks to a living soul
. . . the man leads a life to drive him crazy."

"He was crazy to begin with," said Love. "Look at the
way he collagues with the niggers, calling 'em Mister and
Missis."

"That's political, to hold his office under a Republican
Administration."

"Yes, but he acts like he means it—if it's not put on;
he's crazy, anyway."

"I never had thought of that end of it . . . he may be."

This was a sidetrack from the main theme of interest.
Love came back to it.

"Didn't he have a idyah who he thought told him to tell
you?"

"No-o . . . no . . . he said it was a youngish man . . .
with gray eyes . . . who had come to his death by a gun-
shot."

Love thought this over.

"Handback wasn't a youngish man . . . and he didn't
have gray eyes."

"I'd thought of Handback . . . but who it was doesn't
make much difference. The point is, there's nothing in the
cash drawer except four dollars and a few cents."

For some unknown reason there was something comforting in the fact that Landers' ghostly communication was
proved empty.

"That sort of thing is always a fake," said Love.

"Well . . . no, it isn't," objected the merchant. "When
my brother Polycarp was shot my mother was asleep at
home. She woke up crying and said that Polycarp was
killed."

"Well, I declare . . . and he was killed?"

"Yes, he was killed."

Love himself came around and searched carefully through
the cash drawer.

Colonel Vaiden rode out to his plantation concerned
mostly about his debts, but thinking now and then of

Landers. The postmaster's message had been proved empty, but what puzzled Miltiades was how Landers knew that he was on the edge of ruin? But, of course, so many duns and everything coming through the post office . . . The Colonel dropped the subject.

Miltiades now began thinking how he could get some concealable money out of his holdings before he was forced into bankruptcy. What he could grab promised to be about all he would actually own in his sudden dash for wealth. He rode along now, thinking carefully how to realize as much money as he possibly could.

When the Colonel reached the Lacefield place the first thing he observed was Toussaint's cotton. It was tall, lush, green-black, and starred with white blooms. It ranged from the road clear to the yard of the old manor, a sea of profound green. The sight filled Miltiades with a breath of admiration. It was the kind of cotton the Lacefield place had raised twenty years ago. In its heavy, tangled green, slaves might have been at work. He, Miltiades, might have been a young man again, returning from the fields where he directed an army of negroes, and Drusilla, in her youth, might have been waiting for him on the piazza.

For a moment the heavy cotton erased the war and subsequent neglect and ruin and elevated the countryside to its former glory.

Miltiades rode on to the manor, unable to take his eyes off the field. Then he began to think of his equity in the flowering cotton, and he wondered if he could dispose of it at once.

Gracie, with her dramatic eyes, came out on the piazza, calling out:

"Law, yonder comes Colonel Milt!"

The Colonel called back:

"Howdy-do, Gracie, howdy-do Lucy, you and Toussaint."

He observed that Lucy was heavier than when he had seen her before, and he thought of the rapidity with which negroes multiplied. This youngster, Toussaint, was about to become a father, while he, Miltiades Vaiden, had never had a child.

Aloud he was saying in a serious voice:

"Well, Gracie and Lucy and Toussaint, I've come to see you all, and I don't know whether I'll come any more or not."

Consternation broke out among the tenants.

"Colonel, what's happened?" ejaculated Gracie.

"What do you mean by that, Colonel?" asked Lucy.

"I think I've probably lost the place . . . after I've paid for it in hard money."

"We heard about the lawsuit," said Gracie, "Mr. Ham's deed not being recorded."

"I was just saying what white people did to one another," put in Lucy.

"So I came out here with an idyah of realizing some little money on what I've got here now," explained Miltiades, "the stock, the plows, and the new wagon."

"You're not thinking about selling them!" ejaculated Toussaint, unable to believe what he had heard.

"You don't mean sell the mules and the plows!" echoed Lucy.

"I'm afraid I'll have to," said the Colonel, "if I lose any time, my creditors will levy on everything, and they'll go anyway. . . . I want to come out with something."

"Why, we'll never finish the crop without something to work with," cried Toussaint.

"My loss will be much greater than yours," said the Colonel, looking at the white negro.

Toussaint returned the white man's gaze with incredulity, and then with a growing resentment in his eyes.

"Yes, you'll lose more than we will . . . I see that."

"He loses his whole place," said Gracie, "every cent he paid for it."

"And if I wait till fall to sell my mules and stuff, even if they should not be levied on, the prices will be low then. Half the farmers will be wanting to sell their mules so they won't have to feed them through the winter."

"I don't think that's the point," said Lucy.

Miltiades looked at the distended body of the tan girl.

"Why isn't it the point?" he asked, with a shortening of patience.

"The point is," said Lucy, "you are under contract to furnish us stock and implements and provisions for the year. I don't believe you could legally come in and take everything away from us like that."

Miltiades frowned at the pregnant girl. A slow wrath welled up in him. For a nigger wench to tell him what he could and could not do with the stock on his own plantation . . . to tell him what was "legal" for him to do!

From the interior of the manor a gray-headed, wizened old negro came shuffling out on the portico.

"Look heah, Lucy, de Bible say delivah to Cæsah de things whut am Cæsah's. If dat ain't talkin' 'bout Col'l Milt's mules, whut am it talkin' 'bout?"

"I don't know what the Bible's talking about—I know what I'm talking about."

"I certainly had no intention of starting an argument when I rode out here," said the Colonel drily, "I merely came to tell Toussaint to bring the wagon and mules to town tomorrow and load on as many plows and hoes as he can haul."

The four negroes on the piazza stood silent. Then Lump said:

"Yas, suh, Mas' Col'l, we do dat."

And Gracie said in a pinched tone:

"Yes, sir, Mister Milt."

Miltiades walked back to the gate. Lump hobbled after him to unhitch his horse for him.

As the Colonel drove back to Florence with controlled resentment at Lucy's affront, he met a smallish man just beyond BeShears' store who gave a kind of grin as the horseman went past.

"Hidy, Colonel," he called from the roadside. "Well, I'm back agin."

Miltiades slowed his horse.

"When did you get out, Alex?" he asked without pleasure.

"Today. I tol' the shurf he ort to drive me home. He said he rode me one way in his buggy and he figgered I could walk back. He allowed turn about was fair play." And Alex Cady burst out laughing.

CHAPTER SIXTY-FIVE

PARSON LUMP MOWBRAY was preaching about the wagon and mules.

"De onlies' thing you kin do," intoned the old negro in the middle of the kitchen, "is to take dat waggin an' plow an' evahthing back to Col'l Milt an' gib 'em to him. They's his plows an' mules, an' whut he gibs he takes away."

The Biblical cadences of the old man sharply annoyed the tan-colored girl, who was resting her heavy body in a big home-made chair.

"Oh, hush talking," she said at last to Lump.

"Hush talkin'! You tell a gray-haided man like me—ol' enough to be yo' gran'daddy, to hush talkin'? Whut do de Bible say 'bout gray hairs, Lucy Lacefield?"

"Toussaint . . . you . . . you'll have to give them up," said Gracie shakenly.

"Now, dat's right, you lissen to huh," nodded Lump, pointing at Gracie.

"But, Mother Vaiden," protested Lucy, trying to keep respectful to her mother-in-law, "don't you see all our work here will be thrown away? We won't have anything at all to show for what we've done!"

Gracie looked at her daughter-in-law.

"What colored person ever has anything to show for what he's done?" she asked bitterly. "I've always wanted to go away from here! But you would stay . . . and keep Toussaint!"

Gracie was only a little removed from weeping. Her own shock and loss in the death of Handback had been overwhelming, but for Toussaint, her son, to lose his whole year's work, broke Gracie's heart.

He had worked so hard . . . like a white man. Now to have all his tools taken from him on the verge of a heavy crop. . . .

"But I tell you, Mother Vaiden," repeated Lucy in controlled desperation, "Toussaint doesn't have to take his tools back. Colonel Vaiden is under a contract."

"Contract!" repeated Gracie hopelessly.

"At least he might have spirit enough to ask a lawyer about it before he turns everything over to him," cried Lucy.

"Oh, Lawd, a lawyah!" gasped Lump. "Whut chanst has a niggah got in co't agin Col'l Milt Vaiden?"

A knocking far away at the front of the manor stopped the futile wrangling. All the negroes listened.

"Wondah who dat is?" asked Lump in a low tone.

Toussaint, the keeper of the manor, started toward the front door, thinking of the hazard of trying to make a white man keep his contract with a negro.

"Here, wait," said Gracie to her son, "let me go."

"Why, Mother," ejaculated the youth, annoyed by his own nervousness, "you know *this* can't be anybody already!"

Gracie stopped under the bracket lamp on the wall, listening toward the front.

The person on the piazza proved to have no connection with Colonel Vaiden and his demands. It was Mamie Cady, standing close to one of the columns, almost hiding behind it.

"Is that you, Toussaint? Can I see Lucy a minute?"

"Won't you come in?" asked the white negro.

"No, I'm going right back home."

"Well . . . if you won't come in . . . Lucy, Miss Mamie wants to see you."

The two heard the heavy young wife moving through the darkness of the hallway. When she reached the portico Mamie put two dimes in Lucy's fingers.

"Ain't that what I owed ye?" she asked.

"Yes, but what are you paying me now for?"

"Pappy's come home. I won't git to take no more lessons.

I slipped off and run over here. I'm much obliged to ye for showin' me how to read."

"You're more than welcome. I'm sorry you can't keep on."

"I imagine there is a whole lot more."

"Yes, a good deal."

"Well . . . if Pappy ever gets sent to jail ag'in, I'll take some more lessons."

Lucy stood holding the two dimes in her hand, momentarily touched by the pathos of this poor white girl. When Mamie had gone away she said gloomily:

"Now he'll be putting his nose into our business again, if he can find a way to do it."

Toussaint knew whom she meant.

"Oh, well, his jail sentence will give him a bad name, even among the whites."

This last was the most optimistic view to take of Alex Cady, that he had disqualified himself even for the mean post of general nuisance.

"Toussaint," asked Lucy, shifting back to her major premise, "aren't you going to stand up for yourself in this matter? I—I admired you, Toussaint, in the beginning, because you stood up for yourself—because you knocked down that mean little contemptible bully, Alex Cady."

"What do you think I ought to do, Lucy?"

"Why, tomorrow, when you go to town, see a lawyer. Even the white people can't say there's any harm in asking the advice of a lawyer. Surely we've got a right to do that."

CHAPTER SIXTY-SIX

COLONEL MILTIADES VAIDEN was about a mile out of Florence near the Cypress Creek bridge on the Waterloo road, waiting for old man Erasmus Ham. The Colonel had sent word to old Mr. Ham that he wanted to sell him his mules, and the old man had returned an answer saying that he didn't need any mules but he would buy them on account of the damn fool way he had stove up the Colonel's business.

So now the merchant stood near the bridge pondering what he would ask old man Ham for the mules. Since old Mr. Ham's conscience was forcing him to buy, Miltiades meant to make the price as low as he could. He had paid three hundred dollars for the mules, and now he thought tentatively of two hundred, or two twenty-five.

Behind this mental pricing lay a feeling of futility at what all of his exertions had come to. For a short time he had held a fortune and was now salvaging a few tiny scraps like this.

The reason he was meeting Mr. Ham at the bridge was because he did not want anyone to know that he had sold his mules. The first move he made to get rid of his property would bring a deluge of legal actions against him. His creditors would levy on everything he had, and he would be able to save nothing.

The merchant had been waiting at the bridge for upward of half an hour; now he walked further along the road, scrutinizing every horseman who grew from miniature to natural size out of the distance.

The sun mounted higher and hotter. The long stretch of road began to dance. Drops of sweat started prickling the Colonel's eyes. He grew more and more anxious about

Mr. Ham, because the old man always had been punctual.

Not that the Colonel had set any particular hour. But it was his old friend's custom in the summer time to ride into Florence in the cool of the morning and remain until the cool of the afternoon. If he wanted only a spool of thread, he took all day to get it.

So now Miltiades began to fear that Erasmus was not coming at all. And if the news leaked out that the Colonel had been trying to sell his mules . . . the man in the road mopped his head and frowned at the thought.

He was also on the watch-out for the negro Toussaint and his mules and wagon, but he was not uneasy about Toussaint. Nobody knew when a negro was likely to start to town; the furnace of midday was the same to a negro as the chill of night.

Presently the hour became definitely too late for old man Ham to come at all. The Colonel gave it up and turned toward the bridge. As he retraced his steps he would peer back up the road from time to time, still hoping to see the old man.

As he stood, turned, looking back like this, the patient plodding of a horse in hot weather came up behind the Colonel from the direction of Florence. A loud annoyed voice called out:

"Milt Vaiden, what in the Sam Hill are you doin' out here?"

The Colonel whirled in bewilderment.

"Why, I was waiting for you!"

"What time do you think I come to town on a swinjer like this?" The old farmer's word "swinjer" meant a very hot day.

"Confound it, I knew you come early of a morning. . . . Come on, let's wait down here on the bank of the creek in the cool."

"I ast Dalrymple Love where you was, but the dern shut-mouth wouldn't cheep a word. Fin'ly I cussed him out and started home."

Miltiades saw that his friend was out of temper.

"I asked Love not to say where I was, Erasmus," explained the Colonel. "Ever since that suit went against me, you don't know what a gang is after me every minute of the day. Why, damn it, I can't step in the store to post my books without being pestered to death."

Old man Ham simply nodded at this.

"Come down here on the bank and let's wait in the cool," suggested Miltiades, in a friendly tone.

"Wait for what?"

"My nigger Toussaint, with the mules."

"Yore nigger Toussaint!" cried the old man, exasperated. "Why, I saw that yellow devil in town thirty minutes ago. He was on one of yore mules. I ast him where was you and the other mule, that I'd bought 'em from you. He told me to go see Mr. Sandusky first."

The Colonel's thoughts came to a stop.

"Told you . . . what?"

"Told me to go see that damned little jack-leg lawyer, Sandusky! A nigger, instead of doin' what I ordered him to, tole me—to—go—see—Mr.—Sandusky—first!"

The Colonel stood transfixed.

"The dirty . . . impudent . . . Did he have both mules?"

"I just saw the one he was riding."

"Why, that stinkin' nigger mumbled something last night about not wanting me to sell my mules. . . . I bet, by God, he never brought 'em up at all!"

"Well, I went to Sandusky," continued the old man wrathfully, "and that young spittoon of a lawyer had the effrontery to tell me I wouldn't be allowed to buy yore mules. He said he had got out an injunction against you to keep you from sellin' 'em."

The Colonel turned his head to one side and looked at the farmer.

"How did Sandusky get in on this?"

"Why, the nigger hired him. I ast him what for. He said

the nigger wanted to use the mules for the rest of the season. I says to him, 'By God,' I says, 'kain't a man sell his own stock without consulting the niggers on his place?' and the damn little rat grinned and said, 'I dunno. I'm going to find out.' "

The Colonel began fulminating.

"Damn traitorous yellow snake . . . son of a damned Yankee . . . dirty cutthroat lawyer. . . ."

He started walking rapidly toward Florence.

"Here," cried the old man, suddenly sympathetic with Miltiades in his trouble, "here, put a foot in my stirrup and mount behind me! Hell, me and you used to ride together to keep niggers down. I guess we can still do it!"

The Colonel heaved up. Old Mr. Ham kicked his animal into a reluctant single foot.

"I God!" swore the old man in the midst of this exertion, "what air things comin' to? What'll the new generation of niggers be up to next?"

"What did Judge Abernethy mean by granting any such injunction . . . and to a nigger?" cried Miltiades.

"He ain't granted it yet," explained the farmer; "he's just goin' to hear it."

"Hear hell! Why, if he ever starts hearing nigger injunctions, his damn court will be running over with 'em!"

"It's a funny thing," said old man Ham, "that we've forgot how to han'l' niggers. Me and you knowed how right after the war, Milt."

The Colonel said nothing to this, but helped his fellow rider kick the old horse into a brisker movement through the scorching sunshine.

When he reached Courthouse Square Miltiades found that Toussaint's action had given his mule trade with Mr. Ham the precise publicity he had so wished to avoid.

It turned out in a way not to be such bad publicity after all. When he dismounted in the Square, two or three lawyers who had accounts against him came up to tell him the injunction was a damned shame. They said the dirty yellow nigger had come to them first with his belly-aching, and they told him to get out of their offices and go to hell. Then the nigger had run upon Sandusky, who would defend carrion from buzzards if he saw a fee in it.

"Who served the injunction, anyway?" demanded Miltiades.

"Why, Mayhew."

"Where is he?"

"Hell, don't look him up, let him look you up."

"Where are Mayhew and the mules?" demanded the Colonel bitterly.

"Why . . . at the courthouse, maybe. . . . What are you going to do?"

"I'm going to see Mayhew," said the Colonel, and started for the courthouse.

There were a score or two of men loitering in the shade of the courthouse and under the mulberry trees along Intelligence Row. Now the whole Square began watching the Colonel. They all knew that a negro had enjoined him from selling his mules, and they were curious to see what would happen.

Then they saw angling across from the northeastern corner of the Square, coming toward Miltiades, the Colonel's brother Augustus Vaiden, and his nephew Jerry Catlin.

At this promise of family action everybody in the Square stirred and began moving on the apparent destination of the Vaidens. Their interest rose. The Vaiden boys would raise some sort of disturbance. Suddenly they heard Augustus calling through the hot sunshine:

"Milt! Oh, Milt . . . who you looking for?"

The Colonel glanced around.

"Mayhew!"

"I don't think he's at the courthouse, Milt!"

The Colonel waited for his nephew and younger brother to catch up.

"Let's go down to the jail."

One of the watchers was walking rapidly and paralleling

the course of the Vaidens. He said to his companion in sudden enlightenment:

"They're going to cuss out Mayhew and give that damn nigger a threshing, and he deserves it."

The moment the man said that the Vaidens were going to curse Mayhew and flog Toussaint every man in the Square accepted this as the white negro's deserts. And it picked up their spirits. It was a very hot day. It would be something to look at.

The three men of the Vaiden clan crossed Intelligence Row ahead of the crowd, went down an alley between two offices, and came out between the jail and the fire station on the back street. As they approached the jail they saw Mayhew and Frierson hurry out with rifles, jump onto horses, and start off.

Miltiades ran forward.

"Mayhew! Mayhew! Did that damned Sandusky get out papers to keep me from selling my mules?"

Mayhew paused a moment, thrust a hand into his hip pocket, and brought out an envelope.

"Here it is, Colonel. Judge Abernethy asks you to show cause why you should sell your mules, plow wagons, hoes, and other farm implements."

"What in the hell do you mean accepting such a paper to serve on a white man? You knew it come from Sandusky and a damned nigger."

The Sheriff raised his quirt.

"Can't go into that now, Colonel. See you later. Don't sell your mules!" and he struck his horse.

The animal shot down the back street, followed by Frierson's mount. They dashed around a corner, and the Colonel could hear their hoofbeats receding toward the river. He stood looking blankly at the jail and at the fire station. Inside the station two firemen yawned over a checkerboard.

"What's Mayhew in such a lather about?" asked Augustus indignantly.

"Danged if I know," said the fireman. "What are you-all

going to do about that nigger trying to keep Colonel Milt from selling his own stuff?"

"Do you know whether I'm summoned to a trial or not?" inquired the Colonel. "Mayhew went off in such a rush."

"I don't know anything about the trial. We was just settin' here talkin' about what ort to be done to a nigger like that, when he got a telegram and jumped up and run off like you seen him."

"Mayhew, you mean?"

"Sure . . . Mayhew."

The three Vaidens retraced their steps through the alley to Intelligence Row and then started to the Governor's office.

On the way one of the idlers in the Square called out:

"Are you-all looking for that white Vaiden nigger, Colonel?"

"We'd like to see him," said Augustus in a significant tone.

Two or three men laughed.

"We bet you'd like to see him! He left here ridin' toward East Florence."

"We'll look him up," called young Jerry, with a feeling of holding an important position in the growing complication.

A little farther on the trio reached Governor O'Shawn's office. The doors and windows were open, and they could see the Governor inside at a water cooler making himself a toddy against the heat.

When the three men entered the hallway that led to the office, the Governor called out, as if he had been expecting them,

"Come right on in. . . . My God, isn't it hot today? Do you boys want a toddy? Haven't got any ice. I believe an ice toddy heats you up. And then they're not meant for ice, anyway."

He stood facing them with a red moist face, drinking and

explaining toddies, but appraising his callers and really not thinking of toddies at all.

"Governor, what about that nigger stopping me from selling my mules?" asked the Colonel in a brittle voice.

"Governor," asked Augustus, "do you think there is any wisdom in letting such a case come to court?"

"Now, now, Mr. Vaiden," soothed the Governor.

"You don't think we ought to stop him before he gets into court?" asked Augustus, surprised.

"I do not."

"Why in the devil don't you?"

"Yes, what are you going to do," inquired Miltiades, "when a nigger comes up and tells you you can't sell your mules? Are you going to stand there and say, 'All right, I can't sell 'em'?"

"Certainly not."

"Then what are we going to do?"

"Why, by God, we're going to make the laws of Alabama agree with the actual facts of farm labor in Alabama. We're going to set a precedent," pronounced the chief executive sharply.

"What are we going to do about this particular case?" pressed Augustus.

"Answer the injunction. I was just standing here framing my defense when you gentlemen came in."

The Governor finished off his toddy.

"Of course, I couldn't usually make a *viva voce* plea before an Alabama court," continued the Governor, "but I consider this case so important, so constructive, so grave that it almost falls under the head of state papers, gentlemen. It will stop this kind of petty persecution of white landowners by negro tenants permanently, I trust."

The Vaiden group were greatly encouraged at this pronouncement. The trial was to come off at one o'clock, the hottest hour of the day. The Vaidens separated. Miltiades crossed Courthouse Square to his store to await the hour of the trial.

As Augustus Vaiden set out for home, Gibeon Dalrymple angled across the plaza to ask a question.

"Mr. Gus, the boys want to know what you and Mr. Milt want done about that nigger?"

Two or three other men called:

"Yes, are you jest goin' to let him bring his suit against you-all?"

"Why, Milt and the Governor," said Augustus in a dejected tone, "have about decided to let the law take its course."

"Well, now, Colonel Milt and the Governor ain't the whole population of Lauderdale County," said a countryman.

"That'll jest be baitin' niggers to start suits against white folks," warned Gibeon, in alarm.

"That Toussaint Vaiden has been going around jest baggin' some white man to warm his jacket for him," said Alex Cady.

"You're talkin', Alex," approved a companion.

"Well," said Augustus philosophically, "it's their suit. If Milt and Terry O'Shawn wants to handle niggers with kid gloves, they can do it, but that has never been my ticket."

"Mine neither! Mine neither, Mr. Gus!"

Augustus moved onward up the long shimmering furnace of Market Street. He was very irritable in the heat. One reason why he had been especially desirous of giving Toussaint a whipping and letting him go was because he was Gracie Vaiden's boy. The idea of a son of a Vaiden ex-slave suing one of the white Vaidens was unbearable. Augustus damned the heat.

Courthouse Square was greatly disappointed at the tame outcome of the situation. For the Vaiden boys to submit to being sued by a negro was unbelievable. It was as if a fighting bull should be attacked by a bottle-fed lamb.

"Can you imagine such a thing?" queried Gibeon, blinking his eyes against the heat.

"The rest of us white men," said Alex Cady, "oughtn't

to let a damned yellow nigger get away with anything like that. A bunch of us ort to warm his jacket so he would remember it."

Over in Miltiades' store men would come in from time to time not to buy but to ask what the Colonel was going to do about that nigger who had started a suit against him.

When Miltiades said he meant to defend the injunction, his visitors would say:

"Well, we heard that outside, but we didn't b'lieve it was so."

Over in East Florence, other spiritual preparations were in progress for the coming trial.

In Miss Tony's shack, behind its fenceless gate, Toussaint and Fo' Spot were talking. The powerful, compact roustabout was excited.

"Toussaint, I useter think you was a boy of sense . . . read an' write . . . but, fo' Gawd in hebbm, whut you jumpin' up wid a lawsuit ag'inst Col'l Milt Vaiden fuh?"

"I kain't finish my cotton crop without the mules," repeated the white negro for the dozenth time.

"You expeck to finish it wid de mules?"

"I hope to."

"Toussaint, you is de mos' ongodlies' fool niggah I evah hear spoke. Pickin' out de hones'es' white man in de whole county to sue. Col'l Milt Vaiden, who would gib you a poun' when you bought a poun'. Col'l Milt, who would gib back de right change when you han' him a dollah. An' min' you, he do it in his own sto' same as Mistuh Han'back's. Why, Col'l Milt was de man who bought a place in de country jess to befrien' you an' yo mammy when ol' man Han'back th'owed you-all out. Now he comes wantin' to sell he mules—he own mules—when he needs a li'l' money, an' you raisin' ruptions wid he about hit in de co't!"

The white negro sat in silence for several moments. Fo' Spot's eloquence was the most daunting thing he had heard. The octoroon had never liked Colonel Vaiden, but still, the white man had befriended his mother, and just as incontinently deprived her of the rich cotton crop she and he and Lucy were about to gather. The trouble was, the Colonel did not treat his black tenants like persons with rights, but like children who could be set about anywhere and anyway Now, Cady, the mischief-making Cady, could defy him, draw a gun on him, go into a lawsuit against him, and nothing was thought about it, but if he, Toussaint, merely objected to the Colonel's selling his mules . . . He dropped his thoughts in distaste and asked aloud:

"What time is it?"

Miss Tony, almost hidden in the darkness, peered at a little round clock.

"It's half-pas' twelve," said Miss Tony.

"Well . . . I must go." Toussaint got up from his rickety chair.

Fo' Spot jumped up.

"Look heah, niggah, have some sense," he pressed earnestly. "De *Rapidan* is at de landin' rat now. You slip down wid me an' git on huh. She pulls out at five. I'll hide you ovah de boilahs, an' dey kain't nobody fin' you an' make you sue Col'l Milt. . . . You kin 'scape out o' dis country an' be a free niggah once mo'."

Toussaint shook his head.

"No, I don't want to withdraw my suit."

"Fo' Gawd's sake, if you kin withdraw yo' suit, niggah, withdraw it!" cried Fo' Spot. "You ort to withdrawed hit befo' you evah sta'ted hit."

Toussaint repeated that he would go on with it and walked out of the dark heat of the shack into the brilliant heat of the sun.

"Are you coming to town?" he asked of Fo' Spot.

"You think I los' my brains?" asked Fo' Spot, closing the door and shutting himself inside.

Toussaint started toward old Florence. He had the same feeling of adventure that he had felt when he set forth a long time ago to get sixteen ounces of bacon for a pound.

In the noonday heat everything was intensely quiet. From

the Florence landing came the melancholy organ tone of the *Rapidan*. It was whistling for labor. Then Toussaint noticed that all the shacks along the road were tightly closed notwithstanding the heat; and along the glaring thoroughfare between East Florence and old Florence, not a negro was in sight.

CHAPTER SIXTY-SEVEN

COLONEL MILTIADES VAIDEN delivered his hot store into the hands of Love, his clerk, and set out across the crowded Square to the courthouse. Every patch of shade sheltered its group of men. Numbers of leather-colored countrymen who were accustomed to following the plow stood about in the direct rays of the sun, talking and laughing. Some ate cheese and crackers and bologna sausage for their noonday meal. A sprinkling of men were exhilarated with whisky. A few were quite drunk, staggering about amid a drunkard's atmosphere of stench, slapping everyone on the back in exaggerated friendliness or trying to pick a fight.

One of them called to Miltiades, "Jes' leave it to us . . . jes' leave it to us an' ever'thing be aw ri'." The tippler saluted with unfocused eyes and reeled off accidentally in another direction.

In the courthouse the crowd was dense. The small undramatic chancery court at last had come into public regard. When Miltiades entered the room the benches were full of men and a row stood around the walls. The packed courtroom waited to see a nigger keep a white man from selling his own mules.

The court already was in session. Judge Abernethy was just reading a decree in divorce which had been granted on the grounds of drunkenness, cruel and inhuman treatment, and danger to the petitioner's life.

"Mr. Clerk," directed the chancellor, "call the next case."

"Vaiden versus Vaiden," intoned the clerk.

"That's not another divorce suit, is it?"

Laughter arose in the courtroom.

"No, it's that injunction suit, your honor."

544

"Are the parties ready?"

At the fenced-off enclosure beneath the Judge's stand Sandusky sat at a table. Now the oldish-looking young man got up and went to a window and looked out.

"Your honor, my client isn't here yet," said the young man uneasily. "I'm expecting him at any moment."

"Didn't he know his suit was set for one o'clock?"

"Yes, your honor, he knows that."

"Mr. Clerk, have you the file in the case?" inquired the chancellor.

The clerk produced an envelope containing one or two depositions and pleadings. He ran through these papers and said:

"Your honor, the original bill of complaint is not here."

"Where is it?"

"Sheriff Mayhew has it. He hasn't returned it yet."

"Call the sheriff into court," directed the chancellor.

The clerk stood up in his place and called, "Oh yes, oh yes, Sheriff Mayhew, come into court!" Then he went to the window and yodeled his summons into Courthouse Square.

"Judge," called a voice from the audience, "I saw Sheriff Mayhew and Frierson riding out of town toward Sheffield about an hour ago."

"Did he take the substantial papers of this case with him?" demanded Abernethy of the clerk.

"This is an *ex tempore* proceeding, your honor, and he hadn't served the complaint on the respondent in the case."

Governor O'Shawn arose.

"The respondent is here and accepts service, your honor," he advised.

"But the petitioner and the sheriff are not present?" questioned the court.

"Your honor, it may be," suggested O'Shawn, "that the sheriff has ridden over to East Florence to convoy the petitioner through the crowd into court. I understand the petitioner doesn't come into court with a popular cause."

"It's a just cause," called Sandusky from the window.

"The determination of its justice is the gist of this action," retorted the Governor crisply.

"What's the nature of the suit?" inquired the chancellor.

"Mr. Sandusky's client has enjoined my client from selling his mules because he says he has contracted for the use of said mules."

"And what is your answer?" inquired the court.

"*Nullum pactum*," stated the Governor sharply; "no such agreement either explicit or implied."

"I will extend the petitioner three minutes of time," said Abernethy, drawing out a large gold watch and laying it on his stand.

The audience began waiting the three minutes. Sandusky glanced at the Judge and then peered out the window into the crowded Square again. Two minutes dragged past with the slowness of watched time. Suddenly Sandusky called excitedly from the window:

"My client is coming across the Square now, your honor. The sheriff is not with him, and he's having trouble getting through the crowd. May I ask your honor to send the constable to get him into court?"

At this there was a stir in the courtroom. Those near the window tried to look out. Miltiades himself attempted to peer down into the Square. The hum in the courtroom became silent as everybody listened to what was occurring below.

A drunken cry floated through the open window:

"Lemme git to that black bastard, I'll show him!" More controlled voices interposed, "Let him alone! Let him in! Time enough when he comes out again!"

There was laughter below. It was on the whole a fairly good-natured crowd. From where he stood Miltiades could see Toussaint emerge from a knot of men and push his way toward the courthouse. A certain admiration for the negro went through the Colonel.

"That's the Yankee in him," he thought. "His daddy never was scared."

"Do you still think your client will need the protection of a constable, Mr. Sandusky?" inquired the Judge.

"No-o," hesitated Sandusky, watching the negro through the window, "he seems to be getting in all right."

A voice in the courtroom said *sotto voce:*

"He won't get out all right."

Judge Abernethy rapped sharply with his gavel.

"Order in the courtroom," he called.

After a ten-minute wait, the crowd in the courtroom door stirred, and the white negro, Toussaint Vaiden, entered. There was some scuffling in the hallway. The chancellor directed the constable to keep order outside the door.

Toussaint came on down to the table where Sandusky sat. The young lawyer arose and announced that he was ready to proceed.

For several minutes there were the usual preliminaries of clerk and judge and lawyers, through which the audience waited patiently.

Then Sandusky arose and stated the position of his client, that Miltiades was under a contract to furnish him mules and implements until his crop was gathered, and he prayed the court to restrain the landlord from selling the said mules and implements.

There was some hissing when Sandusky sat down. The Judge quelled this, and Governor O'Shawn arose.

"Your honor," he began, looking first at Judge Abernethy and then at his audience, "I will plunge straight at the heart of this action. Your petitioner, Toussaint Vaiden, colored, asks an injunction on the strength of a contract.

"Your honor, your respondent to this action comes forward and denies that there is or ever has been a contract to furnish the petitioner stock and implements for any specified time. It is a contract, sir, terminable at the will of the respondent. Why do I say that?

"Your honor, it is a well known fact in Alabama that no negro tenant obtains any further returns from the crop he raises than his board and keep

"At the end of any agricultural year, your honor, the negro share cropper comes out exactly even. His account at the store balances with his share of the crop. No one owes him anything.

"Therefore a negro tenant's connection with a plantation may be severed by the landlord at any stage of the planting because the negro has had his board and keep up to that point, and that is as much as he will ever get, no matter how long he toils.

"In brief, your honor, the negro share cropper in Alabama has no share in the crop he cultivates. And any contract which contemplates the negro as having a share in such a crop cannot be made the foundation of a suit in equity."

Handclapping and applause interrupted the orator. Judge Abernethy rapped for order, and O'Shawn concluded his oration:

"The above is the *de facto* estate of the negro in Alabama, your honor; it now lies to your hand to make it the *de jure* estate.

"Let your honor in this decision be the first great jurist to reconcile Alabama's laws and her practice. Let her be the spokesman to the nation for the South that, politically, religiously, socially, and agriculturally, the South is and of a right must be now and forever, a white man's country! I thank you."

The small chancery court broke into a tumult of approval of the orator's sentiments. Judge Abernethy did not attempt to suppress the applause. When it quieted he picked up his papers and announced the court would take a recess until four o'clock, at which hour it would render its decision.

Sandusky, who had been twisting in his seat under the Governor's speech, took his hat from the desk and was about to leave the courtroom.

Governor O'Shawn addressed the court again.

"May I suggest, your honor, that you appoint the constable to keep the petitioner in safe keeping until he returns here at four o'clock for your honor's decision?

"The petitioner in this cause is probably an innocent negro egged on to this foolish action by unscrupulous advice. His cause is most unpopular. He has been threatened with a whipping. Your respondent has no desire for such an outcome. That is why I suggest that your honor offer the petitioner the asylum of the county jail for his own safety and protection."

Judge Abernethy took off his glasses and polished them.

"If the petitioner desires such sanctuary the court is disposed to grant it."

Sandusky leaned over and consulted with Toussaint, and presently announced that his client would accept the court's offer. A few minutes later Sandusky, Toussaint, and the officer pushed their way out of the courtroom together.

Colonel Vaiden was moved at the novel yet logical viewpoint expressed in the Governor's speech. Men from all over the house were pushing their way to O'Shawn to congratulate him on his defense when a larger commotion grew up in the Square outside. Miltiades was afraid that something was happening to Toussaint. He pushed his way to the window and saw a great swarm of men collected around two horsemen and a horse and buggy in the middle of the Square.

In the buggy sat two neatly dressed white men whom the Colonel had never seen before. His own curiosity arose.

"What's the hullabaloo about?" he inquired of the man next to him.

At first nobody knew, but at last Miltiades understood a man shouting from below.

"It's the robbers!" cried the fellow. "Sheriff Mayhew's got the robbers!"

Miltiades stood for a moment staring in amazement into the plaza. The horsemen with rifles and the horse and buggy began moving again, this time toward the county jail, following in the wake of Toussaint and the constable.

Colonel Vaiden immediately began scrambling with the rest of the crowd, trying to get downstairs.

CHAPTER SIXTY-EIGHT

Toussaint's injunction vanished completely from the mind of Florence.

Down the alley to the jail the crowd pressed before and after the buggy containing the two prisoners and around the horses of Sheriff Mayhew and Jailer Frierson.

Voices from the mass shouted to the sheriff:

"Where'd you ketch 'em, Mayhew?"

"What's the reward, Sheriff?"

"How come you to know who they was?"

A few of the crowd called to the prisoners themselves:

"Buddy, where'd ye come from?"

"What's yore name, mister?"

Somebody called out:

"Hell, you know they ain't goin' to say nothin'."

The smaller man in the buggy said:

"He's Mr. Smith. My name's Jones."

Some of the marchers laughed at this evasion, but they accepted the names and repeated them.

"The little 'un's Jones, the big 'un's Smith. I swear they look jest like drummers."

When the procession came out in the back street in front of the jail, the vertical sun beat upon the prisoners and the crowd. Frierson got down from his horse carefully so as not to swing a foot into anybody's face.

"Gangway!" he yelled. "Gangway for the prisoners!"

He went around to the buggy and unlocked the wrists of the prisoners from the supports of the buggy top.

"What are you going to do with this stuff?" asked the large prisoner.

"What the hell difference does it make what he does with it?" growled the small man.

The jailer led the two well dressed men through the crowd into the jail-house door. The sheriff remained in charge of the horse and buggy, which had belonged to the thieves. Since the prisoners were taken away, the interest of the crowd centered on the horse and buggy. The onlookers began asking questions: how did the sheriff know where the robbers were, and how was he sure that these were the thieves? They looked like very well to do men.

For answer Mayhew got into the captured buggy, reached up into the top, and unbuttoned a false lining. He opened it and discovered a glittering loot, watches, rings, bracelets, pistols, small clocks; all hung on rings in the buggy top. It looked like a jeweler's display. He lifted the cushion of the front seat and exposed rings of keys, a jimmy, a steel saw, a slender bag of brown leather stuffed with sand.

Amid all this incriminating evidence, the sandbag caught the imagination of the crowd, because they were not accustomed to sandbags.

To young Jerry Catlin the leathern bludgeon seemed sinister. He could visualize the big man entering a room with noiseless feet, lifting the leather bag to strike a sleeping householder. The picture filled the youth with a kind of revengeful horror.

As Jerry stared at the outfit the sun put a hot brand on his shoulders. The crowd pushed and pulled him. A voice said in his ear:

"Jest look at that sandbag! Somebody ort to tar and feather them damned thieves for that!"

Another voice snapped:

"Tarrin' an' featherin' is too good for 'em!"

"Here! Here!" ordered Mayhew. "No talk like that!"

He closed the flaps, replaced the seat, and started calling for the dense crowd to let him through.

A few men followed the sheriff and the buggy around the block to the courthouse, but the crowd remained in front of the jail, talking of the loot of the thieves and the deadly effect of the sandbag.

"Anybody ought to be shot," said a voice, "that would slip into another man's house at night with one o' them damn things. . . ."

A big red-faced man came pushing through the spectators, calling out:

"Where's Mayhew? What's he done with it?"

"Went around to the courthouse with the buggy," directed one of the crowd.

Young Jerry lifted his voice in explanation.

"He intends to use the jewelry as evidence against them."

The red-faced man turned irascibly on Jerry.

"What the hell do you want to have a trial of them damn cutthroats for? They're guilty. What you want to spend the county's money on 'em for?"

"Why, I'm not saying to spend the county's money!" defended Jerry.

Half a dozen voices in the crowd took it up. "They ain't no use spendin' money on them damn sandbaggers."

The red-faced man was a little drunk. He continued talking in a loud voice and shaking his fist at the jail. A group formed about him listening to him, and they moved through the crowd toward the jail-house door. As they drew away from Jerry, the boy could hear them demanding in loose voices, "What's the use havin' a trial . . . spendin' the county's money on a couple o' damn snakes . . . ."

As Jerry Catlin peered after these trouble makers a sudden question went through him, "Would they do anything?" He began moving after them, squinting his eyes against the glare. He was filled with a fearful and fascinated anticipation. He felt as if the commonplace streets of Florence were about to turn into something dramatic and terrible.

The red-faced man was on the jail-house steps, thumping on the door.

"Hey, Frierson, open up!" he called. "Bring 'em out!"

Three or four voices from the crowd shouted loosely to the

jailer inside: "What's use spen'in' county's money on a couple o' damn san'baggers?"

The big man tried the iron knob of the door. He turned and shook it. It was locked.

One of the firemen in the station next to the jail stepped into the alley and walked quickly through it into Courthouse Square and then ran to the courthouse.

The horse and buggy of the thieves stood at the south end of the building with a group around it. The fireman ran toward this group, calling sharply:

"Where's Mayhew? What went with Mayhew?"

"What's the matter?" demanded a half-dozen voices. "Have they got loose? Did they break jail? Mayhew took the stuff inside!"

The fireman ran up the stone steps into the courthouse. He walked rapidly along the transverse corridor, looking in the doors, trying to locate Mayhew. A passer in the hallway said the sheriff was in the registrar's office. The fireman ran along the main corridor and entered this office. Three or four men stood talking inside, but Mayhew was not among them. The fireman asked in an urgent tone where was the sheriff.

The whole group turned toward the door.

"What's the matter, Bill? Anything happened down at the jail?"

"Here I am in the vault," called Mayhew's voice. "What do you want?"

The fireman crossed to the open door of the vault and stepped inside.

"They're beating on the jail door and yelling for Frierson to bring out the prisoners."

Mayhew sat on a stool, making a list of the watches and rings and jewelry and piling them in a goods box. He got up, looked for a moment uncertainly at the loot.

"Don't spread the alarm any further," he said in a low tone. "Don't get the crowd up here to flocking down to the jail." He stepped out of the vault and said to the men in the office:

"I've got to go to Tuscumbia. I'll leave this truck in the vault and list it when I get back."

As he hurried out, the group called after him in astonishment:

"Mayhew, what's broke loose in Tuscumbia?"

The sheriff and the fireman hurried out of the courthouse toward the jail. Once outside they heard a confusion of noise from the jail street and saw the whole Square drifting in that direction. Some men ran, others walked along, peering ahead curiously, as if they could look through the offices of Intelligence Row.

Mayhew caught the fireman's arm.

"Bill," he called in his ear, "go get the Governor! Tell him to come down to the jail and quiet these damn fools."

The fireman angled across to O'Shawn's office. Mayhew broke into an honest run through the drift of the crowd.

When he came out of the end of the alley the back street was full of noise and confusion. The crowd covered the jail steps. Boys hung onto the bars of the high windows trying to peer inside. Now and then a stone banged against the jail-house door. A louder noise arose farther down the street and Mayhew saw a knot of men dragging something through the crowd, and divined it was a log to batter the door.

The sheriff shoved and strong-armed his way toward the jail, shouting against the uproar:

"Hey, men! Be quiet! Stop!" He jerked a boy around and kicked him. "Lay down that rock!" He began struggling toward the steps, hauling men out of his path by their collars. "Get out of here! Clear out, or I'll land *you* in jail!"

Voices yelled:

"Open the door, Mayhew! Go in there and bring out them damned thieves, Mayhew!"

As the knowledge widened in the crowd that the sheriff was among them, a medley of shouts boiled up:

"Bring 'em out!" "Open the door!" "Let Mayhew to the

door, he's go'n' to open it!" "Let the sheriff to the door!"

The crowd suddenly began pushing him. Mayhew stumbled up the treads and stood above the mob.

"Men! Gentlemen!" he shouted, waving his arms. "What the hell do you mean? What do you want?"

"Them sandbaggers! Them dirty, thievish devils!"

"They'll be tried and sentenced! Let the courts do it! We've got enough evidence against them to send a dozen men to the coal mines!"

The crowd took on a semblance of more orderly determination. The red-faced man called from the foot of the steps:

"Hell fire, we don't want no trial! Bring 'em out, Mayhew, or we'll bust in the door!"

The officer looked over the brilliant packed street for a glimpse of O'Shawn.

"Fellows," he temporized, "you know I haven't got any right to hand the prisoners over to you! The law makes me responsible for 'em! It's my duty. . . ."

Shouts interrupted:

"Hell fire, we know that! Git out o' the way! Bring that lawg on, fellers!"

The knot moved toward the steps through the crowd in a wedge-shaped mass. Everybody lent a hand with the log. Mayhew put a hand to his hip pocket with a notion of firing above their heads, but he knew that at least a hundred men in the crowd were armed. He flung up his hands in a desperate appeal:

"Wait, men! For God's sake, wait one more minute! I sent for the Governor. He's the state of Alabama! You-all elected him!"

The mob roared they didn't need the Governor. The knot with the battering ram reached the bottom of the steps. Just then Mayhew saw the flushed face of Governor O'Shawn. He was pushing his way from the alley along the jail-house wall to the steps. An intense relief flooded the sheriff.

"Here he is!" he shouted. "Men, here's the Governor! Listen to the Governor!"

He leaned down, caught the Governor's hand, and pulled him up, while hands pushed from below.

When Governor O'Shawn faced the mob the uproar in the sweltering street died away in waves. O'Shawn continued holding up his hand until almost a silence fell over the thoroughfare.

"Gentlemen! Fellow citizens! Alabamians! Guards and paladins of the stainless escutcheon of our civic honor! What is this thing you are about to do?"

"Lynch a couple o' damned sandbaggers!" yelled a voice.

"No! *No!* NO!" decried the Governor. "You are lynching the honor and dignity of your state. You are lynching the law which you yourselves enunciated! You are lynching Law, which stands like an angel with the scales of justice and separates men from beasts! What have these unhappy prisoners done?"

"Stolen!" "Robbed!" "Sandbagged!" "Murdered!" yelled a dozen voices.

O'Shawn held up a hand against this new uproar.

"The courts of Alabama will discover those facts just as surely as you! You can't afford, gentlemen, to allow another lynching in Alabama! Right at this moment the newspapers of the North are holding their presses to publish news of another Southern outrage! Don't feed the malignity of the Yankee press with a public murder!"

A chorus of voices broke out:

"Git down, Governor!"

"We don't want to hurt you, Governor!"

A drunken voice bawled:

"Look here, Terry, we done enough fer you when we voted fer you!"

A laugh went up. O'Shawn turned on the fellow:

"Sir, do you want to disgrace the man you elected?"

"We're not disgracin' you!"

"Don't you think it's a disgrace to lynch helpless prisoners in the presence of the Governor of your own state?"

"All right! All right! Git out o' town, then!"

The Governor stood, thinking how to delay the tragedy. "Will you men give me time to get out of town?"

"Hell, yes, we'll give you time!"

A dozen other voices took the matter up quite seriously: "You can have time, Governor!"

"You can get out on the four o'clock train, Governor!"

"We'll wait . . . you make the four o'clock, Governor!"

To this grotesque offer O'Shawn acquiesced.

"That's an agreement!" he called, holding up both hands. "Gentlemen, that's an agreement. I am going to leave Florence on the four o'clock train. It is my hope, it is my prayer to almighty God, that in this interim you will remember your duty as citizens, your fealty to the law, your patriotism to the land for which your brothers and fathers have laid down their lives. Gentlemen, may I beseech you to temper this hot and lawless impulse with the manly restraint of law and decency? I leave your contemplated crime to your consciences!"

O'Shawn climbed down the steps. There was a spatter of applause. Several voices inquired:

"What time is it now?"

The bulk of the mob remained in the heat, where they were waiting for the hour of four o'clock and the lynching.

Governor O'Shawn got out of the crowd and hurried up Intelligence Row. When he entered his office a tall man stepped into his door behind him and caused the Governor to whirl around.

"Hell, you gave me a start, Landers. . . . What do you want?"

The postmaster stood shaken in the doorway.

"I heard your speech, Governor. We've got a two-hour wait if nothing breaks loose. Couldn't we get some of the best men to go down to the jail and persuade the mob to break up?"

"I don't know. You might try. I've got to leave town in a little while." The Governor began making himself a toddy with unsteady hands.

"I'll ask some of the men," agreed Landers. "I don't know whether they'll listen to me or not."

The postmaster went out into the shimmering street again. In his thoughts it was not the death of the two men in jail that sent his thin legs hurrying through the heat: it was the sharp and ruinous dislocation of their lives. For the lives of the thieves to be snapped off in tension and agony and terror and to be begun anew with these horrors trailing after them sickened the mystic. Who would disrupt the unending and mysterious processes of the soul for a handful of watches and rings?

The postmaster stopped at Simpson's drug store, and only old man Simpson was in the place. The old druggist stood in his doorway staring toward Courthouse Square.

"When are they going to hang 'em?" he asked excitedly as Landers came up. "I might as well lock the store."

He looked at his watch and began closing the door.

At the corner of Tombigbee and Market the postmaster almost ran into the Reverend B. Alvin Puckett. The minister ejaculated:

"What time have you got? Isn't this a terrible thing! They say the Governor got them to put it off till four. Such terrible things happen! I feel I ought to get within sight of it. A minister ought to see the sins and cruelties of life in order to strike home at the devil from his pulpit!"

In his heart the Reverend Puckett was glad he had met no person more important than Landers, the Republican postmaster. He walked on toward town through the burning sunshine.

CHAPTER SIXTY-NINE

IN THE two-hour interim young Jerry Catlin hurried up Market Street after his uncle Augustus . . . it would be just like his uncle Augustus to stay at home and never know . . . A voice calling his name checked his stride. He looked about and saw nothing.

The hobbledehoy was trembling. He decided he must have imagined someone was calling him. He started on again when the hail of "Jerry Catlin! Oh, Jerry Catlin!" stopped him anew.

He turned all the way around this time, looking everywhere, when he saw Landers, the postmaster, hurrying toward him on the other side of Market Street. The thin man held up a hand.

"Wait! Wait, Mr. Catlin!"

The title "Mister" was unusual to Jerry. It caused him to feel an access of dignity, even in the heat.

The postmaster came up and began talking hurriedly in the middle of things.

"I've just been to see Judge Ashton. He says there's no use trying to do anything for the white men, but we might get the negro out if one of the Vaidens would go down and ask for him. You see the crowd knows the negro sort of belongs to the Vaidens. They have a right to take him out if they want him."

Jerry instantly perceived the whole situation. Pleasure and anger rose up in him that a negro who had sued his uncle should get himself into this fix.

"That Toussaint nigger doesn't have to stay in there,"

said Jerry. "He went in of his own accord so he wouldn't get a licking."

"I know that, but he can't come out now."

"The crowd's not thinking about him."

"They will think about him if they see him. But you could get him clear away without any trouble—you're Colonel Vaiden's nephew, aren't you?"

"Listen," cried Jerry, "that nigger went into court on his own hook—let him come out on it."

Landers gazed oddly into young Jerry's face.

"Listen," he said. "Suppose I told you that this was for yourself for you to help the colored boy to escape the mob. . . . Suppose I told you it was your own self you were setting free—would you do it?"

The boy felt queer.

"I don't know what you mean by myself," he said, moistening his lips. "He's a nigger."

"But he's a living human being, and so are you! It's the same sort of life in both of you. A part of life happened to flow in his body, another part happened to flow in yours." Landers reached his hand toward the youth. "There's no difference in helping him and helping yourself, Jerry."

There was a cadence in Landers' voice, a something in his manner that moved Jerry in an odd way. And because he was moved about a negro he became bitter at himself; he became furious at Toussaint for hiring Sandusky to sue his uncle.

"Why, God damn it, no!" cried Jerry, "an impudent yellow nigger like that. . . . I wouldn't help him out of hell!"

Landers turned.

"I'll see what I can do myself. I don't think I can do much. I have no claim on the negro . . . he has no claim on me that anyone would recognize. And the people here don't like me, Jerry . . . you know that."

Jerry said he didn't care what Landers did.

As the postmaster turned back toward town the same impulse to go with him seized Jerry so strongly as to be painful. But the boy clenched his teeth and thought:

"No, I won't help a nigger who sued Uncle Milt! If it would help me the same as it would him . . . I'll see us both in hell first!"

CHAPTER SEVENTY

A WAGON, oddly loaded, came rattling and jouncing up Market Street. Over its sides thrust hoes, the handles of plows, rakes, what-not. On the seat in front of the hotch-potch sat two women. One, who might have been a white woman, was driving, urging her blown and lathered mules with a whip. By her side jounced an ashen-hued girl, heavy with child, clutching the seat, on the brink of child-bearing.

The frightened driver turned the wagon across to Pine Street. She laid the whip on the spent mules. The team lurched along far in arrears of her haste. She turned into Pine under the dust-filmed trees.

She drew up her team at the Crowninshield residence and almost fell, scrambling, down over the front wheel.

"You sit here," she gasped to her companion, and went running into the big gate that led around to the side entrance of the manor.

A middle-aged brunette woman, who was not so very unlike the hurried caller, was passing the door that opened on the porte cochère. She stopped and ejaculated:

"Why, Gracie, what are you doing here?"

"Where's Col'l Milt, Miss Drusilla?" gasped the quadroon.

"In the library."

"May I see him, Miss Drusilla?"

"I'll tell him you want to see him," and the white woman turned with unhasting courtesy and disappeared toward the front of the manor.

The quadroon moved about, clenching her hands, pressing her fingers against her mouth, stopping her breathing to listen intently toward town.

The town lay silent behind the southerly trees. Somewhere a red bird swung through the air his silver lash, as if laying it on some bare back.

The Colonel came out with disapproval on his face. He looked the woman over.

"What is it, Gracie?" he asked coldly.

The quadroon rushed out her words:

"Oh, Col'l Milt, get Toussaint out! They're going to kill him just for a lawsuit! Col'l Milt, please . . . please . . ."

She knelt before him, catching his hand and weeping.

Her touch repelled Miltiades. He undid his fingers and wiped them on his handkerchief.

"Get up! Don't be an idiot, Gracie! Nobody's going to hurt Toussaint."

"Isn't he in jail?"

"Yes, he's in jail."

"They . . . put him in jail . . . to . . ." her voice went to a horrified whisper, "to . . . hang him?"

"Who did you hear that from?"

"From the colored people. . . . I met them leaving town."

"Well, no . . . no . . . no . . . no! That's exactly like a lot of damn fool niggers. Get everything wrong. They didn't put him in jail. They're not going to hang him. He went there of his own free will. He can come out any time he wants to."

The mother stared in bewilderment.

"Toussaint went to jail himself? What for?"

"To escape a thrashing, which in my opinion he deserved," stated Miltiades crisply.

Gracie stood looking at her former master with wide, dark eyes.

"Are . . . are there a—a thousand white men around the jail-house with guns . . . waiting for him to come out?"

Miltiades was disgusted.

"I swear . . . did the niggers tell you that, too?"

The quadroon nodded.

"That's what all of them said."

"No! They're not waiting for Toussaint. They've forgot him long ago. They're waiting to get two white robbers that Mayhew caught over about Tuscumbia."

"Are they in jail, too?"

"Yes."

"How long will the men wait?"

"Till the Governor leaves Florence on the four o'clock train."

Gracie became inexpressibly agitated.

"Why, Col'l Milt, don't you know they'll do something to Toussaint? Don't you know? . . . Col'l Milt, go down and get him out! Please! Please do . . . before four o'clock. . . . What time is it now?"

The Colonel drew out his watch deliberately as he answered her.

"I don't know that I have any call to get Toussaint out of his trouble. I didn't get him into it. I told him to bring me those mules. And did he do it? No. Damn his yellow skin. he come up here and started a lawsuit against me!"

"I told him not to! I begged, I prayed for him not to."

"Then what in the hell did he do it for?" cried Miltiades, growing angry again.

"Oh, it was that Lucy . . . What was the time?" gasped Gracie, seeing the Colonel had returned his watch to his pocket.

The Colonel took it out again.

"Oh . . . three forty-five."

A terrible trembling invaded Gracie. She reached for the white man.

"Oh, Col'l! Col'l! Get him . . . get Toussaint out! He can't help being bull-headed and starting lawsuits!"

"Why can't he?" cried the white man. "What's wrong with him?"

Gracie glanced at the empty door. She took a step closer and said rapidly in a low voice:

"Because he's your boy . . . he's your own boy! He's a Vaiden! Whoever heard tell of a Vaiden . . . giving in?"

She fell to weeping silently, like a white woman, her face distorted and tears running from her eyes.

The white man stood incredulous.

"Why, he—he's Beekman's boy!"

Gracie shook her head.

"N-no . . . don't you remember . . . the time you took me . . . in the loft?"

The Colonel gazed at the woman a moment longer. Suspicion of deceit flickered through his head but was instantly gone. Gracie did not lie. He snapped out his watch again.

"Hell, I haven't got time to hitch up the carriage . . . we can't walk to town in twelve minutes!"

"I brought the wagon," hurried the woman, beginning to run back down the driveway.

"What wagon?" cried Miltiades, following her.

"Your wagon. Lump and I brought all your things in it we could load. We got scared about Toussaint."

From the driveway Miltiades saw the grotesque load in the street. He ran down, motioned Lucy over to one side of the seat. He got the lines himself and let Gracie scramble up after him. He began belaboring his exhausted animals, which broke into a weary trot once more.

"Where's Lump?" he asked.

"Oh, he got out on the edge of town!"

As the Colonel drove forward in the heat a kind of pulsing ache set up in his head. The street danced and glimmered in the sunshine. He tried to see to town. The mules seemed to creep.

The grotesque thought stood before him that he was rushing to town in a farm wagon with the quadroon mother of his negro son, trying to save the boy a flogging . . . it might be a flogging . . . it might be nothing at all . . . the mob might not notice him in jail. . . .

"Damn mobs!" he said aloud between lashings of the mules. "You can't tell what the devil . . ." He hushed expressing his fears out of consideration for the mother of his son.

"Will we be in time?" gasped Lucy, clinging to the hard seat.

The Colonel had to guess at the time.

"I . . . think we will. . . ."

He planned what he would do . . . go down through the mob and ask for his nigger. He would say the nigger's mother had brought him the mules. . . .

As these thoughts chased through his mind the Colonel heard the blast of the passenger train blowing for the Tennessee River bridge.

A kind of spasm went through Miltiades. He was just entering the business part of town. It was utterly deserted. As the quivering mules galloped past a side street, Miltiades caught a momentary glimpse of the old Handback store with its door boarded up.

A noise began to grow down the street. It was the myriad noise of a great crowd. It was purfled by shouts, outcries. Its ground tone was a persistent roar. At a certain point came an outburst of yelling, then an abrupt and shocking silence.

The Colonel headed the stumbling mules into the Square. The crowd swarmed around the gnarled and twisted mulberries along Intelligence Row.

On three of these trees, in the center of the mob, swung three figures. Miltiades jerked his reins and stopped his heat-struck mules.

Lucy sat staring and motionless in the seat beside the Colonel. Gracie stepped over the front wheel and leaped to the ground. She fell heavily, but instantly was up, running toward the trees. A big man hung from one tree, a little man from another. Toussaint was in the middle.

From the moment she reached the outskirts of the silent crowd she screamed, "Let me by! Let me by!"

The middle tree was low. The white negro's feet were just off the pavement.

The mob became aware of the woman. They took their eyes off their handiwork to look at her as she pushed her way in. They made way for her.

She reached the body and began clawing at the knot. Her fingers could do nothing. She reached frantically toward the faces around her.

"Gimme a knife! Gimme a knife! Oh, Lordy! Lordy! Gimme a knife!"

Two open knives clattered on the brick pavement in the little open ring around the trees.

Gracie caught up one and began slashing the rope. It was tough. She haggled and haggled with the dull knife. At last a strand held it. Another stroke cut it apart. Toussaint collapsed. His mother, trying to hold him up, fell with him.

A dozen drunken voices in the mob broke into laughter at the downfall of the negro mother and her dead son.

CHAPTER SEVENTY-ONE

THREE or four men bore the body of Toussaint to the wagon and laid it on the hotch-potch in the wagon bed.

Miltiades said to the bearers:

"What did you hang the nigger for?"

And one of the men answered with the detachment of an onlooker:

"Why, I think they done it jest to make a clean sweep of the jail. He was there in a cage, so they tock him along with the others."

"Did he . . . fight?" asked Miltiades, with a queer twinge.

"No, he didn't fight or beg or anything; when Alex Cady tied the rope around his neck, the nigger spit."

The Colonel gave over the wagon and mules to the two colored women. They drove away and left him in the hot Square under the westering sun.

The show was over. The mob had become a crowd again, and some of them were going home. A sprinkling of men flowed away in all directions. Miltiades had no heart to return to the Crowninshield manor. He did not want to see Drusilla or Sydna now. A thought came to him that the negro woman, Gracie, had come closer to some inner reality of his life than any other human being would ever come again . . . his boy . . . their boy . . . had looked at Alex Cady when the hillman put the rope around his neck . . . and had spat. The Colonel bit his lip to imprison within himself a throb of strange and tragic triumph, and his grief.

Out of necessity to go somewhere, Miltiades walked across

the Square to the store. It was locked. Love had gone to the lynching, of course.

The merchant took out his key and let himself into the hot dark interior. It smelled of bacon and calico and coal oil. There were some bolts of cloth on one end of the dry-goods counter. The Colonel lay down on the counter and put his head on the bolts. After a moment he sat up, thinking if his boy had not started an injunction against him . . . if Bradley had not lost the deeds . . . if Sandusky had not been admitted to the bar . . . a long string of "ifs" upon which every life hangs suspended.

The rattling of a wagon outside his store drew the Colonel out of his thoughts and off of his counter. He moved mechanically to the door to attend the wants of a possible customer. Love, his clerk, entered.

Miltiades looked at Love for several seconds. He almost asked, "Did you help hang the nigger?" But instead he made his question:

"Did you drive a wagon to the door just then?"

The clerk nodded.

"Gracie and that nigger girl sent it to you by me."

"Where from?"

"The steamboat landing."

"What were they doing down there?"

"They took deck passage on the *Rapidan*. They're going North some'r's. That little dried-up Parson Lump went with 'em."

"Did—did they have any money?" asked Miltiades.

"I don't think so. Fo' Spot was rousting on the boat. He told the mate he could take their fares out of his pay."

"And the . . . the body?"

"Why, the Cap'n waited for the niggers to bury it. There was a Yankee on board laughin' because the Cap'n held up the boat a hour to give time to bury a lynched nigger. He sad, 'Now wasn't that the South for you?' "

At supper time the Colonel went home. He could eat nothing, but sat out on the front piazza in the cool of the dark ening night. Somewhere among the trees a whippoorwill uttered over and over its curving cry.

The merchant wished the bird would hush, when a rattling of the latch at the small postern gate caught his ears. He looked up and saw a dark form coming up the box-lined path. He thought it was Sam, his negro of all work, coming back after his scare. The figure paused in front of the piazza and called in a hillman's voice:

"Hello! Hello!"

"Why, hello, Stebbins," said Miltiades. "Did you want to see me? . . . Come in."

"Yes, I did, Colonel."

"Come on in and sit down."

The clerk came in and groped for a chair.

"I've got something here I believe is yours, Colonel," he said.

"What is it?"

"Why, I'm still rooming at the Handback store to keep up the insurance. This afternoon I got to rummaging around looking for a pistol to take to the lynching bee, and I found them old deeds of yores stuck away in the old cash drawer."

A sort of weak sensation went over the Colonel.

"Deeds to my place . . . the old Lacefield place?"

"Why, ye-es," drawled Stebbins. "I figgered Mr. Han'-back must 'a' put 'em in there before he started out huntin' last Chris'mus Day. He yelled an' tole Lucius he put 'em in the safe. But instid of that he put five thousan' dollars in the safe, an' he put the deeds in the cash drawer. I've been thinkin' and wonderin' about it. I imagine he got 'em mixed up, somehow. He meant to put the deeds in the safe and the money in the cash drawer. But if he done that he meant to come back. And if he meant to come back, then he didn't kill hisse'f like ever'body thinks; the gun must of gone off by accident, after all. . . ."

The Colonel was paying no attention to the quandary into which J. Handback's former clerk had fallen.

The information which had been given him to find the deeds had been true . . . Landers' message that what he needed was in the cash drawer. Its truthfulness now came to him with a terrible mockery. If only he had known which cash drawer . . . Sandusky's suit would never have overthrown him . . . Toussaint would never have been . . . The closeness to avoiding all that had happened tortured the Colonel.

He pushed aside the strange affliction of a white man who has hanged his negro son. He said aloud in an ordinary voice:

"I must tell Landers about the papers. He came to me one day and said . . ."

"Why, Colonel," ejaculated Stebbins, "hadn't you heard?"

"Heard what?"

"Why, Landers got bad hurt. He was trying to get the men to turn the white nigger a-loose when somebody knocked him in the head with a rock. . . . I—I r'ally guess he's dead now. I heard the niggers mournin' in his house as I come by."